the
goodbye
GIFT

AMANDA BROOKE

HARPER

Harper
An imprint of HarperCollins*Publishers*
1 London Bridge Street
London SE1 9GF

www.harpercollins.co.uk

A Paperback Original 2016
1

A catalogue record for this book
is available from the British Library

ISBN: 978-0-00-811652-1

Set in Sabon LT Std by Palimpsest Book Production Limited,
Falkirk, Stirlingshire

Printed and bound in Great Britain by
Clays Ltd, St Ives plc

MIX
Paper from
responsible sources
FSC
www.fsc.org **FSC C007454**

FSC™ is a non-profit international organisation established to promote
the responsible management of the world's forests. Products carrying the
FSC label are independently certified to assure consumers that they come
from forests that are managed to meet the social, economic and
ecological needs of present and future generations,
and other controlled sources.

Find out more about HarperCollins and the environment at
www.harpercollins.co.uk/green

To my son's anonymous bone marrow donor

1

The Accident

The suitcase lay open on the bed, its yawning mouth revealing neat piles of holiday clothes. There were summer tops and cropped shorts that would fit a twelve-year-old, a collection of child-sized bikinis, a couple of sparkly dresses and a cardigan for cooler evenings. The requisite clean underwear was hiding beneath a beach towel together with a pair of sandals, sun cream and other holiday essentials, all of which took up less than half the case. The remaining space was packed tight with enough medical supplies to keep a small pharmacy in stock for weeks.

Lucy had been dreaming of this holiday, and after going through everything one last time, she closed the suitcase and zipped it up. She took a deep breath, which was hard fought for, as was every breath.

'I think that's it,' she said.

'Are you sure?'

Lucy turned to her younger sister. Hayley was almost a foot taller and although her figure was slender, she was a couple of stone heavier than her petite twenty-four-year-old

1

sister. They each had their mother's dark looks but where Hayley's hair was cropped short to give her an edgy look, Lucy had opted for a longer, more feminine hairstyle. Washing and styling it could be exhausting at times but it was a price she was willing to pay to avoid being mistaken for a boy. 'Yes, I've got everything I need. Any last-minute additions can go in my hand luggage tomorrow. We could take this downstairs now if you like?' she said.

Ignoring Lucy's impatience to get away, Hayley said, 'No, I mean are you sure you still want to go? I know you wanted to prove a point and no one, not even Mum, could deny you've done that, but it's not too late to change your mind. No one would blame you.'

'Are you backing out on me?'

Hayley took longer than Lucy would have liked to answer. 'If something happens while we're away, it's going to be on my conscience . . .'

Lucy could feel her pulse rising from a lethargic plod to a gentle trot – her defective organ was rarely capable of racing, nor was it recommended. She took a couple of strained breaths to fill her lungs with sufficient air to speak with the kind of authority the situation demanded. 'So Mum's got to you then?'

'Look, I would love nothing better than for the two of us to spend a wild and furious week going out clubbing and getting drunk, staggering back to the hotel at dawn and spending the afternoon zonked out on the beach recovering. But that's not going to happen, is it?'

'No, it isn't, because we're going to a quiet resort in Lanzarote. It's hardly Kavos or one of those crazy places you go to with your mates. And it's not even for a whole week, for God's sake,' Lucy said, repeating arguments she had already put to her family. She had been talking about going on holiday for the last six months and had eventually managed to wear down her doctors, but not her parents and especially not her mum. She had followed medical advice and had waited until she was sure she was fit enough to travel before speaking to the nice lady in the travel agent's who had been on standby and had found the perfect package deal for her and her sister. The taxi was booked for tomorrow afternoon and she was determined for everything to go as planned, even if it killed her.

'But you haven't got medical insurance. What if . . .'

'If I don't feel well then I have the travel agent's number and we get on the next flight home. I've been saving up for this for ages, Hayley. It's February and the weather out there isn't going to get any better in Liverpool. I want some sun and I want some fun! Sorry but I am going – with or without you.'

When her warning failed to quell her sister's last-minute nerves, Lucy went in for the killer comment. 'Please, it's my dying wish.'

'You're not dying,' Hayley said quickly.

'No, I'm not, but I am getting tired standing here arguing. Are you going to help me with this, or not?'

Lucy's mum had heard the rhythmic thump of the suitcase being dragged downstairs and stood glaring at it until she was sure she had her emotions under control.

'Lunch is ready,' she said quietly without looking at either daughter.

Before taking a seat at the table, Lucy switched on the

TV. Her mum normally frowned upon watching TV at mealtimes but today they were going to need help filling the uncomfortable silences.

At first the conversation was limited to polite exchanges as her mum served up a Spanish omelette. Lucy made a show of being absorbed in the antiques programme being aired but the programme soon finished and was followed by the lunchtime news. The headlines included reports of a terrible train crash and Lucy caught a look from her mum that she ignored.

'Are you sure you've packed everything?' her mum asked. It was the first time she had acknowledged that her daughter was going to follow through with her plans.

'Yes, Mum. And we have our passports, our holiday money and I've booked the taxi.'

'There's still time for your dad to book a day off and take you to the airport.'

'I know, but . . .' Lucy began and then shrugged her shoulders. She chose not to remind her mum how she had been told in no uncertain terms that neither of her parents would help with the arrangements for their daughter's ill-conceived adventure. 'If he can pick us up when we get home again, that would be a help.'

Mrs Cunliffe nodded with grim determination as if to cement the idea that her daughter would be returning home. It was an impossible task and when she put down her knife and fork, she clenched her fists tightly. 'Is there anything I can do to change your mind?'

'No, Mum.'

'I've already tried,' Hayley offered.

Glancing briefly at the harrowing footage of the rail

crash, Mrs Cunliffe said, 'Please, Lucy.' The firmness in her voice had withered away to nothing. 'What if something happens?'

'I've packed all the meds I need for every eventuality, Mum.'

'What if your luggage goes missing? It does happen.'

'I'll have a couple of days' supply in my hand luggage.'

'Are you *sure* you're well enough?' Mrs Cunliffe asked as she narrowed her eyes. She had twenty-four years' experience of assessing Lucy's current state of health simply by looking at her. She could spot a fever at fifty paces, tell within hours if the latest operation had improved her daughter's condition, and she was always, if not the first, then the second person to know when the latest repair job was failing.

'I'm fine,' Lucy told her honestly.

'But what if you pick up a bug while you're there?'

Lucy lowered her gaze and concentrated on cutting up her omelette, letting her mum know she would answer no more questions. The message was far too subtle and Mrs Cunliffe hadn't finished.

'What if the transplant nurse calls?'

Anger bubbled to the surface and Lucy's weak heart rattled against her ribcage. 'Mum, stop! I'm tired of keeping my life on hold waiting for that call. Chances are it isn't going to come, and even if it does, it's hardly going to happen the minute I step on the plane.'

In the background, the TV reporter had moved on to the travel update with news of yet more accidents including a jackknifed lorry that had closed a motorway and a bus hitting a bridge. Lucy wanted to get up and switch it off but it wouldn't stop her thinking unthinkable thoughts. She had been on the transplant list for eighteen months and the anticipation of receiving that call had been agonizing and distinctly uncomfortable as she waited for someone else to die. She paid morbid attention to the news and thought of herself as a vulture eyeing up the slim pickings. And they were *so* slim. She was tired of feeding off someone else's misery. She needed to get away.

When the cavalcade of ambulances arrived, the air was thick with oily fumes that darkened the day and Anya was momentarily disorientated as she jumped out of her vehicle. The sound of wailing sirens came from all directions and muffled the shouts and cries for help. The accident had been classed as a major incident and she had arrived as part of the emergency response team. Her confusion was compounded by the fact that she had sauntered into work that morning expecting to start her usual shift on a surgical ward only to be reassigned to A & E who were desperately short of staff. It had been a while since she had worked as a triage nurse, but it took only moments for her training to kick in. She was quickly on the move, taking direction from the officer in charge so she could help where she was needed most.

Anya knelt down beside a young woman who she guessed was in her mid-thirties, although it was difficult to tell because her face was smeared with blood and grime. There were others nearby, crying out in pain, but this woman drew her attention first because she was unresponsive.

Unlike Lucy Cunliffe who was watching the reports on the news, it wouldn't have crossed Anya's mind to wonder if her patient was carrying a donor card: her first priority was to save the life in her hands. She would only discover later that the woman was a registered organ donor, as were her companions.

2

Four months earlier . . .

7.30 p.m. tonight in the Elephant. Need you there.

If Julia Richardson were to scroll through her messages, she would find texts of a similar vein to this appearing time and again. The requests weren't so frequent that they became a chore or in any way routine and there had been a couple of years where they had barely appeared at all, although that had been some time ago. None of that mattered, however, because when the call came the response was never in question. Julia sent a message back confirming she would be there and then gave herself time to consider the trickier task of rearranging her other plans. For that, a text message wouldn't do.

'Hi, are you busy?' she asked when her call was answered.

'Oh, you know, the usual. I've just finished one meeting where I've been given a shedload of work and I'm about to go into another which will probably be more of the same,' Paul said, sounding completely disheartened, which was nothing unusual when he talked about his job these days. Her husband worked for a housing association that had dwindling funds and increasing demands on its services, and it wasn't the job he had once thrived on. 'How about you?'

'Nothing nearly as exciting,' she said as she wrapped a stray lock of auburn hair around a long, slender finger. Despite the neutral tone of voice, her green eyes sparkled and the corner of her mouth twitched with the beginnings of a smile. 'I had a new client in this morning who wants a diamond and gold pendant for his wife, and I'm working up some designs for him now.'

Unaware of the ulterior motive behind the call, Paul's ears pricked at his wife's poor attempt to sound dismissive about her latest commission. 'Would this be an expensive design, by any chance?'

The commission in question was from a wealthy businessman who wanted something stunning, distinctive and unique for his wife to celebrate their fiftieth wedding anniversary. Julia had been personally recommended which was how she secured most of her commissions.

'Money no object,' she confirmed.

'Wow!'

'Yes, that pretty much sums up the brief.' Julia was smiling now as she leaned back in her chair, which squeaked noisily.

Her workshop consisted of two rooms above a small art gallery on Bold Street in Liverpool's city centre. The front reception room had been refurbished and was bright, clean and modern to give her clients a good first impression, but it was the room she was in now where the real work took place. It had a fifties feel about it, partly due to the reclaimed furniture which had been in situ when she had set up shop

9

ten years earlier. In a previous life, the offices had belonged to an accountancy firm that had stopped trading many years – if not decades – earlier. The dark wood and green leather furniture smelled of decay and her latest commission could be used to spruce the place up if Julia didn't have other plans for her nest egg. There were some things that were far more important than work.

'So will my talented wife's profits stretch to a celebratory meal after the gym tonight?'

'Ah.'

'What?' Paul asked.

'Would you mind if I gave you a rain check?'

'For the gym or the meal?'

'I can still do the gym if we can meet up at five, but I need to get to the Elephant for seven thirty.'

'Would this be a meeting of the coven by any chance?'

Julia smiled at the note of resignation in Paul's voice. His wife and her two best friends, Helen and Phoebe, were as close as sisters and shared a history that stretched back to their childhood when Julia had been called upon to babysit the other two. She was ten years their senior and although those little girls were twenty-nine now, she was still taking care of them.

'So who's in need this time?' he asked.

'Helen.'

'Man trouble?' Paul asked, pretending he had even the vaguest idea of what the friends talked about.

'In the absence of any man in her life, I shouldn't think so. I don't know what's up, Paul, and I won't find out until tonight, but I have to go.'

'I know.'

Having known Julia for ten years and been married to her for five of those, Paul had long since accepted that although his wife would put him first in all other circumstances, when one of her friends called an emergency meeting, Julia would move heaven and earth to be there. And of course, it wasn't only her friends who made the call, they had been there for Julia too, and Paul had had the vicarious benefit of their small but effective support network.

'You don't mind?'

'I could always spend an extra hour at the gym and get something to eat on my way home,' he mused.

'Burn off enough calories to justify a takeaway, you mean?'

'Hmm, that's an idea,' he said as if it had only just occurred to him.

She smiled and not for the first time reminded herself how lucky she was. There might be areas of her life that were lacking, but a loving husband was not one of them. 'I love you.'

'I love you too, even with all your afflictions.'

'What afflictions?' she demanded.

'Helen and Phoebe.'

Phoebe Dodd was standing in the hallway with her coat on as she debated whether or not to stand outside in the rain for her lift to arrive or wait for the arc of Julia's car headlights to sweep across the front of the house. She opted for the relative safety of the small porch but the moment she pulled open the front door, her nan's psychic ability was triggered.

11

'Phoebe? Are you going now?'

'Yes, Nan, I'll see you later.'

There was the creak of the drawing room door and when Phoebe turned towards the noise, her nan was already in the hallway. Eighty-six-year-old Theresa wasn't exactly nimble and if Phoebe didn't know better, she had been lurking. The two shared a house that Phoebe had lived in for most of her life but there was never any doubt that this was her grandmother's domain. Theresa had been left well provided for by her late husband and the family home had been carefully maintained and extensively improved over the years. The triple glazing and heating system provided a tropical paradise in the midst of winter and was currently making beads of sweat form on the back of Phoebe's neck.

'Is it the Elephant tonight?'

'Yes, I told you,' Phoebe answered patiently, suspecting the question was a test rather than a symptom of her nan's failing memory.

'Hmm. And what time did you say you'd be back?'

'Not late and I've written down where I am on your reminder board in the kitchen just in case,' she said. 'Is there anything you need before I go?'

Theresa sighed. 'No, I'll be fine. You go off and enjoy yourself,' she said and before Phoebe could assure her that she would, her nan added, 'But don't drink too much.'

'I won't.'

'You say that, but you have no self-control.'

Phoebe immediately proved her wrong by swallowing her annoyance and forcing a smile to her lips. 'Stop worrying,' she said. 'Can I go now, Nan?'

12

There was the sound of someone tapping on glass and Phoebe turned to find Julia's bright, cheery face peering beneath her umbrella. Her friend wouldn't think to open the porch door without invitation and such invitations were rare. While Phoebe would happily open up her home to her friends, it wasn't in her gift.

'I thought you said you were going out with Helen too?'

Theresa had crept close enough to spy Julia over Phoebe's shoulder.

'She's meeting us there.'

'Us?'

'Me and Julia.' Phoebe kissed her nan dutifully on the cheek. 'I'll see you later.'

'Hello, Mrs Dodd,' Julia called when Phoebe opened the porch door and stepped outside. 'I hope you're well.'

Theresa had a tight grip on the front door and was eyeing Phoebe's friend with suspicion. 'Don't keep her out late,' she said by way of an answer.

'I won't,' Julia replied even as Phoebe pulled her away.

The scene was reminiscent of Phoebe's childhood. She and her mum had lived with her grandparents until she was nine and both mother and daughter had suffered under Theresa's iron rule. Twenty years on, she still felt a certain giddiness whenever Julia helped her escape her grandmother's clutches. Back then, Julia had technically been Helen's babysitter, but Phoebe had stayed over at her friend's so often that Julia had been obliged to look after them both and she still did.

'I can't stay out long either,' Julia said after they had jumped into her car and escaped the large double-fronted house with its thick sandstone wall that imprisoned a carefully manicured garden.

Giving her the kind of look her nan would be proud of, Phoebe said, 'You're just saying that to make me feel better, aren't you?'

Even in the dim light Julia looked stunning, effortlessly so, with flawless skin that meant few people noticed the age difference between the friends. Her sense of style was timeless too, and tonight she had opted for jeans and a linen top beneath a woollen jacket. By contrast, Phoebe would describe herself as the short dumpy one, a perception that was reinforced, in Phoebe's mind at least, whenever she was in the company of her tall and leggy friends. To deflect her obvious failings, or perhaps to exaggerate them, Phoebe went for a more distinctive look. She might have outgrown her penchant for body piercing in her early teens, but she still liked to experiment with hair colour, or at least as much as her employer would allow. At the moment her short hair was a flaming shade between crimson and orange.

'I'm not, honestly,' Julia said, trying a little too hard to sound genuine. 'I've got a lot of work on at the moment and one of the reasons I wanted to bring the car was so I didn't drink.'

'Sounds like business is booming.'

'I have a new order and, oh, Phoebe, I can't tell you the last time a commission fired me up like this,' Julia began and went on to describe how desperate she was to impress her new client and his wife who she hoped would show off the piece to her friends and secure new orders. She made a steady income resizing rings and replacing missing gemstones to cover the rent of her workshop but this was the sort of work that gave her butterflies. She had until next week to come up with a selection of designs and her head was buzzing with ideas.

As Phoebe listened on, she tried hard to absorb her friend's enthusiasm but it didn't come easily. It had been Julia's love of art that had nurtured a similar passion within Phoebe, having set her two charges little art projects just to keep them out of trouble. Phoebe's dream had been to go into fashion design, but unlike Julia, an artistic career was nothing more than wishful thinking and the closest she came these days to designer labels were the ones she sold as a sales assistant in Debenhams.

'I'm so jealous,' she said, knowing she could speak her mind.

'I know, Phoebes, but your time will come.'

Although Phoebe knew any realistic opportunity had already passed her by, she was tempted to imagine she still had time, until Julia's next comment served up a dose of reality.

'Your nan looks well. How's she doing?'

'She went out shopping at lunchtime and left the grill on. It's a wonder she didn't burn the house down. Everything stinks of smoke now.' She wafted her coat sleeve in front of Julia's face.

'I did wonder about the smell.'

'I've unplugged everything in the kitchen just in case she decides to make some supper for herself,' she said, which explained her need to return home at a reasonable hour.

'Do you have any idea why Helen's called the meeting?' asked Julia.

'No. I take it you haven't either.'

'Well, we'll soon find out,' Julia said.

They were approaching the Elephant, which was on the corner of a row of shops and restaurants that ran the length of the main road through Woolton Village. From a cursory glance, the quaint village with its pretty churches and old-style cinema could be a rural outpost rather than a suburb less than ten miles from Liverpool city centre. Parking was at a premium but Julia spied an empty space in the tiny sunken car park that occupied the site of the old duck pond and was partly obscured by trees and a steep dip in the road. She made a sharp left turn without indicating and then had to swerve out of the path of a couple of pedestrians in her eagerness to grab the space before anyone else.

'Ready?' she asked as she brought the VW Beetle to a screeching halt, making them both lunge forward.

'I think I'd feel safer with my nan at the wheel!'

'She's not still driving, is she?' Julia asked as she rummaged on the floor to retrieve her umbrella.

'She would if she had her way but I've started hiding the keys and the car's been left languishing on the drive since before her knee op. I wish I'd got around to learning to drive,' Phoebe added, voicing another regret.

'I'll teach you if you like.'

Phoebe's look of horror wasn't feigned, but she tried to let her friend down gently. 'I wouldn't want to put you to any trouble and besides, I'd rather have proper lessons than learn your bad habits,' she said, jumping out of the car before Julia could retaliate.

'If you're sure,' Julia said when she rejoined her,

holding out her umbrella so they could both take shelter beneath it.

Phoebe refused this offer too. 'The rain might wash off the smell of smoke,' she said, already on the move.

They hurried across the road and into the pub where the third member of their group was waiting.

Helen Butler was standing at the bar with a half-empty glass of white wine in her hand. When she spied Phoebe at the entrance, she turned her back deliberately on the bloke who had spent the last ten minutes trying to chat her up, and waved at her friend who was busy scrunching up her flattened hair to give it some volume. Julia wasn't far behind but remained at the doorway determined to shake her umbrella dry. Helen surreptitiously picked up her own umbrella, leaving a large puddle on the floor where she had thoughtlessly dumped it earlier. Shaking it, she splashed her uninvited suitor who was forced to take a step back, allowing room for Phoebe to squeeze in next to her.

After giving her friend a hug, Helen handed her the glass of wine she had already ordered before saying, 'You stink by the way.'

Phoebe laughed as she slipped off her coat. 'Long story.'

Although they were the same age, Helen was often surprised at how different their tastes in fashion were. The skater dress and Doc Martens combo that Phoebe had chosen gave her a grungy look that was meant to frighten men off but actually made her look dangerously attractive. Helen, on the other hand, didn't really have a style of her own. Her youth had been cut short by unplanned motherhood and she rarely found time to think through her fashion choices. She had grabbed a lace dress from the laundry pile because it was the only decent outfit she had to hand that didn't need ironing, and had paired it with footless tights and platform shoes. As the mother of an eleven-year-old, she felt a bit of a fraud dressing so young and when she saw Julia's outfit, she wished she had gone for jeans too. They had similar body frames, but where Julia was more catwalk skinny with sleek auburn hair, Helen had softer curves and blonde curls and she knew she could never emulate Julia's air of sophistication, no matter how hard she tried.

After releasing Julia from the requisite hug, Helen said, 'I haven't ordered your drink yet, but I take it you don't want wine?'

'No, orange juice for me, please, with a splash of soda because I like living dangerously.'

Helen had also been offered a lift to the pub, but she had preferred to get there under her own steam. She was a nurse in a cardiology clinic and routinely worked beyond her shift, after which there followed various domestic duties which centred round her daughter, Milly. Things rarely went to plan which inevitably meant she would be the last to arrive. Today, however, the urge for that first glass of wine had spurred her on and she was already contemplating her second.

After ordering Julia's drink and a bottle of wine for the non-drivers, Helen said, 'I've booked a table – we are all eating, aren't we?'

'Oh, yes,' Julia said.

Helen could almost hear her friend salivating. 'Have

we been building up an appetite at the gym by any chance?'

'We? Since when did you go the gym?'

'Life is my workout,' she replied. 'OK, then, have *you* been to the gym?' When Julia nodded primly, she added, 'You and Paul are such fitness freaks, it's not healthy,' but then quickly pursed her lips, regretting the words as soon as they had left her mouth. When Helen spoke again, her usual flippancy had been replaced by the kind of serious tone she normally reserved for work. 'Still, it could be worse.'

Phoebe and Julia shared a look, each waiting for the other to ask why they had been summoned. When neither of them spoke, Helen was relieved. She wasn't quite ready to talk yet.

'Come on, our table's ready,' she said.

Two minutes later they were sitting at a table near a window, glasses in hand and a good view of the passers-by being hurried along by a biting November wind and sheets of icy rain – except Helen wasn't so much looking out of the window as she was peering into the middle distance in search of answers to unfathomable questions.

'So?' Julia said softly. 'We're listening.'

'He died,' Helen said, only then turning away from the window to face her friends.

'A patient?' Julia asked, knowing that if it had been a close relative or family friend, she would have already heard. Helen and Julia's mums were also best friends and their lives had combined to make one extended family. Even though Julia's mum had retired to Spain, it wouldn't have stopped the news from being relayed through the family network by now.

'Craig Winchester was thirty-one years old, a married father of two with another on the way. He was fit and healthy until two years ago when he contracted a virus that left his heart weakened. Surgery did the trick for a while, but things took a turn for the worse . . .'

'My God, he was younger than me or Paul,' Julia said.

'And not much older than us,' added Phoebe. 'It doesn't bear thinking about.'

'That's why it got to me, or at least part of the reason why. I'm thirty next year and I still don't feel like my life's got going properly – excepting the odd false start,' Helen said, referring to the failed marriage already under her belt. Her daughter Milly was the product of an intense teenage romance that had led to a relatively short-lived marriage. John and Helen had stayed together just long enough for her to complete her nursing training before she was thrown into single parenthood.

'And you're not the only one,' added Julia.

Helen wrinkled her nose at Julia to let her know she understood what she meant, and for a moment neither of them realized Phoebe was waiting to be noticed. When they did look at her, she said, 'Some of us haven't even made it to the starting line yet.'

Helen gave her a smile that she hadn't thought she had in her. However frustrated she felt now and again at having her wings clipped too early in life, she was blessed in comparison to the friend she had known since nursery school. It was there that they had formed a formidable friendship, dreaded by their teachers and envied by their classmates, and it had been strong enough to survive a lengthy break. Phoebe's mum had run off with her daughter

20

to Manchester when Phoebe was nine and when they had met up again in their teens, the intervening years had left their mark on both of them. Helen was the not-so-proud mother of a newborn baby while Phoebe was damaged for reasons she would never share. She had been wild and reckless, even by the standards of a teenage mum, and it had taken the determined Theresa Dodd to eventually tame her granddaughter, destroying her free spirit in the process.

'And his wife was pregnant?' Julia asked as the finer details of the stranger's life came into clear focus in her mind.

Helen took a long sip of wine that practically drained the glass. 'Yes, and she was convinced we would be able to save him, especially after he was put on the list for a heart transplant. Craig, on the other hand, took a lot of persuading that he should be considered at all. He was such a lovely person,' she said of the man who had made a lasting impression on her. 'Although I'm sure he thought coming to clinic was a bit like stepping into the confessional. Every time I saw him he'd tell me about some past misdemeanour or other as if to prove how unworthy he was of being a recipient. He told me about pinching his dad's cigarettes when he was a teenager, and how he got so drunk at a wedding that he and his brother did their very own version of *The Full Monty*.' Helen tried to laugh but it was as much as she could manage to staunch her tears. 'I would have liked to have seen that because he looked a bit like Robbie Williams.'

'Your one true love,' Julia said, referring to Helen's teenage obsession.

'Except, dare I say it, Craig was even lovelier. He argued against getting bumped up the list in case he took the place

21

of someone who, in his opinion, might be more deserving. Even in the last month when he was told it might only be a matter of weeks . . .'

'What that family must have gone through. What his wife *will* be going through . . .' Julia said, shaking her head as her words trailed off.

'She was going to be induced on Thursday,' Helen said, then had to swallow hard before adding, 'Just so he could hold the baby.'

Again Helen and Julia held each other's gaze and when Julia looked away, she glanced longingly at the bottle of wine.

'You could always leave the car and pick it up tomorrow,' Helen said. 'Or phone Paul. Couldn't he jog over and drive you home tonight?' She knew Paul well and the suggestion was a reasonable one.

'I shouldn't,' Julia said.

Helen knew there was more to Julia's decision not to drink than simply the car, so she didn't push. As it turned out she didn't have to because within moments, Julia had sent and received a reply from Paul.

'I do love that man,' she said, grabbing an empty glass from the next table. 'He'll pick us all up whenever we're ready to leave.

Phoebe poured the wine. 'You don't know how lucky you are.'

'Oh, yes, I do,' Julia said, took a sip of wine and then added, 'OK, maybe I do take Paul for granted *some*times.'

'We all take our health for granted,' Helen piped up. She spied the waiter coming over and scanned the menu that she already knew off by heart. 'Maybe I should order a salad.'

'What can I get you, ladies?' he asked.

'More wine, please,' Helen said without hesitation and then turned to square up to her friends. 'I said we take our health for granted. I don't remember saying anything about living like nuns. And because we have Julia setting us a good example with her health regime, we're probably entitled to some brownie points just by association. Wouldn't you say so, Phoebes?'

'I'll drink to that!'

There were smiles all around and by the time the waiter had taken their order – which didn't include a single salad leaf – the shadow that had followed Helen from the hospital had begun to recede. But before all thoughts of their fragile mortality could be laid to rest, Julia had an idea. 'I think I'll register as an organ donor.'

'You mean you're not already?' Helen said, genuinely shocked. 'I work in a cardiology unit, for goodness' sake! We're the ones struggling to keep alive the patients who don't get the call from the transplant centre, all because there aren't enough donor organs to go around. Have you not been listening to a word I've said all these years?'

Julia shrugged guiltily. 'I had thought about it, I just hadn't got around to doing it.'

'And what about you?' Helen demanded of Phoebe. Another shrug told her all she needed to know. 'Right, you two, let's do it now.'

Helen took out her phone, opened up the Internet and found the online registration page. 'OK, who wants to go first?' she asked.

They emerged from the pub to find the night as blustery as they had left it, but at least the rain had been swept away. Linking arms, they crossed the road with Helen and Julia teetering like fawns down the steep incline into the car park. If it weren't for Phoebe in her Doc Martens, they would have fallen at least twice and, as it was, Julia only managed to stop herself when she thumped against a car. Thankfully it was hers.

'Had a nice night, ladies?'

The three women were still interlinked and a sudden fit of giggles made the task of detangling themselves doubly hard. Their observer waited patiently. He was wrapped up against the elements with the collar of his heavy woollen jacket turned up and a scarf wrapped around his neck that matched his beanie hat. He was tall with dark features that belied the gentlest of hearts and he was the man Julia had been looking for, although she hadn't known it the first time she had set eyes on him.

Julia had been distinctly wary when Paul had started chatting her up at the gym. She had just turned thirty and was recovering from her break-up with her pathetic excuse of a fiancé, who had waited until a week before their wedding to tell her he wasn't ready to settle down. When she had been playing hard to get with Paul, there had been no acting required. She had been deeply suspicious of his motives, not sure why someone five years her junior would be interested in her, but his deep brown eyes had drawn her to him, as they did now.

'You didn't mind coming out, did you?' she asked.

'That depends. Are you all going to behave?'

'Not if you don't want us to,' Helen said as she took what she intended to be a step forward, except her balance was out of kilter and she tumbled into his arms. 'Hey, watch where you put those hands, pal!' she cried.

Julia gently prised her friend from her husband. 'Excuse me! You watch where you're putting *your* hands.'

'It was worth a try,' Helen said and grabbed hold of Phoebe for consolation. 'Nobody wants us, Phoebes. We've got too much baggage.'

Phoebe and Julia wore identical scowls although for entirely different reasons. 'Speak for yourself,' Phoebe said, 'I'm alone because I choose to be, and my nan wouldn't be too pleased if she heard you referring to her as baggage.'

'And I'm sure Milly would object to being called baggage too,' Julia reminded Helen.

Helen waved her hand dismissively. 'Oh, my little Milly the Millstone has heard me say it often enough.'

'You had better not call her that to her face, Helen!' Julia said, suddenly sobering up. 'I'm not suggesting you have it easy but you shouldn't take her for granted.'

There was a mixture of pain and envy in Julia's face that Helen couldn't ignore. 'I was only joking, Julia, you know what I'm like,' she said. 'Life's too short to be taken seriously, but it doesn't mean I don't love my little—' When she faltered, it was obvious she was struggling to think of a more flattering description for her daughter than one of a collection she would normally use. Sounding distinctly unsure that she had found the right word, she said, 'My little *princess*. Milly is more important to me than life itself and she knows it.' She cupped Julia's face. 'Friends?'

'Always.'

Phoebe cleared her throat. She had been standing to one side looking dejected.

'Come on,' Julia said, tugging her sleeve so they could form an untidy rugby scrum.

Paul was shaking his head and Helen caught him. 'And you too,' she said. 'Come on, don't be shy.'

'Maybe we should let Paul join our other club too,' Phoebe suggested once they were in the car.

'I'm on the case,' Helen said. She took out her phone and her tongue poked out as she tried to focus on the screen. Paul was driving away from Woolton towards their first drop-off point, which was Helen's house. 'Right, what's your full name, Paul?'

'Erm, I don't think so. I'm not signing up for anything until I know what you lot are up to.'

'Paul Ernest Richardson,' Julia said.

'I should have remembered that,' Helen said, and once the sniggers had died down she tapped in the details and ignored Paul's demands to know what she was doing.

'Date of birth?'

Paul pulled up at a red light and turned to glare at his wife. 'No, Julia, not until you tell me what's going on.'

'Oh, don't worry,' she said, leaning over to kiss his pouting mouth. 'We're just making you even more of a hero than you are already.'

When Paul continued to look uncomfortable it was Phoebe who put him out of his misery. 'It's nothing bad. We've all signed up as organ donors, that's all.'

'That's all?' he repeated with a note of incredulity.

Paul was still staring at his wife, his face glowing red,

26

amber, and then green in the reflected light. 'The lights have changed,' she said.

'One of my patients died today waiting for a heart transplant,' Helen explained. 'Julia and Phoebe have registered and now it's your turn. So? Can I have your date of birth?'

Making an exaggerated effort to navigate another junction, Paul let the silence extend long enough to let his reluctance be known. The subject was dropped, and at first the silence was broken only by the occasional hiccup from Phoebe. Eventually Helen started babbling on about Milly's latest antics, stories her friends had already heard but it was better than nothing. But once Helen had been dropped off, it was left to Julia and Phoebe to fill the void, and Paul spoke only when he was asked a direct question.

'Phoebe's thinking of learning to drive,' Julia told him. 'You'll give her lessons, won't you?'

Paul was tapping his fingers on the steering wheel as he waited for another set of traffic lights to change. 'Yeah, sure.'

'Julia, I said I'd sort it myself,' Phoebe insisted.

'Oh, you'd never get round to it if we didn't give you a little push. You've put it off long enough as it is. Helen passed her test when Milly was still a baby.'

'Good for Helen.'

Ignoring the huffing and puffing from her friend, Julia continued, 'All I'm saying is you should have done it years ago.'

There was a deep sigh and when she did speak, Phoebe's voice was slurred and yet still barbed with pain. 'Well, I can't go back and change things, can I? And believe me, if I could then learning to drive wouldn't even make the top ten.'

'Sorry, I know I'm being pushy,' Julia said. Her friend had always played down the struggles she had faced during her early life, and had outright refused to talk about her mum's death, which had prompted her return to Liverpool. But as the years went by and Phoebe's life continued to stall, it was becoming increasingly hard for Julia to stand back and let it happen. 'I won't mention it again.'

'It's OK, Julia, I know you're only looking out for me.'

When they pulled up outside Phoebe's grandmother's house, Julia noticed a curtain twitch.

'I don't mind giving you lessons,' Paul said as Phoebe got out of the car. 'The offer's there if you want it.'

Once she was alone with her husband, Julia said, 'So you do have a heart after all.'

'Yes, and one I intend to use for my own purposes, thank you very much.'

'But why? Why don't you want to register as an organ donor, Paul?'

He squirmed a little in his seat. 'I'm just a bit creeped out by it, that's all. It's the whole idea of bits of me living on while the rest of me is dead and buried.'

'I was planning on having you cremated.'

'You know what I mean.' He visibly shuddered when he repeated, 'It's just the thought of it.'

'But the point is, Paul,' Julia said, trying to form a cohesive argument while fighting through a hazy, alcohol-induced fog, 'you'll be dead so there'll be no "thinking" involved.'

'I know but, I'm sorry, I just don't want to do it.'

'Why not? You're a lovely, sweet, generous man, Paul, and I'm struggling to understand.'

'I don't think I can explain. I wouldn't want someone walking around with my heart beating inside them, and I certainly wouldn't want them walking around with yours.'

'Well, I don't care what you think, I'm registered – and it's my wishes that count.'

'They'd still have to ask for my consent.'

Julia stared open-mouthed at her husband, her expression all the more exaggerated after consuming far more wine than her body was used to of late. 'You mean you'd go against my wishes?'

'It just doesn't feel right.'

'I'll tell you what's not right. People who deserve a chance to live just as much as you and me, are dying when they could be saved. Helen sees it all the time and she was really upset this evening. The patient who died was younger than us and . . .' An image came to mind of three children who would grow up without a father, one of whom hadn't even entered the world yet. 'And his wife's pregnant.'

Paul took a deep breath and his words were released almost as a sigh. 'Is that what this is about?'

The flare of anger came from nowhere, and whereas a sober Julia could dampen her fury, venomous words tumbled out of her mouth unabated. 'No, *that* isn't what it's about! Do all my motives and reactions have to be centred round the fact that I can't have a baby? Am I not allowed to sympathize with a woman – pregnant or not – whose husband has just died needlessly when there might have been a potential donor out there somewhere except he felt a bit "creeped out" about organ donation?'

29

'Julia—'

'Why does it always have to come back to having babies? Why has our whole life been taken over by me getting pregnant? Everything we do, including doing *it*, has to be checked and double-checked against a schedule. I can't look at a calendar without thinking about my monthly cycle or how I'm approaching forty at breakneck speed. I can't put anything in my mouth without considering how it's going to affect my fertility. I'm riddled with guilt just because I had a drink tonight, and I'm sick of it, Paul, sick of trying so bloody hard and getting nowhere. I want the waiting to be over, I can't stand it any more!'

She hadn't noticed that Paul had pulled over to the kerb until he unbuckled his seatbelt and leaned towards her. She wrapped her arms around his neck and held onto him as she began to sob.

'It's all right,' he whispered, 'I know it's hard but we have to keep believing it'll be worth it in the end.'

Julia sniffed back her tears as the embarrassment of making a fool of her drunken self took hold, but her feelings had broken free and it was too late to backtrack now. 'But it's already been two years, Paul. If it hasn't happened by now, maybe it never will.'

'So isn't it time we went back to the doctor and asked for a referral to see a specialist?'

It had been a contentious issue between them for almost a year now. They had gone as far as broaching the subject with their GP and with the help of the practice nurse Julia had thrown herself into learning all the self-help techniques, from ovulation tests to strict diets, relaxation methods to the best positions during sex. They had followed all the advice to the letter and every month they had experienced a fleeting sense of hope when Julia was convinced her body felt different only to realize it was nothing more than the usual premenstrual changes. And this had happened every month without fail since she had stopped using contraceptives more than two years ago, at a point in their lives when they had settled into married life and their careers were established. She had been thirty-seven and she had presumed that the time for children had been right. She had thought they would be planning for baby number two by now, sitting in a people carrier rather than crammed into the VW Beetle that was starting to make her feel claustrophobic.

The next step would be for both of them to go through a series of exploratory tests to identify potential problems, and it was Julia who had been prevaricating, praying month after month that it was an unnecessary intervention. In truth she was frightened about what might be uncovered and every scenario held its own horrors. How would she feel if she were infertile, which was the most likely outcome given her age? Would Paul blame her or at least resent her? He wanted to be a father so much and if she couldn't make that happen, would she be able to live with the guilt? Worse still, how would she console Paul if it were him? And what if the doctors couldn't find a problem, what would they do then? What if there was no quick fix? Would they need to go through fertility treatment? Would they even be eligible now that she was so old? How many more months, if not years, of agonized waiting lay ahead? Would their marriage survive that kind of stress or would she be jilted yet again?

'I can't,' she said, sitting up straight to wipe her eyes and then focusing on the road ahead. She had to place a hand over her chest to calm her racing heart. 'Can't we just go home?'

Paul didn't move. 'I know you're scared, Julia, I am too, but we can't go on like this.'

'The only thing I feel right now is tired and a bit queasy. If you don't get me home soon I just might throw up in the car.'

The threat worked and when they arrived home a few minutes later, the issue was put off for yet another day.

3

The Accident

Anya's patient lay unresponsive on the trolley as she was rushed into the Accident and Emergency Department which was in as much a state of mayhem as the crash site, albeit slightly less chaotic. Anya exchanged brief looks with colleagues she hadn't worked with since transferring to the surgical ward, each registering the shock that she should be back in the thick of it as a triage nurse. But there was no time for chitchat; the pressure was on and they all had a job to do.

As a precaution, her patient had been placed in a back brace at the scene while they treated some of the more obvious injuries, which included a broken arm and a nasty gash to her side. These were superficial injuries in the scheme of things and of more concern was the woman's raised heart rate and falling blood pressure, which suggested a ruptured spleen.

With her condition deteriorating rapidly, Anya made sure she received immediate attention, which wasn't easy with the department at breaking point, but that was the point of triage, to prioritize.

While Anya was updating the team on her patient's condition, the woman began to mumble. Leaping at the opportunity to glean some information from her, she leaned in closer.

'Hello, can you hear me?'

The woman's eyes flickered open but remained unfocused. 'Where am I?' she murmured.

'Warrington General. You've been involved in an accident, but you're in safe hands. We're here to look after you.'

'We were going to London,' she said. 'We shouldn't have . . .'

'It's all right, don't worry about that now,' Anya said as the woman became sufficiently aware to start feeling scared. 'Let's just concentrate on getting you better, shall we?'

The woman remained agitated. 'The others? Where are they?'

'They'll be receiving the best care we can give them, but right now you're my first priority,' Anya told her. 'Can you tell me your name?'

'Phoebe,' she said. 'Phoebe Dodd.'

4

Julia had spent the morning at her workbench finishing off a handful of repair jobs before returning to her desk where she had made a start on the anniversary designs the day before. The workshop was draped in cold wintery shadow with the exception of a warm pool of light cast from a desk lamp onto the unopened sketchpad in front of her. She had lost her mojo and the flashes of inspiration that had fired her up the day before had been replaced by white pain between her temples.

She was sitting in her old leather chair that creaked every time she moved so she moved slowly and deliberately as she opened up the sketchpad. She picked up a fine-tipped pen and pressed down hard against the cream cartridge paper, watching black ink bloom from beneath the nib. By the time she had summoned up the strength to lift it, a nasty inkspot had developed in the centre of one of her pendant designs. Her client's wife was a nature lover and Julia had been working on a modern design in the shape of a chrysanthemum, chosen specifically because it represented fidelity and long life. Dewdrops of diamonds denoted their three children and she had intended to add smaller gemstones to signify not only the three grandchildren they had already, but those that would undoubtedly follow. And that was when her mind had stalled, tripping over the word – *undoubtedly*.

Julia tore the sheet from her pad and scrunched it into a ball. She was too exhausted to throw it at the wall so flung it lazily across the desk before picking up a polishing cloth to drape over the lamp. With her designs consigned to the shadows, she rested her head on her folded arms and closed her eyes. She could hear the hustle and bustle rising up from the street below. This part of Bold Street was pedestrianized and the sound of traffic was no more than a distant hum, so it was the noise from the passers-by that drew her attention. There were shouts and occasional bursts of laughter, a mournful police siren crying from afar and as she strained her ears she thought she heard a baby cry. A familiar yearning began to build deep inside her and she wanted to cry too.

When she and Paul had gone to bed the night before, she hadn't been sure if he was angry with her, disappointed or simply resigned to her obstinacy. She would have liked to have seen him that morning but he had let her sleep through the alarm and had vanished by the time she had rolled out of bed. They had never sat down and confronted their problems head on, not really, and perhaps that was because it had crept up on them so stealthily. She had been thirty-four when they had married and although they both wanted kids, there had been no urgency to start a family. Paul was that much younger so putting it off for a few years seemed the right thing to do, or at least it had back then.

In the early days of trying, there had been disappointment and growing impatience as the pregnancy tests were left unopened in the bathroom cabinet – she was so regular that she could predict her period to the day if not the hour. After six months, Julia had started to worry that something was wrong but had left it another six before she plucked up the courage to raise the spectre of infertility with Paul. He had tried to convince her that there was nothing to worry about yet, but it was his use of the word 'yet' that had made her realize that he was harbouring doubts too. The nearest they had come to an open and frank discussion had been with the GP and even then it was his platitudes about there *probably* being nothing to worry about that they had clung to. But after another year of ever-weakening reassurances, it was impossible to ignore the growing fear that, after a lifetime spent mothering other people in her life, she may never actually get to be a mother.

Julia pushed her face down hard against her arm, the pressure alone holding back her tears. A high-pitched beep from the adjoining room warned that someone had come into the reception area, but she couldn't bring herself to move. It was only when the door to the workshop creaked open and fluorescent light leaked into the darkness that she forced herself to lift her head.

'I thought you might be in need of some vitamin C,' Paul said.

Julia stared at the bottle of orange juice her husband had placed in front of her, if only to block out the sight of the pack of sandwiches lying alongside it, but the

37

astringent smell of mayonnaise was already wafting towards her, making her stomach heave.

'OK, I'll take those away,' he said, retrieving the tuna sandwiches and tearing open the packet as he sat down in the visitor's chair opposite. 'So how are we feeling today?'

Julia mumbled something that even she couldn't understand.

'That good, eh? What happened to treating your body like a temple?'

'I think all the gods have deserted this particular empty vessel,' she said, holding Paul's gaze. Was he admonishing her? She didn't need him to tell her that alcohol affected fertility but she was starting to think she was beyond hope. She wanted to drop her head back down but held her nerve. 'I'm so sorry about last night, Paul. In fact, I'm sorry about everything.'

'It's not your fault.'

Julia was tempted to argue that it might very well be her fault and he had every right to blame her, but these were words she had guarded against, even when she had been drunk. She couldn't argue about where the blame should lie, because what if it wasn't her body that was at fault but his? However unlikely, it remained a possibility. She had to keep telling herself that neither of them was to blame, they had done everything by the book. Like her, Paul had been following all the latest medical advice to improve their chances of conceiving. And while she might have temporarily fallen off the wagon, as far as she was aware, Paul never had – which only went to prove that he wanted this baby as much as she did, if not more so. 'I'm still sorry,' she persisted. 'Do you hate me? Am I turning into a neurotic wife?'

'No and no,' he said, answering her questions in turn, but then his eyes narrowed, letting her know that she wasn't completely forgiven. 'But we do need to talk.'

'I know,' she said weakly.

'You summed it up last night when you said you were sick of getting nowhere. I'm sick of it too. I hate spending two weeks of every month walking on eggshells in case one wrong move wrecks our chances of conceiving, followed by two weeks of dragging ourselves out of the mire so we can gear ourselves up to try again. One of us was bound to blow a fuse and it happened to be you but it could so easily have been me. This is killing me, Julia.'

When he stopped to clear his throat, Julia wanted to leap up and hold him but he hadn't finished what he needed to say and she needed to let him say it. 'I know it's hard admitting that there might be a real problem, especially when we have no idea if that problem will kick parenthood into touch or simply make it a long, frustrating and no doubt costly journey to get there. But,' he added, 'at least we'd be able to look ahead further than the next month.'

'If we have to start fertility treatment, then the going will get tougher. You do realize that, don't you?'

'I know, but let's have the tests first and see what we're up against. If nothing else, it might help manage our expectations, which, if I'm being honest, are already at rock bottom. Even if the specialists were to tell us that there's practically no chance of us having kids, that's more chance than I think we stand right now.'

'You think it won't happen?' Julia asked, her words trembling over her lips. It was one thing to think it herself, but to hear Paul admit it too was unbearable.

'I think it won't happen naturally and . . .'

Julia's head had been throbbing but the pain intensified as her blood pressure soared. 'And what?'

'And maybe we shouldn't even be trying – at least not until we know *why* things aren't happening. We need a break from all this pressure we're putting ourselves under, Julia.'

'You want me to go back on the pill?'

The half-eaten sandwich in Paul's hand was beginning to droop and he shoved it back into its container. 'No, I'm not saying that at all. I'm only suggesting we stop letting it take over our lives. No ovulation tests, no special diets. We eat and drink what we want when we want without feeling guilty, and we have sex simply for the fun of it. I miss that old life, Julia. I miss the old us.'

She didn't answer immediately. Asking her to agree to see a specialist was a big step in itself, but to throw away even one month's opportunity to become pregnant naturally was too much to ask. She couldn't do it – but as she looked at Paul, she could see the pain in his eyes. She wanted to take away that hurt and began wondering how she could keep up with the old regime without him noticing as she said, 'I miss us too.'

When Paul stood up, she took hold of his outstretched hand. He pulled her to her feet and, slipping his arms around her waist, began kissing her neck.

'Don't you have to be back at work soon?'

'Not yet,' he whispered in her ear. 'Don't you remember what it was like?'

'What?' she asked softly.

'Doing it just for fun?' His hands moved down to her hips and he pushed her back against the desk.

She laughed and gasped at the same time. 'Here?'

'Here.'

She was still smiling as Paul kissed her full on the lips. When he lifted her onto the desk and her sketchpad and pens fell to the floor, she didn't care, and for once she wasn't thinking of sex as a means to an end. She hadn't realized how much she had missed making love instead of making babies, and it felt good.

Helen turned her back on the sink full of breakfast dishes. The only soapy suds she was interested in was the long bath she intended to slip into just as soon as she was left to her own devices. It was Saturday morning and the housework could wait, most likely until Sunday evening when it would dawn on her that neither she nor her daughter had clean uniforms to wear the next day.

'Aren't you dressed yet?' she asked Milly when she poked her head into her daughter's room.

The *little princess* made a point of looking her mother up and down before replying. 'Aren't you?'

'I'm not the one due to be picked up in ten minutes.'

Milly was sitting on her unmade bed holding her iPad, which she had used to while away the last hour messaging her friends. Following Julia's advice, Helen set limits on how much time her eleven-year-old daughter spent on gadgets during the week, but she was a firm believer in

41

letting loose a little at the weekend. If anything, Milly was more self-disciplined than her mother. She certainly hadn't been impressed that Helen had nursed a hangover for two full days after the mid-week session with her friends.

Dragging herself off the bed, Milly went to her wardrobe and pulled out a pair of jeans and a jumper. She turned to find her mum still watching.

'Can I have some privacy, please?'

Helen went into her own bedroom to brush the tats out of her honey-blonde hair. Even in her pyjamas, she looked reasonably presentable thanks to smoky eyes that were an accidental result of not washing her make-up off the night before. It was a look that Phoebe would approve of, but not necessarily Julia who was the person she was about to face.

Julia and Paul were planning a day trip to Martin Mere, a wetlands reserve just north of Ormskirk, in search of inspiration for Julia's latest commission. Apparently she wanted to get up close and personal to nature and they had offered to take Milly with them.

Julia was practically a second mum to Milly and had been from the moment she was born. At eighteen, Helen hadn't been prepared for life as a wife and mother. Her own mother hadn't been too impressed at becoming a grandmother either, and while she helped as much as she could, she had expected Helen to face up to her responsibilities. Julia, on the other hand, was twenty-eight, happily engaged, and more than willing to get some practice in, and would look after Milly at the drop of a hat. And even when her fiancé had dumped her, Julia had still somehow been there for her, and Helen had muddled through parenthood thanks in no small part to her friend.

Paul had played an important role in her life too, arriving on the scene just in time to act as mediator between Helen and her soon-to-be ex-husband. Where Helen might otherwise have screamed abuse at John for bailing out on what was undoubtedly a disaster of a marriage, Paul had talked reason, to both of them. The end result was that John was still a key player in their daughter's life and although Helen would never admit it to her ex, she needed him, if only to take his fair share of the burden. Too often, Helen felt old before her time and she savoured those precious moments when she didn't have to be the responsible adult.

Grabbing a handful of rollers she would use to curl her hair while she soaked in the bath, Helen headed back downstairs where she caught sight of a red car pulling up outside. 'They're here!' she shouted up to Milly.

Even as she opened the door, Milly was rushing past her. She had managed to get ready at breakneck speed and was dragging Julia out of the car so she could pull back the front seat and dive in the back.

'Erm, haven't you forgotten something?' Helen asked.

Milly turned slowly, her face a picture of innocence as she looked from the coat draped over one arm to the backpack dangling from the other. 'No, I don't think so.'

Standing on the doorstep of their small terraced house with her arms folded, Helen out-stared her daughter. Milly let out a groan and scraped her feet along the pavement as she returned to her mum, offering up a cheek to kiss. Helen grabbed her in a bear hug and smothered her face in kisses. Despite herself, Milly giggled.

Released from Helen's clutches, Milly made a second dash for freedom and flung herself onto the back seat. 'Go, go, go!' she cried when she noticed her mum coming out onto the street to speak to Julia.

'In a minute, sweetheart,' Julia said and turned to greet Helen. 'You could come with us if you want?'

'Thank you but there's a Lush Bath Bomb with my name on it and the only water I intend stepping into will be blue and glittery, not smelling of duck poo.'

'Having a lazy day, are we?' asked Julia.

'Actually no, I was just off to the shops. I could get away with this look, don't you think?' She opened up her dressing gown to reveal Elmo pyjamas.

'Mum, don't you dare!' Milly cried.

Helen looked confused for a moment and then dug her hand into her pocket. 'Of course, I forgot these.' She took out the hair rollers and proceeded to wrap a lock of hair around one, winding her daughter up at the same time.

'Pleeeease, Mum, just go back inside.'

'OK, but if I'm banned from going out then I suppose I'll have to leave the shopping until tomorrow. You'd have to come with me though.'

'OK,' Milly mumbled.

'And by that, I mean you'd have to help me pack and unpack the shopping.'

Milly huffed a little. 'OK, I'll do it.' She turned to Paul who had been silent throughout. 'Please, Uncle Paul, save me.'

Paul laughed. 'Helen, leave the poor child alone,' he said sternly.

Helen grinned at him. 'I'll leave her in your charge then.

Just remember, don't get her wet and don't feed her after midnight.'

Having never watched *Gremlins*, Milly had even more reason for wanting to escape. 'Please, can't you see she's insane?'

Julia got back in the car and went through a last-minute checklist. 'Got your wellies?'

'Yes.'

'Seatbelt?'

The clasp clicked into place.

'OK then, we'll see you later,' Julia said to Helen as she closed the door.

'Have fun and don't rush back on my account.'

From the way Julia's face lit up the moment she had set eyes on Milly, Helen had no doubt that her friend would thrive on the opportunity to play happy families. She also knew from experience that when they did drop her back off, the sparkle in her eyes would have dimmed as she faced the prospect of returning home to her empty nest.

As they drove away, Milly had her arms folded across her chest. 'Mothers!' she muttered under her breath.

From the corner of her eye, Julia watched Paul struggle to keep his smile in check. It was during these little excursions with Milly that Julia could see the full extent of the shadow that had been cast over their lives. It scared her, because even if she were ever to reconcile herself to a childless marriage, she wasn't so sure that Paul could, or even that he should.

Her husband's tone was firm when he said, 'Good morning, Millicent. Yes, I'm fine, thanks for asking.'

'Sorry. Morning, Uncle Paul. Morning, Julia.'

Julia turned in her seat. Her poker face wasn't as good as Paul's. 'I'm really looking forward to this. How about you?'

'How long will it take to get there?'

'Oh, only about forty-five minutes,' Julia said, hoping the traffic would be on their side. 'Can you cope with being tied to your seat for that long?'

Julia's heart pulled a little when she saw Milly dragging her bag onto her knee and taking out her iPad. She didn't want to fight for the little girl's attention with a flashy piece of technology. If she allowed Milly to be drawn into her electronic world it would be difficult to pull her back and Julia debated whether or not to say something. She wondered if they should set a rule about not using it when they took her out, but she was afraid that laying down the law would put Milly off going out with them in future. Her friend's daughter had no idea how precious this time with her was to them, but it was hardly surprising when, in contrast, her mother made such a big deal of getting rid of her. Helen's love for Milly was never in doubt but Julia wished she wouldn't take her for granted so much.

'I've downloaded an app that lets you record all the different kinds of wildlife we're going to see. Look,' Milly said, turning the screen to show Julia thumbnail photos of various species of birds.

'I don't think we'll get to see many swallows and martins,' Julia warned as she scanned the list. 'It's too cold in this country during the winter. They'll all be sunning themselves somewhere a bit warmer.'

'What will we see then?'

'I'm not sure,' Julia said, which wasn't exactly true. She had never been to Martin Mere before but she had read up about it when she had scoured the Internet for family day trips in the North West. The wetland centre was perfect for their needs. It would give her the inspiration she needed for her jewellery designs as would immersing herself briefly into the family life she and Paul yearned for. 'All I know is there are huge flocks of swans and geese that should be quite a sight around feeding time, but as for the rest, I'm counting on you to do the exploring. Paul's brought his binoculars so we can pinch them off him when he's not looking.'

'It's all right, I've brought my dad's,' Milly said, heaving a large pair out of her bag.

'No wonder that bag was weighing you down – they're huge,' Julia said.

Milly pushed the binoculars between the front seats so Paul could see. 'Looks like I'll be the one trying to nab yours,' he said.

'Dad says we can go birdwatching in the Lake District in the summer if I want. He said it would be good for me to have a hobby,' she said but her voice was already trailing off when she added, 'I think he just wants me to have something to keep me occupied while he's busy . . . You know.'

Julia's jaw tightened as she tried to summon up the urge to say the right thing and not take advantage of an evolving situation. 'I'm sure when the new baby comes along, your dad will be making an extra special effort to involve you. The last thing he'll want is for you to feel pushed out.'

'Do you think?'

'I don't think, I *know*,' Julia said.

If Milly didn't hear the catch in her voice, Paul did. 'It's hard work looking after a baby and for the first few months your dad and Eva are going to be pretty exhausted,' he said. 'Maybe you won't be able to do the kind of stuff you're used to, but it won't be because they don't want to, Milly. I can promise you that.'

'I've told them I can help look after the baby, but I don't think they want me to.'

'Oh, just wait until they're up to their eyes in nappies, they'll be glad of your help, believe me,' Julia said. Her jaw was aching from her forced smile.

'That's what I thought,' Milly said although she didn't sound convinced. 'And it's not like I would want paying to babysit.'

Paul turned his head even while his eyes remained on the road. 'Babysit?'

'Yes. Why not?'

'Because maybe you're still a bit too young,' Julia said. 'And I'm pretty sure it's against the law to leave a baby with a child of your age.'

'I'm not a child, I'm eleven!' When neither Paul nor Julia looked reassured, she added, 'Well, how old do I have to be then?'

Julia shrugged. 'A *lot* older and by that time, babysitting will be the last thing on your mind. I should know, I got landed with your mum and Phoebe when I would have much preferred to be out with my friends.'

'*Boy*friends, you mean,' Paul teased.

'Yes, I do,' Julia said, not afraid to take the bait. 'You have to play the field, Milly.'

'Erm, no, she doesn't,' Paul said quickly. 'Milly is going to be locked in her room until she's at least twenty-one.'

Milly had been making various retching noises to demonstrate her own repulsion at the idea. 'I wouldn't want a boyfriend even then!'

'You don't want to get married when you're older?' Julia asked.

'No,' she snorted, 'and I definitely don't want babies. I don't know why you're so mad about trying to get one.'

The pause was long enough for a lump to form in Julia's throat. 'You might change your mind one day,' she managed to say.

'Hey, look,' Paul said, 'there's the sign for Martin Mere. Right, Milly, I need you to be my navigator – you know how hopeless Julia is, so could you watch out for the signs for me?'

While Milly kept her eyes peeled for the signposts, Paul reached over to squeeze Julia's hand. She kept hold of it for as long as she could and resolved not to let fears for the future interfere with their enjoyment of the day. It wasn't as hard as she expected because Milly's excitement was infectious.

'Feeling inspired yet?' Paul asked after they had taken shelter in one of the bird hides that lined the mere. The temperature outside was hovering just above freezing and the vague white orb of watery light in the sky offered little hope for improvement. The wooden hides were only marginally warmer and despite wearing padded winter coats, woollen hats and thermal gloves, they were all shivering.

'I might take some photographs rather than sketch,' Julia

said. 'There's no way I'm taking my gloves off for more than a few seconds.'

'How about you, Milly? Are you going to be put off by a little frostbite?' Paul asked, having to raise his voice above the cacophony rising up from hundreds of swans and geese gathering expectantly at the water's edge.

Milly had her hands over her ears but her eyes were wide with wonder. 'It's amazing!' she said and then gasped at the sudden thunderclap created by countless wings thrashing against wind and water. One of the keepers had appeared with a wheelbarrow and began flinging shovelfuls of grain into the air. Feeding time.

Amidst the geese and swans, seagulls and shelducks took to the air and fought for their share of the bounty. Julia began clicking away with her camera but the flock was moving fast and it would be sheer luck if she captured individual birds in flight without chopping off heads in her photos. The sights and sounds were thrilling and no one spoke until the noise had died down and Milly checked the guide to choose their next stop-off point.

'Can we go and see the otters now?' she asked, grabbing hold of Paul's hand and pulling him away.

'Hold on, what about me?' Julia's words were muffled by the glove she was holding in her mouth while adjusting the settings on her camera.

Paul and Milly were already on the move and although Julia was quick to follow she didn't rush to catch them up. She was happy to watch her husband being led by the little girl with masses of auburn hair, colouring she had inherited from her father but made it possible for Julia to pass Milly off as her own. Judging by the way

Paul was holding her hand, you would think him the doting father.

Julia lifted her camera to eye level and made no apologies for capturing an image she could hang her dreams on. Paul turned and waved at her and then Milly did the same. Soon they were posing for the camera and pulling faces until Julia couldn't hold the camera steady for laughing. She gave up and went to join them.

'Paul said those two swans over there are in love,' Milly said, pointing to a pair of dazzlingly white birds as they drifted effortlessly across the aptly named Swan Lake, oblivious to the clamour that had so recently erupted from the mere. They had eyes only for each other.

'Mmrph, hurumph . . .' Julia said.

Paul took the glove from her mouth. 'And in English, please.'

'They might just be the inspiration I need,' she said and spent the next few minutes taking long shots and close-ups of the swans while Paul sat with Milly at a nearby picnic table to tick off all the different birds they had spotted so far.

'I don't know about you,' Julia said as she struggled to replace the lens cap on her camera with numb fingers, 'but I'm ready for something to warm me up. How about we get some hot chocolate?'

'But what about the otters?' Milly whined, clearly not feeling the cold as much as her older companions.

'They'll still be there in half an hour,' Paul said, agreeing with his wife.

'OK,' Milly said brightly before darting off in the direction of the café.

Julia was shaking her head and laughing again. 'That took a lot of persuasion, but then of course she'd do anything you asked of her. She idolizes you, Paul.'

'Oh, I'm just a stand-in,' Paul said, looking uncomfortable. 'And I just hope John doesn't lose sight of what he already has when the new baby arrives.'

'I may not be John's biggest fan, but I don't think he will. Besides, how could anyone ignore that ball of energy?'

Paul had somehow been left carrying Milly's backpack and swung it absent-mindedly from side to side. 'But even with the best will in the world, she will get her nose pushed out.'

'And when she does, we'll all make an extra special effort to make her feel wanted and loved.'

The backpack knocked against Paul's thigh as he walked with his head down. 'I hope it's enough.'

Julia kept her eyes fixed on Milly who was waiting at the corner of the visitor centre for them to catch up. 'There's only so much we can do, Paul. She's not ours.'

'I know.'

'I was thinking . . .' she said and could quite easily have left her opening remark hanging. There was only ever one subject that occupied her thoughts, especially now they were no longer actively trying for a baby, as far as Paul was concerned at least. Julia had reluctantly agreed that they wouldn't resume their efforts until they knew it was all going to be worth it in the end, and there was only one way of finding that out. 'Maybe we should make an appointment with the GP sooner rather than later to get a referral to the fertility clinic.'

The backpack that had continued to swing against Paul's leg stilled. 'How soon?'

'I could phone up on Monday?' she said.

'Right.'

Unsure if he was agreeing or simply acknowledging her intent, Julia asked, 'Right as in yes you want me to?'

Paul's posture straightened as he flung the backpack over his shoulder then slipped an arm around Julia's waist. 'You really need to ask? Yes, Julia. Most definitely, yes.'

5

The Accident

Anya eventually made it back to the surgical ward to resume her shift, but it was hardly back to normal with the ward dealing with multiple crash victims who had needed operations. Other than a snatched cup of coffee she had yet to have a break and was feeling distinctly light-headed.

'Go and get something to eat, Anya, before you keel over,' the ward sister said when she spotted her stopping halfway down a corridor and putting a hand against the wall to steady herself.

'I'll be fine,' Anya insisted, aware that she wasn't the only one who had been working flat out.

'That wasn't a suggestion. Go on your break, have a cup of strong, sweet tea and eat something.'

'I was just on my way to check Mrs Richardson's obs; I'll go after that, I promise,' Anya persisted. 'She's just arrived from theatre and is a bit unsettled. She's been drifting in and out of consciousness.'

The sister raised an eyebrow but didn't argue. 'Is she talking yet?'

'Nothing that makes sense.'

'Keep trying, but don't take too long. You've got your break to go on, remember.'

Anya made her way to the side ward where there were eight beds, seven already occupied and the remainder waiting for yet another patient to return from surgery. Julia Richardson was in the bed nearest the door and looked as if she were in a deep sleep, but when Anya slipped the blood-pressure cuff around her arm, Julia opened her eyes. Her lips began to move but she failed to form coherent words.

'Hello there, Mrs Richardson, there's no need to worry. You've had surgery on your legs and you'll still be feeling the effects of the anaesthetic. I'm guessing you're feeling a bit woozy at the moment?'

Julia nodded and directed her gaze down the length of her body. Her stare intensified despite the drugs.

'You're fine,' Anya assured her. 'Broken bones, but nothing to worry about.' She pursed her lips before she had the chance to add the word *hopefully*.

'The others?' Julia managed, her speech slurred and broken.

'They're receiving the best care we can give them,' Anya told her, although she didn't have a clue who Julia meant. It was as much as they could do to identify the victims of this morning's accident, let alone their relationship with one another. Next of kin had been notified and until they arrived, Anya could offer only feeble reassurances that those Julia cared for most were alive and well. There had been fatalities and for others the next twenty-four hours would be critical.

6

Phoebe stood outside the Tate Liverpool, buffeted by strong winds that had picked up speed across the Mersey before slamming into the Albert Dock. Meeting up at the waterfront had been a good idea earlier in the week, but the weather had taken a turn for the worse and winter was making a wet and wild start to the festive season. While Phoebe was relatively snug in the oversized duffle coat she had picked up at a vintage fair, her friend appeared to be faring less well. She watched as Julia trudged towards her with the remnants of an umbrella hanging at her side. Her long auburn tresses had been pulled from a silver clasp and were now plastered across her face.

'Wet?'

'Can we get inside?' Julia replied, her teeth chattering.

The lunch date had been Julia's idea, although Phoebe had been about to suggest the same thing. They were eager to visit the Andy Warhol exhibition and because they both worked in the city centre, they had opted to combine it with a lunch date. The friends still shared a love of art and one of Phoebe's fondest memories was sitting at the dining table in Helen's house while Julia played teacher. She had been as surprised as Julia at her ability to transform blank pieces of paper into vibrant worlds full of colour and excitement with relative ease. It had been Julia's nurturing that had stimulated a natural flair in that timid little girl which might otherwise have gone unnoticed, even by Phoebe.

In her teens, Phoebe had briefly studied fashion design at a sixth-form college in Manchester but she had abandoned her course to return to Liverpool after her mum died. She could have transferred to a college in Liverpool, and perhaps she might have done if her grandad had still been alive, but her nan had recently been widowed and she wanted Phoebe to start earning a living and learn how to provide for herself rather than waste time on some half-baked idea about being an artist. Phoebe's argument that she was learning a trade and hoped to be a fashion designer one day had fallen on deaf ears, and her current career path had begun as a cashier in the local supermarket, but she had refused to give up on her dream completely. She had attended art classes at night school for a while until that had also ended abruptly, like so many other things in her life.

Phoebe didn't have Julia's drive to take her gift and make a career out of it. The nearest she came to being creative in work was helping out occasionally with the window displays at Debenhams, and even that might be coming to an end soon.

'So how long have we got?' Julia asked.

'I have to be back in an hour,' Phoebe replied, but then checked her watch. 'Make that fifty minutes less the ten

57

minutes it'll take to get back, so . . .' She winced. 'Sorry, did you need longer?'

'Oh, don't worry about it. Let's have a walk around the exhibition first and if there's time we can grab something to eat. If not, we'll have to make do with eating a soggy sandwich on the way back, if that's all right with you?'

'I really don't want to rush you, Julia. I could always leave you here so you can have a proper look around,' Phoebe offered. She didn't want her friend to curtail her own enjoyment just for her.

Still dripping wet, Julia was too bruised and battered by the wind to hide her frustration. 'I want you to get the most out of this too. How about we concentrate on what you want to see and then if I'm desperate to hang around afterwards, I will. But let's make time to sit down and at least have a coffee before fighting gale-force winds again.'

'This could be our one and only chance to see this exhibition. I'm sorry we couldn't have arranged it for the weekend, but I've been signed up for Saturday shifts from now until Christmas and I have to take Nan to church on Sundays and then there's the shopping. I wouldn't have had time to get into town. Sorry,' she said again.

They had taken the lift to the fourth floor and as soon as they stepped into the gallery, Phoebe came to a stumbling stop, overwhelmed by the sight of works of art she had spent so much of her life admiring. She had often drawn inspiration from the thought-provoking images, and the dramatic colours used by Andy Warhol had become the palette for so many of her own designs. While she stood in awe, Julia wandered off towards another piece of the exhibit and Phoebe hurried to catch her up. They found themselves in a darkened room that pulsated with throbbing music to accompany a disturbing mix of film clips projected onto the walls. Phoebe was mesmerized once again, but after only five minutes, Julia was on the move again.

'Sorry, I am making you rush, aren't I?' Phoebe said.

Julia let out a deep sigh. 'If you apologize one more time, Phoebe, I swear I'm going to have to take one of these paintings and hit you over the head with it, giving visitors a new display to ponder over.'

'Who rattled your cage?'

'Concentrate on the artwork,' Julia instructed, making a point of peering at the printed description of one of the exhibits.

Phoebe knew better than to argue and leaned in for a closer look. 'I wish I had the imagination to come up with something like this,' she said. 'Something that takes the accepted view of the world and turns it on its head.'

'Have you done any painting lately?'

'God, no, I can't remember the last time I locked myself away in the garage and threw paint at a canvas.'

'But you *are* still making clothes?'

Phoebe wanted to say yes, but it would be stretching the truth too far and it had been a long time since she had been able to get away with lying to Julia. 'I'm still sketching designs now and then and I'll happily make a start at sewing things up, but I never seem to complete anything. You know what it's like. Whenever you get the time, you don't have the inspiration and when inspiration does strike, you're too busy doing something else,' Phoebe said and then stopped as she did a reality check. 'Oh, sorry, that's just me, isn't it? So how's this amazing commission of yours going?'

At first Julia seemed reluctant to show off but in the next moment she was pulling out her phone to show Phoebe photos of the designs she had been working on. 'I was at Martin Mere last weekend and as inspiration goes, it was perfect. I came up with a few options which I've already sent through to the client but this is the one he loved – which is a relief, because it was the one I wanted him to pick.'

At first glance it looked like two interlinked hearts, but the abstract design had been based on a pair of swans, their curved necks and wings creating the heart shapes. The sketch wasn't as simple as it looked and Julia pointed out the subtle references to the brief she had been given, such as the individual feathers that represented the couple's family.

'It's beautiful,' Phoebe said. 'I'd love to see it when it's completed.'

'I'd love you to see it before then. It would be good to have another artist's perspective while I'm working on it.'

Phoebe sighed. 'I'd hardly call myself an artist.'

'It's going to be a great loss to the art world if you never get to apply your talents, Phoebe. You could be the next Andy Warhol, or Banksy, or maybe even a budding—'

'Budding? I'm almost thirty, in case you've forgotten.'

'And? You talk as though you're the same age as your nan. Remember that conversation we had the other week? You said your life hadn't started yet. It's not too late, Phoebe, and the first step is telling yourself there's still time. Plenty of it.'

'But that's it, I don't think there is time, or at least not enough to scrap one career and start again,' Phoebe said. 'I applied for a promotion the other week.'

'And you got it?'

Phoebe laughed. 'This is me you're talking to, of course I didn't.' When Julia looked confused, she added, 'It was an assistant manager post and while I've got the experience, there are plenty of others with more qualifications than I have.'

'OK,' Julia said, letting her words stretch to give her some thinking time. 'When one door closes, another one opens. Use this as the push you need to go back to your studies.'

Julia made it sound so simple but she might think differently if she saw life from Phoebe's perspective. She didn't quite appreciate how opportunities in Phoebe's life only arrived to be snatched away. It wasn't Julia's fault; they were best friends but there were some things that Julia was better off not knowing, things that Phoebe would rather forget.

It hadn't helped that Phoebe's life had been built on perilously weak foundations. Her mum, Eleanor, had been a rebellious teenager who had fallen pregnant and had little choice but to stay at home with her authoritarian parents who helped bring up their grandchild. It was impossible to say if Eleanor's decision to run away with Phoebe nine years later had been a desperate attempt to claim her independence or simply to hurt her parents more. It hardly mattered because the end result would have been the same – Eleanor quickly fell in with the wrong crowd and eventually died in desperate circumstances, leaving behind a seventeen-year-old daughter who, rather than learn from her mother's mistakes, had convinced herself that she was destined to follow the same self-destructive path.

When Phoebe had returned home to Liverpool, her

grandmother had had her work cut out taming the girl who had suffered years of neglect, but Phoebe had eventually stopped resisting and allowed someone to control her and, more importantly, take care of her. And she had been relatively content leading a steady and unremarkable life, but things were changing. At home she was now primary carer while at work . . .

'My manager has already suggested the same thing,' she told Julia. 'They want me to enrol on some management programme starting in April next year.'

'Well, that's good, isn't it?' Julia said, more in hope than with any real conviction.

'I went for the promotion because my nan said I should, not because I wanted it. She's looking to the future when she'll go into a care home and we'll have to sell the house to fund it. There'll be enough equity left for me to get a small house or an apartment but I will have to support myself, and besides, I'm always helping my manager sort out the rotas and the stock sheets, so I know I could do the job. It's just . . .' She looked around the gallery at the prints and paintings hanging from the walls. The vibrancy of the colours hurt her eyes, making them sting. 'I know I should be happy about it. It's a proper job, a proper career.'

'Just not the career you wanted. You could always—'

'No, I couldn't,' Phoebe said before her friend had the chance to finish. She wasn't about to be talked into a sudden change in direction, not by someone who might not have everything she wanted in life, but she certainly had more than Phoebe could even dream of.

Realizing it was an argument that she wasn't going to win, Julia said, 'Time for that coffee now?'

Checking her watch again, Phoebe said, 'I suppose I could *run* back to work. The exercise would do me good.'

After taking a very quick look around the rest of the gallery, they made their way downstairs to the small cafeteria on the ground floor. While Phoebe went to get the drinks, Julia found a table. Her clothes were as damp as her mood and the visit had done little to lift her spirits. She worried about Phoebe.

'Here, I got you a muffin,' Phoebe said as she set down the tray.

'Nothing for you?' asked Julia. 'You're not dieting, are you?'

'Not particularly, why? Do you think I should?'

'No, Phoebe, I don't think you need to lose weight, not at all,' Julia said and not for the first time.

Phoebe had always been self-conscious about her weight and her nan didn't help by making direct comparisons with her two gazelle-like friends. Julia presumed Theresa thought she was helping by telling Phoebe she was just *big-boned*. 'You're perfectly proportioned,' Julia added for emphasis.

Ignoring the platitudes, Phoebe said, 'I'll more than make up for it when I get home later. It's impossible to avoid food living with Nan. She still lectures me on how my leftovers could keep a family in the Third World going for a week. And then she has the nerve to complain when I get fat.'

'You are not fat!'

Phoebe sipped her coffee and steadfastly refused to look at the muffin Julia had broken in two. 'Eat, Julia. You're the one who could do with some meat on your bones.'

Julia had lost her appetite of late but setting a good example, she tore off a morsel of sponge dappled in blueberry juice and dutifully popped it into her mouth. 'Paul and I went to the doctor this week.'

'If that isn't taking coupledom to the extreme then I don't know what is,' Phoebe said. It was offered as a joke although both remained sombre-faced.

'It was a "couple" problem.'

'Ah.'

Phoebe surprised them both by picking up her half of the muffin and taking a bite. Julia waited for her to ask for more detail and when Phoebe didn't, she added, 'We've been referred to a fertility specialist at the Women's Hospital.'

'I suppose that's a good thing,' Phoebe said uncertainly. 'You'll get some answers at least.'

'But I don't know if I'm ready for answers, Phoebe. It sounds churlish, I know, but the last place I want to go is to a maternity hospital where they'll probably tell me I'm never going to need its services.'

Julia wasn't sure what she wanted her friend to say but the silence was perhaps the worst of responses. Her mouth felt suddenly dry and she took a sip of coffee. 'Paul's said we should stop trying so hard to get pregnant and just let nature take its course, at least until we've seen the consultant and we have a plan of action. He thinks obsessing about it is putting us under too much stress.'

'And is it?'

'It's certainly starting to feel that way,' Julia said. 'He's the one who picks me up every month when the latest attempt has failed and I know it's not fair because he's hurting too. I sometimes think he'd be better off without me.' She took a deep breath and shook her head, already disagreeing with herself. 'I won't give up, but the longer we leave it, the older me – and more importantly – my eggs are getting.'

'How long would you have to wait?'

Again Phoebe hadn't offered the reassurance she needed and Julia felt the panic that had been building rise up in her chest, making her heart flutter. 'I don't know exactly, but if we wait until we've seen the consultant, had the tests, gone back for the results, we're talking months.'

'A few months won't make that much difference, surely, and maybe, just maybe, something will happen without even trying. Nan had my mum when she was your age after years of trying.'

'And that's the point, Phoebe, I can't *not* try. I just can't. I've already decided I'm going to have to do it on my own.'

Phoebe stared at her. 'What?'

Julia tried to smile but it was beyond her. 'What I mean is, I'll carry on doing what I've already been doing; taking the ovulation tests to work out when I'm most fertile and then luring Paul into bed.'

'Very romantic.'

'Yeah, well, that's the problem. Sex hasn't been romantic for quite some time,' she said, until a more recent memory came to mind. 'Although . . .'

Phoebe held up a hand in warning. 'Oh no you don't! I do not want to know the details, Julia.'

'Excuse me, but let's not forget that you saw my husband naked long before I did.'

The joke was an old one and Julia wasn't sure why she should mention it now. It had been a long time since she had needed reassurance that there was nothing to fear from the past. When Paul had entered her life, Julia had been nursing a broken heart, but she hadn't been the only one with a past. He had one too, and when the time had come to introduce her new boyfriend to her friends, she had known it would be difficult.

Helen and Phoebe had been intensely protective towards Julia, who had been jilted practically at the altar only the year before, and it was Helen whose approval she had gained first, albeit reluctantly. When the time came for Paul to meet Phoebe, however, her friend had been struck dumb.

'Is there something we need to talk about?' Julia had asked Phoebe afterwards.

'What? No, nothing,' Phoebe had said, her eyes wide but somehow managing to look anywhere except Julia's face.

'It's all right, Phoebe. I know you've probably seen more of Paul than I have – yet.'

The wide eyes turned in Julia's direction. 'You do?'

'Helen told me all about it.'

Phoebe and Paul had met a couple of years earlier when Paul had been between jobs and needed to raise some extra cash. A friend had suggested life modelling and, as much for a dare as anything, he had turned up at one of Phoebe's night-school classes. Their paths had crossed only briefly because, soon afterwards, Phoebe's nan had decided her granddaughter was having too good a time and had made her give up her classes. Julia hadn't been a part of Phoebe's life back then, it was Helen who had first become reacquainted with their old friend and she had told Julia all about her exploits.

'Look, Phoebe, I've only had a handful of dates with him. If this is too weird then you only have to say so and I'll end it here and now.'

'You'd do that?'

'Yes, I would,' Julia had said and she had been sure of her answer while desperately hoping that Phoebe wouldn't put her to the test.

'But you don't want to?'

'No, I don't. I know you and Helen think it's too soon to get involved with someone else, but I really, really like him. I think Paul's a keeper.'

'Then keep him,' Phoebe had said with the same intense blush that was burning her cheeks now.

'Anyway,' Julia said, realizing she had shared as much intimate detail about her sex life as Phoebe could bear, 'isn't it about time *you* got up close and personal with someone? It's been what, three years since you split up with . . . what's-his-name?'

'What's-his-name, exactly!' Phoebe said as if Julia had answered her own question. 'All my relationships are destined to be brief and meaningless. It's too much like hard work for minimum return and besides, Nan's keeping me busier than ever these days.'

'How is she?' Julia asked, letting the conversation slide. 'Not burnt the house down yet?'

'Oh, she's not so bad. I suppose it could be worse.'

Phoebe had been devastated when her grandmother had been diagnosed with Alzheimer's three years earlier and it was why she had dumped her then boyfriend, although Julia suspected she had used the diagnosis as an excuse to push away someone who was a potential threat to the mundane life she had become accustomed to with her nan. But things were going to change no matter how much Phoebe resisted.

'She has the odd *episode*,' Phoebe continued, wrapping the word in quote marks with her fingers, 'but as long as I put everything she needs to know for the day on her reminder board, she can appear as sharp as she ever was. It's more her physical decline that's causing the problem.'

'Her knee?' Julia guessed.

'Her doctor said that if she'd stuck to the physio after her operation, she would be fully mobile by now, but Theresa Dodd knows better. She still thinks rest is best and she won't go out of the house unless she has to.'

'It's such a shame that you have a perfectly usable car parked in the drive and you can't use it. Have you given any more thought to driving lessons?'

'Have you seen how expensive they are? I've dropped a few hints to my nan to see if she'd help, but she didn't take the bait. I don't think she likes the idea of me driving. Too much freedom.'

'Helen and I could buy you proper lessons as an early Christmas present.'

Phoebe shook her head. 'I can't let you do that. It's fine, Julia, honestly.'

'No, it's not,' Julia said, and if there was a fleeting moment when she felt uneasy making the next offer, she ignored it. 'There's nothing else for it. If you don't want me teaching you then it'll have to be Paul. I'll send him over on Sunday afternoon. What time do you and your nan get home from all your errands?'

'About one, but—'

'Great, I'll get Paul to put you on our insurance. Problem solved.'

'But—'

'Problem solved,' Julia said as she shoved the last remnants of the muffin into her mouth. Her doctor had said she was a little underweight and she felt an additional sense of satisfaction as she left the table with nothing but crumbs. Whatever her husband might think, she was still working hard to reach their ultimate goal.

7

The Accident

Lucy tried to have an afternoon nap but nerves were getting the better of her. There had been some truth in what her sister had said about being too stubborn to back down. Her determination to go on holiday was as much about proving she had some control over her life as it was the simple pleasure of spending a few days relaxing by the pool and getting drunk on half a cocktail. If she wasn't being so pig-headed, she might accept that the risks she was about to take were life-threatening. Something could go wrong and she would be thousands of miles from the two hospitals that were key to her survival – Broadgreen where she received her ongoing treatment and Wythenshawe where she might one day undergo a transplant if and when the call came.

Somehow Lucy did manage to doze off, but rather than golden beaches and blazing sun, she dreamt of the smoke that had enveloped the scene of the rail accident reported on the news. The drama was playing out to the rhythm of a strong and steady heartbeat, one that wouldn't judder as hers did, when a series of shrill beeps from her mobile startled her into consciousness. Bleary-eyed, Lucy peered at the phone and, still half-asleep, was momentarily confused that it wasn't a message from the transplant coordinator as her dream had prophesied. It was simply the airline company confirming her flight details.

Relaxing back onto her bed, Lucy stared up at the ceiling and wondered if the call would ever come. She summoned up an image of two lists in her mind, one containing the names of all the people waiting for a transplant, and on the other, those wonderful individuals who didn't deserve to die but would be heroes when they did. The first list was so much longer than the second, and Lucy had no way of knowing if there was a line yet to connect her name to another. And if by some chance there was, she wished she could have just one chance to meet the person whose heart she would eventually be gifted for safekeeping.

8

Julia and Paul went to the gym at least three times a week and had been known to squeeze in extra sessions whenever they found themselves at a loose end. Their workouts were meant to help prime their bodies and give them the best chance of conceiving but it was one part of their lives that predated their present health regime.

Julia's fitness obsession had begun ten years earlier when she had come dangerously close to falling into depression. It was shortly after her fiancé had jilted her and she had faced a choice: to remain in a dark world where she hated men and life in general, or to act – which was always going to be Julia's preferred option. She had joined a gym where she soon met Paul, and although she had initially eyed him with suspicion, he had captured her heart and then mended it.

She supposed she could have settled into a contented life after they had married and cut back on her workouts, but she could never completely lose sight of the fact that Paul was five years younger. She needed to keep up with her training so she could keep up with him.

'Fancy a bike race?' Paul asked as they eyed up the equipment. The gym was relatively quiet for a Saturday morning, which was hardly surprising given it was a month before Christmas. They intended to make the most of the peace and quiet because come January, there would be hordes of new starters determined to keep to their New Year's resolutions.

'I was thinking more of a gentle stroll on the cross-trainer.'

'Oh,' Paul said, unable to hide his surprise. 'It's not like you to turn down a challenge.'

'I'm following your advice about taking it easy for a while, and I think that should include gym sessions,' she insisted, which was partly true. The doctor's comment about her weight was still playing on her mind. She had presumed working out would keep her at peak fitness, but what if she had been pushing herself too hard? What if their healthy eating plan hadn't provided sufficient fuel for strenuous exercise and that had been affecting her ability to conceive? She wanted to rebalance her ratio of energy consumed and expended and at the same time reassure Paul that she was taking his suggestion seriously. To reinforce his misconceptions, she narrowed her eyes when she added, 'I thought you'd approve.'

Paul pulled the sports towel from his shoulder and draped it over the display panel on his cross-trainer. 'All right then, a stroll it is.'

Julia started slowly and at first her husband matched her steady pace. She was looking straight ahead and concentrated on two members of staff who were chatting on the other side of the gym – it would seem it was a slow morning for everyone. From the corner of her eye she noticed Paul's pace begin to creep up as he extended his reach as far as he could. His breathing had also become more intense while Julia had barely broken into a sweat. She suspected all his huffing and puffing was to exaggerate his efforts, to goad her into competing against him, but Julia continued to stretch muscles rather than burn energy.

'Is that the best you can do?' Paul asked after failing to get a reaction from her. 'Come on, Julia, put some effort into it.'

'This is not boot camp, Paul, and you are not my personal trainer. If you want a race why don't you ask one of the staff?'

He slowed down and was quiet for a moment as he watched her. Julia's eyes remained to the front. 'Have I done something to upset you?'

'No,' Julia said in a sharp tone that gave away her true feelings. She was happy to take the pressure off Paul to perform, but what she couldn't do was make her own anxieties disappear overnight. She hadn't stopped wanting a baby and she was annoyed that Paul didn't seem to be considering her feelings as much as she was his. He was familiar enough with her monthly cycle to know that they were reaching the point when they would normally be concentrating on nothing else except trying to conceive. Or was he? Paul had left it to her to take the initiative, to keep track of her hormones and announce when the time was right. Was she in this alone?

'Julia, tell me,' he said softly.

Julia visualized Paul sitting next to her when they had

explained to their GP how they had followed the practice nurse's advice to the letter without result. When the doctor didn't argue about a referral, when he didn't suggest even the remotest possibility of there being nothing to worry about, that was when Paul had taken hold of Julia's hand. The doctor would have presumed her husband was being the strong one, supporting his wife as they were told about all the advances in fertility treatment while facing the possibility of a childless marriage. He wouldn't have noticed Paul's hand trembling as it gripped hers tightly. Yes, he wanted this baby just as much as she did. If it were possible, he might even want it more, which might explain why he couldn't cope with trying and failing every month.

'Look,' she said, before choosing her next words carefully. 'I can't simply switch off my feelings about wanting a baby but I accept that the stress of trying has put us under too much strain. I am trying to do things differently, Paul, so I'd appreciate it if you didn't give me such a hard time.'

'Fair enough.'

He didn't sound convinced and so she added, 'This is my way of coping, that's all.'

'It's tough for me too, Julia.'

She turned to give him a weak smile. 'I know it is.'

Paul had slowed to a stop and picked up his towel to wipe his face. His body glistened with sweat, accentuating his muscular frame. At thirty-four, he was in the prime of his life and looked more than capable of fathering a child. Julia on the other hand was outwardly healthy, but at thirty-nine was she fit enough to carry a child? When Paul returned her smile and it didn't reach his eyes, she wondered if he was thinking the same. Had he chosen the wrong woman to make a family with?

'Would you mind if I coped in a different way to you?' he asked. 'I'd rather come here and work out my—'

'Frustrations?'

'I can't help feeling like I'm letting you down and no, that wasn't an opening for us to regurgitate all those worn-out assurances that it's not me, it's you, and vice versa. We go round in circles, Julia, and that's what I was hoping we'd be able to avoid, for a while at least. It's not working, is it?'

'What goes on in the gym, stays in the gym,' she said firmly. She had kept the cross-trainer moving and was vaguely aware that her pace had become, if not faster, then certainly more forceful.

'In that case, I'll see if I can outrun my feelings. I might be some time,' he warned.

Julia watched as Paul set himself up on one of the treadmills lined up along the opposite side of the gym. It was becoming impossible to ignore that they were dealing with their shared problem in separate ways and she felt an irrational sense of fear that their paths were diverging. Or was it so irrational? She was deceiving Paul, and although she could justify her motives to herself, she wasn't sure Paul would see it that way. Far from letting nature take its course, Julia had used an ovulation kit that morning before disposing of the evidence in next-door's wheelie bin. She intended acting on the results that night by planning an indulgent and distinctly unhealthy meal for two, which would cover up her ulterior motive – which was to get her husband into bed. If the end result were a child to call their own then it would be worth it, and if not, she would face the sense of failure alone. This was her way of coping.

On the other side of the gym, a couple of new arrivals caught Julia's attention. There was a young woman with a child who looked a year or two older than Milly although it was difficult to tell because the girl had her back to her. The gym was strictly adults only and yet both were kitted out in gym gear, and Julia continued watching to see how their arrival played out. If nothing else it was a distraction.

One of the instructors had a clipboard and was taking details from the older woman. Julia presumed she was the mother until she turned, and it became clear she wasn't old enough to have a teenage daughter. They had the same hair colouring, but because the young girl was still facing away, it was impossible to tell if there were any other family resemblances. Her long hair was tied up in a ponytail and it swung from side to side as she took a look around the gym while her companion was otherwise engaged. The moment she turned towards Julia, their eyes locked and it was then that Julia realized her mistake. She wasn't a child at all.

Despite being very slight, the girl had the features of an adult. Her complexion was translucent with more of a hint of blue than pink, and even from this distance, Julia could tell that her dark lips were not due to some dramatic shade of lipstick that Phoebe might wear. The poor girl was obviously ill which made her appearance at the gym on a wet and wild Saturday morning all the more curious.

The instructor finished filling in his questionnaire and after a brief discussion with the first woman, whom Julia now thought might be the sister, he sent her off on a tour of the facilities with his colleague who had been loitering in the wings. The clipboard holder turned his attention to the frail-looking girl who looked distinctly nervous, but not as much as he did. He scratched his head and kept looking around, possibly searching for his manager. At one point, he stared vacantly at his questionnaire, his pen motionless while the young woman waited for the next question. Julia presumed the instructor was still struggling with the answer to the last. It was excruciating to watch.

Eventually the drama drew to a close, but rather than give the woman a tour like her sister, she was directed to a treadmill close to Paul. The gym instructor helped the girl onto the running platform and, after a short exchange, started up the machine at a snail's pace. Paul was running at full pelt, and had been for at least twenty minutes, so at first he didn't even notice what was going on. Julia was watching his reflection in the mirrors that ran the length of the wall in front of him and she saw him glance to his side. Her not-so-subtle husband did a double take and then, recognizing his own rudeness, turned to say something. It made the woman laugh but the smile on her face didn't last. She raised her hands in panic and the instructor practically launched himself at the console to pull the emergency cord and bring the machine to an immediate stop. He helped the woman to a sitting position and she kept a hand on her chest as she perched on the edge of the treadmill.

There was an intense discussion between the two and then her sister arrived. Heads were shaking, perhaps to convince the members of staff that they didn't need medical assistance, and when the argument was won there were slow nods and wafting of hands. She wanted to be left alone.

After another short debate with her sister, the feisty girl won her argument and her sister wandered off to use a rowing machine nearby that allowed her to keep her sibling in her sights. The gym instructors moved to a safe distance too and continued to watch the fragile figure that had turned her back on them all.

Julia was so absorbed by the unfolding drama that she had set aside her own troubles and had even forgotten Paul was nearby until he stepped off the treadmill and sat down next to the girl. He was busily wiping himself down, but his mouth was moving; he was making small talk and, more importantly, making his new friend smile.

Checking the display on the cross-trainer, Julia realized she had been using it for almost forty minutes. The most she would normally do was twenty, after which she would tumble off feeling completely depleted before dragging herself to the next machine, but not today. The only evidence that she had exerted herself at all was a slight looseness in her limbs and a sheen on her brow. Deciding she had worked out enough, she walked over to Paul.

'Hi,' she said. 'I'm done for the day.'

'Oh, hi,' Paul said. 'This is Lucy. Lucy, this is my wife, Julia.'

The woman smiled, her blue lips making her teeth look yellow. 'Hello.'

Julia racked her brain to think of something to say. She didn't have Paul's flair for chatting to complete strangers but she wanted to make the effort. 'Did I see the instructors giving you a hard time?'

Lucy's shoulders folded inwards as if she were trying to disappear like the Cheshire cat, leaving only a blue smile. 'I knew I was pushing it coming here,' she said, the sentence itself taking her breath away. With a painful gasp, she added, 'But a girl has to try.'

'Yes, and you'd better keep trying,' Paul said before pulling himself up. 'It was really nice meeting you, Lucy. Who knows, maybe one day you'll be back here training for a marathon and if that happens then you can hold me to my promise. I'll be your running partner.'

'Thanks,' Lucy said. 'It was nice meeting you both.'

As Paul and Julia weaved their way through the maze of equipment towards the changing rooms, Julia asked, 'What was that all about?'

'She has some heart condition but when her sister announced she was joining a gym, Lucy insisted she could do it too. It sounds like she's getting fed up that she can't do as much as her younger sister.'

'I thought she was just a child when she came in.'

'She's been ill all her life by the sounds of it; I suppose it must have affected her growth.'

Julia had heard many such stories from Helen and it was perhaps a timely reminder that even if she was told that she had faulty ovaries or some other condition, it wasn't the worst diagnosis she could be given. 'That's so sad, and so wrong, but why on earth were you offering to be her running partner?'

Paul hesitated as they reached the doors to the changing rooms. 'She's waiting for a heart transplant,' he confessed.

Julia raised her eyebrows. 'Now do you see why Helen was trying to convince us all to register as donors?'

'Yeah, but it's not like anything's going to happen to us. What are the odds of dying at the right time and place and in the right condition for anyone to want our organs? We're going to be old and decrepit by the time we're ready to meet our maker.'

'But if you're wrong, I'd like to think my life wasn't completely wasted,' Julia said. It was only as she was talking that she realized the connection she was making. If she failed to create a life by her preferred means, couldn't she at least give life another way?

Paul shrugged and she felt a rush of annoyance as she realized it was beyond her husband to make that kind of link. He was probably still thinking how 'yucky' the whole process was, even after meeting Lucy.

'I swear I'll come back and haunt you if something happens to me and you go against my wishes.'

'Would you go against mine?' he challenged, although his question was drawn more from curiosity than anything.

'It would depend if your wishes matched mine I suppose.' She would donate his organs in a heartbeat.

'I'll think about it,' he said.

'Good,' Julia said as if she already had the answer she wanted.

The grey light playing across Julia's closed lids suggested that dawn was approaching and she began the slow process of rousing herself from slumber that matched the pace of the rising sun. She enjoyed waking up like this, remaining quite still while each of her senses came to life. The crisp cotton pillowcase she had laid her head upon had softened overnight and the fresh laundry smell had mellowed and

81

merged with the warm tang of the previous night's exertions. She was lying on her side, facing but not touching Paul, and she could hear his deep, steady breaths although it was impossible to tell if he was asleep or awake. Her husband knew her rituals and she often opened her eyes to find him staring at her. She smiled at the idea, but if Paul was watching her now, his breathing didn't suggest there was a returning smile.

There was a dull ache between her temples that would make her Sunday morning a little less than perfect. She and Paul had overindulged the evening before on delicacies that included scallops, lobster and a less-sophisticated chocolate sponge pudding for dessert, all polished off with a bottle and a half of Pinot Noir. Opening the second bottle had been extravagant by their standards but there was no reason to restrict their alcohol consumption at the moment, was there? Paul hadn't needed much encouragement to have an early night and, if anything, he had been the one to seduce her. Her conscience was clear, except perhaps for a hint of guilt about drinking so much, but abstinence hadn't got her pregnant so perhaps this new, reckless approach might relax them enough to make the magic happen. And there would certainly be no harm in repeating the attempt.

Tensing muscles to untangle stiffened limps, Julia reached out towards the space occupied by her husband, aiming for and touching his shoulder first. Eyes still closed, she trailed her fingers down his bare arm and when he didn't so much as twitch, she knew he was awake. Sneaking a look, her smile broadened and a tingle skipped down her spine when their eyes met.

'Morning,' he whispered.

'Morning.'

Slipping her hand beneath the covers, Julia continued to explore his naked body until Paul grabbed her hand and lifted it to his lips. 'So you're awake, are you?' he asked.

'Almost.'

He leaned over to give her a gentle peck, but as he pulled away Julia followed him, her lips searching hungrily for his. The deeper she kissed him, the more pronounced the smile on his face became and she was forced to stop what she was doing.

'What?' she asked.

'I'm just wondering when my wife turned into a wanton woman.'

'It must have been the wine last night. I think it goes to my head far more quickly than it used to.'

Paul pulled a face as he smacked his lips. 'I suspect most of mine is still coating my tongue. My breath must smell foul.'

It did, but Julia didn't care. 'Mine can't be much better. We probably balance each other out.'

'Well, I didn't like to say.' And with that, Paul was pulling back the covers to get up.

'Don't leave me,' she called, trying to sound dramatic rather than desperate.

Paul was oblivious to his wife's needs and when he disappeared into the en suite, Julia sat up in bed and wrapped her arms around her knees as she waited for him to reappear. She tried to remind herself how much she had enjoyed making love last night. It had been slow and sensual, not perfunctory as it once had been. It was time to let

83

nature take its course, she told herself, but Julia was reacting to fear rather than listening to reason. She strained her ears as she tried to make out if Paul was freshening up or getting ready for the start of the day. The minutes ticked by and she wasn't surprised when he reappeared clean-shaven in jog pants and a T-shirt.

'I thought we could have breakfast in bed,' she said.

'I was toying with the idea of going for a run. If I eat first then there's no time to let it digest, especially if I'm going to pick Phoebe up at one thirty.'

Julia bit her lip. She had forgotten about the driving lesson and was already regretting being so generous with her husband's time. 'Surely the session at the gym yesterday was enough for one weekend.'

'Ah, but that was before the meal last night.'

'Indulgence doesn't have to be paid back calorie for calorie. That's not a healthy way to live.' Detecting a flicker of doubt, Julia pushed harder. 'Please, Paul. When was the last time we spent the morning in bed? I'll tell you what: I'll make us breakfast while you run down to the shops for the papers. We can meet back here in . . . say, twenty minutes?'

Paul was looking at her as if she were a siren of the seas calling him into perilous waters. She held his gaze. Running his fingers through his hair, he said, 'OK, you win.'

Julia had just enough time to freshen up and slip on a silk chemise she knew he liked before putting together the makings of a healthy breakfast that wouldn't make them so sluggish they would fall back to sleep. She was sprinkling pomegranate seeds over yogurt and granola when he returned with an armful of newspapers.

Paul slipped an arm around her waist and whispered in her ear. 'Hello, sexy.'

'Come on,' she said, 'let's snuggle up in bed!'

They sipped their orange juice as they leafed through the papers, sharing stories and making comments as they went. When Paul went quiet and seemed to be absorbed in a particularly lengthy article, Julia took a chance and slipped out of bed to clear away the breakfast tray. She wanted to make room on the bed for her next move while ensuring that Paul didn't see it as a prompt to get up. Walking across the room, Julia put the tray down on the dressing table and picked up a hairbrush. From the outside, she looked oblivious to anyone who might look up and see her adding a layer of shine to her coppery hair while her silk chemise clung to her slender figure, her arms raised to show off her bosom to its best advantage. When she turned towards the bed and caught Paul watching her, she looked surprised.

'You're beautiful. Do you know that?'

Without saying a word, she cast aside the hairbrush and walked slowly towards Paul, gently swinging her hips from side to side. She leaned over him, daring him not to look at her chest, which was heaving.

'If I didn't know better, I'd say you were seducing me,' he whispered before she covered his lips with hers. He pulled her onto the bed and began peeling off her chemise, covering her bare skin with kisses as he did so.

The fears that had taunted Julia slipped away. It was going to work this time and the strain that had been pulling them apart would be released with the cry of a newborn in nine months' time. She just knew it and her relief was visible as Paul raised himself on top of her and caught her smiling. He gave her a curious look. 'What?'

'Nothing,' she groaned then raised herself up to nibble his ear before whispering, 'Is it so wrong for a wife to find her husband irresistible?'

As she wrapped her legs and arms around him in a pincer movement, Paul let his lips hover over the smooth skin of her outstretched neck. 'You usually only want me for one thing,' he said and then waited just long enough for his wife's body to respond to the comment. She tried not to tense but it was too late. 'God, is that what this is all about, Julia?'

As he lifted his head, she refused to meet his gaze.

'Is it that time of the month?' he asked.

Staring at the thin covering of coarse brown hair across his chest, she said, 'How would I know?'

'Because maybe you've been using the ovulation kit like you have every other month. Old habits die hard, don't they?'

'Paul, please . . .'

In one smooth move he lifted himself off her and out of bed. 'So was that what last night was about too?'

'You were the one who initiated sex as I recall. And besides, all that alcohol would hardly have helped our chances,' she argued.

'All the more reason to try again this morning.'

Julia had a choice. She could continue with the lie and face suspicion every time she tried to get close to Paul or . . . 'Oh, for God's sake, Paul, it's not like I'm cheating on you. Is it such a crime to want to have sex and hold onto the hope that one day we'll be parents? I know you want this as much as I do.'

'So were you ever going to take a break? It was for a few months, Julia, maybe not even that. All I asked was that we take the pressure off each other until we know what we're facing. Was that really too much to ask?'

'No!' she cried. 'And yes! You were getting stressed, I could see that, and I thought that as long as you were happy to think we'd taken a break then that worked for you. It just didn't work for me. You're asking me to wait even longer than we already have and I can't bear it.'

'I can't bear it either, don't you see that?' Paul said, the words choking him.

More calmly, Julia said, 'That's what scares me most. I don't just want a baby for me – I want it for you, Paul, because I know what an amazing dad you're going to make. What if you're stuck with me, and only me? What happens if we can't ever have kids? What happens if we can't adopt?'

'I don't honestly know, Julia. It terrifies me too, but what scares me more is that you don't seem to be able to face the possibility of it just being the two of us, not when you can't even give me a couple of damn months.'

'Because I want more for you,' Julia said, her eyes wide with fear. She couldn't help thinking back to the first man who had walked out on her. If it were to happen again, she had to be prepared. 'And I can't help but thinking you'd be better off cutting your losses and—'

Before she could finish her sentence, Paul's temper exploded. 'You really think I'd do that?'

'I'd *want* you to do it!' she cried.

Paul stared at her in disbelief and when he started to turn away, she added, 'I'm sorry. Please, Paul, I know our relationship is about so much more than having a baby and I know I'm being irrational, but I can't help how I feel.'

'But you could lie to me?'

'I know you're angry and I don't blame you, but I was trying to protect you from the stress of it all. And it's not like we were avoiding getting pregnant. We had a lovely time last night and we could be doing more of the same right now.'

Paul was shaking his head as he pulled open a drawer and took out his running gear. 'Funnily enough, Julia, I'm not in the mood any more and I'm not sure when I will be again. At the present moment I feel like a prize bull and I'm about to jump over the fence. But isn't that exactly what you'd expect of me anyway? Isn't that the kind of man you think I am?'

'No, of course it's not. I shouldn't have said that. Please, Paul, stay here. You can't go for a run now, you need time for your food to settle.'

'I'm already feeling sick, Julia. Sick and tired.'

When Phoebe came out of the house, it wasn't until she reached the gate that she spotted Paul further down the road. He had parked out of view of the house and was sticking magnetic L-plates to the VW Beetle. Walking towards him, she played nervously with the checked flannel shirt her nan had just told her made her look like a man.

'You're not expecting me to drive straight away, are you?' she asked. 'I've never been behind the wheel before.'

There was a brief flash of annoyance on Paul's face, but then he remembered himself. 'Sorry, I wasn't thinking,' he said. 'There's an industrial park I know that'll be quite enough. We can start there and go through the basics. Come on.'

Phoebe had had butterflies all morning and not simply at the prospect of driving. She couldn't help thinking how odd it was going to be spending time alone with Paul, something they had somehow managed to avoid for almost a decade, and from the way he was behaving, Paul was feeling just as awkward.

Before getting in the car, Phoebe shoved a carrier bag full of shopping behind the passenger seat.

'We'll only be out for an hour,' Paul said with a hard-fought-for smile. 'You didn't have to bring supplies.'

'That's my alibi,' Phoebe said. 'They're the bits and pieces I told Nan we'd forgotten and I needed to go back to the shops for. She'd only want to know why I was coming back empty-handed.'

'You need an alibi?'

It was a challenge more than a question. 'You know what she's like.'

Paul laughed bitterly as he started the engine. 'Yes, I know exactly what she's like.'

Remarks like this were as near as they got to talking about the past, skirting around the detail and making no more than the occasional nod to the memories they shared. Phoebe didn't expect today to be any different and she didn't want it to be because, assuming her driving skills didn't frighten Paul off after one lesson, they would be spending a lot more time alone together than either were used to. 'Are you sure you're OK doing this?' she asked.

'Yeah, of course,' he said before cursing under his breath

at a driver who had pulled out of a side road without warning.

'Yeah, of course,' Phoebe repeated, mocking his lack of enthusiasm.

Pursing his lips, Paul released a sigh with a long hiss. 'Sorry, Phoebe. As I'm sure you've already noticed, I'm not in the best of moods, but I promise it has nothing to do with you.'

Phoebe said nothing. If his foul temper had something to do with Julia then it didn't feel right talking about it, even if there had been a time when she and Paul had been able to tell each other anything. But that had been a long time ago – before Paul and Julia had become a couple, at which point the past had been rewritten and then ignored. Unfortunately, Paul was too wound up to apply the normal rules and he took Phoebe's silence as an invitation to speak openly.

'Did Julia ever tell you she thinks I'd leave her if we couldn't have kids?'

Avoiding any comment on what Julia had or hadn't said to her, Phoebe asked, 'Would you?'

'Of course not!' he said, but then his body sagged; it was just a little, but enough to notice. 'I'll admit that I can't imagine not ever being a dad, Phoebe. I never realized how much it meant until we started trying.' He took a moment to concentrate on his driving, or more likely to give him time to collect his thoughts. 'It would be a crushing disappointment, no doubt about it, and I'd want us to explore every option before we gave up completely. But worst-case scenario, if we couldn't have our own kids and couldn't adopt, then no, I wouldn't give up on our marriage.

90

So if Julia ever says anything like that, tell her, Phoebe. Tell her I wouldn't leave her and I hope she wouldn't either.'

'She wouldn't,' Phoebe said. She was looking out of the window, feeling distinctly uncomfortable and desperate to change the subject. 'Is that the industrial estate we're going to?' she asked, pointing to a road sign.

Paul indicated and changed lanes, ready to turn into the estate with its warren of side roads and car parks that were deserted on a Sunday afternoon.

'Julia says your car is pretty easy to drive,' Phoebe continued brightly although the tone was forced and just a touch desperate.

'Yeah, you're lucky we didn't opt for the tank of a car we had our eye on last year and I'm glad now that we didn't get it. Too many empty seats.'

They drove on in silence until another wave of frustration washed over Paul. 'You know what gets me?' he said, hitting his palm against the steering wheel. 'I spend most of my working life finding new homes for people who've outgrown their last one. Mothers complaining that they're packed in like sardines, as if their kids are an affliction.' He glanced over at Phoebe and his voice softened. 'Sorry – again. I shouldn't be offloading my problems onto you. I'm here to teach you how to drive. Now there's one problem I *can* solve.'

After parking, the time had come for Phoebe to begin her lesson in earnest but neither of them moved. 'And while I'm in rant mode, do you mind if I say something, Phoebe?'

'That would depend on what it was,' she said, daring to meet his eyes only briefly.

'What happened?'

'Sorry?'

'What happened to the Phoebe I met in those daft art classes? I've always wanted to know.'

'They weren't daft,' Phoebe answered, not sure if it was his dismissal of her craft that angered her or the point he was trying to make.

'And neither are you,' he said softly while looking at her with such intensity that for a moment, Phoebe thought he might just find what he was looking for.

'You used to have this spark,' he continued, then laughed to himself. 'Actually, no, it was way, way more than a spark. You were irrepressible. But two years later it had been snuffed out. You *looked* the same but I swear, I wouldn't have recognized you.' Realizing he was making her cringe, he added, 'I don't know why I felt the need to say that, it's just the mood I'm in, but I'm glad I said it, Phoebe, because it needed saying. You've been smothered for too long and if teaching you to drive can get some of that spark back then at least I'll have achieved something. So come on, Jenson Button, let's get this lesson started.'

When Helen looked out of the window and spied the VW Beetle pull up, she felt a rush of relief to see both Julia and Paul in the car. Julia had been giving Helen a blow-by-blow account of the couple's latest argument, which had continued to rumble on for the past week, leaving Helen with a bad feeling. Julia was Helen's role model and had been for as long as she could remember. For the first time in a long time, Helen didn't want to be in her friend's shoes.

With their two families so close, the two had practically grown up together and it wasn't only the age difference that meant Helen had always looked up to Julia. Her friend was always the one to set the good example, which Helen generally failed miserably to follow, and it was rare for Helen to feel that she had the upper hand. The last time would have been when Julia had been jilted a week before her wedding. Helen was not only a wife but a mother by that point, although she had hardly been proud of her achievements. She might have been the one to make it to the altar first, but she had been slightly stunned to be there, not to mention very pregnant, having been caught two months after her first date with John. Her marriage had been destined to fail, whereas Julia had got it right second time around – or at least that was the script they were meant to be following.

It wasn't entirely for selfless reasons that Helen was happy to see them together, however, and she was momentarily confused when she opened the door to find only Julia on the doorstep. She looked over to Paul who had remained behind the wheel.

'Not coming in?' she called, hoping he would respond to the disappointment in her voice.

'Sorry, I have a date with the gym. I'll catch you later.'

Helen was about to follow through with a more direct plea but the driver's window was sliding back up and Julia had already pushed past her without a backward glance. Helen watched the car disappear before joining her friend in the kitchen. She found Julia admiring the room's various battle wounds which included a broken handle dangling from one of the cupboards, deep scratches on the wooden dining table and a fridge door littered with magnets and notes. It was the home-made calendar Sellotaped lazily to the wall that held Julia's attention for longest.

'I take it you two haven't made amends yet?'

'Paul prefers getting intimate with a cross-trainer these days than with his wife.'

'By that I hope you mean a piece of gym equipment and not an angry gym instructor?'

The scowl that had been fixed on her friend's face softened but she didn't smile.

'He'll have to start talking to me sooner or later,' she said. 'We've just had the appointment through to see the consultant. It's in a couple of weeks and I'm dreading it now more than ever. Can you imagine what the doctor's going to think when he realizes his patients are barely talking to each other?'

'Sit yourself down and tell me all about it,' Helen said.

Julia had already spoken at length about her troubles over the phone but Helen didn't mind hearing it again. It would be good to feel appreciated, something that didn't happen that often in her house. She switched on the kettle and set out two mismatched mugs as her friend took a deep breath. Julia was about to launch into her complaints when there was a loud thump from upstairs. They both looked up to the ceiling.

'Milly, what are you doing up there?' Helen bellowed.

There was a mumbled, incoherent reply.

'What?' Helen screeched.

Rather than a reply, they heard movement as Milly made her way downstairs.

Julia looked understandably confused. 'I thought she was at her dad's this weekend?'

'Now there's a story,' Helen promised but could say no more as a miserable-looking child poked her head into the kitchen.

'I wasn't doing nothing.'

Helen glared at Milly, who was keeping her head down and refused to meet her mother's death stare. 'If you weren't doing nothing, Milly, then you must have been doing something.'

Julia sucked the air through her teeth. 'You don't want

to get caught out by a double negative,' she said in a poor attempt to break the tension.

Milly looked at Julia with tears brimming in her eyes. 'I was only doing my homework like my mum told me to.'

'And what?' Helen asked. 'You were so absorbed in your studies that you fell out of bed?'

'Yes,' came a surly reply.

Helen practically growled her response. 'Go back upstairs and stop messing about.'

'Can't I stay down here with Julia?'

'No.'

Milly turned to Julia in the hope that she would over-rule her mother. Julia shrugged. 'Sorry,' she said.

'Can I get a drink first?'

'No.'

The tears spilled down Milly's cheeks as she pursed her lips. She attempted a response but it came out as a sob and she turned tail and stormed back upstairs, stomping her feet and slamming her bedroom door. Silence followed but brought no peace to the house.

'That was a bit harsh, wasn't it?'

Helen poured their drinks and took out a packet of biscuits from the cupboard, determined to demonstrate how unmoved she was by her daughter's tears. Her jaw clenched when she said, 'She's about to learn that if she insists on staying home with me then she bloody well isn't going to enjoy herself.'

John had Milly every other weekend, a routine that Helen relied upon. It wasn't that she didn't enjoy spending time with her daughter, but she deserved some time to herself. She was still in her twenties and she wasn't ready to spend all her weekends at home avoiding the housework and watching kids' TV. She had planned to go into town that afternoon and pester Phoebe. What was the point in having a friend with a store discount if you couldn't take advantage of it? She needed a new outfit because she was meeting up with the girls from work later and hadn't intended coming home until she was too drunk to remember how good a time she'd had.

Those plans were in disarray and she suspected she would be spending the next two days pacing the floor like a trapped animal and being irritated by her daughter.

'What happened?'

'Eva had a bit of a scare with the baby and ended up in hospital for a couple of days.'

This was news that Helen could have shared with Julia earlier in the week but under the circumstances she had avoided any conversation that involved other people's pregnancies.

'Oh, God, is she all right?' Julia asked, surprising them both by the alarm in her voice.

'I think so, they're home now but they'll have to monitor her blood pressure a bit more closely.'

'She must be, what? Eight months now?'

'She's due a few days after Christmas, so yeah, about that. Knowing my luck, she'll decide to drop it on Boxing Day, which is when Milly should be staying with them. If my darling daughter is in a strop now because her dad suggested they stay home to look after Eva rather than go tenpin bowling, I dread to think what she'd be like if Christmas was cancelled. You might want to keep a wide berth if that happens.'

'It's understandable, though. Milly's been the centre of her dad's universe for so long and she's scared that's going to change.'

'It *will* change,' Helen said, having long since lost sympathy for her spoilt brat who was going the wrong way about convincing either parent that they should be investing more time and effort into her upbringing. 'No doubt about it.'

Julia eyed Helen with suspicion. 'Sounds like it's bothering you as much as it is Milly. It must be weird thinking of John with a brand-new family.'

Helen did her best to look affronted. 'I'm not jealous, if that's what you're suggesting.'

'Aren't you? Just a little bit?'

Helen picked up a biscuit and, rather than put it in her mouth, she snapped it in two. A shower of crumbs fell onto the table while she played with the theory her irritatingly insightful friend had voiced. 'No, Julia, I'm not,' she said before remembering who she was talking to. 'Well, all right, maybe just a little bit – but not over John, I may add. My feelings for that man were overpowered a long time ago by the smell of dirty nappies and baby sick.'

'As opposed to someone whose relationship is being eroded by their absence,' Julia said wistfully, before realizing she had spoken her thoughts out loud. 'Sorry, carry on.'

Helen would much rather revert back to talking about

Julia but her friend waited patiently for her to continue. 'Look,' she said at last, 'if I'm jealous at all it's because I'm condemned to living the life of a lonely spinster while he's starting over again. Blank page, new start.'

'Hardly a blank page,' Julia reminded her by lifting her eyes to the ceiling.

'I suppose.'

'And you're a lonely spinster, are you?'

'I bloody well will be tonight,' complained Helen.

'There's still plenty of time to meet your knight in shining armour.'

Helen gave a derisive snort. 'Do you think? There are slim pickings out there, Julia. Believe me, I've looked, and so far all I've found is the odd court jester.'

'May I remind you that I was around your age when I met Paul?'

Helen was about to argue that Paul had been significantly younger which meant that unlike the candidates she came across, he hadn't yet had the chance to have his fingers burnt by an ex who would leave him bitter and cynical – but then she remembered. Paul did have a history.

The pause gave Julia a chance to reconsider her words. 'Although thinking about it, maybe he's the one who ended up with the court jester.'

'Meaning?'

'I'm a fraud, Helen. I married Paul under false pretences and when we see the specialist I'm going to be exposed. It's terrifying me to the point that I've become a woman possessed. The old me wouldn't have stooped so low as to use tricks like I did the other night. How can I expect Paul to like me when I don't like myself?' She stopped to

99

tap her head. 'There's this little voice in my head getting louder and louder, telling me he'd be better off with someone else.'

Helen had just shoved a biscuit in her mouth and created a fresh shower of crumbs as she almost choked. 'Oh, don't be so ridiculous,' she said, letting her irritability get the better of her. 'If Paul was daft enough to marry you in the first place then he's daft enough to put up with your weirdo behaviour.'

'Thank you for that vote of confidence, but you have no idea how much strain our marriage has been under and it's only going to get worse. That thing you and John managed after a quick fumble in the dark is something Paul and I might never be able to achieve.'

Hearing Julia's sense of defeat was unbearable. It was as if her friend's body had been taken over by someone Helen had never expected to see again, a jilted bride who thought her life was over when her husband-to-be had developed cold feet. The rat had left it to Julia to cancel the wedding arrangements at a time when she had struggled to drag herself out of bed, and for a long time afterwards she had only pretended to function. Helen dreaded to think what might have happened if Paul hadn't come along when he did and she dreaded to think what would happen if he disappeared again. But Paul was better than that, and if Julia weren't being so neurotic, if she weren't so convinced that history was about to repeat itself, she would realize that too.

'Seriously, Julia, I thought I was supposed to be the drama queen. Wait until you've seen the specialist before you start jumping to conclusions,' Helen said, and when her plea failed to give rise to a response, she opted for flippancy which was bound to rile her friend, but anything was better than despondency. 'And what do you mean by that *thing*?' She left a dramatic pause and looked up in the direction of her daughter. 'Actually, you might have a point.'

Julia glared at her.

'What did I say?' Helen asked, her face a picture of innocence.

'You can't leave that poor girl locked in her room all day.'

'Who said it was just for today? She's staying there all weekend!'

'Helen,' warned Julia.

'Look, Milly has to learn that she can't throw a tantrum and expect people to bend over backwards to make her feel better. When John turned up this morning, Milly wouldn't even speak to him or ask how Eva and the baby were. She doesn't realize that he might eventually get fed up and stop making an effort, which is what she was worried about in the first place. It's a self-fulfilling prophecy.'

'And as part of her punishment are you also planning on starving her? Milly only asked for a drink.'

'Ah, it starts with a drink but next she'll be asking for three meals a day.'

Julia didn't so much as blink let alone smile. She knew Helen better than to take her impersonation of a wicked mother seriously but she was happy enough to play along if it made her Milly's saviour. 'I'm sorry, Helen, but if you're not going to let her come down then I'm taking something upstairs and you can't stop me.'

Grabbing the packet in front of her, Helen said, 'She's not getting my biscuits.'

Julia knew her way around the kitchen and poured Milly a glass of juice before shoving an apple and a chocolate bar in her pocket while Helen picked up a gossip magazine and ignored her friend. As she left, Julia made the point of rattling the extra bag of crisps she had taken from the cupboard and Helen simply flicked over a page in response. She allowed herself a smile and hoped the fire she had reignited in Julia's belly would burn long enough to put the world to rights.

Julia tapped lightly on the firmly closed bedroom door. 'Can I come in?'

Taking Milly's silence as agreement, she stepped into the room, which was cast in brooding shadow. If the curtains had been drawn back at any point that morning, they had been pulled over again. Milly was lying on her bed with her back to the door and the only sign of life came from a few sharp sniffs.

'I come bearing gifts,' Julia promised.

When she perched on the end of Milly's bed, the little girl reluctantly turned to face her. 'Is Mum still angry with me?'

'You really need me to answer that one?' When more tears threatened, Julia said, 'Here, you need rehydrating.'

Milly shuffled into a sitting position and took the proffered drink. 'Thanks.'

'And I smuggled up some supplies,' Julia added, digging her hands into her pockets. 'Would you like to go with the healthy option or is it a chocolate fix you need?'

Milly took the chocolate.

'When you've finished that, make sure you eat the apple too. It's one of your five-a-day and it might earn you some brownie points with your mum, just as long as you put the core in the bin and don't leave it rotting under your bed.' After placing the fruit and the packet of crisps on Milly's bedside table, it was time to get down to some serious talking. 'So what happened?'

'I didn't want to go to Dad's because it would have meant being stuck in the house all weekend. I told Mum I didn't want to go and I texted Dad too, but no one ever listens to me. It's like I can't have an opinion of my own and it doesn't matter what I do or say, they think they're the bosses of me. I can't wait till I'm old enough to leave home and then I won't have anyone telling me what to do!'

Milly had been so passionate with her speech that she slopped blackcurrant juice over her jeans.

'Do you want me to get a cloth?'

'Doesn't matter; it's not like I'm going anywhere.'

'So tell me, Milly, how do you think your dad's feeling right now?' Julia asked, even though John's feelings were rarely her concern. Helen was her best friend and her ex generally deserved whatever he got.

When Julia had first heard that John and his new wife were expecting a child, she had reacted as she always did to the countless couples who were popping out babies at an infuriating rate of knots. She couldn't share their joy when she was consumed with so much envy, and she couldn't wish them happiness when she was too busy trying to work out why they deserved to be parents and she and Paul didn't. John already had a daughter; he was just being greedy and obviously hadn't considered how this new addition would affect Milly, as her current behaviour clearly demonstrated.

But while her jealousy ate away at her insides, the last thing Julia wanted was for any harm to come to Eva or the baby. 'He must have had quite a scare this week. They don't send people to hospital for the fun of it, you know,' Julia said, trying to find a safe middle ground between making Milly understand the seriousness of Eva's condition and worrying her too much. 'There are going to be times, Milly, when your dad will put you first without question and there will be times when he'll have difficult choices to make. I'm sure he didn't want to let you down but this was serious stuff.'

'Do you think the baby could have died?'

'I think it's a relief for everyone that they didn't need to keep Eva in hospital but your dad will be worrying until the day that baby's born. Of course, then he'll carry on worrying as he or she grows up, just like he worries about you.'

Milly's lip trembled. 'I don't see why things always have to change.'

'I'm sorry, but you're old enough to know by now that that happens.' When it was clear that her words didn't provide the balm Milly needed, Julia added, 'But look at all the changes you've already been through, like when your dad met Eva and you had to get used to having a stepmum. You were scared then too, remember?'

Milly nodded.

'But you came around to the idea eventually. You like her now, don't you?'

Milly nodded again. 'I like her a lot.'

'But not enough to care about her going into hospital?'

From the silent flow of tears, Julia was afraid she had pushed too hard. She held her tongue for a while and was relieved when the tears gradually slowed to a trickle. From downstairs, they heard the doorbell ring and Milly's eyes opened wide. She pushed her glass into Julia's hand before jumping off the bed and pulling back the curtains.

'Daddy's here!' she cried.

Milly bolted towards the door but then did an about turn. She rushed over to her dressing table, grabbed her backpack and an overnight bag and then she was hurtling towards the door again. Julia smiled as she heard the little girl screech to a stop on the landing, followed by a loud thump as she dropped her bags, then a whirlwind of motion as she ran back into her room where Julia had remained still throughout. When Milly flung her arms around her, the blackcurrant juice sploshed on Julia this time.

'Thank you, Julia,' the little girl said and then she was gone.

Again Julia didn't follow. She stayed where she was and listened to the sound of two shocked parents laughing at their daughter's sudden change in attitude. Looking around the room, Julia took in every detail of Milly's world, the posters of her favourite boy band that all but obscured the wallpaper she and Paul had hung for her when she had been young enough to still like pink. There were piles of schoolbooks and laundry scattered about the place that Julia was tempted to start tidying away until she remembered it wasn't her job.

'Bye, Julia!' Milly shouted up to her. 'I love you!'

'Not as much as I do,' Helen added in a singsong voice.

Julia smiled and ignored the ache in her heart.

10

The Accident

Routine operations on the surgical ward had been cancelled to deal with the sudden influx of patients, but staff were still under immense pressure and Anya had accumulated more work than she could handle. When she wasn't taking care of her patients, she was taking care of the paperwork in an attempt to keep records up to date. As the shock had begun to wear off, some of the accident victims were more coherent and the arrival of families had allowed the medical team to fill the gaps in their knowledge, but it was still very much a work in progress.

'I need to see Helen,' Julia Richardson whispered when she heard Anya close by leafing through her notes. She spoke without opening her eyes.

'Is she a relative?' Anya asked as she went through a mental checklist of all the patients who had been brought up to the ward. The name wasn't a familiar one.

Julia's brow furrowed as she fought through a morphine haze to find her words. 'Helen Butler – a friend,' she said.

'Was she . . .' Anya paused to frame her words carefully. 'Was she travelling with you?'

'Yes.'

'I'll see what I can find out.'

For a moment, Anya thought Julia was drifting off again but her eyes flickered and she managed to open them. 'Phoebe,' she said.

'Do you mean Phoebe Dodd? Is she another friend?'

Julia frowned as she struggled for an answer, but then gave a tentative nod.

'She's still in recovery,' replied Anya, who had kept track of the patient she had brought in earlier. 'The surgeon's been able to mend the small tear in Phoebe's spleen but they were monitoring her closely. I expect she'll be brought to the ward soon and I'll let you know when that happens.'

Julia didn't respond and although she had managed to keep her eyes open, she was staring off into space. Before she drifted off again, Anya said, 'Your husband is here. I thought you might—'

'No!' Julia cried out before Anya could finish. Her previously sedate patient began thrashing her body around, which was no mean feat for someone with multiple leg fractures, not to mention other injuries including a couple of broken ribs. Even with pain relief it would undoubtedly be excruciating for her to move. 'I don't want to see him and I don't want him knowing anything about me! Please, I can't face him.'

'It's OK,' Anya said in a soothing voice as she attempted to calm her patient. 'You don't have to do anything you don't want to.'

It took a minute or two for Julia to settle and not before

Anya had administered an extra boost of morphine. She wiped Julia's sweaty brow and smoothed away hair that was still matted in blood. Slowly, her patient began to drift off to sleep but not before she made one final plea.

'Find Helen . . . I need Helen.'

Anya returned to the nurses' station and found Helen Butler's records with relative ease. Another piece of the puzzle had been uncovered but the nurse couldn't quite work out yet how everything connected. She wondered what the little group had been doing earlier. Had it been an average day or had they been planning something special? Whatever the reason for their travels, it was frightening to think how quickly things could change. Where hours earlier they would have been looking to the future and the arrival of a new baby, the best they could hope for now was to survive through to the next day.

11

Standing naked in front of the bathroom mirror, Julia scrutinized her body until her reflection was obscured by steam rising from the shower she had yet to step into. Even without the benefit of the mirror, she continued to examine herself. She had put on a little weight in the last month, only a couple of pounds, but it had given her new curves. There was a dull ache in her lower abdomen and when she pressed her palm against it, she felt the pain intensify slightly. Moving her hands upwards, she cupped her breasts in a slow, perfunctory motion. They were fuller and slightly tender.

These were all signs and symptoms she was used to immediately before her period. What wasn't normal was the absence of the period itself. She had woken up before the alarm and had beaten Paul to the bathroom on the pretext of wanting to get to work early. It was partly true because she did have a meeting arranged to hand over her completed anniversary pendant to her client, but right now jewellery making was the last thing on her mind. She was two days late.

Julia frowned as she checked herself one more time. Was there something different? Could the slight cramping be a symptom of her body adjusting to being – she stopped herself short of even thinking the word and her stomach heaved. She felt sick.

This latest sensation was scrutinized too. Could her nausea be a result of nerves or could it be – again she caught the thought before it had time to develop, but the butterflies in her stomach were building up a storm and she gripped the side of the basin to keep her balance. Leaning over, she let her head drop and squeezed her eyes shut before she could catch a glimpse of the white plastic stick propped against the porcelain.

It had been a while since she had got as far as needing to use a pregnancy test. In the early days she had been known to use three or four every month but that had been back when she and Paul had thought their only problem was impatience. More recently they had let time rather than a test reveal their bitter disappointment if for no better reason than to keep their dream alive that little bit longer. Today she felt justified in resurrecting that hope and part of her wanted Paul to share in the moment, but what if she was wrong? What if it was a false alarm? The disappointment would be felt all the more keenly and she wanted to spare him that.

As she waited for the test to consider its verdict, Paul lay in bed only feet away unaware of his wife's anxiety. He would know soon enough she told herself as she peeled open her eyes and searched out two blue lines.

* * *

111

Emergency meeting 7.30 p.m. The Elephant

'Damn, damn, damn, damn, damn,' Helen muttered under her breath as she read the message from Julia.

Feeling a pair of curious eyes upon her, she turned to the woman sitting next to her on the bus and made the mistake of giving her an apologetic smile. Helen was a seasoned commuter and the twenty-minute ride home from Broadgreen Hospital was her chance to divest herself of her professional persona by becoming absorbed in irreverent banter on Facebook or watching inane YouTube videos of cats falling off shelves. After the awful day she'd had at work, she was desperate to set free her careless and carefree nature and the last thing she needed was someone spotting her uniform and taking up the entire journey telling her about their ailments. It did happen occasionally and there had been one man in particular who had gone as far as opening his shirt to show her his impressive rash. She had got off the bus two stops early just to escape him.

'Trouble?' asked the woman who appeared to have just completed a marathon Christmas shopping expedition. She looked harmless enough.

Taking a chance that her fellow traveller might offer a friendly ear, Helen said, 'The usual balancing act of coming to a friend's rescue and finding a babysitter at short notice.'

'How many have you got?'

'Just the one, thank God,' she said, catching herself as soon as she said it then relaxing when she realized Julia wasn't in earshot.

Her new friend introduced herself as Beryl and as she began reeling off all her children, grandchildren, not to mention one great-grandchild, Helen surreptitiously glanced at her phone again to check the date. It was the first week in December and it didn't take a genius to work out what Julia's emergency might be. Helen was far more familiar with Julia's menstrual cycle than she ought to be and her heart sank. It would be another bitter blow and perhaps this one would be especially hard given that marital relations were at an all-time low.

'Sorry, I just need to text my mum to see if she can look after Milly,' Helen said as her fingers tapped out the cry for help with practised ease.

'What would we do without them, eh?' Beryl said and by the time Helen's phone beeped with a response from her mum, she was more than familiar with the list of children Beryl looked after and how often.

'Bugger,' Helen said when the text from her mum wasn't the reply she wanted. 'Right, let's try someone else.'

Beryl waited for her to finish texting and then tipped her head towards the uniform peeking out beneath Helen's coat. 'So you're a nurse then?' she asked.

Here we go, Helen thought, and took a breath. 'Yes, I work in Broadgreen. In the cardiology department.'

'How old's your daughter?' Beryl asked, contradicting Helen's presumptions by keeping the focus of the conversation on children and not raising the ugly spectre of varicose veins or athlete's foot.

'Milly's almost twelve. She's OK getting to and from school on her own, but not quite old enough to trust home alone. She stays with Mum until I get back from work and I was hoping she'd keep her.'

'All of mine were latchkey kids. I had a cleaning job at

113

the school so I was leaving as they were coming home, but that was the good thing about having four. My eldest had the joy of looking after the younger ones.'

'If that's meant to be a selling point for having more kids then I think I'll pass.'

'You and your husband don't want any more?' Beryl asked, a little too casually.

'I'm divorced,' Helen said.

Beryl's eyes lit up. 'My youngest lad happens to be back on the market if you're interested? He has a few miles on the clock but he's done all right for himself. He's a financial adviser,' she said proudly, 'and his kids are almost grown up, so he's pretty much a free agent.'

Helen was laughing at the blatant sales pitch as Beryl searched for photos on her phone, but when she was shown the image of a distinguished-looking man in his late thirties, she nodded approvingly. 'Very nice, but don't you think he might have something to say about his mum palming him off on a practical stranger?'

'Oh, a little matchmaking does no harm, and my fees are reasonable compared to one of those online dating sites. A glass of Baileys will do me.'

Glancing at her own phone, which had beeped again, Helen sighed. It was a reply from John to say he couldn't help because he was taking his mum out for her birthday, which meant her third and final resort was also unavailable. 'This son of yours doesn't do babysitting, does he?' Helen asked, only half-joking.

For a minute it looked as if Beryl might actually consider putting in an offer, but then the bus turned a corner and the opportunity was lost.

'Sorry, this is my stop,' Helen said, forcing Beryl to juggle shopping bags to give her enough room to slip past. 'It was nice meeting you.'

'You too,' Beryl said and the expression on her face suggested she would have liked time to develop the acquaintance more.

When Phoebe arrived at the pub, Julia and Helen were already there. There was something about the sight of the two huddled together that made her feel a little resentful. Helen had been Phoebe's best friend in school, but during her years of absence it was Helen and Julia's relationship that had strengthened as the age difference became less of a hindrance. They had both welcomed Phoebe back with open arms, but there was still a gap that had never been completely bridged, and at times like this, as she watched Helen reach over the table to give Julia's hand a fierce squeeze, Phoebe felt it most keenly.

'Sorry I'm late,' she said.

'I've only just got here myself,' Helen said.

Paying more attention to the expression on Julia's face than Helen's reply, Phoebe was prepared for the news her friend was about to impart.

'No blue line,' Julia said with tears brimming in glistening pools at the corners of her eyes. 'I know I should have learned my lesson by now but I was two days late. I did a test but it turned out that if I'd waited another half-hour, I wouldn't have had to. I came on.' She took a juddering breath then added, 'So be warned, as well as being mightily pissed off, I also have the worst case ever of PMT to contend with.'

Helen took a deep breath and they both watched her purse her lips to form the letter M. Julia knew what she was about to say.

'Don't you dare say "Maybe next time," or I might just hit you.'

'OK, I won't,' Helen said with a shrug before pouring a generous glass of wine for Phoebe and sharing a look with her that suggested they were in for a rocky night.

'So what happens now?' Phoebe asked, taking her seat next to Julia and putting her hand gently on her back. 'You see the specialist next week, don't you?'

Julia shrugged her friend's arm away. 'For what good it'll do. I can't even mention it to Paul without him bristling. Has he said anything to you, Phoebe? Does he talk about stuff like that when you have your driving lessons?'

'Mostly he has his heart in his mouth so he can't say much at all,' Phoebe said a little too defensively. She had only had a couple more lessons with Paul and he hadn't been as wound up or as open with her as on that first day, but they did talk with a level of intimacy that she wasn't sure Julia would approve of.

'No, how silly of me,' Julia said. 'Why would he tell you how he feels when he won't even speak to me?' She lifted her glass of wine and swirled the contents until she had created her very own whirlpool. 'I hate what this is doing to us. I haven't even mentioned that I took the test because it would only open up another argument about how we're not supposed to be trying.'

'But only for another week,' Helen said. 'Once you've seen the specialist you can resume romping around the bedroom, can't you?'

'We haven't *romped* for years. That was the problem Paul was trying to fix until I messed up,' she said bitterly. 'Our sex life had become a tightly choreographed event, and now it's nonexistent. Our problems aren't going to be solved by one appointment, Helen. It's only an initial meeting and Paul is determined that we wait until we've had all the test results before we start thinking about babies again.'

Helen looked as irritated as Phoebe by Julia's snappiness but whereas Phoebe could disguise her feelings, Helen could not. 'I know this has been another setback but honestly, Julia, you need to get it into perspective. Just try spending a day at my clinic,' she said before sitting back and folding her arms.

When the ensuing silence became unbearable, Phoebe said to Julia, 'You and Paul are both under a lot of pressure at the moment, that's all.'

'And it's going to stay that way until I get pregnant or Paul walks out on me!' Julia cried. Her eyes narrowed as she looked over at Helen. 'Yes, I know there are worse things in life, but you have no idea what it's like to lie awake at night longing to hear a child call out to you, instead of cursing when they do. I'd give anything to hear someone call me mummy and the silence is killing me, Helen, and it might just be killing my marriage. Remember how devastated you were when John left? At least he didn't leave you completely alone. What happens if Paul and I do break up? Who else is going to be interested in me if I'm barren?'

Helen glared back at her friend. 'Do you really need me to tell you how wrong that statement is on so many counts?'

117

Julia tried to maintain her steely expression but her emotions weren't up to it and her face crumpled. 'Our marriage might not have reached breaking point yet but I have,' she said. 'I want to be a wife *and* mother. Is that too much to ask?'

Phoebe couldn't have felt more awkward and wanted to put her arm around Julia again but she had already been pushed away once and so resisted. Julia was an emotional mess and Phoebe knew that Paul was too. He had explained to her that he wanted a break so he and Julia could remind themselves that there was more to their relationship than having children. So far, that plan was failing and he was scared, but however much Phoebe wanted to tell Julia this, she couldn't. She had a feeling her intimate knowledge of Paul's feelings wouldn't allay Julia's fears at all.

Helen released a sigh and the tension along with it. 'I'm sorry, Julia, ignore me. It's no excuse but I'm at the tail end of a crappy day myself.'

'Why, what's happened?' Julia asked.

Phoebe began pouring the last of the wine into their glasses. She would need some fortification if she was going to hear the story Helen had already shared with her earlier. Helen had phoned to warn Phoebe that she was struggling to find a babysitter and might not be able to make it to the pub. She had mentioned how desperate she was for a drink and went on to explain in graphic detail how she had ushered an elderly gent in to see the consultant with a smile on her face that gave no clue to the devastating news that awaited him, and how utterly dignified her patient had been. The worst part had been when he cracked a joke as they left simply to cheer her up.

'I met an interesting lady on the bus today,' Helen began.

Julia looked almost as puzzled as Phoebe. 'How awful for you.'

'She tried to palm me off with her son. I only saw a photo but he looked hot.'

'I say again,' Julia said. 'How awful.'

'Helen?' Phoebe asked, reminding her that she knew what was really on her mind.

'Sorry, it's just that if I'm going to leave Milly to her own devices then it has to be for good reason. Either we sit here and listen to Julia offload in the hope that she'll go home feeling marginally better, or we put aside our troubles and have a good laugh so that we can all go home feeling better. What I'm not prepared to do is sit here dishing out more doses of misery.'

'You left Milly home alone?'

Helen looked at Phoebe for support and then said, 'So that I could come here to support you – *yes*.'

'I'm sorry I asked now. I'd rather you had let me down than abandon Milly.'

'It's partly my fault,' Phoebe added. 'I was the one who convinced her that Milly could be trusted on her own. If anything, I'm the one who shouldn't be leaving Nan without supervision.'

'Do you know,' Julia began, 'I sometimes wonder if you two can be trusted on your own either!'

'It's no big deal,' Helen said and then began counting out the positives on her fingers. 'Milly's almost twelve; she has the house to herself, tons of junk food to gorge on, full control of the TV remote and she can go to bed a bit later than usual. She wasn't complaining, Julia.'

'She's *eleven*, Helen,' Julia corrected.

'Shall we order?' Phoebe asked when her friends entered into a staring competition.

'How about we skip starters? I don't want to stay out long,' came Julia's clipped response.

With their orders taken and a fresh bottle of wine in the cooler, Phoebe tried to move the conversation on. 'Speaking of my nan, she's announced that it's time to think seriously about moving into residential care.'

'Really?' chorused Helen and Julia.

'She drew up a shortlist of potential homes within weeks of being diagnosed and now she thinks the time is right.'

'I never expected it to be so soon. You said she was doing OK,' Julia said.

Her surprise was hardly unexpected and not even close to Phoebe's own sense of shock. 'I think almost setting fire to the kitchen the other week made her realize she has to do something.'

'You could get carers in to help you.'

'But I'd still be expected to look after her and you know how she is, Julia. She likes being in control and her disease is going to take that away from her, it already has to some degree. And while she can accept the inevitable, she can't accept that it will be me controlling her when that happens.'

'She doesn't trust you to take care of her?' Julia asked in disbelief.

'In some ways she does. She's given me power of attorney so that when the time comes I can take future decisions about the finances.'

'Like selling the house?'

'Her savings will cover the fees for a couple of years,

but eventually, yes. Her decision to leave now is more a matter of dignity. She'd rather have strangers seeing to her most intimate needs than her granddaughter.'

'Well, thank God for that,' Helen said. 'I would have placed bets that she'd want you at her beck and call until her last breath.'

Phoebe ignored the jibe, knowing that any defence of her grandmother's good character would fall on deaf ears. 'Paul said he has dealings with a few of the homes on her list. One or two are really popular and I'm hoping he can use his influence to bump her up the waiting list if need be.'

'He never mentioned it to me,' Julia said.

Helen gave her a warning glare, letting her know that she wasn't allowed to dwell on the failings of her marriage or her husband, to which Julia gave a dismissive shrug.

Phoebe was more than happy to avoid the subject too. 'Anyway, like Helen said, let's not spend any more of the evening making each other feel miserable.' She looked from one face to the other but neither Helen nor Julia was showing signs of letting go of the tension that had been building between them. 'We should be cheering ourselves up, not going for each other's throats,' she reminded them.

Julia sniffed the air and when Helen poked out her tongue, Julia gave a begrudging smile. The two had known each other forever and had plenty of practice in recovering from arguments, even the unspoken ones. Reaching over, Helen grabbed Julia's hand and in all seriousness said, 'I really am sorry for snapping at you, Julia, and I want you to know that if it comes down to it, I don't mind renting out my womb. You can even have my eggs if you want them.'

Julia gasped in mock horror. 'Do you really think I'd

want a child of mine inheriting your questionable personality traits?'

'Such as?'

'Your warped sense of humour, for one. And what about your penchant for meeting strangers on the bus and offering yourself to their sons?'

'He was offered to me,' she said primly, 'which means I'm obviously a good catch. Besides, look at Milly. I didn't do too badly with her, did I?'

Phoebe had been pushed to the sidelines of the conversation but when she saw her chance, she jumped in. 'I think Milly has John's genes to thank for that.'

Helen's eyes widened in shock. 'Don't you start picking on me too!'

'Sorry, I couldn't help it and in fairness, Julia would have said it if I hadn't.'

The waiter arrived with their main courses and with the atmosphere thawing, they tucked into crispy battered fish and in Julia's case, a loaded hamburger with extra mayonnaise.

'Actually, I do have some good news,' Julia said. Her cheeks were glowing from too much wine and perhaps a dose of pride too. 'That commission I was working on? Well, the client loved it and now he wants me to do some smaller pendants for each of his daughters. For Christmas.'

'Bloody hell, that's going to be a bit of a push, isn't it?' Phoebe asked, knowing how much work would be involved.

Julia shrugged. 'I know, but I have the time and he's willing to pay a premium.'

'Oh,' Helen said, 'that follows on nicely to what I was just thinking.'

'You, thinking?' Julia asked.

Helen pulled a face. 'Since you'll be able to splash the cash and Phoebe has access to her nan's savings, I say now would be a good time to decide what to do about our birthdays next year. I have some savings and we said ages ago that we should do something special for our joint one-hundredth birthday. Time is running out, ladies.'

Julia wiped a trail of mayonnaise from her mouth. 'OK, but only on the condition that we don't call it our hundredth birthday, and you have to do as I say because I'm the majority shareholder.'

'You don't have more years if me and Helen form a coalition,' Phoebe countered.

'Do you want *another* argument?' Julia said and without waiting for a response, added, 'I thought we might spend a long weekend in Spain. We could pack Mum off and have her villa to ourselves.'

'A long weekend in Spain?' Helen asked and shook her head with disappointment. 'We have to think bigger.'

'I did have an idea,' Phoebe began hesitantly. 'But I didn't think it was worth mentioning because of how things were with Nan. But if she does go into a care home, then I could certainly do it, although, for the record, I would fund it myself. I'm not going to break my nan's trust and spend her money the minute I get control of it. I'll just have to work all the overtime I can get to afford it.'

Two expectant faces stared at her and then Helen asked impatiently, 'Afford what?'

'A road trip,' she said. 'I haven't exactly worked out the details but I was thinking we would head to London to catch a West End show and see the sights before taking the Eurostar to Paris. We could do a tour of all the galleries and indulge in some fine dining before catching a flight to New York, where we would end the holiday with a shopping trip before coming home again. I know it might be a bit expensive but I'm pretty good at searching out a bargain.'

'And you haven't worked out the detail?' Helen said, clearly impressed. 'But if we go to Paris then I want to go to Notre Dame – the location of the best Disney film ever in my humble opinion.'

'*The Hunchback* does not beat *The Little Mermaid*!' Phoebe said.

Before the argument could escalate, Julia interrupted. 'Anyway, children, exactly how long will this trip take, including a trip to Notre Dame?' she added for Helen's benefit.

Phoebe was starting to blush. She had dreamed up the plan without ever really believing it would happen, and it was probably only the wine talking now. 'We wouldn't want to spend all our time travelling so I'd say two weeks, or at a push we could condense it into ten days.'

'When?' asked Helen, already sold on the idea.

'That would be entirely negotiable.' Phoebe was feeling giddy now. Her dream holiday was taking shape. 'We'd have to factor in taking time off work and all our other various responsibilities, but I thought it would be best to do it before my birthday in March or after Julia's in October so we've either all hit our milestones or none of us have.'

'I'd prefer to go sooner rather than later,' Julia mused.

'How about February?' Helen asked. 'It's half term so

John would probably be looking after Milly then anyway – well, that's the plan now.'

Phoebe was still in shock. She had expected her friends to dismiss the idea. 'Look, all of this is dependent on my nan following through with her own plans.'

'Now don't go getting cold feet on us, Phoebes,' Helen warned. 'Some care homes arrange short stays so even if your nan hasn't moved by then, she could always try before she buys.'

'I suppose.'

'Does that mean we're all up for this?' Helen asked, excitement flushing her face.

'It's tempting,' Julia said, 'and you're right, we could do with something to look forward to, but I don't know what might be happening with me. There could be appointments, treatment . . .'

'We wouldn't have to book it straight away and could easily work around your plans if necessary,' Phoebe offered.

'Is that a deal then? Shall we go?' Helen asked, already raising her wine glass.

Julia and Phoebe raised theirs a little more hesitantly, but with a tinkling of glass the plan was sealed and they were all a little stunned as they continued with their meal. Phoebe promised to put together an itinerary and get an idea of costs so they could do a reality check, but as they chatted about ideas for their trip, it was clear that a lack of money wasn't going to stop them. They were going, come what may.

When the plates had been cleared and desserts ordered along with another bottle of wine, Julia excused herself and went to the bathroom. Helen immediately reached under the table for her bag.

'What are you up to?' Phoebe asked as she watched her friend fumble with her phone.

Helen was tapping away even as she spoke. 'Checking that Milly's OK. I wouldn't dare show Julia I was worried.'

Once the text had been sent, Phoebe asked her next question. 'You were a bit harsh with Julia before. Is everything all right between you two?'

'Of course it is,' Helen said confidently but then her shoulders sagged. 'I don't know, Phoebe. I feel for Julia, really I do, but ever since she started getting panicky about having a baby, she's made me feel so bloody guilty about having Milly. I don't remember anyone feeling envious when I found myself knocked up at seventeen. Julia was all prim and properly engaged at the time and didn't approve one bit of me and John rushing into things.'

'I suppose that's the problem with us three. We either start too early or leave it too late.'

'I know,' Helen said, 'and given what Julia's going through, I really am glad I have Milly, but that doesn't mean I can't have a bit of a moan now and again. Being a mum might be a blessing but it can also be bloody hard work, especially on your own and especially with a wannabe teenager.'

'I'm always available if you want to talk.'

'I might just hold you to that.'

Julia looked a little unsteady on her feet when she returned to the table and had only just flopped back down on her seat when Helen's mobile beeped. 'Who's that? Is it Milly?'

Helen checked the message before answering. 'She says,

and I quote, "I've posted a party on Facebook and now the house is being trashed by drug-crazed teenagers. Don't come home until the police have cleared the area."' Helen left a pause before adding, 'Yes, Julia, she's fine.'

'Sometimes the big lies hide the smaller ones,' Phoebe offered.

'Thanks for that, Job's comforter!'

'We should leave soon,' Julia said as she stabbed her chocolate gateau with a fork. 'I'm already regretting falling off the wagon again and besides, I can't keep up with you two. I'm not sure I'll be able to walk in a straight line if I drink much more.'

'I hate to break this to you, Julia, but I think you're way past that point,' Phoebe said and then, as tactfully as she could, added, 'Will Paul be picking you up?'

Julia shook her head solemnly but appeared to have lost the power of speech.

Fuelled by alcohol, Phoebe wanted to shake some sense into her friend. Why couldn't she see what she had instead of acting like she had nothing? Compared to Phoebe, Julia had everything. 'Maybe you should phone him,' she tried.

'He might say no.'

'Of course he won't. Paul would do anything for you, Julia, he loves you,' Phoebe said without a shadow of a doubt. She knew how much Paul wanted a baby, but he would give up his chances of fatherhood for his wife in a heartbeat. He had told her as much – hadn't he told Julia too, or was she determined not to listen?

'The way I've been lately, I don't deserve his love,' Julia continued.

Helen had remained silent and when she did make a

contribution, it certainly didn't help matters. 'You're really convinced Paul would be better off without you, aren't you?'

Julia's lip began to tremble. 'I don't know . . .' she said. 'I just want him to be happy and if I can't give him children, if it's too late for me, then why should it have to be that way for Paul?'

'You'd break up with him?' asked Phoebe.

'It has to be better than waiting to be dumped again. I think that's why I'm freaking out about seeing the specialist. I'm sure they'll do their best, but if whatever treatment they suggest fails, then that's one door closed. Adoption's another possibility, but what if that doesn't work out either? The only thing I know for sure is that Paul deserves to be a father. I can't let him make that kind of sacrifice for me.'

Phoebe wondered how two people who wanted to make each other happy could get it so wrong. She wanted to cry and had to keep her lips pursed to hold back the sob.

'That is utter bollocks,' Helen said. 'I won't insult your intelligence by telling you it won't be hard for both of you, Julia, but you and Paul were meant to be together, come what may. He loves you with every bone in his body and I'm going to prove it.' She picked up her mobile and made the call.

'I have your wife with me,' Helen announced, 'and she's a teensy bit worse for wear. For some reason, she's under the impression that you wouldn't want to pick her up.'

After sorting the details, Helen put down the phone and folded her arms. Julia didn't look any more assured.

'Was he angry?'

'Not as angry as I'm getting,' Helen said. 'He'll be here

in five minutes, so for God's sake cheer up or he might just drive past. Come on, let's get some fresh air.'

The fresh air in question was accompanied by torrential rain so they were forced to wait at the entrance where the doorman pretended not to notice how drunk they were. Julia wobbled like Bambi and, despite heavy boots, Phoebe was no better grounded and stumbled into the door when Julia knocked into her. They giggled together while Helen peered out into the gloom. She was marginally less inebriated than her friends, something she wasn't particularly used to, and eager to find reinforcements. 'Here he is,' she said.

When Helen pulled Julia from the shelter of the pub, Phoebe was dragged along with them and they all screeched as the shock of the cold rain hit them. Paul watched from the safety of the car, which they were getting no closer to because as Helen pulled them in one direction, Julia and then Phoebe teetered in another.

Eventually, Paul stepped out into the downpour and his light grey T-shirt became pitted with dark splodges that merged until it was completely sodden and clung to his shivering body.

'Need some help?' he asked while checking all three women in turn to work out who he was more likely to get a coherent response from. It was clearly not his wife and when his eyes settled on Phoebe for a moment, all she could give him was a woozy smile. He opted for Helen and was about to ask her something when Julia began to sob.

'I came on,' she cried. 'I wanted to tell you this morning, but I couldn't.'

'It's all right,' Paul said in a low voice, concentrating on his wife and trying not to acknowledge the doorman standing only feet away. 'It's not your fault.'

'But it is,' Julia said, taking a step towards Paul that somehow resulted in her taking two steps back.

Paul handed Helen the car keys. 'Take Phoebe and get out of the rain.'

Helen took hold of Phoebe's arm and dragged her away, but Phoebe was more interested in looking back.

'See, he does love you,' Phoebe said as she watched Paul scoop Julia up into his arms.

'Go!' he said, when he noticed they had come to a standstill.

Phoebe would have to wait until they had sobered up before her friend would tell her how right she had been. Julia would go into exquisite detail about the rush of relief she had felt when she looked up into her husband's eyes. Paul hadn't looked sad, or annoyed, or any less in love with her than on the day he had vowed to take her as his wife, for better or for worse, till death do us part.

12

Helen was overdue her coffee break but with waiting times in the clinic lengthening as the morning wore on, she had to settle for a quick drink of water from the cooler while fetching another for a patient.

'Here you go, Lucy,' she said, returning with a plastic cup.

The young woman who thanked her had been a regular since transferring from Alder Hey Children's Hospital where she had been cared for since birth. After a lifetime of challenges, Lucy's treatment options had gradually diminished and it had been at least a year ago, probably closer to two, when her consultant had concluded that a heart transplant was the only real option left.

In the five years that Helen had worked in cardiology, she had met more patients than she could possibly hope to remember, but there were some she would never forget. Craig Winchester had been one and Lucy Cunliffe was another. The young woman was stronger than her failing organ gave her credit for. She never complained about the endless wait and refused to let it show when the short walk to the consultation room was ready to defeat her. She always remained remarkably calm while her mum fussed around her and more than anything, Lucy tried not to act like a patient, but rather the young woman her health would otherwise deny her.

'Do you think we'll be much longer?' Lucy's mum asked Helen.

'You're next on the list, Mrs Cunliffe.'

'You mean, *I'm* next on the list,' Lucy corrected.

Mrs Cunliffe seemed about to argue but was silenced by her daughter's warning glare. 'OK,' she said. 'But you know where I am if you need me.'

Two minutes later Lucy's name was called and Helen remained with Mrs Cunliffe while they watched Lucy walk carefully down the corridor. Like Lucy's mother, Helen had to fight against the urge to rush to help her.

'She'll be fine,' Helen said.

'Will she?' Mrs Cunliffe asked, mostly to herself before aiming the next comment directly at Helen. 'Do you think we'll ever get the call?'

Helen tore her eyes away from the now empty corridor and sat down next to Mrs Cunliffe. The plastic seat that Lucy had occupied only moments earlier held no residual warmth as if she had never been there at all. 'You know I can't answer that,' she began. 'It's closer to a lottery than any of us would like, and some people are luckier than others.'

'Our Lucy hasn't been blessed with luck, I'm afraid. She doesn't deserve any of this, spending all her energy fighting for every breath while her friends and her sister sail through life. Not that I wish ill on any of them,' she added quickly.

'I thank God every night that Hayley's healthy and happy, but is it too much to ask the same for Lucy?'

'No, of course it's not,' Helen said, putting her hand briefly on Mrs Cunliffe's shoulder and giving it a squeeze.

'And I wouldn't wish ill on anyone else either, but there lies the problem.'

Helen knew what she meant and made it easier for her. 'Don't think you're the only one to sit in that chair and wrestle with conflicting emotions. You just have to keep telling yourself that the people who donate organs don't die so that someone else can live: they die because of what happened to them. Whether their organs are harvested or not, the outcome for them remains the same. They still leave behind families who will grieve their loss. The only crumb of comfort is that the donor leaves an amazing gift of life, to be given to people like Lucy.'

Mrs Cunliffe refused to be comforted. 'When I listen to the news, my ears prick up whenever I hear there's been an accident. I can't believe I'm even admitting this but I get this tiny buzz of excitement when a fatality is reported because I wonder if we're going to get the call. Can you believe how heartless I've become? I certainly can't,' she said bitterly, 'and I hate myself for it.'

'I have a daughter too. Milly is eleven going on twenty and I can't think of anything I wouldn't do for that child. No matter how crazy she drives me, I'd wish ill on my best friend if it meant saving her life.'

'Lucy can drive me mad too.'

'And you'd do anything for her,' Helen said, her words slow and purposeful.

133

Mrs Cunliffe sniffed and then sat up a little straighter. 'Sorry, I talk utter nonsense sometimes.'

Helen knew the signs. It was time to step back and brush off Mrs Cunliffe's temporary lapse. 'If we're giving out awards for talking a load of rubbish then you'll have to join the queue. It's a wonder I've managed to keep my job this long given some of the things I come out with before I remember to engage my brain.'

'You have a job because you're good at it. I've dealt with a lot of nurses in my time and, don't get me wrong, there are plenty of good ones, but occasionally there are one or two that stand head and shoulders above the rest, and you're one of them.'

Despite the lack of caffeine and with little prospect of snatching more than twenty minutes for lunch, Helen felt re-energized as she got back to work. She couldn't wait to get home and tell Milly how amazing people thought she was, although given her daughter's current mood, Helen might have to resort to taking Mrs Cunliffe home with her before Milly would be convinced.

It was the week before Christmas and Phoebe was meeting Julia and Helen for some last-minute shopping in an effort to get Helen organized. Phoebe had already bought all of her Christmas presents in a single lunch hour, although in fairness, her list hadn't been a particularly long one. All she would be looking for now were some last-minute bargains to revamp her wardrobe and she could do with her friends' help. She might know instinctively how to find the perfect outfits for customers, but when it came to picking something out for herself, she had a tendency to dress down rather than up. Julia always complained about her wearing black and she needed a firm hand to stop her from reverting to type.

'Aren't we waiting for Julia?' Phoebe asked Helen, raring to go after they had met on the corner of Lord Street.

'Sorry, it's just me. I thought it would be easier,' Helen said.

'You didn't ask her?'

'You know what Julia's like,' Helen answered curtly. 'She'll want me to spend a fortune on my already spoilt child and I'd rather save up for our holiday. I've told Milly not to expect the ridiculously expensive iPod she's been asking for. She's getting a mid-range one, which is more than she deserves, but if Julia were here . . .'

'I suppose,' Phoebe said. Every once in a while she enjoyed being with just one of her friends so she didn't feel the need to compete for attention, but she didn't like the idea of anyone being excluded, if only because she wouldn't want it to be her.

'Shall we head straight off to the shops or do you fancy a caffeine fix first?'

'Caffeine,' Phoebe said with more than a hint of desperation.

'Bad night?'

'Nan was wandering about at two o'clock in the morning, wanting to know where Grandad was.'

'She's getting worse, isn't she?' Helen asked.

'It's only once in a while. Most of the time she's fine.'

'Liar.'

Phoebe fell silent as they queued up in the nearest coffee shop.

'Any progress on getting her into a home?' Helen asked after she had ordered coffees and a couple of Danish pastries.

'We've been back to see a couple and now it's just a matter of waiting until one of them has a vacancy. Even when we do get offered a place, it's still Nan's choice, and I'm not going to push her. It has to be her decision and it's going to be a hard one.'

They settled at a table with a good view of the Christmas-crazed shoppers sweeping past the window in waves, although Helen was more interested in her friend. 'I know you owe your nan a lot, Phoebes, but if she thinks it's the right thing to do then so should you. You haven't had a life of your own since . . .' She paused as she tried to do the maths but then gave up. 'Since forever.'

Phoebe didn't want to talk about it. There was a part of her that was looking forward to having so much freedom, but there was another part that wondered if she could adapt to a new life on her own. Selling the house and finding a little apartment she could finally call home was both thrilling and utterly terrifying. The last time she had had that much freedom was when she was a teenager, fighting against her nan's control, and that had gone badly wrong. Her nan had said often enough that she couldn't be trusted on her own and all evidence so far suggested she was right.

'And I'm sorry for dragging you out. You could probably do without this right now,' Helen continued. 'I know I can be high maintenance, just ask my beloved ex-husband.'

'No, it's fine,' Phoebe said with a smile and enough

conviction to put Helen's mind at ease. 'I'd rather do this than stay at home watching Nan like a hawk. I think she'd rather I went out too. Are you sure Julia won't mind that we didn't ask her?'

Helen wiped froth laced with chocolate from her upper lip. 'Of course not, stop worrying about it. Look, if Julia were here she'd only be trying to make us stay sensible, while I was thinking maybe we could stop off for cocktails on our way home as a reward.'

'I can't stay out late.'

'Not a problem. I was intending on being drunk by four o'clock anyway.'

'Julia definitely wouldn't approve of that,' Phoebe said with a guilty smile. It was as if they were little schoolgirls again, conjuring up tricks to annoy their babysitter.

'She need never know,' Helen replied, but then saw the look of concern reappear on her friend's face. 'Stop worrying, Phoebe. If anything, Julia will relish the prospect of telling us off if she does find out – which of course she will.'

'I don't know how you two do it. You're at each other's throats one minute and the next you're so close I couldn't separate you with a crowbar.'

A frown began to form as Helen asked, 'You do know that you can do the same, don't you, Phoebes?'

And yet, Phoebe never had. If there was a difference of opinion, it was second nature for Phoebe to back down because she had been brought up in a household where her opinion rarely counted. The last time she could remember arguing with one of her friends was when Helen had tipped a pot of paint over one of her drawings in Mr Whitwell's class when they were eight.

'I don't like falling out,' she said.

'We don't fall out,' Helen insisted. 'We fight like cat and dog and then we get over ourselves.'

'Are you sure about that?' Phoebe asked. 'This whole baby thing is getting to you, isn't it?'

'Isn't it getting to you?'

Phoebe shook her head, not because it wasn't, but because she wouldn't dare acknowledge those feelings. 'I'm just worried that it's created a wedge between you and Julia. Is that the real reason you didn't want her to come today?'

'Look, I love Julia to bits and even though I'll admit it's a bit tense at the moment, I wouldn't let anything break up our friendship. I promise.'

Phoebe pulled a sliver of buttery pastry from her Danish and decided to let the matter rest. 'So how are things at home?' she asked. 'Is Milly any happier about becoming a sister?'

Helen snorted and almost choked on a mouthful of pastry. 'John and Eva took her shopping the other day to pick out baby clothes. They've known the baby's sex for a while and were intending on keeping it a secret, but with Milly as she is, they thought it would be nice to go into the baby section of John Lewis and start picking out blue vests and dungarees.'

Phoebe smiled. The idea sounded sweet but judging by the face Helen was pulling, not to Milly.

'By the time they left the shop, Milly had made her position clear. She didn't want anything to do with a smelly, stinking brother.'

'Oh dear.' Phoebe was still smiling.

'It's no laughing matter,' Helen said coldly. 'If things get much worse then there's a chance Milly won't want to spend as much time with her dad, which means I'll have more childcare headaches than I do already. And it would be muggins here who has to manage Milly through her teens.'

Phoebe was crestfallen. 'Sorry, I didn't mean to laugh. I just didn't realize how much of a problem it would cause.'

Helen fixed Phoebe with a glare. 'Oh, for goodness' sake don't apologize. What I really need is for someone to tell me I'm overreacting.'

'You're overreacting,' Phoebe said quickly.

Maintaining her glare, Helen continued, 'I know Milly will come to her senses eventually and even if she doesn't, there's no way she would cut John out of her life completely. For one thing, John wouldn't let her.'

'It sounds to me like you don't need me to tell you you're overreacting after all,' Phoebe said, relaxing a little.

After draining her coffee cup, Helen said, 'Maybe you're right, but enough talk about the annoying stuff. Have you researched our holiday yet?'

'I've had a quick look and I think ten days is doable if we want to keep to a tight budget. I don't see any point in adding extra days if it leaves us too broke to do anything with our time, but the final bill is going to be dependent on the dates. Nan hasn't been able to think up any objections so far and I've checked with work and it looks like I'm OK for any time in February.'

'I've already got the February half-term holiday booked off and I don't think there'll be a problem asking for a few extra days. My biggest problem will be convincing John to have Milly – or should I say, convincing Milly to stay at her dad's – but I won't take no for an answer. That just leaves Julia, and she can suit herself about taking time off, so let's go ahead and book it,' Helen said with growing decisiveness.

'No, let's wait. We said we'd fit around any appointments Julia might have.'

Helen raised an eyebrow at Phoebe's assertiveness, making her friend blush. 'OK, but at least it sounds like we're getting there.'

'As long as the final bill doesn't end up being extortionate – I'd like to keep something in reserve for proper driving lessons.'

'Things not working out with Paul?'

'No, far from it, but he's the first to admit he can't teach me all the proper manoeuvres you get tested on these days.'

Helen was thoughtful for a while. 'Paul *does* talk to you, doesn't he?'

Phoebe had managed to sidestep Julia's earlier remark in the pub, but she wouldn't be able to fob Helen off so easily. 'A bit, but you can't blame him. Julia has us to talk to. All he has is his mates, and you know what blokes are like.'

'I wasn't blaming him,' Helen said as if there hadn't been a hint of an accusation in her question. 'As a matter of fact, I've had the odd private conversation with Paul myself, although I can't say I've been able to get him to open up. What exactly does he tell you?'

'No more than we already know,' Phoebe replied. 'He feels under pressure just as much as Julia, and it only seems to be building.'

'I'd be lying if I said I wasn't worried,' Helen said. 'But there's not a lot we can do except be there for both of them. Oh, and for me not to moan so much about Milly the Millstone.'

Phoebe was relieved that Helen hadn't launched into a thorough cross-examination. She wasn't ready to admit that she looked forward to her driving lessons far more than she should. 'Julia really doesn't like it when you call her that,' she said.

'I know, which is why I'm glad she's not here to listen to me complaining about all the little extras my precious daughter has added to her Christmas list. I'm afraid I've reserved that particular pleasure for you.'

'And on that note, should we get going?'

Helen picked up her bag and took out her phone to check for messages before they left. Phoebe glimpsed a screen full of missed calls and texts, some from John and others from Milly. 'You're popular,' she said.

'Oh, bugger!' Helen said as she opened a text from John. 'Eva's gone into labour.'

'Is she all right?'

'I think so,' Helen replied as she opened up the last message from her daughter. 'But I need to pick Milly up from the Women's Hospital. Sorry, Phoebes, I'm going to have to get moving.'

'No need to explain, just go,' Phoebe said and when Helen remained rooted to the spot, unsure of what to do next, she added, 'Go, Helen!'

Milly was sitting alone in a row of chairs running along the corridor. Leaning forward with her elbows on her knees and her chin propped on her hands, she stared intently at the wall opposite and didn't notice Helen approaching. Even when she recognized the sound of footsteps, she turned in the wrong direction towards what Helen presumed was the labour room where John and Eva would be.

Helen was almost at her side by the time Milly turned towards her mum, lifting her head to reveal red puffy eyes brimming with fresh tears. The questions that Helen had been ready to fire at her daughter were immediately swallowed back.

'It's all right,' she said, sitting down and wrapping her arms around her little girl who had shrunk to such an extent that Helen was reminded of the sweet little toddler she had once been able to rest on her hip. She kissed the top of Milly's head. 'I'm here now.'

Milly's shoulders began to shake as she buried her head. 'Everyone keeps saying it's going to be OK, Mum, but I don't believe them. Dad looked so scared and so did Eva. Is she going to die?'

The only information Helen had gleaned so far was that Eva had gone into labour and they were concerned about her blood pressure. 'I'm sure she'll be fine. People have babies every day,' she said and tried not to think of her own experiences as a nurse which had taught her that life was far from risk-free, even new life.

As she rocked her daughter, Helen looked up and down the corridor. At first glance she had thought the nurses' station deserted but then spotted a nurse coming out of the backroom.

'Shall I go and find out what's happening?' she asked,

although the real question was whether or not Milly was willing to let go of her.

'Yes, please.'

Despite the seriousness of the situation, Helen found herself smiling at her daughter's new-found politeness as she approached the nurse.

'Hi, could you tell me what's happening with Mrs Butler?' Helen asked, trying to ignore how odd it felt using her own name to describe John's second wife, the mother of his new baby – hopefully.

'Are you a relative?'

'That's my daughter,' Helen said, nodding towards Milly who was watching them keenly. 'I'm here to take her home but I'd like to be able to give her some reassurance that her stepmum and the baby are all right first.'

'I don't think there's anything to be too concerned about. Do you want me to let them know you're here? Mr Butler's been worried about leaving Milly out in the corridor alone and he'll be relieved to know you're here.'

Helen wanted to say no. She hadn't wanted to be at the hospital at all and intended on leaving as quickly as she could. She had never expected to be this close to the birth of John's new family. 'All right, but tell him he doesn't have to come out,' she managed to say. 'Tell him to stay with Eva but if he has a message for Milly, that might be good.'

Returning to her daughter, Helen began pacing the floor while Milly resumed her previous pose of staring blankly at the wall. Helen had expected the nurse to return almost immediately but the minutes dragged on and when she did reappear, she gave Helen an encouraging smile that might have been a suggestion of good news or could just as easily

143

have been hiding bad – Helen had offered her fair share of both. 'He won't be a minute,' she called down the corridor and then quickly disappeared behind the nurses' station again.

'Is something wrong?' Milly asked when she saw the unease on her mum's face.

Helen gave her own version of a false smile. 'No, of course not. She would have come over and said something if there was,' Helen said to convince them both.

There was a gentle creak of a door and then John appeared. He was tall with unkempt russet hair and his usual pale complexion was blighted with bright red blotches that made his cheeks glow, exaggerating the beaming smile on his face. He bounded towards them and was looking at Helen when he said, 'She's had the baby and they're both fine.'

Thankfully for both of them, John remembered to turn his attention to his daughter and he knelt down in front of Milly to cup her face so she would keep his gaze. 'I've only ever felt this happy once before and that was the day you were born, Milly.'

Helen pressed her lips together in a tight line that rippled with emotion, the smile she had been trying to maintain all but forgotten. She could remember that day so perfectly and even though she and John had barely been more than children themselves, they had both immediately recognized how momentous the occasion was. While they had been terrified and even a little reluctant to become parents, they hadn't taken their new roles lightly. The pregnancy had been a mistake, as was the marriage, but there was a part of Helen that didn't mind the fact that she had apparently skipped her youth and was fast-forwarding into middle age. She might complain but she wouldn't have it any other way. The day Milly had been born remained by far the best day of her life.

That pink bundle of delight was a person in her own right now, someone who formed her own views and opinions, and Helen focused on working out how Milly was dealing with the news.

'They're not going to die, are they?' she was asking.

'Eva is a bit knackered but she's fine otherwise, and the baby was balling his eyes out as soon as he was born. Do you want to see him?'

Milly's eyes widened and at first Helen thought it was with horror but then she said, 'Can I?'

John pulled himself up and Milly along with him, no longer holding her face but her hand. After taking only a few steps, however, he stopped and turned to Helen who hadn't moved.

'Aren't you coming?'

Forcing herself out of her stupor, Helen remembered herself. 'Seriously?' she scoffed. 'Your wife has just given birth and you think she's going to appreciate her husband walking back into the room with his ex?'

'She wouldn't mind,' John said. 'You two get on well and she might even appreciate your support right now.'

Helen shook her head in reproach while wishing it was only Eva's feelings she was trying to protect. 'You really are a man, aren't you, John?'

The proud father gave her a smug smile. 'Yes.'

If Milly hadn't been within earshot, Helen would have made some cutting remark about his manhood, but she was forced to bite her tongue. 'I'll wait here,' she said simply.

The expression on John's face changed and it was as if he had been blessed with an insight that had eluded him during their brief marriage. As he watched her wrestling with unwelcome emotions, Helen felt exposed and wished he would go away. It took a tug of the hand from Milly to get him going.

'Has he got a name yet?' Helen asked quickly before they disappeared.

'Oliver,' John said and then looked down at his daughter for her approval.

She shrugged. 'It could be worse.'

It was John rather than Milly who gave Helen one last look before disappearing into the labour room. It was a look that rooted Helen to the spot long after the door closed and the pale cream corridor began to ripple behind a film of tears that had washed over her eyes. She inhaled deeply and cursed under her breath. Why the hell was she being so emotional?

It wasn't as if she had feelings for John any more and it had been a long time since Paul had needed to act as their go-between. They had settled their differences and maintained a fairly close relationship, not so much like brother and sister but distant cousins perhaps. She had genuinely been happy for John when he remarried, if not a little concerned about its impact on Milly, and again, the same feelings when he announced they were having a baby. So why on earth did she want to burst into tears? Why did the thought of going into that room and seeing John's second child all brand new and wrinkly give her palpitations?

Ignoring the sign that told her not to use her mobile, Helen quickly texted Phoebe. Her hand was shaking as she

146

sent her friend a message telling her the news and apologizing once again for leaving her high and dry. She then scrolled down to find Julia's number. This was news that couldn't be delivered by text but neither could she make the call, even though of everyone she knew, it was Julia she wanted to speak to most. She needed an adult to make sense of feelings that felt distinctly adolescent, but there was a chance if she phoned now she would burst into tears and make a fool of herself.

There was the now familiar creak of a door as Milly reappeared, thankfully on her own. She held her body taught with her shoulders hunched, and judging by the smile on her face, she was a tense ball of excitement. 'Oh. My. God!' she exclaimed as quietly as she could. 'He's sooooo adorable. They let me hold him and he was crying but then he stopped and he was looking at me and I thought he was going to smile but then his lip started trembling and it was really funny when his face scrunched up and then he started crying so I gave him back to Eva quick and then he really started crying and they—'

Helen put her hand on her daughter's arm. 'Milly,' she said slowly, 'remember to breathe, sweetheart.'

There were a couple of gulps of air and more than a hint of the melodramatics when Milly raised up both hands before lowering them slowly with palms down as she released a long, slow breath. 'OK, I'm fine. I just . . . I just love him, Mum. He's my brother and I love him and I don't care what I get for Christmas now because this is the best present ever!'

Helen did her best to ignore the hurt. She sighed dramatically and said, 'And there I was thinking you could come back into town with me so I can resume my Christmas shopping. Instead of hiding your presents this year, I thought you might want to help pick them – unless you *want* a surprise?'

Milly gave her a knowing look. 'Not your kind of surprises, Mother.'

'OK then, and maybe afterwards we can call in to see Julia and Paul,' said Helen, trying not to think about the cocktails she had been planning with Phoebe, which would go down a treat right now.

'I can show them the photos of the baby, look,' Milly replied, taking her phone from her pocket.

Helen had no option but to look and she wrinkled her nose. 'You've got to admit, newborn babies are pretty ugly.'

Milly rolled her eyes. 'Muuummm,' she said in one lyrical note.

'OK, he's gorgeous, I'll admit it but can you do me a favour? Let's not shove this under Julia's nose, or Paul's for that matter. You know how much they want a baby of their own and even though it's wonderful news and everyone's happy for John and Eva and you, it's still tough to hear when someone else gets the one thing you want more than anything else.'

Milly was looking at the photo of her brother again and held the phone as if the baby were still in her arms. 'Understood,' she said.

'Good girl, now come on, sister Milly. We need to hit the shops before everything's sold out.'

Leaving the hospital, Helen felt an unexpected sense of emptiness and again her thoughts turned to Julia. Her friend wasn't the only one capable of feeling broody and at least

Julia was trying for a baby whereas it was going to take another Christmas miracle for Helen to conceive a child.

As these desires wrapped around Helen's chest and pressed against her aching heart, Milly was wrapped up in her own thoughts and completely forgot that she was too old to hold her mum's hand. Never was it more noticeable how fast her daughter was growing up than when she held her hand. Milly was no longer reaching up, and they both had to twist their arms to match each other's height. It was still a lovely feeling and one she knew she should appreciate more. This was what Julia was missing and little wonder she got so mad when Helen started complaining. This sudden epiphany did have a downside, and as they headed into town, Helen had a feeling that Milly was going to get all the Christmas wishes her credit card would allow.

When Julia had read the text from Helen proposing to call in that afternoon with Milly, she had been expecting the worst. Milly was supposed to be at her dad's so she warned Paul that they may have to intervene once more.

'You two look in need of something to revive your energy levels,' she said brightly when they arrived laden with shopping bags. 'And fortunately for you, I've been baking.'

Milly's eyes lit up. 'Chocolate cake?'

Julia lifted up the skirt of her apron, which was covered in dark chocolatey smears and a dusting of icing sugar for good measure. 'What gave it away?'

'Great, I'm starving!'

'I just hope Paul hasn't eaten it all.'

'I heard that.' Paul had appeared from the kitchen and raised an eyebrow at Milly. 'Hello, trouble,' he said and then turned to Helen. 'Hello, double trouble.'

'I don't know what you mean,' Helen said primly.

When the two shared a look that Julia couldn't interpret she felt unnerved. 'What? What am I missing?'

'Nothing,' chorused Paul and Helen.

Their open smiles suggested that whatever it was, it didn't deserve the bad thoughts that had briefly invaded Julia's mind and she silently admonished herself for letting her growing sense of insecurity get the better of her. Her inability to produce a baby for her husband was slowly turning her into someone she didn't recognize any more.

'You didn't mind us calling around, did you?' Helen asked when Milly had disappeared into the kitchen with Paul. 'Not frantically wrapping up last-minute Christmas presents?'

'Unlike you,' Julia said, cocking her head towards the mountain of shopping bags Helen had dumped in her previously uncluttered hallway, 'I had Christmas boxed off at the end of November.'

'You missed some good bargains then,' Helen answered smartly.

Julia caught herself before launching into a lecture about being more organized. It wasn't simply the difference in their personalities that meant Julia was the more prepared of the two. They had distinctly different lifestyles too; where one needed more hours in the day, the other had both time and love to spare. You only had to compare their homes to spot the differences. Unlike the homely chaos that greeted visitors to Helen's home, the house

Julia and Paul had moved into a year before they married was all clean lines and understated style. The sum total of Julia's Christmas decorations amounted to a handmade wreath on the front door, the requisite tree which wouldn't look out of place in a department store window, and a lush garland of holly and ivy draped over the mantelpiece with twinkling crimson lights that gave a gentle, sophisticated nod to the season. There were no garish strips of tinsel, tacky dancing Santas or musty handmade decorations like the ones Milly insisted on putting up each year, some of which Julia had helped her rescue from the bin last January when Helen had tried to throw them out.

'Come on,' Julia said and was about to lead her friend into the kitchen when Helen put a hand on her shoulder to stop her. From the kitchen, they could hear Milly's excited chatter and while it was impossible to follow the one-way, high-speed conversation, the word 'baby' was being mentioned often enough to forewarn Julia. She braced herself for the news, and to her shame felt a twinge of disappointment that her friend's visit wasn't to give Milly another dose of her motherly advice after all.

'Eva had the baby,' Helen said softly.

Julia let her head drop forward. 'Oh,' she said simply.

Helen squeezed her shoulder and by some small miracle, when Julia lifted up her chin there was a smile on her face. 'Are they both well?'

Nodding, Helen said, 'I wanted to tell you in person although . . .' Her eyes were drawn in the direction of her daughter's voice. 'I hadn't expected Milly to get so excited.'

'I'm fine, Helen, and it was nice of you to think of me,

but I'm not so wrapped up in my own world that I can't be happy for someone else.'

'Nice speech,' Helen sniffed. 'Shame I don't believe it – and if it helps, I'm feeling a bit shitty about it too.'

The comment took Julia by surprise and she was about to ask her what she meant but Helen was already pushing her towards the kitchen. Unlike Julia, her friend wasn't going to find catharsis by talking through her issues. She preferred distraction.

'Come on, I want cake,' Helen said.

There was still enough mess to prove that Julia had indeed made a cake from scratch and not simply put a shop-bought one on a plate and dusted the counter with icing sugar to suggest otherwise – as Helen had been known to do. The only deceit in Julia's kitchen was that she'd had no intention of baking that day until Helen had sent the text message.

'The kettle's on,' Paul said to Julia.

She held his gaze and wouldn't have been surprised if there had been an audible buzz to trace the telepathic messages streaming between them. After the drunken debacle at the Elephant, Julia and Paul had settled their differences and there had been no acting involved when they had presented themselves as a united front during their consultation with the fertility specialist earlier that week. They hadn't expected to be given answers there and then, nor had they received them, so although she and Paul were now speaking to each other and living for the moment, their plans for the future were still a sensitive issue and one to be avoided. They relied on non-verbal messages to understand how the other was feeling and they were

152

becoming quite adept. When he blinked, she knew he was asking if she was all right, and her pursed lips let him know that she was holding up. Julia had had worse days.

Oblivious to it all, Milly said, 'Did Mum tell you, Julia? Eva had the baby this morning and they've called him Ollie.'

'Oliver,' Helen corrected.

Milly huffed. 'Well, I'm calling him Ollie – and probably other things too when he starts being a proper annoying boy. But he's so *tiny* and I was allowed to hold him,' she said to Julia. 'I think he's just so perfect with tiny, tiny fingers, but Mum says he's ugly.'

Julia turned to Helen. 'You've seen him?'

'Only a photo.'

'Here, look,' Milly said.

It wasn't only Julia who tensed, but Paul and Helen too as Milly turned her mobile towards her. There was a blur of pink flesh and blue blanket but Julia's focus fell short of the screen and she concentrated on the impassable space between herself and the newborn.

'He's lovely,' she said.

'Hey, why don't we go into the living room, Milly?' Paul asked. 'I was about to watch *Elf* if you're interested?'

Once Julia had handed out generous slices of cake, Paul disappeared with Milly while she and Helen sat down at the kitchen table. Facing each other with their elbows resting on the table and their hands wrapped around mugs of coffee, there was no escaping each other's scrutiny and it was Helen who beat Julia to the first question.

'Are you OK?'

'I'm happy for John and Eva, although I might hate their

153

guts just a little bit for making it look so easy. So what's your excuse?'

'Oh, I don't know. Nothing probably.'

Julia waited for a better response.

'You don't have a monopoly on being broody, you know. I went to the hospital to pick up Milly and when I saw John there, it brought back memories, that's all. Memories I know I'm lucky to have,' she added, reacting to her friend's thoughts before Julia had even acknowledged them herself.

'You don't have to apologize for having Milly,' Julia said as kindly as her frayed nerves would allow.

'Well, I do have to apologize for my daughter's insensitivity. But enough about John and bloody Eva! Tell me more about your visit to the clinic. What haven't you told me?' Helen asked, clearly dissatisfied with the updates Julia had provided so far.

'Nothing, more's the pity, unless you want me to repeat our consultant's quite lengthy description of a sperm's epic journey to the egg, which he compared to jumping into the Mersey and swimming to New York?' When Helen shook her head, Julia said simply, 'There's no magic solution on offer, Helen.'

'Not yet,' Helen said.

Helen spoke with a confidence that Julia would once have shared but not of late. Time, and more specifically, Julia's age were against them and she didn't need a consultant to tell them that their options would be limited. 'If you say so,' she managed to say. 'First, we both have to undergo all kinds of tests where we'll be thoroughly prodded and poked, or in Paul's case, he'll do his own prodding.' They both pulled a face before Julia continued,

'And we'll know more when we get the initial results, hopefully by the end of January.'

'Initial results?'

'There could be more tests and there could be drugs we could take. There are procedures we could go through or there could be more radical options. Could be, could be, could be,' she said with a sigh.

'And until then, your decision to hold off trying for a baby continues.'

'For Paul's sake, and the sake of our marriage, yes,' Julia said. 'But we're such a long way off from knowing what treatment we can have, if any, not to mention whether or not we would want to pursue it. If we do go for fertility treatment and that fails, on top of the time we would have wasted trying, we would then have to wait for up to a year before we could be considered for adoption. Part of me – the impatient part of me – is tempted to accept it's all my fault, give up trying and go straight to plan B.'

'I know I joked about it, but maybe I could be some kind of surrogate. You want a baby and I'm feeling broody. You have a husband and I don't have the means to have another baby. We could share!'

For the first time since arriving, the smile on Julia's face reached her eyes. 'You want to share my husband?'

Helen's face contorted with disgust. 'Have you never heard of a turkey baster?'

'I have one.'

'There you go then, we're already ahead of the game.'

'And what about the baby?' Julia said in a tone that made it clear that she wasn't taking Helen's suggestion at all seriously, although a part of her was sorely tempted.

'Oh, I don't want the baby, not really,' Helen admitted. 'Seeing John today just made me realize how much I want what he has, the same as what you want, really. A nice, neat family package. We each have one half of that.'

'Ah, so you are talking about sharing.'

'We already do, don't we? I borrow your husband when I need a man with power tools and you enjoy spending time with Milly.'

'Sounds like we should be grateful for what we have.'

Helen lifted up her mug. 'I'll drink to that.'

Gales of laughter erupted from the living room. 'Shall we join them?' Julia asked.

Once Julia had settled into an armchair with her half-eaten cake on her lap and a fresh cup of coffee, she felt a certain sense of fulfilment that surprised her. Helen's arrival with glad tidings ought to have floored her but there had been something in Helen's summation of the four of them that comforted her. They were a family unit of sorts, and when Helen caught her watching them rather than the TV, there was something in her eyes that suggested she recognized it too.

13

The Accident

Two hours after her shift had officially finished Anya was ready to leave, but rather than heading home she felt compelled to pay a quick visit to the Critical Care Unit. Julia Richardson had been drifting in and out of consciousness all day and each time she woke she asked about her friend. Anya had done her best to put her mind at ease but could offer only limited comfort. The reports on Helen Butler were far from promising, and Anya faced the prospect of a sleepless night herself unless she found out a little more about this friend who Julia appeared to have much more of a connection with than she did the husband she was still refusing to let near her bedside.

Anya's feet and calves ached as she hurried through the hospital while chomping on a Mars bar and swallowing it back with a double espresso to give her enough energy to keep going. Turning the last corner she spied a dishevelled-looking man outside the CCU. He had his eyes closed as he rested his forehead on the wall with his hands in his pockets.

Although she had no idea who he was, Anya immediately recognized him for what he represented. He was one amongst many other relatives roaming the corridors in confusion and in some cases, despair. Without exception, they wore dazed expressions that suggested their brains hadn't quite caught up with the day's events. They couldn't yet comprehend how it was possible that the loved ones they had casually waved off that morning should now be fighting for their lives, or worse.

At the sound of her approach, the man straightened up and turned towards her. Seeing only the uniform, his eyes widened in fear and apprehension. 'My wife . . .' he began and then shook his head. 'I mean, my *ex*-wife and her friends were involved in the accident. What should I do? I don't know what to do.' He glanced over his shoulder, drawing Anya's gaze to another figure approaching from the opposite direction.

Anya watched the young girl walking slowly up the corridor. She had her head down as she gave her undivided attention to the two plastic cups in her hand. Nothing else existed except those cups of water; nothing else was going to invade her consciousness or add to the distress that had already turned her complexion ghostly white and her nose bright red.

'What do I tell my daughter?' John asked.

14

Christmas in the Butler household was pretty much the same as always; lots of frantic preparation and panic followed by a general sense of anticlimax. Milly had been spoilt rotten despite Helen's best intentions and this fact was driven home on New Year's Day when Helen was searching for her gloves and found her daughter's brand-new and ridiculously expensive iPod shoved down the side of the sofa. In Milly's eagerness to get to her dad's the day before, she hadn't thought to pick it up. It was becoming more apparent by the day that Milly hadn't been exaggerating when she had said the baby was the best Christmas present ever.

'Do you want to borrow my gloves?' Phoebe asked as they strolled around Sefton Park Lake, her words floating on a cloud of crystal white vapour.

'No, you keep them. I'm fine.'

Ignoring her, Phoebe peeled off her green and orange striped mittens and handed them over. Helen was too cold to object. 'All right, but you can have them back just as soon as I get the feeling back in my fingers.'

Even as Helen was pulling them on, an arm extended into the space between them. At the end of that arm was a broad, bare hand holding out a pair of men's leather gloves. 'Here, Phoebe, wear these. I've got padded pockets.'

When Phoebe looked as if she were about to refuse, Helen made a grab for them and forced them on her friend. 'There, I can keep yours now,' she said.

'If I'd known you needed gloves, Helen,' Julia said from behind them, 'Santa could have brought you a pair.'

'I'd say Santa was generous enough as it was,' Helen replied.

They continued their walk in a silence that was broken only by the occasional quack of a disinterested duck, which had already been overfed that morning. It had been Helen's idea to go for an early morning stroll followed by breakfast in a local café, but things hadn't exactly gone to plan and Helen was blaming her daughter. Milly had declined the invitation to join her for the usual raucous New Year's Eve party at Helen's mum's in favour of a quiet evening in with John, Eva and the baby. Helen's lack of maternal responsibilities had resulted in her waking up in an empty house on the first day of the year with a stinking hangover that she had well and truly earned the night before. She could vaguely remember playing vodka roulette with her cousins and dancing barefoot in the street. By the time she could focus her bleary eyes on her phone, she had already missed numerous calls and texts from her friends asking where the hell she was. It had been one o'clock by the time they had reached the park, at which point their favourite coffee shop had already closed up for the day. They were going to have to make do with bacon rolls back at Julia's, which was fine by Helen. Anything was better than going home alone.

'I'm starting to think we should have borrowed a dog from someone,' Helen said as she cast an eye around the park. Without exception, all the other visitors were walking dogs, pushing prams or chasing after their offspring. It made their own little group look a little conspicuous and for various reasons, they all felt uncomfortable.

'Weren't you thinking of getting one?' Phoebe called behind her.

'Were we?' Julia said, directing her response to Paul.

'I was trying to think of something different to get you for Christmas and I asked Phoebe if she had any ideas. I think *she* was the one who suggested a dog.'

Phoebe laughed softly. 'I was only thinking it would be nice if one of us had one and I can't because of Nan's cat.'

'For the record, Phoebe, I would have killed Paul if he had presented me with a puppy on Christmas morning. Since when have I been a dog person?'

Paul gasped. 'Don't blame me; I wasn't seriously considering it. It was Phoebe's idea!'

'Thanks, Paul!' Phoebe said with mock horror that didn't quite hide the smile on her face. 'Drop me in it, why don't you!'

Looking over her shoulder towards Paul, Helen met Julia's gaze first and was glad she couldn't read her thoughts. In the last ten years, Helen could be forgiven for forgetting there had ever been a previous connection between Phoebe and Paul. She felt distinctly unsettled that she should be reminded of it now.

* * *

Julia hadn't realized she was wearing a frown until she saw it reflected in Helen's face. She hadn't meant it to form and quickly tried to recover. 'What's wrong, Helen?' she asked with a forced grin. 'You're not the one who's thinking of getting a dog, are you?'

Helen tried a little too hard to smile back. 'Not unless it can be trained to walk itself while I laze in bed.'

'Which I presume is where you would rather be now,' Julia concluded, to which she received no more than a grunt.

Whatever had just passed like a shadow over the group had been swept to one side although Julia hadn't completely erased it from her mind. As she walked along the side of the lake she crunched gravel underfoot but it might as easily have been eggshells. More than ever, she had to consider everything she said in front of Paul, so when the subject of a puppy had been raised, she had stopped herself from accusing him of thinking a puppy could be their substitute baby. She didn't want to suggest that the aching void in her life couldn't be filled, that they were unfixable, and she certainly didn't want Paul to think the letter they had received from the hospital a few days earlier was a game changer.

And while this editing process of what she should or shouldn't say had been going through her mind, Helen had turned to look at her and Julia had found something else to worry about. Something was bothering her friend and Julia wondered if it should bother her too. There was nothing unusual about hearing playful banter between Paul and her oldest friends; it was just that it was usually Helen and not Phoebe giving him a hard time.

162

'How are the driving lessons going, Phoebe?' Julia asked. 'Are you getting more confident?'

Phoebe glanced over her shoulder and looked to the man whose arm his wife was holding onto tightly. 'I think you'd better let Paul answer that one.'

'Judging by the way my husband comes home needing a stiff drink I'd say there's still plenty of room for improvement.'

'Shouldn't you be starting proper lessons by now?' asked Helen.

'No, not yet,' Phoebe and Paul answered together.

'But you're right,' Phoebe continued, 'I do need to get a move on. I need to make it a priority now Nan has a moving date.'

There were gasps from both Julia and Helen.

'Would this be to the home in Gateacre?' Paul asked, sounding the least surprised and the most knowledgeable.

'Yes, all thanks to you putting in a good word for me. They have a resident who's relocating at the end of Jan— I mean the end of this month. Good grief, it's not that far off, is it?' Phoebe sounded terrified.

Julia pushed her way through the group so she could slip her arm into the crook of Phoebe's elbow. 'It's going to be such a change for you, isn't it? Do you think you'll be OK on your own?'

'I don't know . . . I don't like to think about it, but I suppose I'm practically on my own now as it is. Nan likes to spend most of her time locked away in the drawing room while I watch my *mindless entertainment* on TV. We don't even eat together, but still, the idea of letting her be cared for by someone else just doesn't seem right.'

163

'Let her go,' Julia insisted. 'She doesn't want to face the humiliation of her granddaughter taking care of all her intimate needs and she doesn't want to be a burden to you. She knows her own mind.'

Phoebe lowered her head. 'Not all the time.'

'All the more reason for you to let her do things her way while she can,' Helen offered. 'She wants to make this choice on her own terms and you have to let her.'

Julia had hooked arms with Helen too, and as they walked, she did her best to ignore the irritatingly complete family group coming towards them along the narrow path circling the lake. They were still some distance away but it was close enough to feel the glare from what she perceived as unnecessarily smug grins. 'It's a new year and a new start for you, Phoebe, and given you have a couple of years before you have to sell your nan's house, maybe now is the time to rethink your career. Before you commit to this management programme at work, why don't you look at other options? The way things are going with my jewellery commissions, I could even take you on as my apprentice,' she said, thinking how well received her latest pieces had been, and she had already had enquiries for more.

'I don't have a clue how to make jewellery,' Phoebe reminded her.

'And you don't want to,' Julia said, hearing what Phoebe was too polite to say. 'And maybe I am jumping the gun about apprenticeships, but the thing is you have options. And not just career-wise either. I think Helen and I are going to have to remind you that there's more to do on a cold winter's evening than curl up with a cat on your knee watching *The X Factor*. We're going to have to get you out more and I don't just mean driving.'

Helen was following her train of thought and added, 'We could always put your details on a dating site.'

Phoebe made a move to unhook herself from Julia's clutches, but Julia refused to let her go. Phoebe was a problem that needed fixing. Her friend was far more attractive than she gave herself credit for but she had approached every relationship so far with the same level of expectation; that there was no one out there who would think her worthy of emotional investment, and meaningless sex was a fair exchange for a little attention now and again.

Julia was more determined than ever to help Phoebe embrace the brave new world that awaited her, and that included finding the *right* man, not *any* man. 'After everything you've said about those sites over the years, Helen, I don't think that's what we want for Phoebe.'

'I only tried it once, no twice, and that was years ago. I'm sure they've improved loads since then.'

Phoebe was still resisting as Julia pulled her friends into a huddle, allowing the oncoming family just enough room to squeeze past. 'If you're that much of a fan, Helen, you can do it too. You could go on a double date so you can watch each other's back.'

Helen craned her neck to look back at Paul. 'Help!' she cried.

Paul didn't have a chance to respond because Julia was on a mission. 'Why not, though? You're both still young. Don't wait for life to happen, go out and make your own opportunities. If I could have the last ten years over again, I wouldn't have wasted my chances.'

'Me neither,' Phoebe said wistfully and then blushed when she saw the curious looks from both her friends. 'But I'm set in my ways now, Julia,' she said, recovering herself. 'I like my own company and I'm not looking for anyone.'

'Come on, Julia, leave the poor girls alone,' Paul said as he pulled at his wife's arm. 'And then perhaps you'd like to tell me all about those wasted opportunities you've had while we've been together.'

Julia was annoyed at herself for the slip, which she should have known Paul would misread. Returning to his side, she looped her arm in Paul's and rested her head on his shoulder. 'I only meant that I shouldn't have been so cautious. I should have known from the start that you were the one for me.'

'Or maybe you should have checked for faults first,' he muttered under his breath.

Julia matched his low voice and said, 'You're perfect in my eyes.'

'I don't think the consultant sees it that way.'

'We don't know what he thinks, Paul, not yet.'

Helen and Phoebe were walking ahead and refrained from looking back or joining in the conversation that was decidedly awkward for all of them. Even so, their unspoken questions couldn't be ignored.

'I've been recalled for more tests,' Paul announced. 'Apparently my first sample wasn't good enough.'

'Paul, you don't need to—' Julia started.

'What? Share my humiliation with your friends? It had to happen at some point, Julia, and I don't mind that it looks like I was the problem all along,' he said, his voice softening. 'I'd hate you to feel like I do.'

166

It was Helen who turned first. 'It could just mean that the first sample was contaminated or they could have simply messed up the test,' she said and allowed a wicked smile to form. 'You could have been too hot to handle.'

Phoebe joined in next. 'Helen's right, it must be a mix-up at the hospital. It can't be you.'

While Phoebe's words stung, Julia had to agree with her. Of course it couldn't be Paul; it had to be Julia. Wasn't that what they had all been thinking? 'It's too soon to jump to conclusions,' she said.

When no one could think of anything else to offer, Julia simply repeated her previous statement. 'You're perfect to me, Paul. And I want the same kind of match for my friends.'

Paul kissed the top of her head. 'I'm afraid when they made me they broke the mould.'

'Oh no, Phoebes, all the best ones have been taken!' Helen cried, following Paul's lead and doing her bit to break through the tension. 'There's nothing left for us sad old spinsters so we might as well throw ourselves in the lake!'

As she pulled Phoebe towards the water's edge, Helen's giggling was infectious and the frown that had been furrowing Phoebe's brow began to soften. Julia, in her best schoolmarm voice, told them to be careful as they teetered towards the frozen edges of the lake, but even as she spoke, Phoebe had stepped onto an icy puddle and lost her balance. Paul pulled himself from Julia's grasp and rushed to catch her even as Phoebe righted herself.

Julia watched as Paul guided her to safety before being forced to return to fetch Helen who had decided she too was a damsel in distress. Once his heroic deeds were accomplished, Julia reached out an arm, inviting her husband to return to her side. 'I'd say it's about time we headed home,' she said.

'Yes, please,' Phoebe replied. 'How about I drive back to get in some practice?'

'Erm, I think we've had enough danger for one day,' Helen said and Julia agreed.

'Don't you listen to them, Phoebes,' Paul said. 'You'll be driving better than either of these two before the end of the year.'

'I'd do it even quicker if you could manage a few more lessons,' Phoebe said. 'Aren't you off work this week?'

Even as she felt her hackles rise, Julia questioned her reaction. There was no reason to be concerned by the evolving relationship between Paul and Phoebe – she trusted them both implicitly. The root of her anxiety had nothing to do with them and everything to do with her own feelings. It was wrong that Phoebe should suffer because of Julia's growing insecurities, but she was already trying to think up excuses to put Phoebe off when Helen cut in on her behalf.

'I'd have thought Paul would want to spend precious time off work with his wife.'

'Sorry, yes, of course,' Phoebe said, but turned to Julia in the hope that she might reject Helen's argument.

'I don't know . . .' Julia said and was about to suggest that Helen had a point when Paul cut in.

'I could spare the odd hour. It's not a problem.'

As they headed back to the car, Paul's words were ringing in Julia's ears. There wasn't a problem, was there?

* * *

The mound of laundry hidden beneath a strategically positioned tablecloth had grown so large that to the untrained eye it could be mistaken for a piece of furniture. Helen had intended to work her way through it while she was off, but there was something wrong about spending a much-deserved Christmas break doing housework. And so it had been left to grow and if she didn't do something about it now, she was going to need a bigger tablecloth.

Helen would argue that she was not a slob. She liked the idea of a tidy house, it was just putting that notion into practice that she had a problem with, but enough was enough, and she set aside her Sunday morning to clear the backlog. She had dragged herself out of bed deliberately early, switched on the radio, and two cups of coffee later she had so much fresh ironing that she had run out of space to put it all.

Gathering up as many garments as she could carry, Helen was surprised to note it was already half past ten. She hadn't heard a peep out of Milly and took great pleasure in striding into her daughter's darkened room and shouting, 'Wakey, wakey,' at the top of her voice. She kept moving until she reached the window and then used her elbow to prise apart the curtains.

'Mum, I'm having a lie-in!' came a muffled protest from beneath the bedclothes where her daughter had retreated.

'Well done, you've achieved that – now get up.'

'In. A. Minute.'

'Milly, look at me,' Helen said as calmly as she could manage.

Her daughter flung back the covers and tried to scowl at her mum but the light was stinging her eyes. 'What?'

'I want this laundry put away carefully, because if it gets creased again you'll have to either go to school in a crumpled uniform or iron it yourself.'

Helen placed the pile of clothes proudly on the bed, forcing Milly to draw up her legs.

'And after that, I want you to tidy your room.'

'But I thought we were going to the cinema today?'

'And we will, once all the housework is done. It can be our reward.'

'It's not fair. I don't even get to sleep in at Dad's any more,' she grumbled, 'but at least there I get to do interesting stuff like dress up the baby.'

'And I suppose I have it easy, do I? What with working all week so I can spend my weekends washing and ironing my ungrateful daughter's clothes?' Completely unfazed by the withering look her daughter was giving her, Helen continued, 'Come on, you'd better move these clothes because I'll have another pile to bring up to you in an hour.'

Returning downstairs to the kitchen, Helen took a deep breath of warm air laced with the scent of fabric conditioner. She considered having breakfast but was scared she might lose momentum, so she picked up the next item from the pile. It was the dress she had been wearing when she had gone to Sefton Park with her friends. Two weeks had passed and the outing was still playing on her mind. Phoebe had most definitely been acting strangely. She had been what Helen could only describe as giddy around Paul, and she had to describe it like that because she didn't want to use the word flirty. And why, after witnessing first-hand how Julia and Paul were going through testing times, did

Phoebe think it would be a good idea to take up more of Paul's time with driving lessons when he should be at home talking things through with his wife?

Phoebe and Paul's history was meant to be buried in the past but Helen had been carrying out an exhumation of the past over the last week or so. When Helen had stumbled upon Phoebe again after a nine-year gap in their friendship, much had changed. Phoebe had been working behind the till in a supermarket when Helen rolled up with a trolley full of nappies, a bawling baby under one arm, and a look of surprise on her face – which had as much to do with her own circumstances as it did with seeing Phoebe again. Helen had felt tired, isolated and out of sync with her other friends who had sailed off to university while her own plans to be a nurse had run aground. Phoebe's life hadn't gone to plan either, and the two had quickly resumed their friendship.

'Remember the life model I mentioned?' Phoebe asked when visiting Helen one day. Her friend had a sleeping Milly in her arms and was sitting in one of the second-hand armchairs that John's grandparents had donated to help them set up home. The chairs made the room smell of stale tobacco, but as with most things in Helen's life at that time, there were no alternatives.

'How could I forget after seeing your sketches? He's gorgeous, Phoebe,' she had said with a groan. 'I'm tempted to join you at your art class just so I can get up close and personal.'

'John wouldn't be too pleased if he knew you were ogling someone else.'

Helen had snarled when she answered, 'Like I care what

he thinks. He's not the one home all day with nothing to do but feed, burp and change the baby. Anyway, I thought we were talking about your model, not my boring husband?'

Phoebe kissed the top of Milly's head and smiled. 'Did I tell you he followed me home?'

Helen's jaw had dropped. 'Erm, no, Phoebes. I think I would have remembered that!'

'Only in the last couple of weeks. We've all been going to the pub after class and Paul's been tagging along. He offered me a lift and when I said no, he followed me on foot. He said he wanted to make sure I got home safely.'

'OK, so now he's gone from an Adonis to sounding more like a weirdo.'

'No more than any of the other blokes I've known in my time.'

'You haven't got in his car, have you?' Helen had asked. She was becoming more anxious by the minute.

Phoebe looked as if she were about to say no, but then nodded.

'And?'

'And nothing happened! Jesus, Helen. I'm eighteen, not a child. It's bad enough that Nan doesn't think I'm allowed out on my own, but you too? When I was in Manchester I did what I wanted and, believe me, I can take care of myself. What's the worst that could happen?'

Helen looked from Phoebe to the baby she was cradling. 'You really need me to spell it out?' she asked. 'And that reminds me, I won't be dragging you along to see Westlife after all.'

172

'Thank God for that. You really do have bad taste in music, Helen.'

'Count yourself lucky there's no chance Take That will ever get back together, because believe me, there's no way anyone would stop me going to see *them*.'

'Wow, and there I was thinking I had no luck.'

'The point is I can't go to *this* gig. And do you want to know why?' Her pitch had risen and she was griping now. 'One, I can't afford the ticket and two, I can't find a babysitter because John's working and, oh yes, everyone else has a life.'

Rather than looking dismayed, Phoebe stared in awe at the baby's tiny hand wrapped around her finger. 'My mum was around our age when she had me. I've always wondered what it must have been like for her, and if having me so young made her the way she was.'

'That doesn't mean you have to try it for yourself,' Helen had warned. 'If you need to know how demented having a baby can make you then look no further than me.'

When Phoebe looked up, Helen had crossed her eyes and was pulling a face, making them both laugh. 'Seriously though,' she said when they had settled down again, 'this Paul does sound a bit creepy.'

'You think I should keep away from him?'

Helen began to squirm. 'Don't look at me to tell you what to do, I don't know! It's your life, Phoebes.'

Helen had felt out of her depth. She knew so little about what had happened with Phoebe's mum other than she had had a mental illness, and she couldn't begin to imagine how it had affected Phoebe, but her friend had certainly changed. The timid little girl had turned into a feisty teen and Helen wasn't sure if she should admire Phoebe or fear for her. 'You should talk to someone though, someone older and wiser.'

'I don't get to do much talking with Nan, I'm just forced to listen,' scoffed Phoebe.

'God, I didn't mean someone *that* old,' Helen said. 'But Julia's been asking about you. Maybe we could have a little reunion?'

'Is she still as bossy as ever?' Phoebe had asked suspiciously. When Helen refused to answer, she added, 'Look, I'd love to meet up with Julia again but not until I've got my act together. She's only going to give me an earful about dropping out of college otherwise.'

'Yes, probably, but—'

'Please, Helen, don't tell her. This is between you and me.'

It felt now that those past secrets were coming back to haunt Helen. Was she wicked to even think that those old, buried feelings might be rising to the surface? Phoebe wasn't that reckless teenager any more, she preferred her own company these days and she had said she wasn't looking for love. More importantly, she wouldn't betray one of her best friends.

And what of Paul's intentions? Even if his marriage was under a lot of strain, it was only because he and Julia loved each other so much. They wanted the same things out of life and they wanted each other, anyone could see that.

The smell of fabric conditioner intensified, pulling Helen back from her thoughts. Lifting up the iron, she discovered a shiny triangular mark on her dress.

Refusing to let her mind wander again, Helen ploughed

on until the only thing left in the laundry pile was the tablecloth that had been hiding it all. With a swell of pride, she practically glided upstairs and after dropping off a mound of freshly pressed clothes in her bedroom, she slipped into Milly's room. She tried to keep her temper in check as she stormed across the room to open the curtains for the second time that day, but halfway to the window she stumbled when her foot caught on something. Whatever she had tripped over hadn't been there earlier and Helen had a sinking feeling she knew what it might be.

As soon as the late morning light flooded into the room, Helen took a deep breath, but rather than calming her, it gave her the lung capacity to scream at Milly.

'What the hell are you doing?'

Milly had been fast asleep, lying on her back with an arm dangling over the bed and her mouth wide open. She must have jumped at least an inch off the bed and when the look of terror faded, it was replaced by one of fury that was a match for her mother's. 'What did you do that for? I was asleep!'

Helen's heart was hammering and her eyes widened as she looked from her daughter to the clothes strewn across the floor. There was some vague suggestion that they had once formed a neat pile of laundry but nearer the bed they had merged with dirty clothes that hadn't yet learned the technique of getting up and walking themselves to the laundry basket. 'Look!' she screamed. 'Look at the mess!'

'I'll clear it up in a minute.'

'Four hours it's taken me to iron all of that and you've just – you've just flung it across the room without a thought. You can't even tell what's clean and what's dirty now!'

The look of pure disdain on Milly's face made Helen's blood boil. 'You didn't spend all that time doing my clothes. You must have been ironing your stuff too.'

Helen's jaw locked and it was a small miracle that any noise came out of her constricted throat at all. 'Get out of bed now and clear up this mess.'

Milly flung back her covers and scooped up an armful of clothes. Shoving past her mum, she fumbled to open her wardrobe and then squeezed the crumpled mess onto a shelf before forcing the door shut. 'There!' she said, putting a hand on her hip. 'Is that better?'

'You little bitch!' Helen said. She never swore at Milly and she hated people who cursed in front of their children, let alone directed such abuse at their offspring. A red haze had descended and the next thing she knew Helen was hurling the pile of laundry still in her hands directly at her snarling daughter with enough force to make Milly stumble backwards. 'Don't you think I have a hard enough job working full-time, looking after you and looking after the house?' she said before pausing to take a gulp of air. 'And now, if that isn't bad enough, I have to do the fucking housework twice! Do you think I'm some kind of doormat you can walk over? I'm sick of it, Milly! I'm well and truly sick of it!'

'Well, I'm sick of you! I *hate* living here! It's so *boring* and you never want to do anything. The only time I get to do something interesting is when your friends take me somewhere and even then you just stay at home!'

'So going to the cinema is nothing?' Helen demanded. To her credit, she was talking more calmly in hope of reining in her emotions. 'Oh, well, actually, it is nothing

176

now because you're not going. You're not going anywhere.'

'I am! I'm going to my dad's!'

'No, you're not. The last thing he'll need under his feet is a stroppy little madam like you – and besides, it's not your choice. You're grounded and that's all there is to it.'

Helen's calmness was making Milly all the more furious. 'You can't keep me locked up! It's against the law.'

'I'm going downstairs to make myself breakfast. When I come back up, this room had better be tidy.'

Milly was oblivious to the angry tears sliding down her cheeks. 'You can wait all day! I'm not doing it. I don't care how messy this room is because I'm leaving! I'm going to ask Dad and Eva if I can live with them.'

'No, you're not,' Helen said and turned her back on her daughter.

'You can't stop me.'

Helen didn't acknowledge the empty threat and left the room, closing the door behind her.

'I hate you!' Milly screeched after her. 'Did you hear me? I hate you, Mum!'

Returning to the kitchen, Helen put away the iron and ironing board and set about preparing the cooked breakfast she had been looking forward to, all the while knowing that neither she nor her daughter would be able to stomach it, or each other for that matter. She grilled sausages and bacon, fried tomatoes and mushrooms and even made eggy toast, which was usually only reserved for high days and holidays.

Helen had never argued like that before with Milly, but

it had been building for some time. Milly's anticipated rejection of her new sibling might have failed to materialize but they were still going through a period of change and that had put family relationships under considerable strain.

For a moment, Helen wished that Milly had refused to have anything to do with the baby because her daughter's actual reaction was far more difficult to contend with. Milly loved her little brother and she thrived on being a member of John's perfectly balanced family unit. From what Helen had gleaned from John over the last few weeks, Milly couldn't be more helpful, whereas Helen was lucky to raise a smile from her daughter.

Once breakfast was prepared, Helen went upstairs and, with each purposeful step, she told herself over and over again not to lose her temper no matter what she found. Helen wasn't particularly good at the serious stuff and she tried to imagine how Julia might handle the situation. If Milly had retreated beneath the bedcovers again then Helen would peel them back and gently persuade her daughter downstairs. Barking orders hadn't worked so far and it was hardly a good foundation for the open and frank discussion she wanted to have with her daughter.

She knocked on the door before opening it a crack. 'Can I come in?'

There was no answer so Helen pushed open the door until she could see Milly standing in front of her wardrobe. The curtains had been drawn wide and Helen had a good view of the bedroom with its neatly made bed and a relatively clear floor with the exception of one corner of the room.

'That's all the stuff I want to throw out,' Milly said when

178

she noticed her mum examining the newly constructed mound of clothes.

'Oh, all right. I'll get a couple of bin bags and we can drop them off at the charity shop.'

'Whatever,' Milly said with a shrug. She had her hand resting on one of the interior shelves, her fingers playing with the corner of a precisely folded T-shirt.

'You've done a good job in here. I hardly recognize the place.'

The smile she offered wasn't returned and Milly appeared in no hurry to say anything else.

'I've made breakfast,' Helen added. 'Do you want to come down?'

'I'm not hungry.'

'I know, and the last thing you want to do is to look at my ugly mug, but I'd really like you to come downstairs, Milly. Please.'

Casting her gaze to the floor, Milly remained stubbornly silent.

'Don't make me beg, sweetheart.'

To her surprise, there was a catch of emotion in Helen's words. Milly had heard it too and although it didn't tempt her to look up at her mum, she did accede to the request and slipped past Helen with her head down.

Helen took her time following Milly downstairs. She was overcome with a sudden urge to cry and had to wait for the pressure building at the back of her nose to subside. It was ridiculous to be so upset over a silly argument with an eleven-year-old child, even one fuelled by unrestrained anger on both sides. And it wasn't as if it was the first time that Milly had said she hated her; in fact it was such a regular occurrence that Helen had once threatened to have a T-shirt made for Milly with the words 'I hate my mum' emblazoned on the front. This time, however, it felt different and she had a bad feeling about how the next conversation with her daughter was going to play out.

Milly was sitting at the table with her arms folded when Helen came into the kitchen.

'What would you like?' Helen asked as she heated a container of baked beans in the microwave.

'Coco Pops.'

'But I've made a cooked breakfast.'

'I did say I'm not hungry.'

'I've made eggy toast,' Helen said, aware her voice had gone up an octave.

Milly was concentrating on straightening the cutlery in front of her and, without looking up, she said, 'Then I suppose I'll have to eat what you want me to. I'd forgotten I didn't have a choice in this house.'

'Milly . . . Please, I'm trying to make things right. Couldn't you at least meet me halfway?'

The silence that descended was leaden and Helen would have liked nothing better than to drop into a chair and admit defeat, but she pushed on and plated up two breakfasts. When the microwave beeped, it had the effect of a gunshot with Helen so tense that she almost dropped a plate.

'What do you want to drink?'

'Whatever you want me to have,' mumbled Milly.

With a fixed grin on her face and a look of panic in her eyes, Helen made a fresh cup of coffee for herself and poured a glass of juice for Milly. When she was ready to sit down, her daughter had a knife and fork in her hands but had so far refused to touch her food. She reminded Helen of an automaton – one she had somehow lost the key to operate.

As she began cutting into a slice of bacon, Helen counted to ten. When she was sure she could keep her voice level and calm, she said, 'Look, Milly, I'm sorry I flew off the handle before, but you're old enough now to realize that I'm not a machine programmed to do everything a perfect mum should, or say the right things all the time. I'm as flawed as the next person and it's hard for me sometimes. It's scary being a single mum, not having anyone else to back me up or share the load, or someone who can step in and take over when I'm feeling under pressure.'

'It's not like Dad doesn't help.'

Milly had kept her head down as she spoke, so Helen found herself talking to the top of her scalp. 'I know, but it's not the same as being a couple. You're lucky we get on so well.'

'I don't feel lucky.'

'I know it can't be easy for you, especially with a mother from hell.'

Aware that she had cut her bacon into tiny slivers, Helen put a morsel in her mouth and then struggled to swallow.

'Please, Milly,' Helen said, 'could you at least look at me?'

When Milly lifted her head, Helen wished she hadn't. There was no pain in Milly's eyes and certainly no love. There wasn't even anger. Her daughter's expression was devoid of emotion. 'I want to live with my dad,' she said.

The piece of bacon Helen had swallowed lodged in her

181

throat and she almost gagged. Taking a gulp of air, she said, 'Well, I don't want you to.'

'Dad said I can.'

'Oh, really? And when exactly did he say that?' Helen asked, then immediately dreaded the answer.

'I phoned him before.'

'And said what?'

Milly cocked her head. 'I didn't tell him you assaulted me, if that's what you're worried about.'

'I didn't assault you, Milly!' Helen said and then remembered she was supposed to keep the conversation calm. 'I might have thrown a handful of T-shirts at you but I hardly think that constitutes *assault*.'

'You threw what happened to be in your hand at the time when you lost it. What happens next time if you're in the kitchen and you have a knife in your hand?'

Helen narrowed her eyes. 'I hardly think I've reached the point where I'd be throwing knives at you, and what's more, Milly, I don't think you believe that either.'

There was an imperceptible shrug of the shoulder. 'I still want to live with Dad. You said how hard it is looking after me and now you don't have to. Everyone would be happier.'

Helen only realized her jaw had dropped when she managed to close her mouth. The saltiness of the bacon had left her lips parched. She lifted her mug to her mouth and noticed how the surface of the coffee trembled in her grasp. 'I'd never be happier without you, Milly,' she started and then, recognizing too late how she had fallen into a trap of her own making, quickly added, 'For all my complaints, I love being your mum, your full-time mum. I'm already dreading you going off to university.'

'See, you don't even know me. I don't want to go to university. I want to go to art college like Julia did.'

'I don't want to lose you, Milly. I won't agree to you living with your dad. I can't,' she said, the words catching on the lump still lodged in her throat.

The stony expression Milly had been so intent on keeping, dissolved beneath a gentle stream of tears. 'But I want to go, Mum. Please don't stop me.'

'Why, Milly? Am I that bad?'

Milly twisted in her chair. 'It's not that . . . I do love you, mostly. It's just that I'm happier with Dad and Eva. My friends live nearer to them and besides, I want to help look after Ollie. It's not fair that we'll hardly see each other. I'm his sister and I want to be around him, I want to be around a family.'

'You're happier there?' Helen said, needing to repeat the words that had already kicked her in the stomach. It was all her fault. She had assumed that the love and adoration of her daughter was a given. Daughters always wanted to be with their mums, didn't they? Helen hadn't had to put the effort in because she had never felt there was a competition. What the hell had she done?

Milly put her hand over her mouth to hold back a sob. 'Please, Mum, don't cry,' she begged.

Helen's whole body was shaking and when she tried to pinch her nose, she was surprised how wet her face was. She wanted to say something only she couldn't think what that might be. She couldn't browbeat Milly into believing she wouldn't be better off with her dad, not when the evidence was already damning. 'I don't blame you for hating me.'

'I don't hate you!' Milly cried.

She shot up out of her chair and rushed into her mum's arms where Helen clung to her as if she were drowning.

'I'm sorry I said that, really I am, Mum. I do love you. I'll *always* love you.'

Milly's words cut into her. She had heard John say pretty much the same thing when he had left her and it made Helen's blood run cold. She hadn't thought it possible to hear a heart break but she swore she heard hers crack. She didn't know what to do next. Was Milly supposed to sit back down so they could eat their breakfast while discussing the new arrangements? Did she agree to all of Milly's demands while working out how she could persuade John to refuse her request? Or should they try to salvage the rest of the day so she could prove what a fantastic mother she could be and then leave it to Milly to reach the same conclusion? In the end she did none of these things. She simply clung to her daughter and tried to convince herself that she would never have to let her go.

Phoebe walked into her bedroom and rested her back against the door, taking a moment to soak in the silence which would inevitably be broken by the insistent thump of a walking stick or, worse still, the crash of something falling as her nan fumbled about on her own downstairs. Her grandmother, Theresa, was a proud woman but while she didn't like admitting she needed more help these days, she still expected her granddaughter to be at her beck and call.

Phoebe's bedroom was her private retreat and she had pasted its walls with sketches of long, lithe figures dressed in haute couture designs of her own imagination. Some of her creations had been brought to life, and Phoebe had worn them with a mixture of pride and disappointment. These were designs that deserved to be draped over six-foot models strutting down the catwalk, not someone whose life never quite lived up to her imagination.

Looking at herself in the full-length mirror, Phoebe was aware of her hunger pangs and it felt strangely comforting. She imagined her body as a chrysalis and that the fat, frumpy Phoebe of old was slowly being gnawed away until one day a new woman would emerge. She was hoping this new woman would bring something back into her life, something she hadn't even realized was missing until Paul had pointed it out. She was looking for that spark he remembered and she still hadn't found it.

For a spark to catch there needed to be at least a smouldering ember but Phoebe's life had been reduced to ash. She had surrendered her dreams a long time ago in return for the security and permanence that a life with her grandmother had offered. She had learned to fear change and had not only turned her back on opportunities to establish a career, she had thrown away the chance to grow, to be a wife, a mother.

Staring at her reflection, Phoebe was aware that things were changing whether she liked it or not. She was a grown woman and as she turned from side to side, she tried to imagine what a man might see. She was average height and, despite losing weight in the last couple of months, she knew she would never be in the same league as her two friends. She might have ten years on Julia but she was no competition and never had been, not really.

185

A man like Paul would choose Julia over Phoebe any day, whether that was a decade ago or last week. Phoebe and Paul had met eleven years ago to be precise, during that brief time when Helen had re-entered her life but she had yet to re-establish her friendship with Julia. Perhaps if Julia had been an influence in her life back then, if she had been there to tell Phoebe not to give up, then she might have finished her fashion design course and perhaps even gone on to art college instead of a half-hearted attempt at night school. She might have stood up to her nan and by now have what Julia had. She might even have more.

She could remember the first time Paul had showed up in her evening class and how her hand had trembled as she attempted to sketch his semi-naked body. She had been going through a phase of wearing T-shirts emblazoned with her own outlandish designs, wanting to make a statement, and the general theme was, 'Take me on at your own risk.' To her surprise, it was a challenge that Paul took up. When their art class had decamped to the pub, Paul had followed and continued turning up even on those nights when he wasn't modelling.

She would never know if their brief liaison would have developed into something more because she hadn't been brave enough to fight for what she had wanted. She had let Paul go and if ever there was a moment when she realized her life was no more than a string of bitter disappointments, it was when Paul had re-entered her life two years later – although technically he had entered into Julia's life. Phoebe's first reaction was to distance herself from them both, but she had slowly become accustomed to seeing Paul with her friend, and their happiness had proved that they were destined to be together. But they weren't happy now. No one was.

As she cast a critical eye over her five-foot-four frame, Phoebe's frown threatened to turn into a scowl. Her jeans had once pinched at the waist giving her a muffin top but the midnight-blue satin shirt she was wearing fell smoothly over her distinctive curves. Not that Phoebe saw those curves as anything but layers of fat clinging to her with grim determination. She had thought losing a stone would do the trick but no amount of dieting was going to help her grow taller.

Phoebe was desperate to reinvent herself; into what, she couldn't quite say. Why she was doing it at all was an even more difficult question to answer. She had started her diet in earnest after her nan had announced she wanted to move into a care home. Being on her own, taking control of her own life, was a daunting proposition for Phoebe but while it terrified her, she wasn't completely opposed to the idea, she just needed to prepare herself.

Except, she reminded herself, this version of events wasn't quite true. Phoebe had become a little more particular about her appearance some time before her nan shared her plans. It had been around the time Paul had started giving her driving lessons. He had said he missed her spark and he had made her want to find it again. But her efforts had been wasted today, as they had been for the last couple of weeks, because despite his promises on New Year's Day, Paul had so far failed to deliver. She wasn't sure if this was a blessing in disguise. It had been awful to watch him wrestle with the possibility that he was infertile, and she was desperate to talk to him, but what could she say? What comfort could she offer him?

As guilt began to rise like bile into her throat, Phoebe's phone began to ring, giving her a start.

'I'm not disturbing you, am I?' Helen asked.

'No, I was just about to put on my pyjamas and read a book,' Phoebe said as she turned her back on the reflection and concentrated on her friend. 'So what's up? How was your weekend?'

'Oh, you know,' Helen said.

Before Phoebe could ask why there had been a catch in her voice, Helen quickly continued. 'How was your driving lesson?'

'What driving lesson?' Phoebe said, trying not to sound as frustrated as she felt.

'Another no-show?'

'They were at some antique fair in St George's Hall, so he couldn't fit me in.'

'Good,' Helen said.

'What do you mean *good*?'

'Sorry,' she said before clearing her throat. She sounded as if she were coming down with a cold. 'I just mean it's good to hear Julia and Paul are busy doing stuff together. Don't you think?'

The question was a probing one and it wasn't the first time Phoebe had sensed that Helen was a little unsure about Paul spending time with her. 'Of course I do,' she said and was thankful that the old Phoebe was still there deep inside, the one who wouldn't have felt burning jealousy at the sight of her friend making up with her husband on New Year's Day, the one who wouldn't dream of coming between them, but would put her friend's needs before her own. 'I just hope it lasts.'

There was a break in the conversation as Phoebe waited for Helen to say something. She didn't.

'Helen?'

The only response was a weird strangled noise. Helen was trying to speak but she couldn't get the words out.

'Helen, are you OK?'

'No,' came a whispered reply and then silence again.

'What's happened?'

After a couple of gulps for air, Helen said, 'I screamed at Milly today.'

'You scream at Milly most days, Helen,' Phoebe said with a nervous laugh.

Helen released a long, painful wail. 'I know! And now she doesn't want to live with me any more. She says she's going to move in permanently with John and Eva.'

'Well, she can say that all she wants,' Phoebe said, sounding more like her nan than she would like. 'Tell her she can't go picking and choosing where she lives, there are other people to consider. Besides, John wouldn't agree to it, would he?'

'He already has.'

'You mean it's really going to happen?'

Helen hiccupped as she fought to bring her sobs under control. 'I've just got off the phone with him. He says Milly's been more of a help with the baby than he could have imagined. He says that with Eva taking the next year off on maternity leave, they could easily manage school runs. He's got it all worked out.'

'And I don't suppose it's a great hardship for him financially if he's not giving you child support,' Phoebe said with more than a note of cynicism.

'I know,' Helen added, 'which means I might have to downsize, but to be honest, that's the least of my problems.' There was another painful sob and then, 'I'm going to lose Milly, Phoebe. I'm going to lose my baby girl and I can't bear it. I just can't.'

Phoebe dropped down onto her bed. Her understanding of the bond between a mother and child was mostly theoretical, but when she heard the desperation in her friend's voice, it sent shock waves through her body.

'Do you want me to come over?' she asked.

'No, I'll be fine,' Helen said when she could speak. 'And I'm sorry for blubbing like an idiot.'

'I don't blame you. So what happens now?'

'I don't know. I haven't exactly been in the mood to reason with John, or Milly for that matter.'

'Where is she?'

'Up in her room. I've been holding back the tears all day, Phoebe, and I'm sorry you've had to take the brunt. I'll wait a few days and then talk to her again when we're all calmer.'

'What does Julia say?'

'I haven't spoken to her yet. You know what she's like. She'd adopt Milly given half a chance and she'll be just as upset.'

'No, she won't. She'll be devastated for you and she'll want to support you as much as I do. Would you rather I told her?'

To her surprise, Helen said, 'Would you? I can't bear to talk about it any more, and I certainly don't want to think about what it will be like having Milly as a visitor by arrangement in my life.'

190

'It won't come to that,' Phoebe promised. 'It's probably just premature teenage histrionics from Milly and nothing will actually change.'

After ending the call, Phoebe needed a moment to collect her thoughts before phoning Julia. Helen had called Phoebe first; one of her friends had needed help and they had turned to her. It was a good feeling. Her friends meant everything to her. How could she even think of risking what they had? Nothing was going to threaten that; she wouldn't allow it.

15

The Accident

Anya delayed going into the CCU so she could comfort the man standing outside. She placed her hand gently on his arm. She couldn't tell him what he should say to the young girl walking towards them. Even if she were familiar with his ex-wife's condition, she would have no magic words and the best she could offer was an apology. 'I'm so sorry,' she said.

There was a soft clatter as two cups of water hit the linoleum floor. The girl who had been carrying them still had her hands outstretched and her fingers coiled as if still around the drinks that had already spilled onto the floor. She stared at her father with unblinking eyes and held herself so still that Anya suspected she wasn't even breathing.

When the man took a step towards her, it jolted the girl out of her trance. 'Is Mum dead?' she asked bluntly in a way that only children could.

'What? No! Good grief, Milly, no,' John said, dropping to his knees and seeming not to care that he was kneeling in the puddle of water.

Milly didn't believe him and turned to Anya for confirmation.

'I'm sorry if I gave you a fright,' she said. 'I'm a nurse from another department and I don't have any news of your mum, not at all. I really am sorry.' She glanced at John before saying the one thing she usually avoided because her words would be faithless. 'But I'm sure she's going to be fine.'

'My mum was a nurse,' Milly said and immediately took a sharp intake of breath, her swollen eyes wide with horror. 'I mean she is! She *is* a nurse.'

This new knowledge made the circumstances all the more painful because Anya could see the parallels with her own life. She too was a mother and her son Jacob would be at home waiting for her, insisting on staying up past his bedtime until he knew his mum had arrived home safely. He was a few years younger than Milly, but still . . .

Milly's lip trembled. 'What if she dies and she doesn't know how much I love her?'

'She knows, Milly,' John said as he tried to wipe away fresh tears, but the dam had been breached and there was no stopping the flow.

'But I said I hated her, Dad. I said it all the time.'

'And you've told her you love her plenty more times, and I know which she believes,' her father said.

'Have you been able to see her yet?' Anya asked.

Milly shook her head while searing, heartfelt pain contorted her features.

'They've said we should be able to see her soon,' John explained to Anya. When he stood back up, his jeans had wet patches from where he had been kneeling and he gave his daughter a look of reproach. When he winked at her, he managed to tease an apologetic smile.

'If you like, I could find out what's happening? Do you want to wait in the family room?'

The man shook his head. 'There are so many people in there already, including her mum and dad. We wanted some space and they said they'd come and find us if anything changed.'

'Would you like me to see if I can find anything out?'

'Please. Her name is Helen. Helen Butler,' he said and then, seeing the look of recognition on Anya's face, asked, 'Do you know her?'

'I have another patient, Julia Richardson, who's been asking for her. That's why I'm here, to find out how she is.'

'Is Julia going to be all right?' Milly asked. She had taken a step closer to her dad and leaned in so he could wrap an arm around her.

'She has some pretty serious injuries,' Anya said, daring to be as honest as she could, 'but she's receiving the best of care. We've given her some pretty strong painkillers so I'm hoping she'll have a peaceful night.'

'I saw Paul before and he's in one hell of a state, a complete mess,' John said, shaking his head. 'Helen and her friends were all setting off on a little world tour this morning. It's so scary how things can change in a heartbeat.'

A few minutes later Anya had found Helen's bed in the fully occupied CCU, and she stood listening to the hiss and sigh of the ventilator. Milly's mum was in a medically-induced coma and from the machines tracking her vital signs, she was holding her own. On one of the screens, Anya's eyes followed the thin line tracing her heartbeat. Helen Butler's ex-husband was right; things could change so easily.

16

The cardiology clinic was busier than usual thanks to the post-Christmas catch-up combined with the arrival of the flu season, which meant not only more patients needing care but fewer staff to deal with them. Despite this, Helen was thriving on the pressure that gave her no time to wallow in self-pity, not when she was looking after people who would gladly swap their problems for hers.

'You look as bad as I do and that's saying something,' Lucy said when Helen escorted her from the consultant's room back to her mum. Lucy had been struck down by a virus over Christmas and was struggling to recover to the point that even the short journey to the waiting area required a little help. Talking at the same time was completely beyond her so she stopped to catch her breath before adding, 'And I hope you're going to tell me it's from nonstop partying.'

'That's exactly what it is,' Helen said. 'It wasn't even worth going to bed by the time I got in this morning and

I'm still wearing my going-out gear underneath this.' She lifted the collar of her uniform and Lucy played along by pretending she had spied her outfit.

Mrs Cunliffe stood up as they approached. 'Do you want to have a rest before we go, love?'

'No, the less time we spend here the better. No offence,' Lucy said to Helen.

'None taken.'

Before checking the next patient on her list, Helen paused to watch Lucy's stop-start progress out of the clinic. She used the time to remind herself that Milly wasn't only strong-headed, she was strong and healthy. There were worse ways to lose a child.

Caught up in her thoughts, Helen continued to stare down the corridor long after Lucy had disappeared and it took a moment for her to react when another familiar figure appeared around the corner. Julia was already offering her a smile by the time Helen's thoughts caught up and the shock transformed to one of suspicion when she spotted Phoebe behind her.

'What's going on?'

Two innocent faces looked back at her. 'We were just passing and thought we'd invite you to lunch. I hear the hospital food here is delicious,' Julia said.

'Scrummy even,' Phoebe added.

Having a lunch hour was a luxury the department could ill afford and the refusal was already forming on Helen's lips when another nurse patted her shoulder.

'You need a break, Helen. We'll manage.'

'Can she go now?'

Her colleague was already taking the patient notes Helen was holding. 'Of course she can. She's not indispensable even if she'd like to think she is.'

The three friends made their way through the maze of corridors to a small café. Helen hadn't eaten much during the last few days but along with her coffee, she picked up a packet of crisps she knew she wouldn't be able to finish. She found a table while Julia and Phoebe made their own selections before proceeding to argue over the bill.

'Who do I owe money to?' Helen asked when her friends had joined her.

'Put that away,' Julia said, glaring at Helen's purse. 'This is our treat.'

'*Your* treat,' Phoebe corrected.

Pulling apart the packet of crisps, Helen felt a now familiar wave of nausea begin to build. It wasn't the smell of cheese and onion, but a certain sick feeling that arrived every time she thought about Milly. Her stomach was guaranteed to do a somersault the moment some well-meaning friend made her talk about it.

'Phoebe told me what's going on,' Julia started. 'Why didn't you tell me, Helen?'

'I was hoping it would blow over.'

'And has it?'

Helen shook her head. 'I spoke to John again last night.'

'And?'

'No one's rushing into anything. We both know what Milly's like.'

'Exactly! Look at the way she was with the baby,' Julia said. 'One minute she was determined to have nothing more to do with John and his new family, and the next . . .'

198

Helen knew exactly what Milly was like and there was a grain of comfort in Julia's words. Anything could happen, and she had to keep believing that. 'We've agreed not to do anything until half term. She was going to stay with John then anyway, and if she doesn't want to come home afterwards, well . . . She won't.'

'And is Milly OK with leaving it until then?' Phoebe asked.

'Despite appearances,' Helen said, 'Milly does not rule the roost.'

'She'll come home again,' Julia added firmly. 'She has to.'

The agony Julia was trying so hard to hide was deep enough to be a mother's pain and Helen was finding it excruciating to watch. 'I hope so, Julia. Oh, God, I hope so. I have one month to convince her that I'm the best mum in the world, and that spending time with me is far better than living with a screaming baby. Just you wait until the first time Ollie pukes up all over her favourite trainers. You can bet there'll be hell to pay.'

Julia's lip trembled and it was impossible to tell if it was at the thought of losing unlimited access to Milly, or simply the picture Helen had been painting, which would be pure bliss to her friend. Helen wasn't strong enough to offer assurances of her own and felt a sense of relief when a waitress arrived with three piping hot paninis to distract them.

'I didn't want anything,' Helen said.

'Mother Julia insisted,' offered Phoebe. 'You look like you're about to waste away.'

Julia pushed the food a little closer to Helen. 'And we're not leaving until you've cleared your plate.'

With little chance of winning the argument, Helen tore an inch off the end of the roll, pulling at strings of cheese and ham as she went. Rather than endure having her friends watch her every mouthful, she diverted attention to Phoebe. 'You look like you've skipped a meal or two.'

'New Year, new diet.'

'And you're growing your hair out too,' Julia noted. 'Are you going for a complete makeover?'

Phoebe shrugged and wouldn't meet her friends' gaze. 'Come next week, everything's going to change.'

'I hope that means your nan's still going,' said Helen.

'Next Monday. Her bags are packed and there's no talking her out of it.'

Helen couldn't remember the last time she had seen Phoebe's grandmother and was in no rush to do so. The drugs Theresa was prescribed to combat Alzheimer's meant she was even more cantankerous and obstinate than ever, and that was saying something. Helen had never liked visiting the Dodd household at the best of times. When they were children, Phoebe's mum could be fun when she wasn't hiding away in her room, but the grandmother had always terrified her and still did. 'You never could argue with her once her mind was settled.'

'I still feel guilty though.'

'Don't,' Julia insisted. 'If I know your nan, she's doing this as much for herself as you. If she felt capable of staying put so she could carry on dictating your life, then she would. She's only going now because she can't face having the tables turned.' When Phoebe could only shrug in response, she added, 'You've got exciting times ahead, Phoebe, and I think we should go out and celebrate.'

'Not me,' Helen said. 'I'm a stay-at-home mum until further notice.'

Julia and Phoebe looked at her, not quite believing what they were hearing.

'What?' Helen asked, looking at Julia in particular because she would be the hardest to convince.

'And exactly how long is this saintly attitude going to last?'

'Forever, Julia,' Helen said in a tone that she had heard Milly use so often.

'But you can still go out when Milly's at her dad's,' Phoebe said. 'How about this weekend? Milly need never know.'

Julia pulled a face. 'Sorry, I can't. Paul and I are going away for a theatre break.'

'That's news to me!'

Julia and Helen both gave Phoebe a quizzical look but it was Julia who replied. 'I didn't know I had to run all our trips past you first?'

'Sorry, it's just that I was counting on Paul being able to give me a driving lesson. It's been ages, Julia, and I really do need to keep up with the lessons.'

'Isn't there someone else you can ask? I know it was my idea,' Julia said, 'but I hadn't realized how much I liked having my husband to myself at the weekend.'

'Maybe it's time to start proper lessons,' Helen said.

'I'm saving up for our holiday, and speaking of which, I think it's time we booked.'

'I can't help wondering if it was really meant to be,' Julia said with a note of finality. 'You can't afford it, Helen won't want to leave Milly, and I go back to see the consultant at the end of the month. I don't know how the results are going to go and I don't want to leave Paul.'

'You mean you do know how the results will go and you want to hang around to console him,' Helen corrected.

'You can't prejudge the results,' Phoebe told her.

'Although some people seem to be giving it a good try,' Julia said, looking at Phoebe rather than Helen who had come closest to voicing a prediction.

The atmosphere had turned decidedly tense and it was left to Helen to raise their spirits. 'Hey, I thought we were going to celebrate our one-hundredth year in style. Julia, I know we're all facing major change in our lives but we won't hit these milestones again and we need to seize the moment.'

She looked from one friend to the other and for a split second she thought she glimpsed a hairline crack in their friendship. It was a crack that had been papered over once already and she needed Julia and Phoebe to concentrate on the feelings they shared for each other, and not for someone else. 'OK, so I hate the thought of leaving Milly right now but she'll be spending that week with John irrespective of what she decides to do long term. And if she does choose to abandon me, then I'm relying on some damn good memories of our trip to keep me warm at night.'

Phoebe had bowed her head and was playing with her fingernails. 'I still want to go,' she said.

'Julia?' Helen asked.

With an imperceptible shrug, Julia said, 'Whatever the results from the consultant, it's going to take time to digest the information and decide our next plan of action. Maybe it would be good to have some time apart to collect our thoughts.'

Helen leaned back in her chair and sighed. 'Well, now that we're all raring to go,' she said in a monotone voice, 'I can't wait. This trip is going to be unforgettable.'

'Oh, for goodness' sake, *yes*, of course I want to go,' Julia said before stuffing the remainder of her panini in her mouth.

It was only when they were all ready to leave and Phoebe had nipped into the ladies, that Helen had a chance to speak to Julia alone. 'You really don't want Paul giving Phoebe lessons, do you?'

'Is it that obvious?'

'Well . . .'

Julia busied herself slipping on her gloves and arranging the scarf around her neck.

'Julia?'

'I swear this baby thing has turned me into a neurotic wife.'

'What do you mean?' Helen asked, even though she could guess the answer.

'Things between me and Paul are OK at the moment, but it's taking a lot of effort from both of us to make it work and I don't know, Helen . . . Sometimes I wonder if the past is catching up with us. I never expected Paul to be so eager to give Phoebe lessons, and I know it was probably only because he found it easier being anywhere except with me for a while, but even so . . .' She took a breath and then said, 'It really pissed me off that he was actually enjoying being with *her* and I was jealous. There, I've admitted it and I'm not proud, which is why you can't

203

say anything to Phoebe. I know it's not being fair to her. I'm being irrational and that's why I'm trying to tackle things subtly by making Paul too busy with me to have any time for anyone else. Is that really bad of me?'

'No, of course not, it sounds exactly the right thing to do.'

'But I am awful for even thinking there's something to worry about, aren't I?'

'No,' Helen said while thinking she must be equally as bad. But the problem wasn't in the present, it was in the past and what had been done couldn't be undone.

It had been awkward for everyone when Julia had started dating Paul, especially when it turned out that he was a pretty good catch after all rather than the creep Helen had assumed him to be. But it wasn't as if Phoebe and Paul had been involved in some passionate affair, and once it had become clear that Paul was as much in love with Julia as she was with him, Phoebe had been as relieved as Helen that she had found 'the one' to mend her broken heart. There had never been the slightest suggestion that she had still been nurturing feelings for Paul. Phoebe was their friend.

'It's my own fault,' Julia said. 'I've been so convinced that it was my age stopping us getting pregnant and convincing myself I would be able to set Paul free to be a father with someone else if I had to, that I never seriously considered what would happen if it was him. We still don't know but it *could* be and what happens then? Would he feel obliged to set me free?'

'Seriously, Julia – and I don't say this very often but I'm going to enjoy it – you're being childish! Neither of you would ever give up on each other, and I think you know that. Isn't that why you're being paranoid? You're jealous and I think it's quite nice that you should be so possessive of your man. You and Paul were made for each other and whatever happens, you can't lose sight of that.'

'I lost sight of everything except having a baby for a while,' Julia admitted. 'But Paul was right all along. Taking a break from *trying* has taken some of the pressure off. I won't deny it's still there in the back of my mind every time we have sex, and when I came on again last week I was as heartbroken as always, but the rest of the time, it's good, or at least it's getting better.'

When Phoebe reappeared, she was oblivious to the conversation that had just taken place and gave them both a determined smile. 'I was thinking I might take a trip to the travel agent's next week and see what's on offer.'

'Do you think you'll be able to book something?' Helen asked.

'I'd rather just pick up some ideas first, like the best places to stay. I know we need to watch our pennies but I have a feeling you two will kill me if we end up in a fleapit.'

'We wouldn't. I trust you implicitly,' Julia promised her.

'Me too,' Helen said and let the relief wash over her. Everything was as it should be and if they had been musketeers they would have lifted their swords and made some exclamation about being all for one. Instead they hugged each other tightly.

'I'm really glad you came,' Helen said. 'I don't know what I'd do without you both.'

* * *

Julia's eyes were heavy as she sat in the back of the taxi, her head resting on Paul's shoulder as they pulled away from the station in the direction of home. It had been a hectic weekend and the train journey back from London had seemed to take twice as long as the one going out. She wanted to be home in her bed, even if her sheets weren't going to be as starched or as white as the ones in the hotel they had stayed in the night before.

Paul kissed the top of her head. 'Are you falling asleep?'

Julia closed her eyes. 'No,' she said with a soft groan and then fell silent.

Before she could drift off, he whispered, 'I love you.'

'And I love you. So much, Paul.'

'I enjoyed our little trip.'

'Me too.'

'We should do stuff like this every weekend.'

Julia groaned again. The three-day trip had been a heady mix of shopping, fine dining and visits to the theatre, two museums and one art gallery, but it wasn't something she would want to repeat again in a hurry.

'OK, maybe not *every* week,' he conceded when he noticed his wife's head lolling.

Julia tried to stay awake. 'And not forever. Only until . . . things change,' she said, leaving a pause because she was too sleepy to edit her words quickly enough.

'Hmm,' he said.

The sound Paul made held too much uncertainty for Julia's liking. 'Don't give up, Paul, not yet.'

He kissed her head again by way of an answer and then lifted his arm so Julia could snuggle closer. She felt warm and contented until a cold, insidious doubt made her wonder if this was how the rest of their life was meant to play out. Would it be so bad to have so much free time and spare cash to spend on each other instead of the children they seemed destined not to have? No, it wouldn't be so bad, it would be *good*, she told herself. The problem was that while she could learn to live with the emptiness, she couldn't pretend it wasn't there. Even the little girl who they borrowed now and again was slipping from their grasp.

'Maybe we should invite Helen along on one of our trips,' she said. 'If Milly leaves, she's going to have more time on her hands than she knows what to do with.'

'Hmm,' Paul said again. 'You'll be suggesting we invite Phoebe next. Don't forget she's going to be on her own too after tomorrow.'

Julia hadn't forgotten about Phoebe, she simply hadn't had a good enough heart to include her. She wished she could ignore her paranoia, but it had gained strength simply by hearing Paul speak her name. 'Would you really want to come away with all of us?' she asked.

She felt his body shake as he laughed softly. 'No, I suppose not.'

Letting her mind go off at a tangent without warning Paul, she asked, 'Don't you feel guilty?'

The laughing stopped. 'About what?'

'About letting Phoebe down over the driving lessons.'

With her ear pressed against his chest, she could hear his heart beating that little bit faster. 'It's been good taking time out to indulge ourselves, Julia,' he said. 'We shouldn't feel guilty about that.'

Julia wanted to lift her head and look into her husband's

eyes when she asked the next question but she wasn't that brave. 'But you do feel guilty about something?'

Paul took his time answering and there was a moment when Julia thought he wouldn't, but then he said, 'Isn't it obvious?'

She managed to raise herself up so she could face him as he made his confession. The irrational part of her which had been ruling her emotions told her to prepare for her worst nightmare, something worse than facing a life without children – facing a life without Paul. But as she caught the pained expression on his face, she didn't just wake up, she came to her senses. Enough was enough. She had been letting her insecurities eat away at her belief in her husband and if anyone was feeling guilty now it was her. 'You haven't done anything wrong,' she told him.

'That's a matter of medical opinion.'

As confrontations went, this was a tame one, cowardly even, but it had at least brought her some resolution.

'I'm so sorry,' she said.

'And what do you have to be sorry for?' he asked.

'Everything.'

Helen began the following week in relatively high spirits thanks in part to her friends, but also her mum who had cosseted her over the weekend while Milly was at John's. The cherry on the cake was when Milly had returned home and had actually looked happy to see her.

That good feeling lasted all through her Monday shift and when she boarded the bus home, she happily returned the smile of a fellow passenger.

'Hello,' the lady said. 'It's . . .'

'Helen,' she offered when she had come alongside her.

From the puzzled look on Helen's face, the woman guessed she was at a loss and said, 'I'm Beryl.'

It was of no help but then Helen recalled fragments of a conversation on her commute home before Christmas. 'Of course,' she said with a wide grin. 'And don't worry, I'm not looking for a babysitter this evening.'

Helen took the vacant seat immediately behind Beryl who craned her neck so they could continue talking. 'Did you manage to get out to see your friends, then?'

'Yes, I did, thanks,' she said and immediately felt a twinge of guilt as she remembered how quick and eager she had been to leave Milly home alone that evening.

'A night out with the girls, wasn't it?'

'Erm, yes.'

'Still no boyfriend, then?'

As she spoke, Beryl made eye movements to point to the man sitting quietly next to her, making Helen cringe even more than she might have done at this relative stranger's comments alone.

'Erm . . .'

The man turned sharply towards Beryl and the two shared a wordless exchange.

Helen presumed this would be where Beryl turned back around and left her in peace, but instead, Beryl said to the man, 'This is my friend, Helen. She's a nurse.'

The man tried to turn but he was sitting directly in front of Helen and they only managed to share a brief look of embarrassment. 'Hi,' he said.

'Hi.'

'This is Chris. He's my youngest,' Beryl told her.

Helen glanced at the back of the poor man's head, but it was the unmistakable glint in Beryl's eye that made him immediately recognizable as the son she had been trying to palm off on Helen. Chris's hair was a mass of short-cropped curls and his shoulders were broad. Even sitting down Helen could tell he was tall, although from his posture he looked desperate to shrink from view.

With Chris looking straight ahead again, Beryl mouthed the word 'divorced,' to Helen.

Feeling her cheeks burning, Helen scrambled in her bag for her phone, willing it to burst into life and save her from what was becoming an increasingly awkward situation.

'Sorry, I'll leave you to it,' Beryl said, taking the hint, or so Helen thought until she saw her lean over to her son and in a loud whisper say, 'That's what you need. A lovely young lady like Helen.'

Helen was still too far away from home to justify getting off the bus early so she did her best to focus on the message she was about to send Milly to let her know she was on her way home. This was something she had stopped doing when Milly started high school, where her daughter had quickly learned that replying to your parents was not the done thing. When Helen had resurrected the messages last week, she had been surprised to receive not only prompt replies, but ones that were civil and occasionally ended with an 'x', sometimes two.

She was halfway through the message when the bus jolted to a halt, making her look up. The two passengers in front of her were engrossed in a whispered conversation and as Helen looked out of the window, she tried to keep her ears closed. They were on Allerton Road and had hit a queue of traffic. The night had arrived prematurely and the glare of shop displays along the busy high street stung her eyes.

Glancing down one of the side roads, Helen watched a woman pushing a pram laden with shopping. The young mum had to manoeuvre her buggy past an obstruction that turned out to be someone sitting on a wall. Helen could make out the legs of a woman in jeans and stiletto-heeled boots, but the upper part of her body was obstructed from view by overgrown shrubbery. As the bus began to creep past, the woman on the wall leaned forward and looked up the road in Helen's direction. The flaming orange hair caught alight beneath the beam of the streetlamp, making Phoebe's features immediately recognizable even from a distance.

Her friend was too far away to catch Helen's eye and then the bus was picking up speed, leaving Helen wondering if it really had been her. For one thing, Phoebe didn't wear stilettos and besides, Theresa was moving into the care home that afternoon and Phoebe had been expecting to stay and help her nan settle in. Helen quickly finished tapping out her message to Milly with the intention of sending another to Phoebe to see if everything was all right.

She had been meaning to text her anyway and debated whether or not to mention she had just seen her doppel-gänger. As she considered what to write, Helen turned her attention to the other side of the road where the oncoming traffic had come to a halt at a pedestrian crossing. Again there was a sense of familiarity as she spied a bright red Beetle. Paul and Julia often travelled to and from work together but with a job that required a fair amount of travel around the city, it wasn't unusual to see Paul alone in the car, although she was surprised to see him travelling in the opposite direction to home at this time of night.

As Helen sat mulling over this latest piece of a puzzle she was in no mood to solve, there was a message alert on her phone. Milly wanted to know if they could have takeaway pizza. This was usually a weekend treat and the Helen of old would have told her daughter in no uncertain terms that she would have what she was given. It took two seconds to type OK and three kisses, which left plenty of time for Helen to wonder again if the past was coming back to haunt her – to haunt them all.

'Another dilemma?' Beryl asked.

Helen hadn't even noticed that she was being watched. 'Erm, you could say that.'

'Anything we can help with? My babysitting rates are reasonable, or if you need a plus one for some party or other, I can always recommend someone.'

Beryl did that thing with her eyes again to point to her son as if Helen hadn't already worked out the subtext.

Before Helen could respond, Chris had also turned around and he twisted his body to make sure they kept eye contact this time. 'I can only apologize unreservedly for my mother. She's like this all the time and it's a wonder I subject myself to being out in public with her any more.'

To Helen's surprise, Chris had the most beautiful eyes she had ever seen with dark eyelashes that any woman would die for. His gentle smile was captivating and despite her growing unease about what may or may not be happening only a few streets away, she found herself smiling

212

back. 'So she's not picky, then? There I was thinking I was special,' she said, glancing back to Beryl.

Beryl grinned and didn't look in the least bit abashed. She nudged her son. 'She's not only beautiful, she has a sense of humour too.'

'Mum, enough,' Chris growled softly.

'What? You have to grab every opportunity, son. You might not get a second chance.'

But sometimes you might, Helen thought as her attention was pulled in the opposite direction. Chris noticed the distracted look on her face and misread it. 'I really am sorry for this. If it helps, I'm mortified too. Next time my car's in the garage, I'm going to insist I hire a car to take Mum on her errands,' he said and then not only turned his back again but began to stand up, forcing his mum to do the same. 'Come on, Mum, this is our stop.'

'We're off to see one of my friends. Did I tell you Chris is a financial adviser? He's going to help her sort out her pension,' she said proudly.

'I wish someone would sort out my finances,' Helen said almost to herself. She would be stepping into a financial minefield if Milly did move in with her dad and she was the one who ended up paying child support instead of receiving it.

'Give her your card, quick!' Beryl said.

As Helen shoved the business card in her bag, she would have liked nothing better than to indulge in a little daydream about the services Chris might be able to offer, but she still had the small matter of texting Phoebe. She supposed she didn't have to check up on her. There was enough going on in her own life, and Julia's for that matter, without seeking out more problems. And besides, she only had to look at the evidence to rip her malicious theory to pieces. Paul couldn't have been that interested in Phoebe in the first place because he had been quick enough to back off when Theresa had told Phoebe to stop seeing him. He would never have given up on Julia that easily, they were perfect for each other, and even if things had been rocky of late, why should that make any difference? What mattered was that Julia was Phoebe's friend; they were practically sisters. She wouldn't hurt her like that. She couldn't.

Phoebe was shivering and her bottom had turned numb. The stone wall she was sitting on felt more like a glacier but she had no intention of getting up until she felt the warmth from the headlights of Paul's car. Looking up the road, she could see a sluggish trail of traffic slithering along Allerton Road. What if Paul had decided against meeting her? What would she do then? She couldn't face going home.

Risking frostbite, Phoebe slipped off her gloves and checked her phone in case she had somehow missed a text message. She hadn't, and after reading Paul's original reply once more to reassure herself that he was on his way, she looked at the message below it.

Emergency meeting at the Elephant tonight 7.30 p.m.

The message had a bright red background because although she had typed it out, she hadn't sent it. She hadn't made the emergency call to her friends because she didn't want to burden them. She was actually being thoughtful, she told herself, preferring not to acknowledge any other motive for turning to Paul first.

214

Before her mind could lead her towards dangerous territory, her phone played a jingle alert and a new message flashed up. To her shame, her heart sank a little when she realized it was a message from one of her friends and not a friend's husband.

How did it go today? Are you still there?

Phoebe glanced up and down the road again. Satisfied that there were no other demands on her attention, she sent Helen a quick reply.

Absolutely awful. Busy now but promise to catch up later. P x

Feeling a shiver that had nothing to do with the cold, Phoebe put her phone away. A decade's worth of guilt pressed down against her chest, but it was immediately washed away by the arc of a VW Beetle's headlights turning the corner. Phoebe was already at the kerb when Paul pulled up in front of her.

'Are you OK?' he asked, letting the car idle as Phoebe slipped into the passenger seat beside him.

'I'm absolutely freezing.'

Paul ramped up the heating then put his hand on the gearstick but didn't drive off. 'That wasn't what I meant.'

'I'm fine,' she said, not sure if her lip was trembling because of the cold or because she felt anything but fine.

'Liar,' he said softly. 'So, where do you want to go?'

Phoebe didn't have an answer and so asked, 'Did you tell Julia you were picking me up?'

'No.'

Paul had avoided looking at her when he replied but she could see the look of doubt on his face. Like Phoebe, he didn't really know what he was doing or, to be more precise, what he intended to do. Instead, he put the car in gear and drove away with neither of them sure where it was leading. It wasn't until they were back on Allerton Road that Paul spoke again.

'Go on, tell me what happened.'

'I was convinced she was going,' Phoebe said with a note of disbelief. 'We had a lovely evening last night and we actually sat down and had a meal together. We stayed in the same room all evening which hasn't happened since I don't know when.' Phoebe was staring out of the window as she spoke and the bright lights of a pharmacy caught her attention. She had spent half her life collecting prescriptions, becoming such a regular that the chemists knew her by sight. The irony was that Phoebe was one of the healthiest people she knew. 'I thought I'd escaped all of that,' she said.

'Sorry?'

'I know I didn't want my nan going into care and I was fully prepared to look after her for as long as I could, it was the least I could do, but . . .' She stopped staring out of the window and turned to Paul. 'I was looking forward to being in control of my own life for once. I thought it was what she wanted and even this morning she was barking orders at me to help with the last-minute packing, not to mention giving me instructions about what she wanted me to do after she'd moved out. It was still going to be her house, whether she was there or not,' she added with a laugh.

'So what changed?' Paul asked.

'She went quiet at lunchtime, wouldn't eat and started muttering to herself. She does that when she's about to have an episode and I knew then that things might not go to plan. You know that feeling you get when your stomach starts twisting with a mixture of excitement and cold dread?'

He simply shrugged, but of course Paul knew what that felt like. It was exactly how he described the monthly routine of hoping that Julia was pregnant and fearing that she wasn't. Phoebe had found it difficult to listen when Paul voiced such intimate thoughts as if the intimacy was theirs. It could have been once, but like so many of Phoebe's dreams, it had been no more than a tantalizing precursor to what would ultimately turn into crushing disappointment.

'We were supposed to be at the home for two o'clock and I'd ordered a taxi,' Phoebe continued, 'but when I told Nan it was outside, she just flipped. I know the doctors had warned me that she might experience changes in her personality but I think even they would be shocked to see how bad she can get. She told me what a conniving bitch I was and that she wasn't ill at all. She denied ever seeing a doctor and said it was all a scheme I'd dreamt up to get at her money. Then she threatened to cut me out of her will and leave everything to the cat. It wouldn't surprise me if she already had,' she added.

'And what happens now?'

The bright streetlamps were beginning to blur as Phoebe's eyes filled with tears of resignation. They were driving down familiar roads and although they hadn't agreed where to go, in a few minutes Paul would pull up outside her grandmother's house. What other option did she have? 'She stays, and I carry on looking after her.'

'But she only refused to go because she was confused. Once your nan's thinking straight, she'll be as determined as ever to go and I'm sure the home will understand why there's been a delay.'

Phoebe sighed. She had a sinking feeling that, sensible though she knew it was, her grandmother had never wanted to go in the first place. And of course she enjoyed testing her granddaughter. 'I've checked with the home and because we've already paid the first month's fees, they can be flexible up to a point, but if I can't get her there in the next few weeks then they'll offer the place to someone else. I shouldn't be so disappointed, I know that, but I can't help the way I feel,' she said, looking at Paul for the longest time.

Paul took his eyes off the road to meet her gaze. 'And how do you feel, Phoebe?'

Her thawing cheeks were starting to burn as she remembered a time when she had been able to tell Paul anything. Was history about to be repeated? 'Remember the old me? I thought I was getting her back. Well, maybe not exactly,' she said, thinking of how hard she had been working on a new image, whereas her younger self had relied only on her youth and . . .

'The spark,' Paul surmised.

'Yes. I think I understand what mum went through now. She took us to Manchester because she was convinced she was well enough to look after us both. She'd come out of a dark period of depression and she couldn't face being beaten back down again by Nan. I know now that's not

218

how it works and she was never going to outrun her illness, but that was how she felt. And I feel the same.'

'You want to run away?'

'I want to stop playing it safe. I want to break out of this invisible straitjacket my nan's made for me.'

Paul pulled up to the kerb and switched off the engine. They were still some distance from the imposing four-bedroom house that had been the Dodd family home for four generations. In spite of this, Phoebe would have had no qualms about selling up when her nan's savings ran out, and she had actually been looking forward to apartment hunting. That wasn't going to happen now and in all likelihood the house that had never felt like a home would one day pass to Phoebe – or the cat, of course.

'I want to help,' Paul said. 'We all do.'

Thinking of the message she had drafted but not sent to her friends, Phoebe said, 'I don't think the others understand, not like you do.'

'Then tell them, Phoebe. Tell them what you went through in Manchester; explain what happened to your mum. I can't believe you never told them.'

'Talking about it didn't help,' she said, and then stopped herself from asking if it was her revelations that had frightened him off. 'I thought it would be better to put everything behind me. It was just something that happened and I got over it.'

'Except you didn't, did you? Talk to them, Phoebe.'

'I can't,' Phoebe said. 'With everything else that's going on, the last thing they need is my problems too.'

'It's not supposed to be one way. They would want to help. I know Julia would.'

'Would she? What would she say if she knew you were here with me now?'

'We're not doing anything wrong,' Paul insisted, although he didn't sound as confident as he should.

'But you won't tell her, will you?' Phoebe asked, feeling too tired and beaten to dance around the issue. 'Is she worried about you and me? Is that why the driving lessons stopped?'

'She's feeling vulnerable at the moment,' Paul explained. 'After everything that's been going on, I suppose it's natural for her to feel insecure. She sees any woman as a risk, and that includes you.'

'It can't be easy for you,' she said, making an opening for the conversation she had wanted to have with Paul for weeks. 'You shouldn't worry so much about the results.'

Paul was shaking his head as he stared straight ahead. 'Of course I should worry. I don't know how I'll live with myself if it turns out I'm responsible for all the pain Julia's been put through.'

Before Phoebe could interject, he said, 'But I couldn't bear it either if it turns out that Julia's the one with fertility problems. The only thing I am sure of right now is that there is a problem and it doesn't really matter where the fault lies. What we desperately need is someone to tell us how to fix it, which is hopefully what we're going to hear next week.'

'I hope so too,' Phoebe said. She looked again towards the house. Theresa was all the family Phoebe had left; she had never known her father who had been little more than a passing fancy in her mother's troubled life. Phoebe couldn't turn her back on her grandmother and leave

220

empty-handed, she had suffered the consequences once before when her mum had walked out. 'I'd better go,' she said.

'Are you sure you're ready?'

Phoebe laughed softly. 'What other choice do I have?'

Paul's features deepened with worry. 'Don't give up,' he said and then bit his lip before adding, 'Look, I'll see what I can do about the driving lessons. I could always forgo the odd session at the gym.'

'You mean go behind Julia's back again?' Despite herself, the idea gave Phoebe a certain thrill and lifted her spirits ever so slightly.

'She would want me to help you if she was thinking straight and we can tell her after the fact. After you've passed your test.'

'Thank you, Paul,' Phoebe replied and leaned over to kiss his cheek. She kept her body close to his a fraction longer than she needed but Paul didn't object. Even so, neither made eye contact as she turned away and got out of the car.

When Paul drove off, Phoebe was reminded of all those other times he had taken her home. She kept looking over her shoulder until the car disappeared around a corner, which summed up Phoebe's problems in general. She spent half her life looking back.

17

The Accident

When Anya returned to the ward to collect her things, she saw a man loitering behind a laundry cage and recognized him immediately. She had already told Paul Richardson on numerous occasions that his wife was refusing to see him. 'You're not supposed to be here,' she said. 'If Sister catches you, you'll be in so much trouble, and now that I've found you, so will I.'

'I need to see my wife,' Paul said, his voice shaking almost as much as the rest of his body.

Anya had seen a lot of people in her time emerging from shock only to be consumed by varying degrees of pain, grief, or guilt, but this man appeared to be carrying more than his fair share. Helen Butler's ex-husband had described him perfectly. He was a mess.

'She's resting now,' Anya said. She took his arm and guided him gently towards a nearby chair. 'Please, just give her body time to recover from the traumas of the day and her mind will catch up. Tomorrow.'

'I phoned her mum,' he said. 'She lives in Spain and was

ready to camp out at the airport until she could get a flight home. I told her to wait until tomorrow too. I did the right thing, didn't I?'

Anya's answer wasn't as quick as it could have been. Her experience of working in A & E in particular had taught her that there were no guarantees. 'She's still on IV meds because we can't get her to tolerate food or liquids but we'll try again tomorrow,' she explained in spite of his wife's instructions not to give him any information on the state of her health. 'There's nothing more to be done tonight, but we'll let you know if anything changes.'

Paul pressed his fingers hard against his lips to stifle a sob. His hand trembled and it took a couple of painful gulps before he could speak. 'It's all my fault!' he cried, his voice so weak it was a whisper. 'And I don't blame her for not wanting to see me. But I do need to explain. I have to tell her how sorry I am.'

Anya had no idea what could have happened between the couple that would make Julia reject him so completely, but she could hazard a guess. Anya had been married for eight years and had had her fair share of marital challenges. She still hadn't completely forgiven her husband for what he had done to her, and although Julia was barely conscious, Anya thought she recognized that same depth of pain that only came from betrayal. She knew she shouldn't jump to conclusions and it wasn't her place to judge the man sitting next to her based on so little evidence, but as she opened her mouth to speak, the words wouldn't come. There was nothing she could say to ease Paul Richardson's conscience and she doubted anyone could, except his wife. The only comfort she could offer was to place a hand on his back and begin to rub.

'What about the others?' he asked, and when Anya's hand paused, his body immediately tensed. 'Are Phoebe and Helen all right?'

'I've just been to see Helen and she's critical but stable.'

Paul was looking at her intently. 'Phoebe?'

'She had some post-operative issues,' Anya said carefully. The repair to the tear in her spleen had taken two attempts and there was still a chance it would have to be removed. 'But I should think she'll be transferred to the ward at some point this evening, all being well.'

'Will you tell me when that happens?'

'I'm afraid I'm about to go home and get some sleep. There's nothing more you can do tonight, other than grab some sleep yourself.'

'No, I can't. I won't rest until I know everyone's going to be OK. It's all my fault,' he said and then, in case Anya still wasn't getting the point he was making, he added, 'It's all my stupid, stupid fault.'

18

Phoebe opened the front door without a sound and just as silently, slipped into the house. The thick pile carpet cushioned her socked footfalls, her boots already left on a rack in the enclosed porch, and the only sound came from a radio deep inside the house. The background noise should have disguised the creak of the first step on the stairs, but her grandmother's hearing was not one of her failings.

'Is that you?'

Phoebe tried to analyse the intonation of those three words. She had become expert at judging her grandmother's mood by the tone of voice and it presently suggested that she was feeling uncharacteristically vulnerable. This only happened after one of her episodes and even then, rarely so.

'I was about to get changed,' Phoebe said when she poked her head into the drawing room. Her nan was in an armchair, a blanket covering her legs, and a book open on her lap. One of Phoebe's duties was to go to the library every week and select half a dozen titles. The choice these days was irrelevant because her nan's imperfect memory meant that she struggled to follow the plot, but so far that hadn't deterred Theresa from the practice of reading and, with dogged determination, she always kept a book to hand.

'Why am I still here?' she asked as if Phoebe were to blame for the afternoon's debacle.

'You didn't want to go, Nan.'

'Rubbish!'

'No, Nan, honestly. You outright refused.'

The creases on Theresa's already furrowed brow deepened and then she released a frustrated sigh. 'I don't remember. Are you sure?'

'Yes, Nan.'

'You should have made me go, Phoebe. I've told you before, you need to be more assertive. How can I leave you to take care of things if you let a frail old lady ride roughshod over you?'

Theresa's eyes had narrowed as she searched her granddaughter's face for answers that her own memory refused to provide and Phoebe withered under her gaze. If there was one person she would never be able to stand up to, it was her nan. When she had been in the peak of mental health, there had been few people who could win an argument with Mrs Dodd, and her illness had only served to strengthen her stubborn streak. What the seemingly frail old lady was blissfully unaware of was that when she wasn't being her usual supercilious self, she was someone far worse. Someone Phoebe feared.

Failing to receive an answer from her granddaughter, Theresa reached her own conclusions. 'That's it, isn't it? You didn't want me to go,' she said, her voice a mixture of resignation and condemnation.

'If you want, we can try again tomorrow.'

'Is that what *you* want?'

Phoebe could feel her answer choking her and when she failed to answer again, Theresa shook her head. 'Oh, Phoebe, you really are a lost cause. Just like your mother.' She placed her book on the side table and then pulled the blanket from her lap. She began to fold it, struggling to find the corners but determined not to let her confusion get the better of her. 'It looks like I'll have to stay around a bit longer, doesn't it?' she said. 'Come on, it's six o'clock and you haven't even started making dinner yet.'

'I wasn't expecting you to be here, Nan so there's nothing prepared. There's some stew in the freezer I could defrost.'

'We'll be living on ready meals next,' the old lady muttered as she reached for her walking stick. She stood up but it was some time before she could straighten and when she placed her full weight on her bad knee, she winced in pain.

'Sit back down, Nan. I won't be long.'

As she left the room, Phoebe heard the thump and shuffle as her grandmother ignored her suggestion and followed her into the kitchen. By the time she arrived, the stew was in the microwave, which was humming noisily.

There was a dining chair in the corner of the room, placed there specifically so Theresa could supervise Phoebe's every move. She sat down and said, 'Make sure it's defrosted properly.'

'I will. Do you want a cup of tea while we wait?'

'I'll only have to go to the little girl's room in ten minutes and right now I haven't the energy. You've exhausted me.'

'I could always help you to the toilet,' Phoebe said quite

227

deliberately to remind her grandmother of what lay ahead if she did stay at home.

'I manage well enough while you're at work, Phoebe. I'm not decrepit just yet. I can't allow myself to be. I need to stay here and look after you, remember?' she asked before adding under her breath, 'And I thought I was the one with the bad memory.'

'I can manage, Nan.'

'So now you're trying to get rid of me? Make your mind up, girl!'

Phoebe had been slicing bread and put down the knife before turning to face her grandmother although it was Theresa's reminder board on the wall that caught her attention first. It was a simple wipe board that Phoebe had used for the last couple of years to write down important daily prompts for her grandmother such as medical appointments, where Phoebe was, and when she would be home. There were only two words on it now, and they mocked her: 'Moving Day.'

'I'm not trying to sway you one way or the other, the decision is yours,' she said patiently. 'I'm only repeating the arguments you've already made yourself. When was the last time you had a proper wash? How long will it be before you can't get to the toilet in time and pee your pants?'

Her prim grandmother's face contorted in disgust. She felt uncomfortable even talking about bodily functions and hated the idea of needing someone to assist her. She had made it clear she didn't want that person to be Phoebe. 'Do not use that kind of language in my house, Phoebe.'

'I've spoken to the home,' Phoebe continued slowly, 'and

228

as long as you're willing to let them keep the first month's fees then your room can remain available, for a few weeks at least. It's your choice, Nan. If you want to go ahead with the original plan then let me know and I'll phone them. If you don't, then can we at least think about what help you might need?'

'I won't have you as my nursemaid.'

Phoebe was tempted to tell her she already was but chose instead to put forward another proposition. 'We could always arrange some home help again.'

'What? Have strangers waltzing around the house and helping themselves to goodness knows what while I'm . . .' She paused, trying to find the right word. 'Distracted.'

'I know you didn't like it last time,' Phoebe said, referring to the carers Theresa had allowed to attend her when she was recovering from her knee operation, 'but if you want to stay here, then you have no choice. I'm going on holiday next month so we'll definitely need to arrange something for then.'

'Holiday? What holiday?'

'I'm going to London with Julia and Helen for ten days,' Phoebe said without elaboration. She had already told her nan about her plans and she would forget them again in an hour.

While Theresa started grumbling, as much to herself as her granddaughter, Phoebe continued to prepare their meal. She heard the clatter of the cat flap followed by a gentle thud. A moment later, a warm feline body pressed against her leg and even above the hum of the microwave she could hear Leonard purring.

'Hello, my little man,' crooned the old lady, her voice

softening to a tone that matched the cat's purr. 'Come to Mummy.'

Phoebe looked down at the ginger cat winding itself around her legs, oblivious to his mistress's calls. He looked up at Phoebe and meowed. She both loved and resented the various cats her grandmother had doted on over the years. Without fail, they had received her grandmother's unconditional love and none of the judgement she reserved for the people in her life. Phoebe had a clear recollection of pretending to be a cat when she was possibly no more than three years old, only to receive the sharp point of her grandmother's shoe in her side.

It was Phoebe who gave the cat a gentle shove now, knowing how irritable her grandmother would become if Leonard paid her too much attention. The cat thumped his shoulder against her calf one last time and then padded over to his mistress.

'You're another one who'd miss me, aren't you? Oh, yes you are,' her grandmother told him. 'You're such a good boy.'

And Phoebe, by comparison was such a bad girl and for once she didn't need her grandmother's help picking out her failings. After serving dinner, which Theresa ate with only the cat for company, Phoebe allowed herself a half portion of stew in the kitchen before escaping upstairs.

In her bedroom, Phoebe picked up a discarded piece of chiffon from a design she had been working on and draped it over the mirror so she didn't have to look at herself. The sewing project was for a jumpsuit, which would accentuate her narrowing waist, but she wondered now if she would finish it. The world she thought was opening up to her had been closed over again. Who cared how she looked? Who was she trying to impress?

Curling up on her bed, Phoebe's thoughts turned to the secret driving lessons Paul had offered and she allowed her mind to wander. Her furtive imagination blocked out the rhythmic thump of a walking stick downstairs that became more and more persistent. It was the first time Phoebe had ignored her grandmother's demands for attention, and the longer she left it, the less inclined she was to face her grandmother's mounting fury. It was only the sound of her mobile ringing that forced her back to reality.

'Hi, how's it going?' asked Helen.

'I suppose I've had worse days,' Phoebe said, her voice calm and almost detached.

'What's going on, Phoebe?'

'Nan refused to leave the house. She had one of her episodes and now she thinks staying here is for the best.'

'So have you been home with her all day?'

A little surprised by a question rather than the sympathy she had been expecting, Phoebe asked, 'Mostly. Why?'

'Oh, nothing,' Helen said in a way that suggested it was something. 'I thought I saw you in Allerton at teatime, that's all. I was on the bus.'

'No, it couldn't have been me,' Phoebe said quickly, hoping that the uncertainty in her friend's voice meant she hadn't been sure.

'Oh.'

In the silence that followed a thought suddenly occurred. What if she had been in Paul's car when Helen had spotted them? She briefly considered telling Helen the truth. Paul was right, they weren't doing anything wrong – other than

231

the small matter of meeting without Julia's knowledge or approval, and of course there were her secret fantasies about an alternate life where Paul had persevered with the young woman who had opened up her heart to him rather than marrying her best friend.

Helen would surely understand, at least up to a point. She had known how Phoebe had felt about Paul at the time.

'You're *still* seeing him?' Helen had asked when Phoebe had called around to ask her advice. Milly was asleep on her mother's shoulder and jerked at the sound of her sharp tone. Lowering her voice, Helen had added, 'The weirdo who followed you home from class?'

'He walked me home and he's not a weirdo,' Phoebe had said before making another correction. 'And we're not seeing each other, Helen. We've had drinks in the pub and he's given me a lift home a few times, that's all.'

'Stalked you, you mean.'

'It isn't like that. The first couple of times he followed me on foot just to make sure I was safe. He had to go back for his car.'

'No, that doesn't sound like stalking at all,' Helen had scoffed. 'I can't believe you got in his car. He could have kidnapped you and locked you away in his basement for years.'

'Seriously, Helen, you're watching way too many day-time soaps.'

'What else have I got to do? Going out has to be perfectly synchronized between feeds and nappy changes. I might as well be in prison!'

Phoebe had been watching the way Helen was

232

absent-mindedly rocking Milly; she really didn't have a clue what she had. The young mum complained constantly about her sorry circumstances and Phoebe had used her friend's unhappiness to dampen her own maternal feelings, but was it so wrong to want something of her own – *someone* of her own? According to her nan it certainly was.

'Stop it!' Helen had snapped.

'What?'

'Staring at the baby like you want one. It's not all it's cracked up to be.'

'It doesn't matter now anyway. Last night Paul made the mistake of pulling up too close to the house and Nan spotted me in his car. I'm under strict instructions not to see him again.'

'You're eighteen, for God's sake. She can't boss you around like that,' Helen had said, forgetting her previous reservations about Paul which were undeserved anyway. She had never liked Theresa and would disagree with anything she said.

Phoebe had been standing at a crossroads in her life. She had needed Helen to tell her to go behind her grandmother's back and carry on seeing Paul, to take a chance and follow her heart. But even at eighteen, Phoebe had had enough failed relationships to know that her heart wasn't a reliable organ to judge the character of a man.

'Could you meet him for me?'

'Me? Why?'

'I'm not allowed to go to art class any more, and I don't have his phone number. I didn't give it to him either because *someone* told me to be cautious,' she told Helen pointedly. 'But you could pass on a message. Tell him I'm

233

sorry and I know it's all a bit weird with my nan but I still want to see him. Tell him we could meet up after my shifts at the supermarket, assuming he hasn't been frightened off, that is.'

Helen hadn't been convinced and so Phoebe had added, 'Please, Helen. Talk to him and see for yourself that he's not some psycho.'

'What, you mean interview him?' Helen's eyes had lit up then. 'It could be a bit like *Pop Idol*. Yes, Weird Stalker-man with the gorgeous body, you're through!'

Phoebe had no idea if Helen had tried her hardest to persuade Paul to see her again, or if his mind had already been made up. The end result was the same and Phoebe could only imagine how different her life might have been, which she did more often than she should.

Still tempted to make her confession to Helen, Phoebe held her breath, but then a series of thumps rocked the house and she inadvertently released a sob.

'Phoebe?'

'I'm going to spend the next God knows how long trapped in this house, Helen. I know Nan means well, but she wears me down. She *has* worn me down and I'm scared I'll never get the chance to build a life of my own. If this is how Mum felt then just shoot me now.'

'Hey, it's not that bad. Your mum was ill and she needed your nan to take charge of her life, but you don't. You have options.'

'Do I? Oh, Helen, I don't know what to do,' Phoebe said, curling herself up tighter on the bed.

'Do you want me to come and get you?'

'What can you do? What can anyone do? Nan doesn't

want anyone taking care of her and she's going to hate whoever it is that does. And it looks like that person is going to be me.'

'It doesn't have to be. If your nan is so determined to stay then good luck to her. *You* can leave though,' Helen said bluntly.

'No,' Phoebe said, shocked by Helen's ruthlessness.

'Look, from what you've said she's got enough money squirrelled away to afford all the help she needs if she does stay at home. She doesn't appreciate you, so why not leave?'

'I can't, Helen. Even if she were capable of making all her own arrangements now, there'll come a point when she won't be able to make even the simplest decisions. She took me in and cared for me. I owe her.'

'Take it from someone who's watched from the sidelines, Phoebes, you've more than paid your dues. Why didn't you finish off your design course when you came back to Liverpool? Why weren't you even allowed to carry on going to night school? I'll tell you why. Because your nan took over your life and made you afraid to take risks. This is your chance to start with a blank canvas.'

'I don't know—'

'Of course you know!' Helen said, having lost patience. 'I was scared of going it alone too when John left, but I had my friends to support me and so do you. Start believing in yourself, Phoebe, and for God's sake, stop listening to your nan.'

Before Phoebe could answer, there was another series of thumps. She stood up and pulled the drape from the mirror. She didn't like what she saw. 'I have to go.'

Whether it had been the creak of the bed or the tone of

Phoebe's voice, Helen knew her arguments were falling on deaf ears. 'If you won't leave permanently then you at least deserve a break. Milly's at home this weekend so how about we have a pyjama party?' Before Phoebe could throw cold water over any suggestion of leaving her nan alone overnight, she added, 'You could still be home by midnight, Cinderella.'

'Maybe.'

'No maybes. I want to see you at my house at six o'clock on Saturday. I'll ask Julia along too and we can order pizza.'

Phoebe was forced to agree to Helen's demands if only to get her off the phone, and then immediately scurried downstairs to silence the menacing thump of her grandmother's walking stick.

'Have you been crying?' Theresa asked.

Phoebe rubbed at the smeared make-up under her eyes. 'No, I was asleep.'

Her grandmother eyed her with suspicion but didn't challenge her. 'I know it's early but I've had an exhausting day, which hasn't been helped by using this to get your attention,' she said, lifting the walking stick. 'Half an hour I've been calling you, Phoebe.'

'Sorry, I didn't hear you.'

'Selective hearing more like,' her grandmother replied and shifted in her seat. 'I've seized up so I need your help.'

Spurred on by the prospect of being dismissed early for the evening, Phoebe helped her nan to her feet, and once she was up, Theresa used Phoebe and her walking stick for support. 'You're a good girl,' she said surprisingly softly. 'I know I'm becoming a burden to you and given how I've been the one looking after you for most of your life, it must be hard.'

Phoebe's response was exactly as they both expected. 'It's all right, Nan. Don't worry about me.'

'But I do worry about you. I worry about what's going to happen when I'm not here.' Her grandmother stopped and let go of Phoebe long enough to tap a finger against the side of her temple. 'Or here,' she added solemnly. 'But something stopped me leaving today, and I think it was meant to be. You shouldn't be on your own, not yet. You're not ready and I expect you're feeling relieved that we won't have to face the prospect of selling this place. I know how much you love this house.'

The cat followed the two shuffling figures into a room at the back of the house that had been converted into a downstairs bedroom, weaving between their legs and making the task doubly hard. When Theresa eased herself onto the bed, Leonard jumped up next to her and they both watched on as Phoebe flitted here and there. She fetched a glass of water and set it on the bedside table next to her grandmother's reading glasses and a stack of books, and then laid out a clean nightdress taken from the suitcase she couldn't face unpacking yet.

'Do you need help getting to the bathroom?' Phoebe asked. Her grandmother normally managed well enough on her own but Phoebe was making a point.

'I'll be fine on my own,' Theresa said with steely determination. 'Here, take Monty.'

Leonard's predecessor, Monty, was buried in a far corner of the garden but Theresa wouldn't take kindly to being corrected. Phoebe did as she was bidden but as she pulled the cat from the bed, his claws pulled at the brocade bedspread, making Theresa tut.

'Sorry,' Phoebe said as she unhooked a particularly stubborn claw.

Her grandmother tugged at the pull in the fabric. 'It's all right, I'll fix it. You go and have some time to yourself,' she said, and then fresh worry creased her wrinkled brow. 'You will be all right on your own, won't you?'

'Yes, Nan, stop worrying,' Phoebe said, swallowing back her frustration which scratched at her throat.

Once she had closed the door to her grandmother's room, Phoebe let Leonard drop to the floor. She focused her creative mind on summoning up an alternate reality where she could believe she was alone in the house and in control of her own destiny, but unfortunately even Phoebe's imagination had its limitations.

19

The Accident

In the dead of night there was one heart that beat loudest and demanded the most attention, but this was nothing unusual for Lucy Cunliffe. She was used to the unsteady rhythm of her defective organ, only this time it wasn't her heartbeat that woke her up but something else. For the briefest moment the remnants of her dream lingered and when she opened her eyes, she expected to find herself in a hotel room in Lanzarote. But she was still at home, lying in her bed in a room bathed in soft light from the streetlamp outside. Despite the familiarity, she felt unsettled and tried to work out what it was that had roused her from sleep and then she heard it again. It was the sound of someone breathing.

'Mum?' Lucy asked when her eyes had become accustomed to the light and she could make out the figure sitting on the wooden chair by her dressing table.

Her mum's chin had been resting on her chest and she had been softly snoring until the sound of Lucy's voice jolted her from her own dreams. 'What? Is everything all right?'

'I don't know, is it? What are you doing in here?'

'Sorry, I must have dozed off.'

Her mum stood up and stretched her spine.

'But *why* are you in here?' Lucy asked, although she could hazard a guess. It wouldn't be the first time her mum had kept vigil at her bedside, clinging to every minute as if it were the last she would spend with her daughter. It was what her mum was doing now except rather than dealing with the latest medical crisis, she was battling with her daughter's stubborn determination.

'I just wanted to . . .' Her mum's words trailed off and there was a catch in her throat before she continued. 'I just wanted to watch you sleep, that's all.'

Lucy could have cried. She could have crumpled along with her resolve and told her mum that she had come to her senses and yes, it was foolish to take such unnecessary risks. But Lucy couldn't bring herself to do that, not even for the amazing woman who had held her hand for the last twenty-four years and was refusing to let go. Instead she smiled and gave a soft laugh. 'Well, you didn't do a very good job. You woke me up with your snoring.'

Leaning over, her mum planted a kiss on her forehead. 'Then I'd better leave you in peace. Sleep tight, my darling. Tomorrow's a big day.'

The palpitations in Lucy's chest were a regular occurrence, but only very rarely was it excitement that made her heart race. 'I know, Mum, and I can't wait.'

Pausing at the door, her mum looked back and stared at Lucy as if committing the image to memory. 'I'm going to miss you,' she said.

'I *will* come back, Mum,' Lucy said. 'I'm going to be the bane of your life for a long time yet.'

'Promise?'

A saying came to mind, one her mum had scolded her for using once when she was a child. She couldn't cross her heart and hope to die. That would be up to someone else if Lucy were ever to keep her promise to her mum.

20

As Julia waited for Helen to answer the door she felt a surge of nostalgia. Life had become too complicated of late and a part of her wished she were back in her teens, about to spend the evening babysitting two troublesome girls and pretending she hated every minute of it. Helen and Julia's parents had done everything together and, as young parents, they thought Saturday night was their chance to kick loose while the kids stayed at home, but in truth, their daughters had claimed it as their own. Julia and Helen loved having the house to themselves, even if the age difference meant they had opposing views back then about what to do with their freedom. By rights, Phoebe shouldn't have been there, but she always was. She and Helen were inseparable, just as long as Helen didn't have to spend too much time at Phoebe's house with her scary grandmother and unpredictable mother, and Julia didn't mind looking after Phoebe – she was never the troublemaker.

'Don't stand there like a dummy. Get in,' Helen ordered when Julia struggled to emerge from the reverie and was a little dazed to see her friend as a fully grown woman.

Helen hadn't been joking when she said it was a pyjama party and had answered the door wearing a Winnie-the-Pooh vest top and shorts, paired with what could only be described as novelty slippers.

'Your feet could do with a shave,' Julia said, stepping into the hall and slipping off her coat. She was wearing a jersey dress that was a little more forgiving than the jeans she had originally tried on.

'You look nice,' Helen said.

Julia wasn't sure if it was the dress or her newly acquired curves that Helen was admiring but took the compliment anyway. 'Some of us like to make the effort,' she said before slipping past one friend, to be confronted by another. Phoebe had poked her head out of the living room and her eyes widened in fear when Julia added, 'And I have a bone to pick with you.'

'Why? What have I done?'

'You didn't tell me what was going on. I had to wait for Helen to fill me in. You should have called an emergency meeting.'

'I said that,' Helen agreed.

'I didn't want to bother you,' Phoebe said, still looking flustered. 'And besides, Helen couldn't leave Milly.'

'*I* could have met you,' Julia said.

'And I can look after myself. Mum's done it before,' Milly said. She had squeezed past Phoebe to greet the latest arrival. Helen's daughter was wearing similar-styled pyjamas to her mum and identical monster feet slippers.

243

'I heard you had one of those Facebook parties last time and trashed the place,' Julia said.

Milly rolled her eyes. 'No one uses Facebook any more.'

'Yeah, Julia,' Helen said in a childish tone, 'you must be really ancient if you still use Facebook.'

'At least I know how to send a text message,' Julia said, directing the comment at Phoebe.

She wished Phoebe had gone against her natural instincts, that she had been selfish for once and bothered her friends. If nothing else, it would have given Julia some reassurance that her recent neuroses hadn't damaged their friendship.

Phoebe gave Julia an apologetic look. 'I really am sorry, Julia.'

'Well, we're here now.'

'So let's get this party started,' Helen said, grabbing her daughter's arm and dragging her towards the kitchen. 'You two make yourselves at home while we get things ready.'

'Do you get the feeling we're a little overdressed?' Julia whispered.

Phoebe tugged anxiously at the soft lamb's wool jumper she was wearing which had ridden up above her waist, exposing her midriff.

'Pastel colours really suit you,' Julia said. She had also wanted to tell Phoebe that she looked stunning but knew from experience that such a compliment would never be accepted and would only serve to embarrass her friend.

'I was going to wear something black – I know, for a change,' Phoebe said, beating Julia to it. 'Something to match my mood.'

'Come on.' Julia put an arm around Phoebe and gave her a gentle squeeze as they slipped into the living room. 'Tell me what's been happening.'

Phoebe flopped down onto an armchair while Julia poured herself a glass of wine from the bottle that had been left amongst a pile of DVDs on the coffee table. They were all Disney movies.

'I refuse to bring the mood down,' Phoebe started, 'so let's just say that all of Nan's things are unpacked and she's now of the view that we've both had a narrow escape. There, enough about me, tell me what's been happening with you.'

Julia stared at the glass of wine in her hand and felt a familiar sense of disappointment in herself. If she knew for certain that refraining from the odd glass or two would get her the baby she craved, if it were that simple, then she wouldn't touch a drop. But the last two years had taught her that there were no simple solutions and no guarantees in life. 'Now that would definitely bring the mood down,' she said before taking a sip of wine.

'Still problems between you and Paul?'

'No,' she said a little too defensively. 'Or at least we're not at each other's throats, far from it. But it's not going to be easy until we know what's ahead of us, which is why we've been making an extra effort to do more fun things together, and that's why he's not been able to help with your driving lessons lately.' Julia winced. 'You don't mind, do you?'

'No, of course not.'

'If there's a problem with Paul and me,' Julia continued, 'it's that we're trying too hard to convince ourselves that we could be happy without kids. And while I think we could . . . God, I'm not ready to accept that as an option, not yet.'

Julia could easily have said more, but the smell of freshly popped popcorn heralded the return of Helen and Milly. She turned to the door in time to greet them with a smile and in a lighter tone added, 'And in the meantime, it's my adoptive daughter who's going to fill the breach.'

Milly ignored the stares as she placed the bowl of popcorn on the table and proceeded to sort through the DVDs, making a good act of being oblivious to the question mark hanging over Julia's statement.

'Are you sure you want to watch cartoons?' she asked them. 'We could stream a movie from the Internet. Something a bit more grown-up?'

'Oh, no, I want to revert to my second childhood,' her mum insisted.

'*Second* childhood?' Julia asked.

While Helen poked out her tongue at Julia, Phoebe was more interested in the DVDs Milly was sorting through. 'I see you've got *The Hunchback of Notre Dame*, Helen, but have you got—' Her eyes lit up when she saw the next one come into view. '*The Little Mermaid*! I used to love watching that.'

Helen began laughing. 'Mum used to have it on standby whenever she knew you were coming over. I think you wore the first video out.'

'Video? As in old-fashioned video tapes?' Milly asked. 'I suppose it was in black and white then too.'

'Less of the lip, young lady,' Helen replied. 'You've heard our selection, now come on, set it up.'

'What? Am I your servant tonight, or something?'

Helen started to speak, then stopped, but only briefly because she went on to say it anyway. 'I might as well make the most of you while I can.'

The rebellious streak her daughter had been displaying vanished in a moment and it was a young girl with a flush of embarrassment on her cheeks that switched on the DVD player.

When the film started, Milly looked for somewhere to sit. Julia made a space between herself and Helen on the sofa and Milly launched herself between them. When she chose to cuddle into Julia, Helen folded her arms, but Julia felt only a small twinge of guilt as she enjoyed the small victory. It didn't matter where Milly lived, Helen would always be her mum, but Julia needed moments like this.

While Milly settled down between Julia and Helen, Phoebe sat quietly on the outer edges of the group, which was her natural position and one she was more than happy to occupy. When the opening music to *The Little Mermaid* began to play it was enough to pull her back to her formative years. Her best memories always seemed to be in someone else's house.

'I always loved your mum,' she said.

'*My* mum?' Helen gasped.

Phoebe had taken a sip of wine and let it warm on her tongue before she swallowed and replied, 'Or Julia's for that matter.'

She had been expecting Julia to reply with equal flippancy but instead she asked, 'Anyone's mum except your own?'

'Oh, Mum wasn't that bad really,' Phoebe said with a shrug before remembering what Paul had said about telling her friends everything. 'She just wasn't that good at looking after anyone, not even herself, especially not herself.' Her voice trailed off as she recalled a vivid memory of sneaking into her mum's bedroom unbeknownst to her grandmother. The sunlight was streaming through the cracks in the curtains as she peaked beneath the bedcovers to reassure herself that her mum was still breathing. This wasn't a single memory but rather an amalgamation of a recurring theme. 'When she was well, she was the sweetest, kindest person you could imagine. Her problem was that the world frightened her most of the time.'

'Or your nan did,' Helen said wryly.

'Nan frightened everybody, even Grandad. But you shouldn't be so harsh, she kept us all safe, Mum included. She was the only one who could make her take her medication.'

This would have been the perfect time to continue, to tell them the things she had only told Paul, but Milly was listening intently. When everyone else had fallen silent and pretended to revert to watching the film, it was the youngster who asked, 'What was wrong with your mum?'

'She had manic depression, what they would call bipolar today,' Phoebe explained while looking to Helen. She wasn't sure how much an eleven-year-old would or should understand but Helen simply gave her a nod of encouragement. 'Which means she had a horrible, horrible illness that sometimes made her so sad she couldn't get out of bed for days, weeks even.'

'What made her so sad?'

'It doesn't quite work like that, honey,' Helen said. 'It was an illness; one that meant her brain didn't work the way healthy people's do. Bad things didn't have to happen for her to feel like the whole sky had fallen down on her.'

'It's a wonder she ever had the strength to up and leave when she did,' Phoebe said.

'She left you?' Milly asked, her eyes wide with shock.

'No, she took me with her. You see, as well as the times when she was desperately sad, there were times when Mum was really happy and optimistic – too optimistic. She convinced herself, and me, that she could stay well as long as we found a new place to live, which is what we did.'

'And did she stay happy?'

'No, Milly, she didn't and I had to learn to look after us both.'

'How old were you?'

'Nine.'

With the little mermaid singing away in the background, Phoebe imagined herself back in a threadbare flat in Manchester, sitting in the dark because there was no money to feed the electricity meter. It was during those times that she held onto her precious memories of sitting with Helen watching videos of gurgling sea monsters while in reality, it was the sound of her rumbling tummy.

Milly innocently pressed on. 'What happened to her?'

No one was pretending to be interested in the DVD now, Milly was asking the questions that Helen and Julia had never been given complete answers to. When she had reappeared in their lives, Phoebe had avoided talking about her missing years and her friends hadn't wanted to press her for information. Over time, those unspoken questions had been buried and forgotten.

'When we arrived in Manchester, Mum was convinced the new start was all the medicine she needed. When you're as ill as she was, it can be hard to recognize your own symptoms.'

'Did she ever get better?' Milly persisted as if she couldn't comprehend such a sad story without a happy ending.

'We managed for a while, eight years in fact, but . . . No, I couldn't save her in the end.' Before continuing, Phoebe needed to take a sip of wine, but her words were still hard fought for. 'I came home from college one day and she was gone.'

'Gone?'

Phoebe looked again to Helen and this time Helen answered for her. 'She died,' she told Milly softly.

'How?'

For this, only Phoebe could answer because her friends had never been told the details. Even so, she had to edit her words carefully. 'She took her own life,' she said and thankfully only she could conjure the sight of what had awaited her when she stepped through the door. She had tried to grab her mum's legs to take some of the strain from the belt she had used as a makeshift noose, and even though she knew it was too late, Phoebe had kept hold of her because she couldn't bear to let her mum's body drop again. Thankfully a neighbour had heard her screams and it was a paramedic who had prised her from the body.

'Jesus,' Julia whispered as if she could see the image in

Phoebe's mind's eye but then she added, 'Are you sure it wasn't accidental?'

'Oh, it was deliberate,' Phoebe replied with a warning glare that no more should be said in front of Milly. The child had lifted herself off Julia and was now snuggling into her mum who held her tightly.

Ariel was singing again, going on about wanting to be part of someone else's world. It could have been written for Phoebe. 'Now, if you lot were meant to be cheering me up, can I just say that you're failing miserably?'

Suddenly everyone was trying to do something – anything – to dispel the air of desolation. Julia grabbed the bowl of popcorn and offered it to Phoebe while Helen, still pinned down by Milly, scrambled for something to say. 'We must have some good news to share.'

'What about Olly?' Milly said, but even she noticed Julia freeze momentarily. 'Or not.'

Julia had quickly recovered herself. 'No, don't be daft. Or at least I don't mind,' she said, looking over to Helen to check how she felt about it.

Helen sighed. 'Oh, go on, Milly. Bore everyone to tears by describing every burp and fart of your new brother.'

Milly gave her mum a look which said, well, you asked, and then launched into a lengthy description of Oliver James Butler. Helen had been right about the level of detail but the look of love and delight on Milly's face was enough to forgive her the lengthy descriptions, and half an hour later it was new life and not death that surrounded them, giving them all a little more hope for the future even though it still felt beyond their grasp.

* * *

251

Helen was glad she had invited Julia and Phoebe over. It had been a while since they had shared a cosy evening in and she had forgotten how much she enjoyed them; it was certainly much less fraught than an emergency meeting at the Elephant and more relaxing than a snatched lunch or a hectic night out. It was a good reminder of the foundations their friendship had been built on, if not quite enough to reassure Helen that it could withstand the kind of threats she had been imagining since spying Phoebe hiding down a side street off Allerton Road.

As the evening wore on, the three friends, four including Milly, alternated between quiet reflection and gentle chitchat as they watched one animated film after another. With the air thick with nostalgia, Helen began reflecting back on simpler times when boys were still a mystery.

'Remember when I kissed David Sanderson?' she said to Phoebe.

'When? You never did!' cried Julia.

'It was when I was in reception, just before we were due to go into proper school,' Helen admitted. 'We were breaking up for the summer and I was so upset because I wasn't going to see David again for weeks, which is forever when you're four.'

'If it's the boy I'm thinking of,' Julia said, 'wasn't he kind of . . . weedy?'

Helen shared a look with Phoebe and they both laughed.

'He was quite short,' Phoebe added, 'even for a four-year-old.'

'I can remember being in the cloakroom putting on my coat,' Helen continued. 'David had shoved past me and I just kept thinking how much I was going to miss him.'

'I saw it all,' Phoebe said. 'Helen was maybe a foot taller and while David was distracted putting on his coat, she bent down and kissed the top of his head.'

'Mum, you didn't!'

'He didn't know a thing about it,' Helen said. She still had her daughter wrapped in her arms and wrinkled her nose at her. 'But when I kissed him there was a strong smell of grease in his hair which really put me off so that little crush was long forgotten by the time September came round.'

'Is that how you pick your men now?' Phoebe asked. 'By sniffing their hair?'

Milly gasped. 'What men?'

'There *are* no men in my life,' Helen said slowly and deliberately so her friends would get the message that this wasn't a subject she wanted to discuss in front of her daughter. The last thing she needed was another reason for Milly to think she would be better off at her dad's.

'Yes, I don't blame you,' Julia said. 'It's bad enough that you have to be jostled on the bus home by *people* with smelly hair.'

Helen glared at her. 'They're not all bad.'

'You must bump into those same people again though.'

'No, Julia,' Helen said, thinking of the business card from the newly divorced financial adviser that was still languishing at the bottom of her bag. 'I can't remember the last time I saw a familiar face.'

'But it *might* happen?'

'I suppose it is possible,' Helen conceded.

The conversation trailed off and by the time the latest DVD had ended, Milly was fast asleep with her head on her mum's lap and her feet across Julia. She didn't so much as stir when the doorbell rang.

'That'll be the chauffeur,' Julia whispered. 'Could you do the honours, Phoebes? I'm a bit stuck.'

'Paul's picking you up? I thought we were sharing a taxi?'

'Don't worry, we'll be dropping you off too.'

Phoebe had drunk a little too much wine to conceal her feelings and Helen wished she hadn't noticed how her friend's face lit up as she hurried out of the room. Groaning, Helen made a point of needing to stretch her spine.

Using a cushion to replace her lap as Milly's pillow, she stood up and said, 'I'll see if Paul needs anything.'

Julia was preoccupied with making a restless Milly comfortable again and thankfully didn't pick up on Helen's unease. 'OK,' she whispered with a half-drunken smile, her eyes never leaving the little girl.

Helen stepped quietly into the hall in time to hear part of a whispered exchange between Paul and Phoebe.

'Hi, Paul,' she said to let them know she was there. 'Fancy a coffee to warm you up?'

'I think I'd rather be getting home if it's all right with you. Me and Julia have an early gym session planned for tomorrow morning.'

Helen rolled her eyes in the direction of the living room and his wife. 'Good luck with that one.'

'She hasn't crashed out again, has she?'

'No, but Milly has. I know she's a big lummox now, but do you think you could help get her to bed?'

As Paul walked past Phoebe, she was stroking her hand

254

softly across her bare midriff and it drew his gaze. That one look was all it took for Helen to stop doubting herself and begin seriously doubting her friend. Phoebe and Paul had unfinished business, business that Helen had put an end to once and she was prepared to do it again.

The first time she had come between Phoebe and Paul, Helen's intentions had been noble. Paul might not have turned out to be the crazed stalker she had imagined, but he hadn't been right for Phoebe back then. In fact, Paul's suitability hadn't really been the issue at all; Phoebe was the problem. She had been desperate for someone to take care of her, someone other than her nan, and she hadn't cared who that was or how it happened. The chances that this man she barely knew would be the one to save her, the one who would stand by her if she 'accidentally' got pregnant, were remote, and if Helen felt guilty at all, it was that Phoebe hadn't been given the chance to reach that conclusion herself. It had been decided for her.

'What should I do?' Paul had asked when Helen had turned up at night school to act as Phoebe's go-between. What Phoebe hadn't known was that, by that point, Helen was a double agent. 'I don't want to cause any more trouble than I already have, but I like Phoebe and . . .'

They had been sitting in a large dining hall that would normally be groaning with teenagers during the day but was only partly lit during the evening to accommodate what were significantly more mature students. At that present moment, most of those students were still in class so Helen and Paul had the hall practically to themselves.

'I heard about her nan catching you,' she had said.

'She's bloody terrifying, isn't she? She came at me with her walking stick and dragged Phoebe out of the car.'

Helen had been genuinely shocked since Phoebe had spared her the finer details of the confrontation. 'You were lucky she didn't. Theresa's quite quick on her feet and the walking stick would have been Phoebe's grandad's. Now there was a man she probably did use it on,' she had added, lowering her tone. She wanted Paul to feel unnerved. He had already been frightened off and now he had to be frightened off for good.

'But I'd still like the chance to see her again. I take it that's why she sent you?'

'Look,' Helen had said, taking a deep breath to steel herself for the lie she was determined to tell, 'the way Phoebe sees it, the incident only forces an issue she would have had to face anyway. She likes you, but as far as she's concerned it was never going to go any further. She isn't looking for complications and she certainly isn't looking for anything serious.' Helen had held her breath as she checked Paul's response. Her script was a well-rehearsed one and she didn't think she could wing it if she had said something that contradicted what Paul already knew of her friend. Thankfully he didn't look as if he was about to correct her. 'Phoebe's still trying to work out who she is, and she doesn't need you to help her do that. But she *does* need her nan.'

'Is she telling me to back off?'

'Will you?' Helen had asked, deftly avoiding an outright lie. 'For Phoebe's sake?'

If Paul had been devastated by the proposition, he hid it well, which was enough to convince Helen that she wasn't betraying Phoebe but protecting her – from herself as much as anyone. And as if she needed reminding about what could happen if emotions were allowed to run free, Helen heard the distant cry of a baby. Like Pavlov's dogs, her breasts began to tingle as they prepared for feeding time. If she didn't move fast, she would face the humiliation of saying goodbye to this decidedly dishy bloke with two large damp patches on her T-shirt.

'If I'm honest, I got the feeling she wasn't after anything serious, just a shoulder to cry on,' Paul said, 'but she's a nice girl and you can't help but want to look after her.'

'I know,' Helen had said, already standing up and bringing the summit on her friend's future to a close.

Phoebe's reaction later on had been equally subdued. When Helen had told her that Paul hadn't wanted to cause a family rift, Phoebe had quietly accepted defeat. She had cut herself off from Helen for a while, but when she returned she was more like the Phoebe of their childhood. She had been tamed at last, and was finally ready to accept Julia back into her life, little knowing that her old friend had been taking care of her from the wings anyway.

For good or bad, Phoebe's fate had been sealed a long time ago and there would be no second chances, not if Helen had anything to do with it. While Paul and Julia took care of Milly, Helen grabbed the opportunity to tackle Phoebe alone in the kitchen.

'What was all that about?' she demanded.

Phoebe had been putting empty wine bottles in the recycling bin and turned to question why her friend's tone should sound so hard. 'What do you mean?'

Helen arched an eyebrow to punctuate her words. 'You and Paul, whispering in the hallway?'

Phoebe did her best to look affronted, but she sounded apprehensive when she said, 'It was nothing, we were just saying hello.'

'I heard you, Phoebe. What was it that Paul told you not to mention to Julia?'

'I don't know . . .' Phoebe said. 'Something about not minding picking us up probably.'

'Really?' Helen said, spitting the word out like an accusation, which was exactly what it was.

'Seriously, Helen, I don't know what you're getting at.'

Helen wished she hadn't drunk so much wine. This was a conversation she ought only to have when sober, but she wasn't renowned for holding her tongue at the best of times and couldn't bring herself to put it off for another day. 'OK, let me spell it out for you. I saw the way you got all giddy when you went to answer the door, I've seen the way you've been flirting with Paul and I've just heard you whispering secrets to each other,' Helen said, counting out the evidence on her fingers. 'Oh, and let's not forget about you hiding down a side street in Allerton when coincidentally Paul drives along in his car.'

Phoebe dropped the last bottle into the bin and it surprised them both that it didn't shatter. 'I'm not listening to this,' she said. 'You're drunk and you'll be embarrassed about it in the morning, so let's not make it any worse than it already is.'

Phoebe went to march out of the kitchen but Helen grabbed her arm. 'I know what I saw, Phoebe. How can you do this to Julia?'

Phoebe shrugged her off. 'I'm not doing anything.'

'But you want to, don't you?'

When Phoebe refused to even look at her, Helen said, 'My God, I'm right, aren't I?'

Again she was met by silence.

'Julia's at her lowest right now and she thinks her relationship is hanging by a thread,' Helen continued. 'You've seen what she's like.' She stopped what she was saying and shook her head. 'Of course you have. That's exactly what you've been doing, isn't it, Phoebe? Circling like a vulture while you wait for their marriage to fail? Please, tell me I'm wrong.'

Helen had let go of Phoebe's arm but rather than try to escape, Phoebe pursed her lips before blurting out her confession. 'I love him,' she said quickly before she lost her nerve. 'I never stopped, Helen.'

'Don't be ridiculous! Don't go telling me you were in love with him all those years ago. You didn't know him, Phoebe, you never even had a proper date.'

'But I know what he could have been, what *we* could have been together. I wish I didn't feel like this and I'd stop it if I could, but it's too late.'

Helen's heart skipped a beat. 'So there *is* something going on?' she asked, not sure if she was ready for the answer.

'No, of course not!' Phoebe cried. 'I wouldn't do that. I swear to you, Helen, we haven't done anything wrong.'

'But you *have* been meeting up?'

'No,' Phoebe said before crumbling under Helen's withering glare. 'Only that once, and only because I had nowhere else to turn.'

'You had *me*! And you had your other best friend! You know the one? She's married to the man you're claiming to be in love with.'

'I can't help the way I feel.'

'And what about Paul? Does he feel the same?'

Phoebe's eyes were brimming with tears and a couple slithered down her cheeks. 'He doesn't know how I feel, Helen. He loves Julia, anyone can see that, and he hasn't encouraged me at all. If anything, he just feels sorry for me and guilty about stopping the driving lessons. He told me how Julia's been a bit paranoid lately but that if she were in a better frame of mind she would want him to carry on helping.'

'Except she isn't paranoid, is she?' Helen said. Her tone was still harsh, but her anger had been tempered by her own culpability. If Paul and Phoebe's relationship had been allowed to run its course, if it had been a fair fight, then Phoebe might have outgrown her feelings and they wouldn't be in this mess.

'I swear I wouldn't do anything, Helen,' Phoebe continued. 'It's just that I feel . . . I feel as if I'm trapped in a life I don't belong in. I keep thinking back to what might have been, what Paul and I might have had if Nan hadn't frightened him away. She tied me up in her apron strings and squeezed the life out of me, Helen, just like the belt Mum tied around her neck. No wonder she preferred that to going back home to Nan.'

Helen's blood ran cold. 'Your mum hung herself?'

When Phoebe nodded, Helen didn't want to make the next chilling connection. 'And you were the one who found her?'

260

With tears rolling freely down her face, Phoebe whispered, 'Yes.'

'Jesus, why didn't you ever say?'

Sobbing openly now, Phoebe continued with her confession. 'The only person I ever really told back in the day was Paul. I opened up to him and, eleven years on, when he needed someone to talk to, he turned to me. And it felt good, Helen. I was needed. *I* wasn't the victim; *I* wasn't the one being pitied. For once I felt like a real person.'

Phoebe was shaking now and Helen surprised herself by grabbing hold of her again only this time it was to enfold her in a hug. Her friend buried her head in Helen's shoulder. 'I didn't mean for my feelings to get out of hand, but I swear to you, I haven't acted on them. You have to believe that.'

'I do,' Helen said as she gently rocked her friend. 'I do.'

Phoebe lifted her head. 'You won't tell Julia, will you?'

Helen smiled. 'I should think that's the last thing she'd want to know right now, but things can't go on like this. You may not have control over your feelings but you most definitely have a choice when it comes to acting on them or not. Promise me, Phoebe—'

Before Helen could finish her sentence, the door opened and Julia entered, closely followed by Paul. The broad smiles on their faces froze in perfect synchronicity as they took in the scene. Phoebe's smudged make-up had left dark puddles on Helen's vest top. 'What is it?' Julia asked and was already putting her arms around her two friends before either had a chance to reply.

'It's nothing,' Helen assured her. 'Phoebes is a little

overwrought. In my medical opinion, it's too much wine and, unless I'm mistaken, not enough popcorn and cheesy puffs to soak it up.'

Phoebe turned her head away from Paul and began wiping furiously at her panda eyes. 'I had a bit of a wobble, but I'm back on track now,' she said, pausing until she was looking at Helen. 'I promise.'

21

There was something about opening her heart to Helen that made Phoebe feel a little better about herself. Her guilty secret had stopped eating away at her because it no longer controlled her. As Helen had so aptly pointed out, Phoebe had choices and she was considering her options as she strolled home from the library laden with a fresh pile of books for her nan.

It was Tuesday lunchtime and, having worked a weekend shift, Phoebe was enjoying a well-earned day off, although enjoying might be a bit of an exaggeration. The whispered conversation Helen had overheard was Paul promising to phone her so they could fit in a secret driving lesson and she had been waiting for that call like a lovestruck teenager. The sick feeling in the pit of her stomach annoyed her, and as she approached home she decided to take matters into her own hands. If he hadn't called by the time she reached home, she would phone him.

Opening the door to the small porch, Phoebe set down the heavy tote bag containing the books next to a large yucca that had been a Mother's Day present for her nan years ago, back when it had been small enough to fit into a carrier bag. After kicking off her shoes to place on the rack, she rummaged in her handbag for her front door keys but her hand closed around her mobile phone first. There had been no missed calls in the five minutes since she had last checked which presented her with her first choice. She could step inside the house and give Paul more time while she made lunch for her nan, or she could get it over with now.

She had Paul's mobile number but chose to phone his office to avoid the risk of ringing when his wife might be there. It also left no trace of the call for Julia to find.

'Can you talk?' she asked when Paul answered after two rings.

'Oh, hi Phoebe. I've been meaning to phone you.'

From the tone of his voice, Phoebe had the distinct impression that he hadn't been looking forward to making the call. 'About our driving lesson by any chance?' she asked stupidly. Why else would he want to speak to her?

'Erm, yeah, the thing is,' he began. She could hear papers being shuffled while he left a pause, and then he added, 'I've been having second thoughts. I'm not sure we should be doing this.'

'I know,' she said softly with a note of acceptance that had yet to be felt in her heart. 'I was thinking the same thing.'

'I want to help, really I do, and especially now. How are things?'

'Nan's being Nan. She has plenty of moments when she's just a doddery and overprotective grandmother, and then there are the other times.'

'I don't know how you do it,' he said. 'And I think you

need our support more than ever, the other night proved that.'

Phoebe tried to laugh. 'I did make a bit of a fool of myself, didn't I?'

'You didn't. It only made us all realize how strong you're being the other ninety-nine per cent of the time. You're a formidable force, Phoebe.'

'Just one who won't be passing her driving test any time soon.'

'Yeah, I'm sorry about that, but the point I was trying to make, hopelessly as usual, is that you need Julia and Helen in your life right now, certainly more than you need driving lessons. If Julia ever found out that I'd been seeing you without telling her, she'd jump to the wrong conclusions.' He gave a short laugh. 'Daft, I know.'

His laugh, awkward as it was, cut her. While she accepted that they weren't allowed to acknowledge their past intimacy which had been too brief to be called a relationship, it had happened and it had meant something, at least it had to Phoebe.

'We can convince ourselves that there isn't an ulterior motive,' he continued, 'but I'd struggle to justify the secrecy to Julia. I've felt bad about not telling her about the other night and I think there's a reason for that. It's wrong, Phoebe, no matter how we try to package it up.'

Phoebe was playing with the leaves of the yucca plant as she let Paul's words wash over her, but it was one particular sentence that kept coming back in gentle, hopeful waves. He had said that they could convince themselves that there was no ulterior motive. What did that mean? Was he trying to deny his feelings too?

She smiled and her vision shimmered with tears. 'You're right, Paul, of course you are. Don't go beating yourself up about it. You have enough to deal with. I'm not the only one who has to be strong, am I?'

'I can't tell you how much I'm dreading the appointment with the consultant tomorrow. I really don't know what to hope for. I suppose the best outcome is that it is me if only because that's the answer I'm most prepared for.'

Phoebe wanted to tell him again that it wouldn't be him but he had made it clear he didn't want the finger pointed at Julia either. 'If your consultant is anything like the ones my nan goes to, you probably won't get a definitive answer either way, just plenty of theories that you'll be sent away to disprove.'

'Which means we'd be no further along. It's a lose-lose situation whichever way you look at it.'

'I'll be thinking of you,' Phoebe said, then quickly added, 'I'll be thinking of you both.'

There was a long, drawn out pause which could easily be filled by either of them saying goodbye and yet the only sound came from the shuffling of more papers on the other end of the line and the faint scratch of a fingernail being drawn along the sharp edges of the houseplant's succulent leaves.

'I'd better go,' Paul said.

'Me too.'

'Bye then.'

'Bye, Paul,' she said and was about to take the phone from her ear when she felt a rush of panic. 'Let me know how you get on tomorrow.'

'I'll get Julia to phone you,' he said carefully.

'Yes, of course. I meant Julia.'

There had been no 'of course' about it and when the call ended, the power Phoebe had convinced herself she had over her life wasn't even strong enough to turn the key in the front door. Her hand shook as she put all her effort into staunching her tears and composing herself before daring to enter the house. She didn't want her nan asking her what was wrong. She might just tell her.

After a few minutes, Phoebe took a deep, juddering breath, held it and then imagined releasing all of those inappropriate feelings that had been contaminating her heart. It didn't work, but it was a nice idea, she told herself as she pushed open the door and stepped over the threshold to face an entirely different kind of pain.

The house was quiet which immediately struck Phoebe as odd. Theresa was a creature of habit and while she didn't spend all day glued to the TV, she liked to watch the lunchtime news, which should still be on. Straining her ears, Phoebe heard a gentle thud as Leonard jumped down, probably off a chair, and a moment later he prised open the door to the drawing room and sauntered down the hallway. Ignoring the cat winding around her legs, Phoebe crept along the narrow passageway with growing dread. 'Nan?' she called out softly.

Phoebe looked through the half-open door as she waited for a reply. She couldn't see the far side of the room where her nan would be sitting although she could just make out the blanket that would normally be draped over her legs. It was lying on the floor.

She strained her ears but the only sound Phoebe heard

was the hiss of rising blood pressure as countless scenarios played out in her mind. Her nan might have had an accident and could be lying on the floor unconscious, or she might have had a stroke or heart attack. What if her life had been slowly ebbing away while Phoebe had been browsing bookshelves? It wouldn't be the first time she had arrived home too late to save someone she had loved and she didn't think she could face it a second time.

Phoebe pushed open the door gently and called out again. 'Nan, it's me. Are you all right?'

Terrified of what she might find, Phoebe looked tentatively around the door. For a brief second she felt a rush of relief when she spotted her nan standing behind her armchair, using one hand to support herself while the other was raised over her head. There was a pink blur as something flew through the air and Phoebe barely had time to avoid the china figurine before it smashed against the wall with enough force to break it in two. She stumbled back into the hallway, tripping over the cat that was rushing for cover, before thumping her back against the stairs. Little Bo Peep's head rolled to a stop only feet away.

'Get out of my house!' Theresa screamed. 'I've called the police and they're on their way! Get out now!'

Her heart thudding, Phoebe returned to the doorway but remained out of sight for the time being. 'It's me. Phoebe,' she explained quietly and calmly. 'Your granddaughter.'

'Rubbish! I don't have a granddaughter! My husband will be home soon and he's built like a brick shithouse. I'm warning you, if you don't walk away now, you won't be walking anywhere when he's finished with you.'

Despite herself, Phoebe smiled. Her nan's episodes were

not only accompanied by confusion about where she was and when, but often a dramatic change in her character too. She said things that even someone as outspoken as her grandmother would be horrified to hear, let alone utter.

'It's all right, Mrs Dodd, no one's going to hurt you. I'm here to help. Your husband sent me to check you were OK.'

'I don't believe you!' the terrified lady yelled.

'Please, Nan,' Phoebe said as she stepped tentatively over the threshold with her hands lifted in supplication.

Theresa had moved from behind the safety of her armchair and, with the help of her walking stick, had crept along the edges of the room. She had been lying in wait and when Phoebe came through the door, the crack of the wooden walking stick across her brow made Phoebe's teeth crunch. Again she stumbled back only this time she couldn't save herself and fell to the floor.

Phoebe knew she didn't have time to get up again because her nan was moving faster than her weak knee should allow. She could only manage to put her arms over her head before a set of fresh blows rained down on her.

'It's me, Nan!' Phoebe screamed. 'Stop it! For God's sake, stop! I'm your granddaughter. I'm Phoebe.'

Still crying out, Phoebe began crawling down the hallway on her knees, one hand over her head while the other kept her balance. Despite another blow that flashed pain across her back, Phoebe managed to gather enough momentum to outrun her nan and when she reached the front door she used a side table to get to her feet. She turned and despite the pain in her left hand where she had received a nasty blow, Phoebe made a grab for the walking stick that was about to come down on her again.

269

'No!' she cried as she took hold of the weapon tight with one, then both hands so she could fight back.

Fuelled by a rush of adrenalin, Phoebe had to remind herself that she was still dealing with a frail old woman whose bones might easily shatter if she were knocked down with the kind of force Phoebe wanted to direct at her assailant. Theresa put up more resistance than she expected, however, and she had to push fairly hard against the walking stick until she had her nan pinned against a wall. Once she was sure she was in control, Phoebe looked into her grandmother's terrified eyes and searched for the merest flicker of recognition, but soon her vision blurred from the stream of blood trickling down her brow.

Still holding fast to the walking stick, Phoebe dropped her head and began to sob. Her body was shaking uncontrollably and it took all her strength not to fall to the floor. She didn't know what to do next. Her nan's episodes could last for hours, and even when she did come out of her mental fugue, it was a slow and painful process. Phoebe's first thought was to go upstairs, pack a bag and leave. She couldn't take this any more.

Wiping her eye as best she could against her shoulder, Phoebe could see that her nan was crying too. Theresa had stopped fighting back and while there was still no sign of recognition, she had at least recognized defeat. Using the last remnants of composure, Phoebe said, 'I want you to go into the drawing room and sit down in your armchair. Do you understand?'

Theresa nodded.

'I'm going to take your walking stick away and you can use my arm for support. Will you do that?'

Another nod.

'I'm not going to hurt you as long as you do as you're told,' Phoebe warned as she assumed the role of the house invader her nan perceived her to be.

When Phoebe removed the walking stick from her grasp, her nan's body sagged a little. Theresa had been carried along by her own rush of adrenalin and it had left her completely spent. Her hand trembled when she took Phoebe's arm as instructed and the walk from the hallway to the drawing room was a slow and solemn journey.

To Phoebe's shame, once the old lady had been returned to her chair, she felt no warmth of feeling towards the cruel monster that had invaded her nan's body. She could offer no words of comfort as she left the room, only a cold warning. 'Don't move,' she said.

Closing the door, Phoebe told herself not to crumble. She went into the kitchen and ran her injured hand under the cold tap to ease the throbbing and then used kitchen towels to staunch the blood from the wound to her forehead. She didn't look at herself until she was in her bedroom and when she did, she didn't simply cry; she began to wail. The sobs racked through her body and, as if she wasn't hurting enough, Phoebe felt fresh pain as her cries tore at her vocal chords. Her body juddered and she could barely breathe as she dropped down onto the bed and curled up into the foetal position. She pressed her eyes tightly closed and the darkness confirmed what she already felt. She was utterly alone.

Helen was humming to herself as she made her way to the hospital pharmacy to pick up a prescription for one of her

271

patients. Her steps were light as she swayed her hips to the beat of the music, but no matter how hard she tried to pretend she was carefree, she was far from happy. Her usual remedy of taking a look around the clinic and telling herself how fortunate she was hadn't put so much as a dent in her despondency.

She had never been a worrier and wasn't used to the tightness she felt in her chest as she tried to form a psychic connection that would give her the first clue as to what might be happening in another Liverpool hospital. She imagined Julia and Paul sitting in a consulting room, gripping each other's hand tightly as the consultant delivered his verdict. When no message came through, Helen was forced to take out her phone and let technology do what her nonexistent psychic powers could not, but then surprised herself by phoning someone else.

'Hi, Phoebes.'

'Any news?' her friend asked nervously.

'I was about to ask you the same thing.' Helen sighed as her pace slowed to a crawl. 'All this waiting is killing me.'

'Do you think Julia will get around to letting us know today?'

'She doesn't have a choice. I know there's going to be a lot to take in and they'll need time to digest all the information before they're ready to start talking to anyone else about the delights of ovaries and sperm counts, but their appointment was at ten o'clock and if Julia hasn't been in touch by lunchtime then I'm going to give her a ring.'

'And you'll let me know as soon as you've spoken to her?'

'Yes, of course I will,' Helen said. 'Are you in work? It sounds quiet.'

'I'm on paperwork duty today. Part of my new training,' she muttered. 'How about you?'

'I've just got a quiet five minutes picking up prescriptions.'

Helen hadn't spoken to Phoebe since the previous Saturday night. They had swapped the odd text message, tentatively testing the water with each other until Helen had been satisfied that she hadn't pushed Phoebe too far. Now that she had that assurance, she decided to push again – just a little.

'How are you feeling about everything? About Paul, I mean.'

'I spoke to him yesterday.'

'Oh,' Helen said. She hadn't wanted the remark to sound suspicious but what other reaction could Phoebe expect?

'I phoned him to say I didn't want any more driving lessons.'

'Oh,' Helen said again, still suspicious, 'but they'd more or less come to a stop anyway, hadn't they?'

'They had,' Phoebe said carefully, 'but like I told you, Paul was feeling guilty and . . .'

'And what?'

'He was going to find a way of giving me lessons anyway.'

'By going behind Julia's back again?' Helen said, surprised that she could feel any more shocked by Phoebe's behaviour than she already was – or Paul's, for that matter, which led to her next question. 'You don't think . . . I mean . . .' She sighed as she tried to find a diplomatic way of speaking

273

her mind, but she had no choice but to say it as it was. 'You've admitted you were developing feelings for Paul and now you've done the right thing. *You've* put Julia and your friendship first, but what about Paul? Do you think he might have wanted to resurrect things, find a familiar port to escape a stormy marriage?'

'He's done nothing wrong! He loves Julia, we both know that.'

A voice in Helen's head told her to stop pushing now, but her mouth had its own ideas. 'I'm sorry, Phoebe, but I disagree. He *did* do something wrong.'

She heard Phoebe take a sharp intake of breath but before she could get the words out, there was the creak of a door and then a voice in the background said, 'How are you getting on, Phoebe? If your hand's still troubling you then you ought to go home.'

'I'm fine, honestly,' Phoebe answered. 'But if you can check some of the figures I've inputted later, that would be a help.'

'Will do,' the woman replied.

When she heard the sound of the door closing again, Helen asked, 'Who was that? What's wrong with your hand?'

'It was one of my managers, and I banged my hand on a door, that's all.'

'In the shop? I hope you've filled in the accident book.'

'No, not here,' Phoebe said. 'It happened when I was leaving the library yesterday.'

'How bad is it? I bet you haven't complained to the library, have you?' Helen asked. 'I know what you're like, you won't want to make a fuss, but I can.'

'Stop,' Phoebe said and there was a distinctive catch in her voice. 'Please, Helen, stop.'

'Phoebe?'

'Everyone keeps telling me to sue the council but I can't because I made the story up. The truth is I was hurt in a bit of a scuffle yesterday.'

Helen couldn't help herself. She laughed. 'You haven't been fighting with the customers, have you?'

'No, with Nan,' replied an unamused Phoebe.

She was most likely expecting more derision but Helen spoke softly when she asked, 'Another one of her episodes?'

'A bad one, Helen. It was horrible and I'm in agony, and what's worse is that I feel so humiliated. I was beaten up by a pensioner and I can't cope with her any more.'

'This is exactly what your nan didn't want you to go through. She might have had cold feet about going into the home, but she must see now how it's affecting you.'

'She doesn't remember a thing about it. Like everyone else she thinks I hurt my hand at the library. She even told me off for breaking one of her ornaments when she was the one who threw it at me. I don't know what to do, Helen. Even though she was back to her old self this morning, I'm scared to leave her on her own any more. And what happens when I can't leave her? What will I do then?'

'Oh, Phoebe, you have to tell her. I know I'm the first to complain about how overbearing she can be, but even I can accept that it's only ever been because she's so protective. Well, you need protecting now and there's only one way she can help you.'

'It would kill her if she knew what she was like when she gets confused.'

'Oh, for heaven's sake, you can't shield her from the inevitable. Did I just hear your manager say you could go home? Well, go home now, Phoebe Dodd, and tell your nan what she's been putting you through.'

'I can't, not yet. I need time to prepare myself. Maybe at the weekend.'

'OK, but make sure you do, Phoebe, because if you don't, I will.'

'Thank you,' Phoebe said, her voice wet with tears. 'Thank you for being such a good friend – I don't know what I'd do without you.'

Ending the call, Helen wondered if Phoebe would think her such a good friend if she knew she was partly responsible for her present heartache, but there was no point in looking back. What mattered now was what the future held for them all. They would get through their current trials and tribulations just as long as they stuck together.

22

The Accident

When Anya arrived for duty at Warrington General the next day it felt as if she had never been away. She certainly didn't feel as if she'd had a full night's sleep, and even if Jacob hadn't snuck into her bed at two o'clock in the morning, Anya wouldn't have felt any more rested. She supposed she was lucky that her husband was still sleeping in the spare room and that for once it wasn't the state of her marriage that had kept her mind turning through the night, but rather the traumas of the previous day. Every time she had closed her eyes she had flashbacks to the scene of the accident.

Anya had thought her days of working in A & E were far behind her after transferring to the surgical ward eighteen months earlier, but when the call had come through for more emergency staff, she had volunteered without hesitation. She missed the drama and the challenges that came with emergency care, although not the accompanying shock and distress shared by patients, families and staff alike, but she was relieved it had been a temporary return and was looking forward to what she hoped would be a less eventful day on the ward. Her first task was to satisfy herself that her patients had made it safely through the night.

'Any problems?' she asked one of the night staff as soon as she came through the door.

'It was a busy one, I'll tell you that much. There were one or two who had us worried,' her colleague said, 'but we haven't lost one – yet. Let's grab a coffee and I'll take you through the notes.'

'I will. Can I just check on someone first?'

Anya wasn't sure why she had made such a strong connection with Julia Richardson. Perhaps it was because they were around the same age but there were other parallels too. The accident had been a random and devastating event, but her patient's distress appeared to have roots that went back further than the crash itself, and that was why Anya found herself standing in front of her sleeping patient's bed checking her notes.

Julia had got through the night without incident, but Anya wouldn't begin to relax until she was off IV meds and eating and drinking normally.

'Hello again,' Julia murmured as she peeled open her eyes. She still sounded a little woozy but at least she recognized Anya from the day before.

'How are you doing?'

'I think I should hurt more than I do.'

'That'll be the drugs. They're doing their job.'

'I don't want any,' Julia said. 'I'd rather live with the pain.'

'I'm pretty sure you wouldn't. Let's just see how you get on today.'

When Anya leaned over to straighten her pillows, Julia frowned. She was trying to focus on the gold pendant dangling from the nurse's neck. 'I must be hallucinating,' she said.

'Sorry, I should have taken that off.'

'I don't think I'll be married much longer,' Julia said, as if she knew the meaning behind Anya's necklace which had been a Christmas present from her dad and matched the pendant he had commissioned for her mother in celebration of their fiftieth wedding anniversary. Her dad was still under the misconception that her own marriage would be blessed with the same longevity.

'Your husband is desperate to see you,' Anya told her.

'I don't care,' Julia said.

Anya was trying to hide her curiosity but Julia had seen it anyway and added, 'Honestly, there's no point. But what about my friends?' Pursing her lips, Julia fought to correct herself. 'My *friend*.'

'Helen Butler?' Anya guessed. It had been an image of the woman's young daughter that had contributed to her restlessness the night before and she wondered how mother and daughter had fared through the night. 'I saw her last night and she was stable, which is as good as the doctors can hope for right now while they wait for the swelling on her brain to reduce. I'll check again for you just as soon as I can, but I do have news about someone else you were asking about yesterday.'

'Phoebe?'

Anya stepped back and invited Julia to follow her gaze. Phoebe Dodd was lying in the bed next to her, completely still with her eyes wide open. She had been listening to every word that had passed between them.

Julia turned and lifted her head slightly so she could look at her. Phoebe was covered with cuts and abrasions, her left arm was in plaster, but to the untrained eye, she appeared to have come out of the accident relatively unscathed. Her visible injuries certainly didn't explain the look of abject pain on her face.

'Is there something you'd like to tell me, Phoebe?' Julia asked.

23

The Elephant 7.30 p.m. Please come.

It was late Saturday afternoon and Phoebe was in the kitchen, within shouting distance of her nan in case she was needed but not under her feet, which was how they had always preferred to live their lives together. She had just been wondering what to make for dinner when the idea for an emergency meeting struck her and she had sent the message before there was a chance to change her mind.

Phoebe had spoken only briefly to Julia in the last few days, a five-minute conversation where Julia had offered only the salient facts. She had told Phoebe the results of the tests and said she and Paul needed time to digest the news and formulate a plan of action. Phoebe had been desperate to know more but even Helen had been unable to glean further detail. With nothing left to do but wait it out, Helen had redirected her focus on Phoebe's issues, as was evident by the speed of her friend's reply seconds later.

Problems? I'll be there! H x

While waiting for Julia's response, Phoebe checked her reflection in the hallway mirror. With the help of a minor adjustment to her fringe and carefully applied make-up, the injury to her forehead had been easily covered up. The worst of the bruising was on her back, and the only obvious sign that Phoebe had been in the wars at all was the damage to her hand. Her fingers weren't as swollen as they had been, but the skin was broken in places and the rest a patchwork of bruising in varying shades of black, green and blue.

Not that Phoebe had to disguise her injuries at home any more. Today had been one of her nan's better days, or at least it was until her granddaughter had taken Helen's advice and told her about the attack. Phoebe didn't hold back on the detail and had even gone so far as showing Theresa the injuries to her back. Helen had been right: it was the only way to convince her nan that staying at home wasn't in her granddaughter's best interests, but the anguish Phoebe had caused by telling her nan the truth was almost as painful as the beating she had received.

Theresa had been quiet ever since and when Phoebe went to check on her, she paused at the door. She doubted she would ever be able to walk into that room again without tensing in fear, but when she did step inside, she was glad to see clear recognition on Theresa's face. Her grandmother's favourite radio programme was playing in the background and she had been busily writing, using a lap tray balanced on her knee for support.

'I'm going out for dinner, Nan, but I'll make you something first. What do you fancy?'

'Oh, I'm not that hungry. I'll heat up some soup when I'm ready.'

'It's no trouble; I'll do it before I go,' Phoebe said, choosing not to remind her nan that she couldn't be trusted near the cooker or the microwave. 'Just give me a shout when you're hungry.'

Phoebe had been about to turn and leave but her nan raised an eyebrow and drew her granddaughter's gaze to the letter she had been writing.

'What is it?'

'It's a letter to myself.'

'Oh, right,' Phoebe said. Her grandmother's illness had led her to say and do some very odd things and Phoebe was prepared to add this to the list. But for once, Theresa was thinking more clearly than she had in weeks, if not months.

'Don't give me that look! I know what I'm doing. I'm going to keep this on the bureau over there and when I need to, I'm going to read it.'

'Why? What does it say?'

It looked as if Theresa was going to hand over the letter but she thought better of it and gave a short summation of its contents instead. 'It tells me who I am for those times when I forget,' she began, 'and I don't just mean the basic facts like my name and where I live. This tells me who Theresa Dodd is.'

'And who are you, Nan?' Phoebe asked with a note of challenge that she might not have used before the attack.

Her grandmother scanned the contents of the letter and her voice was choked with the kind of emotion her written words were undoubtedly laced with. 'I'm someone who has spent her entire life looking after her family and for the most part getting it wrong. I failed your mum, Phoebe, and

283

it's about time I admitted it. Eleanor was little more than a child when we realized she had an illness and I took it upon myself to look after her, to be her pillar of strength so she didn't have to be for herself. I didn't give her the chance to be strong, to be a person in her own right, and no wonder she left. I smothered her and, in some respects, I've done the same to you. Only you're not your mum, Phoebe. You're stronger than I gave you credit for.' She picked up the letter and it trembled in her hand. 'I wrote this letter to remind me that I can't fail you in the same way I failed my daughter.'

Despite the outpouring of emotion, Phoebe couldn't help but feel a little disappointed. This wasn't the solution she had been hoping for. 'I know it's a lovely idea, but when you have one of your episodes, Nan, I'm not sure you would be convinced by a letter, or even if you could manage to read it.'

'It's worth a try and I might not need it anyway. I want you to make the arrangements at the care home, Phoebe. Assuming they'll still have me.'

'Are you sure?'

'What I did to you was unforgivable. I'd rather die now than risk doing that again, and I rather think I might.' Her voice had ebbed away to nothing but after taking a breath her next words would not be brokered with. 'Eleanor ran away from me and I'm scared you might do the same. I'm a proud woman and sometimes that's stopped me saying what needs to be said. I *need* you, Phoebe. You're all I have and if you were to go, then there would be nothing left for me.'

'I wouldn't leave you,' Phoebe answered, casting aside her previous temptation to do exactly that.

'But I shouldn't make it so hard for you to stay. Make the arrangements for next week and if I happen to be playing up when the time comes then show me this letter. If that fails, then when I'm able to listen again, I want you to tell me exactly what I was like, *exactly*, Phoebe. If I'm the kind of monster who could read this and not be moved, then you have my permission to use physical force.' She was holding the letter so tightly now that it twisted in her hand. 'From the look in your eye, I'd say you already know that's what I am. Send me away, Phoebe. You have my blessing.'

Phoebe took the tray and the letter from her nan so that she could kneel in front of her and rest her head on her lap. She had done this only once before, not long after her ill-fated liaison with Paul had been brought to an end and there had been other choices to make.

'You'll be all right, Phoebe,' the old lady said as she stroked her granddaughter's hair. 'I've been telling you that you won't cope without me because it's what I wanted to believe. The truth is, you don't need me any more. You have a full life ahead of you and there's still so much you could do, things you shouldn't have sacrificed for the sake of a silly old lady. I wish you would find a man – I think the time is right for you – but even so, you have some lovely friends. Go out and enjoy yourself tonight, think about the future, and don't you dare fret about me.'

But as Phoebe sat in the Elephant waiting for her friends to arrive, the new life that awaited her couldn't have been further from her mind. She couldn't discard her old life so easily. She still worried about her nan, and she worried about her friends too – especially the one who hadn't replied to her text. Phoebe kept her eyes on the entrance and waited.

'I didn't think you were coming,' Phoebe said with a rush of relief.

'How many times have you been here for me?' Julia asked. 'And it's not often I get to return the favour so of course I was coming.' In truth, she had been glad of the excuse to get out and was almost looking forward to being presented with a problem that she might have some chance of fixing. 'Sorry, I didn't text you, did I? My head's been in the clouds lately.'

'It's all right, you're here now.'

Phoebe picked up the bottle of wine on the table and was about to fill a second glass when Julia said, 'Not for me, thanks. I'm driving.'

'Oh, all right then,' Phoebe said and although she didn't ask why, the question hung in the air.

Julia caught the eye of a waiter and asked him for a glass of sparkling water. He also gave her a curious look, possibly recalling the night Julia had staggered out of the restaurant, which made her all the more determined not to repeat the performance.

'It's not fair on Paul being my chauffeur all the time,' she told Phoebe, 'and besides, I'd rather cut back for now.'

Again there was a lull in the conversation where Julia would normally start talking about her obsession with getting pregnant, but she wasn't ready to talk about what the consultant had said, and more especially how she felt about it, which was what her friends would want to know. She didn't know where to begin and for a moment, she was lost in her thoughts. It was only when Phoebe began to fidget uncomfortably that Julia realized she had been staring at her friend's hand. It took another second to react to the sight of her injuries.

'My God, Phoebe, what happened?'

Phoebe covered up the bruises with her other hand and shrugged. 'It's nothing.'

'Bloody hell, let me see,' Helen said, having just arrived.

Despite wearing a gypsy shirt over torn jeans, there was no doubting Helen was a nurse. She took hold of Phoebe's hand and turned it this way and that, manipulating digits and applying pressure to the area around Phoebe's knuckles. 'You're lucky it's not broken,' she said and, turning to Julia, added, 'Did she tell you what her nan did?'

'No! When did this happen and why on earth didn't you tell me?' Julia began but then stopped. She didn't need to be reminded how she had been hogging centre stage over the last week, if not longer.

'It's nothing,' Phoebe insisted.

'It took me ages getting it out of her,' Helen said. 'Her nan thought she was an intruder and attacked her.'

Julia couldn't hide her confusion as she tried to imagine how Theresa could inflict such an injury.

'She used her walking stick.'

Helen was still inspecting her patient, only now she was looking at Phoebe's face. She tenderly pushed her fringe to the side to expose the gash beneath. 'And exactly how many times did she hit you?'

Phoebe jerked her head away and readjusted her fringe. 'I don't know. It doesn't matter.'

'It doesn't matter?' Julia challenged. 'Your nan assaulted

you and you're going to carry on as if nothing's happened? I won't stand for it!'

'Honestly, Julia. It's all right.'

'Then why have you called this meeting?' Helen demanded. 'What's going on?'

By way of an answer, Phoebe looked directly at Julia and Julia's heart sank even as it filled with warmth. 'You called the meeting for me, didn't you?'

'There's only so much space we could give you,' Phoebe said. 'How are things?'

'Oh, no, I'm not so wrapped up in myself not to care about what's happening in my best friends' lives. Tell me what's going on, Phoebe. Tell me what you need us to do.'

As Phoebe smiled, she fought the urge to cry. She didn't deserve Julia's sympathy. 'Nothing,' she said.

Ignoring the comment, Julia said, 'What does your nan think? She must be mortified.'

'She won't tell her.'

'I said I'd tell her and I have,' Phoebe said to Helen. 'And it had precisely the effect you said it would.'

'She's going into the home?'

When Phoebe simply nodded, Julia shared a look with Helen. They were both thinking the same thing but it was Helen who said, 'We've heard that before, Phoebe. It doesn't mean she'll actually go through with it.'

It was then that Phoebe told them about the heart-breaking letter her grandmother had written and even Helen couldn't think of a smart remark.

'That's so sad,' Julia said at last.

'I'm almost tempted to tell her to forget it, which shouldn't be too difficult with my nan.'

'You'd better not,' Helen warned. 'And yes, it is incredibly sad and I'm not belittling the magnitude of the decision she's taking . . .'

'But?'

'But she's not some sweet-natured old lady we should all feel sorry for, and she never was. I don't doubt that she loved you all very much, but she controlled your family through bullying and intimidation, even your grandad. The reason you were always invited around to my house to play, Phoebe, was because I was terrified of her. She frightened off *all* your friends.'

Thinking back, Julia would be hard pressed to name any of Phoebe's other friends, although being that much older she had never taken much notice of Helen and Phoebe's peers – the two girls had been enough of a handful. But what Helen said rang true. 'And I always had the impression she hated you, Helen.'

Phoebe silenced her friends with a withering look. 'Today my grandmother told me how lucky I was to have such wonderful friends. If only she knew!'

Julia had the good grace to blush but Helen simply shrugged. 'Anyway, now that's sorted, let's turn our attention to the next item on the agenda. How are things in the "low-sperm-count household"?' she asked.

At that precise moment the waiter arrived and, with a wry smile, asked, 'And what can I do for you ladies this evening?'

Even Julia managed a smile and after their orders had been taken and they were on their own again, her friends waited patiently until the forced grin had faded to nothing.

'The consultant didn't rule out the possibility that I might have unexplained fertility issues that are contributing to our problems, particularly given my age, but . . .' She grimaced and wouldn't look at her friends but rather a spot in the distance where Paul's face materialized in front of her, complete with a look of utter devastation. 'Based purely on Paul's results, the odds of us conceiving naturally are pretty dismal. To use another of our consultant's analogies, if Paul's little men were footballers, they'd be lucky to make the Second Division, let alone the Premiership.'

'Shouldn't you ask for a second opinion?' Phoebe asked.

'Why?' Julia said, allowing her friends to hear the pain she had been trying so hard to hide from her husband. 'The fact that we haven't been able to conceive is proof enough that something's wrong.'

'But—'

Helen interrupted her. 'And how are you feeling about it, Julia?'

'I feel – everything,' she said simply and then, knowing the answer wasn't good enough, added, 'I'm relieved that I could carry a baby, theoretically at least; I'm hopeful that there are enough options available so it might happen one day; I'm frustrated that we have to wait for a follow-up appointment before we can decide which way to go; but most of all I'm absolutely gutted that, as far as Paul sees it, the blame for all of this has landed at his feet and there's nothing I can say to make him realize that we're in this together, we always were, and the results don't change a damn thing.'

'Poor Paul,' Phoebe said.

Helen reached over and cupped Julia's face briefly in her hand. 'And poor you.'

Julia offered them a trembling smile. 'It will happen one day, that's what we have to hold onto.'

'Until you're holding your baby,' Helen said. She raised her glass and with more hope than confidence added, 'Here's to new beginnings, for all of us.'

Three glasses were lifted into the air but they couldn't bring them together so readily. Words were easy to say, more difficult to put into action, and they knew it. Only when Julia tipped her glass towards her friends, did they complete the toast.

Deciding enough time had been wasted on the imponderables of biological functions, Julia tackled one of the more pressing challenges of motherhood. 'So, Helen, what new beginnings are you looking forward to? Has Milly changed her mind yet?'

Helen's bright eyes dimmed. 'I'm afraid not. We're getting on better than ever, but I can't compete with cute little Oliver.' She pulled a sad face but her playfulness couldn't disguise the fact that she was hurting.

'Well, I still think she'll come to her senses,' Julia told her. 'She takes you for granted right now, but just you wait.'

'It's half term in two weeks. Time is running out.'

Julia held back from insisting everything would be OK. Wasn't she sick of hearing the same thing herself? And thankfully, Helen's comment prompted another discussion that was well overdue. 'Speaking of which, what about our holiday? Don't we need to stop prevaricating and book it? If we don't get a move on then it could be my fiftieth and your fortieths we're celebrating.'

Helen was counting on her fingers. 'And that would be

our combined one hundred and thirtieth. It just doesn't have the same ring to it, does it?'

'And it's got the number thirteen in it,' Phoebe said, 'and we're not exactly known for our good luck and fortune.'

'We *are* lucky,' Julia insisted. 'We have each other and I know there's been a lot of crap thrown at us all lately but isn't that all the more reason to make this happen? We've been distracted by all our troubles but maybe this is perfect timing. You and Phoebe will be divested of your caring responsibilities and I'm yet to acquire some, so . . .'

When her call to arms was met with stunned silence, she added, 'Seriously, what's stopping us?'

Phoebe shrugged. 'Nothing.'

Helen's mouth twitched. 'I suppose it would be good to regroup and get our acts together.'

'And while we're away,' Julia said, looking straight at Phoebe, 'you and I are going to work out what you want to do with the rest of your life. It's not too late for a career change and with my help, we will make it happen.'

Julia looked from Phoebe to Helen until all three faces were alight with excitement.

'But honestly, could we still do it?' Helen said. 'It'll take a lot of organizing in such a short space of time.'

'I've already done all the hard work,' Phoebe said. 'We know what we want.'

'So?' Julia asked.

Phoebe smiled. 'Assuming my nan does move out, it would be some start to my new life.'

'Exactly,' Helen said. 'Fresh start, clean sheet.'

Typical of Phoebe, she wouldn't let the excitement over-power her sense of the practical. 'We might be restricted on the availability for flights and hotels, but there'll be alternatives if you don't mind me tweaking the itinerary here and there. But I'd rather wait until Nan's actually in the care home, which means it would have to be very last minute.'

'Not a problem,' Julia said.

'I can't guarantee the prices won't have changed from when I last checked, but if I get the travel agent on the case, who knows, we might be able to take advantage of some late deals.'

'Don't worry,' Julia said, 'even if it does cost more, we're still going.'

'Hold on, if it's too much over budget, I might have to consult my financial adviser,' Helen said.

Julia was the first to pick up on her friend's throwaway comment, which had a hint of an announcement. She narrowed her eyes and kept them on Helen as the waiter arrived with their food. 'So there *are* new beginnings afoot,' she said once their food had been served.

Helen picked up a crisp, golden chip and took a bite as if her next words were nothing special. 'There might be.'

'The bloke on the bus?' Phoebe stuttered. 'You're going out with him? Why didn't you say something?'

'Because I'm not going out with him,' Helen said as if she were utterly offended by the remark. 'I simply met him to review my financial position in light of the impending changes to my household.'

Julia cocked her head. 'Met him where?'

'His office is in Chester so it was a bit awkward to get there.'

'Met him where?' she repeated.

There was a hint of a smile when Helen said, 'In a very nice restaurant in the city centre.'

'Which one?'

'The Carpathia.'

'Isn't that part of a hotel?' Phoebe offered and shared a look with Julia. They were both enjoying the sport now.

'It was a business meeting.'

'Yeah, yeah,' chorused her friends.

'You two have minds in the gutter. We talked business.' Rather than more questions, it was her friends' refusal to comment that finally made Helen cave in. 'All right, it might have started out as a business meeting but I suppose it's entirely possible that it did progress towards something that might loosely be described as a date – by which I mean we got personal but not *that* personal.'

'And when are you seeing him again?'

Helen winced. 'I was supposed to be seeing him tonight.'

Phoebe's jaw dropped. 'You should have said! I wouldn't have called you out if I'd known.'

'I did it for you,' Helen said purposefully, 'and I did it for Julia. I put our friendship before any man.'

Phoebe didn't hang about sorting out the holiday arrangements and by the following Wednesday she was already making her second visit of the week to the travel agent's. The first had been during her lunch break on Monday to briefly run through her requirements and set the agent to work sourcing out the best available offers. Her return trip was intended to close the deal.

Phoebe had taken a day off work, but not simply to visit the travel agent's; in fact, not even because of it. If

294

she were being honest, she had been fully prepared for all her plans to come to nothing, but after an extremely busy morning she found herself walking down Lord Street shaking with a mixture of excitement and trepidation. Outside the travel agent's, passers-by had paused to check out the latest deals on display in the window, and even though Phoebe's choices had already been made, she paused with the crowd. She could feel her heart thudding against her chest so hard that it made her nauseous. A smile was forming tentatively on her lips as if it were shocked to be there. She had never thought this day would come.

Eventually her gaze was drawn inside the shop and she made eye contact with the travel agent who was expecting her.

'I have some great news for you,' Lorna told Phoebe as she took a seat opposite her. 'I've managed to match your original itinerary as far as travel arrangements go – that's including the train to London, the Eurostar to Paris and the flights you wanted to New York. I couldn't get you into the Paris hotel you wanted but the one I'm suggesting is only around the corner. It's a tad more expensive but it has a spa and their offer comes with a complimentary treatment. Train tickets are also a bit more expensive than you originally anticipated.' She stopped reeling off the list to check her client's reaction. 'Overall, I couldn't get you quite within budget but it's not far off. Everything is available if you want me to book it today. It's up to you.'

Phoebe looked at the printout Lorna had passed to her with the final figures. The cost had already been eye-watering and the hike only added to the pain. 'It's not only up to me. I need to consult my friends.'

Lorna glanced over Phoebe's shoulder towards the waiting area where new customers had appeared. 'It's less than two weeks away and I can't guarantee availability or prices if you were to leave it any longer, and to be honest, finding alternatives once these options go will be tricky.'

'It shouldn't take long, but I really do need to check with them first.'

'I'll tell you what, why don't you take a seat and make some calls? When you've got your answers then give me the nod and we'll take it from there. It looks like it's going to be a fabulous trip and I really don't want you to miss out.'

Returning to the waiting area, Phoebe pulled out her phone. She got through to Julia immediately who confirmed that she still wanted to go and then asked a more pertinent question. Was Phoebe able to make the trip, or did she still have certain responsibilities? Phoebe said that she could, but offered little else.

Helen was a little more difficult to get hold of so Phoebe was forced to leave a voicemail message and then followed it up with a text for good measure. She hoped the clinic wasn't so busy that Helen would miss both. All she could do now was wait, and as she did she watched other customers book their holidays with relative ease compared to what had been a long and difficult journey for herself and her friends. It was only when she spotted a young girl coming into the travel agent's that she realized it wasn't necessarily plain sailing for everyone else either.

The girl was small and slight with the body of a child but had the presence of someone who had already lived a lifetime. There were no more seats available and without hesitation Phoebe stood up and offered hers. A middle-aged man who had been sitting next to Phoebe jumped up at the same time and there was a brief argument before he got his way and the two ladies took their seats.

'Thank you,' the woman with blue-tinged lips said to them both when she could catch her breath.

'I'm surprised it's so busy,' Phoebe said to her.

'Have you seen the weather out there? I can't wait to get away.'

'Where are you off to?'

The woman was looking straight ahead, staring at a poster of golden shores cooled by crystal blue waters. 'Somewhere warm. Anywhere that isn't here.'

'You have a point,' Phoebe agreed.

'So what about you, then?' the woman asked and when Phoebe gave her the edited highlights of her trip, her eyes opened wide in wonder.

'I wish I could do something like that but my mum is already throwing a fit about this trip. She doesn't think I'm well enough, but I've gone past the point of caring. Life's too short to have regrets.'

'Is your mum going with you?'

'God, no. She'd have me panicking the whole time and thankfully she's terrified of flying. I'm taking my sister Hayley and we only want to go away for a few days, not even a whole week. I've never been abroad before and I'd like to go just once. I'm hoping we can get away soon, just in case things change.'

Phoebe could only imagine what challenges the young woman faced but she envied her attitude. 'I wish I had your determination.'

'You're about to set off on the trip of a lifetime and you don't think you're determined?'

'Ruthless maybe, but not determined,' Phoebe said. The look on the woman's face invited her to say more and Phoebe was about to shrug but then carried on talking. 'I've lived with my nan for most of my life and it's just been the two of us for a while now. Her health started to deteriorate, and then she was diagnosed with the early stages of Alzheimer's – except maybe it isn't early stages any more. I think we've both been fooling ourselves. She forgets who she is and who I am so I can terrify her simply by walking through the door.'

'Is she going into a home?'

'She's already there, as of this morning. And here I am, jetting off on my travels. It feels unreal,' Phoebe said and then, checking her feelings, corrected herself. 'And it feels liberating. I know my nan spent her life looking after her family and I should be eternally grateful – I *am* grateful – but I gave up a lot too.' Phoebe had already given a similar speech to the staff at the home, and there was no reason to explain herself to another stranger but she supposed if she justified her actions often enough, she might be convinced by them too. 'If things had been different, I could have been jetting off regularly to Paris and New York, I could have been living in London.' She released a deep sigh. 'Actually, there's a lot of things I could have done but didn't. So why should I feel so guilty about one holiday?'

'But you do,' the woman said. 'And you're not the only one who feels guilty.'

'About your mum?'

'She's worried I won't make it home again, and it *is* a risk, but I'd rather die knowing I tried to live. Unfortunately, I don't think that would give Mum much comfort.'

'But it's not going to stop you doing it,' Phoebe concluded.

'No, and I'd say we both need to stop feeling guilty . . .' She paused, waiting for Phoebe to offer her name.

'Phoebe.'

'I'm Lucy,' she said. 'We should be living for the moment and to hell with the consequences if it means we can turn an ordinary day into one we'll never forget.'

'This is most definitely a day I'll remember.'

Lucy gave her a smile. 'Me too.'

That short conversation wasn't quite enough to absolve Phoebe of her sins, but it gave her the impetus to book the holiday once Helen had phoned back and asked what on earth she was waiting for, of course she still wanted to go. Her friend's excitement was contagious and on the way home, Phoebe started making a mental list of all the things they needed to do. There were practical considerations like travel insurance and visas and then there were the more complicated decisions about what to take. She would have to be selective if she was going to leave enough spare capacity in her suitcase for the spoils of their international shopping trip, but she had advised customers often enough on how to put together a capsule wardrobe for their holidays and was looking forward to applying those skills to herself for a change.

Phoebe was so absorbed in this mental task that she didn't think about her nan until she stepped into an eerily quiet house and felt a cold shock of fear, her body reacting to the memory of the week before when the silence had been the precursor to an attack.

Standing in the hallway, the stillness was so heavy that it crushed her buoyant mood until all she felt was emptiness. Even the cat was nowhere to be seen and she couldn't blame him for snubbing her. Leonard would be farmed out to a cattery, which meant there would be no one to welcome her home when she returned from her travels. Helen might be coming home to an empty nest too, of course, but at least she had an extended family who would have missed her and, by the sounds of it, an admirer too. Who did Phoebe have except an indifferent cat? Her nan might miss her now but in time her memory would fail and Phoebe would be erased from the old lady's life. At that moment, it felt like her nan had already been expunged from hers.

It was only when her mobile began to ring and she saw the name on the screen, that a smile was tempted from her lips.

'Hi, Julia,' she said as she stepped deeper into the house.

'It's only a quick call. I was just thinking how strange it's going to be for you tonight. If you want to, you could always come over for dinner?'

Phoebe's smile broadened but there was pain in her eyes that Julia couldn't see nor would she suspect. Now was not the time for Phoebe to observe the comfortable machinations of a married couple, especially one that involved Paul. 'That's really sweet of you, but I need to get used to being on my own, and besides, I promised the home I'd go back this evening to see how Nan's settling in.'

'OK, if you're sure,' Julia said. 'But just so you know,

300

this is an open offer. Any time you feel like you need some company, you only have to ask.'

'Thank you, Julia. Maybe after we get back.'

'Or before,' Julia said with the kind of tone that suggested she already had plans that her friend wouldn't be able to wriggle out of so easily. 'Will you be home on Sunday morning?'

'Erm, I suppose so.'

'Well, make sure you are. Expect a visit at about ten.'

'What? Why?'

'Never you mind, just be ready.'

Sunday was little more than a week before they were all due to set off and it came around faster than Phoebe would have liked. There was still so much to do. She had hauled an old suitcase out of the loft and had it open in the middle of the floor in the smallest of the three empty bedrooms. The room had been hers when she was a little girl, but its previous life of lavender walls and My Little Pony accessories had been erased with a coat of cream paint and a beige carpet that left it a blank canvas, much like Phoebe's life.

She had already started packing the case with clothes including a simple yet daring bodycon dress which she had picked out merely because it was lightweight and then was pleasantly surprised when she had tried it on. With little to no appetite, her dieting was really showing results and when she held the taut turquoise material against her body now, she felt something stirring deep inside that she hadn't felt for years. Could it be that she was getting her spark back?

Folding the dress, she glanced out of the bedroom window and saw a red car pull up. She hoped there would be two occupants but to her surprise there was only one, and it wasn't the one she had been expecting.

'I thought Julia was coming?' she asked, aware that her voice was trembling after rushing downstairs at breakneck speed and opening the door before her visitor had a chance to knock.

Paul had stepped into the porch but seemed reluctant to go further. There was a look of confusion on his face. 'Didn't she tell you? I'm here to give you a driving lesson,' he said, dangling his car keys in front of her.

Phoebe stared at the keys. 'But . . . I thought she didn't . . .'

'So did I.'

Judging by the wry look he gave her, Phoebe quickly gathered that it hadn't been his idea. 'If you don't want to do this, Paul, I don't mind. I'm going to start proper lessons when I get back from holiday,' she said and was pleased that she sounded quite genuine when the last thing her heart was telling her to do was send him away. She wanted him to see the new, improved Phoebe and the fine-knit dress she was wearing had been chosen specifically to show off her smoothed-out curves. Even though she would no longer be ruled by inappropriate feelings for her best friend's husband, she still wanted him to want her – just a little, just once.

'Well, I'm here now so come on, get your coat and let's go,' he said with a distinct lack of enthusiasm.

Sitting behind the steering wheel, Phoebe felt the same awkwardness she had felt in those very first lessons, which had nothing to do with the prospect of driving and everything to do with the enforced intimacy of the lesson. The

302

only difference was that this time Paul showed no signs of wanting to open up. He was brusque and businesslike, which made Phoebe increasingly tense.

'Are you looking forward to ten days to yourself?' she asked when they were travelling along a stretch of road that gave her a moment's reprieve from the mechanics of driving.

'Concentrate on what you're doing, Phoebe. We're coming up to a junction and I want you to turn right. You need to start moving into the outside lane.'

'Looking forward to it that much, are you?' Phoebe said before tapping on the indicator. An intermittent click sliced through the silence that Paul refused to fill.

After a couple more failed attempts to start up a conversation, Phoebe got the message. He didn't want to be there. He had barely looked at her twice and she wished she didn't feel so hurt by his indifference. She had had her chance with Paul and she had thrown it away, along with the future they might have shared. He was undoubtedly hurting after being told he was infertile, she knew that, but what could she do? What could she say?

Phoebe knew exactly what she could say, but for once she listened to the warning voice in her head. Ignoring Paul's next instruction to take a turn that would lead them further away from home, Phoebe pulled over sharply to the kerb and said, 'I want to go back.'

'But we've only been out fifteen minutes.'

'It's obvious you don't want to do this, Paul, so please, take me home.' She had twisted in her seat and was pulling on the door handle when Paul reached over and grabbed her left hand tightly.

'Ow!' she cried as he crunched bruised fingers and pain shot up her arm.

'Oh, God, Phoebe, I'm sorry. Are you all right?'

Shaking her throbbing hand, Phoebe turned to him with tears stinging her eyes. 'Please, Paul. I'm sorry I've wasted your time. Just take me home.'

When she made a move to open the door again, he said, 'Wait, Phoebe. It's me who should be apologizing. It's my fault. I shouldn't have come over given the mood I'm in.'

Phoebe reluctantly settled back in the driving seat but made no comment.

'I suppose you know what happened with the consultant,' he said. 'It's because of me that we can't have kids and in a matter of days we've gone from comforting each other to Julia comforting me. No, actually that's wrong. Not comforting – *pitying* me. I'm a complete and utter failure, Phoebe, and I see it in her eyes every time she looks at me. Take the other night when you all went out to the Elephant. Apparently I'm too fragile a soul to go out into the cold to pick you up any more. I had a go at her for it and now she's trying to prove the opposite by coming up with ways for me to feel useful, like giving you lessons again.' He laughed bitterly before continuing. 'Only a month ago she was worried I might be enjoying your company a little too much and now she's practically gift-wrapping me for you.'

Inside Phoebe's head, she was screaming at herself to get out of the car. She cared so much about Julia and she didn't want to hurt her or see her hurt, but she couldn't be expected to sit there and listen to Paul's problems as if her feelings didn't matter. Had he really managed to convince himself that what had gone on between the two of them had never happened, or did he just not care?

'You and Julia aren't the only ones with problems at the moment, Paul,' she said, not resisting the surge of anger when it came. 'I'm sorry you're struggling to have a baby, but you still have each other. If you weren't so self-absorbed and focused on what you don't have, then maybe you could start appreciating what you do have. I'm sick and tired of looking after other people, of putting their feelings before my own. Years of not meaning anything to anyone!' She was glaring at him, willing him to look at her, willing him to *see* her, but he had put his hand over his face. Her body was shaking but surprisingly not her voice when she added, 'I can't do this any more. Sort your own lives out, Paul, and leave me out of it.'

She had jumped out of the car before Paul could stop her this time, only to find him blocking her path when she ran around the back of the car. 'For fear of repeating myself, Phoebe, I'm sorry. I know I'm an idiot and I stick my head in the sand and don't see what's going on around me. But I'm not as self-absorbed as you think.'

He was looking straight at her, only now she wished he wasn't. She was looking at him too. 'I shouldn't have said all of that,' she offered as she waited for the guilt from one or both of them to sever the connection between them that had no right to be there.

He took a step closer. 'I deserved it. I shouldn't be burdening you with my problems, it's not fair.' With that, he took hold of her left hand gently in his and examined her injuries, which were still painfully apparent. 'I felt awful when Julia told me what your nan did, I still do. I was nearly on the sharp end of that stick once, remember?'

Phoebe's skin prickled with goose bumps. It had been the last time Paul had taken her home, the last time they had been able to show their feelings for one another. Even their break-up had been via a third party.

'You had a lucky escape,' she said.

'Did I?'

Phoebe blinked and tried to remember what Helen had said about putting friendship before any man but it was Lucy's words that came back to haunt her. Making mistakes was simply a way of proving she was still alive and up until that moment she hadn't realized how dead she had been feeling inside. When Paul lifted her hand to his lips every nerve in her body began to sing and she didn't pull away, in fact, she did the opposite. She moved closer until she could feel his jacket pressing against her chest. Paul let go of her hand so that he could cup her chin and lift her face towards his. Looking into his eyes, she could see he was fighting with his own emotions, but now that he was looking at her, *really* looking at her, he couldn't turn away, not now.

'We can't,' she said and with those words still wet on her lips, he kissed her.

The sound of traffic speeding past was drowned out by the frantic beating of her heart, which was sending all the blood to her head. She closed her eyes and concentrated on every detail of that kiss, the warmth, the taste, the sensation of his breath on her lips. She wanted Paul to pull her back into the car, to push her down on the back seat and let his hands slide up her dress. It didn't take much imagination to picture how that might play out, it had happened once before and had ended badly for her, and it would again if only for entirely different reasons.

Paul felt her tensing and he pulled away, forcing them both back to reality. He looked as horrified as Phoebe and even went so far as to wipe his mouth with the back of his hand as if that could erase the last few moments. 'I don't know why . . . I never meant to . . . Phoebe, I'm sorry. I love Julia.'

Phoebe was shaking her head as she took a handful of steps back, completely unaware that she was heading towards oncoming traffic until Paul lunged at her and pulled her back. She shrugged him off. 'Go away, Paul.'

'I can't. We can't leave things like this.'

A new wave of anger slammed into Phoebe and words that she never thought she would utter to a living soul poured from her mouth. 'Of course you can! You found it easy enough first time around, didn't you? And like you said, you love Julia and so do I. Don't you worry about the mess you're leaving behind,' she said, spitting the words out with venom. 'I suppose I should count myself lucky. At least this time I'm not pregnant!'

'What?'

'If I were you I'd ask those doctors to rerun their tests, Paul. You weren't always firing blanks.'

Phoebe went to walk away but he put a hand roughly on her shoulder. 'No, Phoebe! You don't just drop a bombshell like that and walk away. You . . . We had a baby?'

She sneered when she said, 'No, Paul. Like everything else about us, it was aborted before it had the chance to develop.'

Paul shook his head as if her words didn't make sense. 'Why the hell didn't you tell me?'

307

'You weren't there. You'd made your choice and I was left to make mine, limited as it was.'

Paul's body went limp and he didn't protest when Phoebe stormed off. She began walking in the direction of home although at that point she didn't care where she was heading as long as she was putting more distance between them.

24

The Accident

Every time Anya walked past the side ward, she glanced towards the two beds nearest the door. Julia Richardson and Phoebe Dodd had spoken only briefly after Anya had left them earlier, and were now behaving as if they were complete strangers.

Phoebe was the more alert of the two, while Julia spent most of her time sleeping, having again complained of feeling far too nauseous to stomach food. It was only when Anya or one of the other nurses checked on her that she had opened her eyes. Her gaze would inevitably settle on Phoebe and then she would close her eyes tightly again, as if desperate to return to her dreams.

After catching up on paperwork, Anya should have taken her break but chose instead to make a call. She had promised Julia she would check up on her friend in the CCU and she wanted to give her some news, even if it was simply confirmation that there had been no new developments which, given Helen's condition, was the best they could hope for at present.

On her way back to deliver the message, Anya was confronted by another familiar face and before he had the chance to speak, she said, 'I'm sorry, Mr Richardson, but you can't see her.'

'And I'm sorry, but I don't care whether I have Julia's permission or not,' he said, 'or yours for that matter.'

Turning his back on Anya, Paul headed down the corridor. Despite his strong words, his steps were tentative and when he reached the open doorway to the side ward, he remained on the threshold where Julia would have seen him if she hadn't been sleeping.

'Maybe you should come back later,' Anya suggested.

Paul appeared not to hear her. His wife held his focus as he approached her bed. He reached out and touched her hand so gently that she would barely have felt it.

'You told her, didn't you?' he said quietly.

Anya only realized the question had been directed at someone other than herself when that person spoke.

'Yes,' Phoebe said.

'Did you tell her everything?'

Julia peeled open her eyes and recoiled from her husband's touch. 'You tell me,' she said.

25

Julia set about making dinner as if she were a white witch concocting a magical potion to right all wrongs. The sun had set, and as she chopped vegetables and ground herbs, she kept to the warm pools of light from downlights that left deep pockets of shadow all around her. She was preparing a hearty stew that she would keep simmering on the stove until Paul came home.

He had gone to the gym straight from work, having kept to a demanding regime despite losing his tag partner. Julia's decision to slow down and relax had been an attempt to help her conceive and now that she knew her fitness wasn't the main problem to be solved, she had lost her mojo. After going to the gym once already that week, she felt no inclination to return and with the holiday only four days away, there were more important things to do, and that wasn't even including her packing.

It had been two weeks since they had seen the consultant and Julia still wasn't sure how Paul was dealing with the news; she wasn't even sure how she felt for that matter. Their relationship had been under constant strain and it seemed as if each time they righted themselves after a wobble, something else came along. She couldn't remember the last time she had felt contented and it was taking a concerted effort from one or both of them to do what had once come naturally. Julia's stomach churned as she continued to grind the herbs using a large pestle and mortar. Something felt wrong; something that went beyond their physiological problems and it was unsettling her.

She was busily stirring her Teflon-plated cauldron when she heard the front door open, followed by a shock of cold air that rushed down the hallway to stir up the cloud of steam rising from her witch's brew. Pretending not to have noticed his arrival, Julia lifted a wooden spoon and blew gently before tasting. The herbs she had been prescribed by the Chinese herbalist a customer of hers had recommended purported to promote male fertility and was one of the few remedies they had yet to try. It wasn't meant to be an overnight cure, but adding it to food two or three times a week might help improve the odds, just a little. Mixed with all the other herbs and spices in the stew, it couldn't be detected and while she knew she ought to mention it to Paul, it smacked of desperation.

Julia and Paul had been putting off talking about the full implications of the hospital results. They had said the things they were supposed to say to each other: how it was good knowing what they were up against, how they wouldn't rush into making hasty decisions, and how, whatever they decided, it would be a joint decision. What that decision might be was the part they hadn't yet faced.

'That smells nice,' Paul said.

He was standing behind her and slipped his arms around her waist. His peppermint-scented breath warmed her ear. 'So do you,' she said.

'I wouldn't be too sure about that. Have I got time for a shower?'

'Didn't you have one at the gym?'

'Too busy,' he said. He kissed her neck, his lips lingering on her flesh for a moment as if he were so drained he needed to absorb some of her energy. He took a breath as he straightened up. 'I won't be long.'

By the time Paul returned downstairs, dinner was ready and before he could suggest crashing out in front of the TV, Julia had set the table.

'Have we had a power cut or something?' he asked, looking suspiciously around the kitchen-diner where tealights twinkled on the table.

'Ambience.'

His smile almost hid the frown. 'Am I being seduced?'

'Do you want to be?' she asked, knowing how he would be visualizing a calendar in his head, counting out the days. 'And no, this isn't a trap, I'm not *ovulating*. That particular window of opportunity has come and gone – and for the record, I didn't check. There are no ulterior motives, Paul. I just want to remind my husband of what he'll be missing next week.'

'I already know what I'll be missing,' he said as he went over to the stew bubbling on the stove and tested a spoonful. He closed his eyes in pure ecstasy and groaned. 'The most amazing home cooking for one thing.'

'It had better be more than my culinary skills you'll miss.'

Paul watched as Julia went to the fridge and took out a fancy fruit cordial packaged up like a bottle of wine but fooling no one. 'I hope you realize I'll be living off takeaways and crates of lager while you're away.'

Gritting her teeth, Julia said, 'I don't suppose I can argue with anything you do. You're a free agent for ten whole days.' As she scrutinized his face, the paranoia she had thought she had conquered returned with a vengeance and she felt the need to add, 'As long as you don't forget you're a married man.'

Paul blushed. 'Excuse me, *you're* the one who's about to gallivant around the world while I'll be coming home from work to an empty house. Shouldn't I be saying that kind of thing to you?'

Their playful teasing had an edge to it and Julia had learned of late that it didn't take much to tip either of them over the edge. 'I really am going to miss you,' she said and felt her heart ache a little. 'I don't even know why I agreed to go.'

The pain she felt was reflected in Paul's words. 'Because you deserve a break from your fraud of a husband.'

'You're not a fraud, Paul,' Julia said, knowing it was a label she would have readily applied to herself if the results had been different. 'You are everything I could ask of the man I want to spend the rest of my life with. I'd be lost without you.'

'Does that mean I should worry about you finding your way back home?' Paul said, trying to keep the conversation light.

He wouldn't look at her and was edging towards the dining table to escape the conversation he had inadvertently opened up until she put a hand on his arm. 'No, never,' she said.

Paul's shoulders sagged and she could see his jaw clench as he wrestled with his thoughts. When he spoke, there was such a clear note of defeat in his voice that it frightened her. 'I'm sorry, Julia. I'm just so sorry.'

'For what?' she asked with a horrible, sinking feeling.

He shook his head. 'Nothing,' he said, but then added, 'But we do need to talk.'

'Yes,' she said, although suddenly it was the last thing she wanted. She had an irrational fear that Paul had more on his mind than she would want to know.

They held off speaking again until the food was served and they had settled at the table with candlelight between them and shadows all around.

'I've made such a mess of everything, and I know we're not supposed to apportion blame, but it *is* my fault,' Paul began, and when Julia tried to object he held up a hand. 'Please, let me do this, Julia. I feel like we've been fighting against the tide for so long, in fact we still are, and I'm the one that's dragging us down. We can skirt around the issues all we like and you can tell me that it's a joint effort but the facts speak for themselves. For my sins, Julia, I can't give you babies. I'm the one at fault, and it's left me feeling . . .' He dug his fingers into his eyes and when he dropped his hand, he was looking straight at her. 'Emasculated, I suppose. I've let you down in the worst possible way and I can't make things right.'

A thousand thoughts buzzed inside Julia's head and she struggled to grasp even one that might give Paul a response that would make him feel better. She wanted to tell him that it was completely and utterly wrong for him to blame himself, but she had already told him so on more than one occasion and it had done nothing to ease his conscience. The cause of their infertility could so easily have been rooted with her and for the last two years, that was what she had feared. 'If you want me to say I think it's your fault then I'm sorry but I can't,' she said. 'However, I will accept that it's a physical fault in your body that's made it difficult for us to conceive a child, but it's still *our* problem, Paul, not yours alone. We have to work through this together. We have to find a solution that suits us both, be that assisted conception, IVF, artificial insemination or even adoption. And if any or all of those options don't work for us then I won't blame you because it's *our* problem, our joint responsibility. The only possible issue I'd have is if you didn't want to try any more. We've had our break like you wanted but when we go back to see the consultant we need to give him an answer. We need to know what we want. I know what *I* want, Paul. Do you?'

'I want *you*, Julia. I know that now more than ever and I'll move heaven and earth to make you happy,' he told her but there was still that note of defeat in his voice as if he thought he had already lost her.

'This isn't just about me, Paul. What makes you happy? Do you still want kids?'

'What if I don't deserve them? What if I don't deserve *you*?'

'Don't you dare say that!' Julia said, only just managing to keep her voice low. 'Don't let these stupid fertility results convince you that you're any different to the man

I married. You would make the most amazing father if only you had the chance. So, I ask again, do you still want kids, Paul?'

'Yes.'

'And are you willing to go through all the stresses and strains that are bound to come with whatever option we choose?'

Despite Julia's outburst, Paul looked all the calmer for it. 'I can't promise I'm going to find it easy, but then I don't think you will either. If we go for medical intervention then it's going to get very clinical and intrusive, and the more effort – and possibly money – we put into it, the more devastated we're going to be if and when it doesn't work. Are *you* ready for that?'

'No,' she said honestly. 'But at the moment I feel like we're dealing with this separately. We need to get back to a place where this feels like we're in it together. We have to be open and honest with each other.' As she spoke, her words became awkward and a flush rose to her cheeks.

'What is it?'

'I came across a herbal remedy.' She looked meaningfully over at Paul's half-eaten stew.

'Why should I not be surprised,' he said and thankfully laughed.

'So do you have any confessions?' she asked, wondering if he'd had a quick pint on his way home and that was why he had been eating mints before coming inside the house.

Pushing his chair back, Paul got up and moved towards Julia. Dropping to his knees, he took her hand in his. 'I love you, Julia. That's my only confession.'

She leaned towards him until their noses were touching. 'And I love you so much it takes my breath away.'

'Like this?' he whispered and pulled her closer.

Even as they kissed they were tumbling onto the floor, giggling like teenagers. When Paul lifted himself over her, Julia wrapped her arms around his neck and ran her fingers though his hair before grabbing his deep brown locks in her hands. She made him hold her gaze until his eyes cut so deep into her she felt them slice through the problems she had allowed to wrap around her. 'I lost you for a while, didn't I?' she asked.

'But I'm back now,' he whispered.

As he kissed and caressed her, Julia felt more complete than she had for years. In that moment, she didn't want for anything else and she believed that Paul felt the same.

While Paul spent the rest of the evening dozing on the sofa, Julia carried on with her packing. She was running out of time to get everything ready and still had one last day to spend at work, which was going to be a busy one. Her bespoke anniversary jewellery had become a phenomenon and she had already adapted the design in such a way that kept the anniversary pieces unique to her client while meeting the increasing demands for what was becoming a range.

She wasn't even going to have time to squeeze in some shopping in her lunch hour the next day because she had agreed to meet Helen. Her friend had already finished work because she needed the time to organize not only her own packing but Milly's too and, understandably, it was breaking her heart. It was breaking Julia's too although she knew her feelings were inconsequential in the scheme of things, and she would have to appear strong and resolute for Helen's sake.

Focusing on the matter at hand, Julia had her suitcase splayed out on her bed and was scratching her head as she tried to work out what she needed as opposed to what she wanted to take. Her wardrobe doors were open and she was desperately searching for a particular black dress that she could match with various accessories to suit different occasions, but it wasn't there. When she had all but given up she found it crumpled at the back of the wardrobe, having fallen off its hanger where it had remained in the shadows gathering dust.

'Damn, damn, damn,' she said as she held it up to the light. She considered sponging the marks, but when she lifted it to her nose it had acquired a distinct mustiness that wasn't going to be disguised by perfume.

Even in her haste, Julia wouldn't waste a wash cycle on one garment and hunted around for anything else to add to the load. The laundry basket was half-full, but still not satisfied, she went through Paul's gym bag which he had left unopened in the bedroom on his way to the shower. She pulled out a scrunched-up grey T-shirt first and was about to fling it into the laundry pile when something stopped her. She unfolded it, not sure at first what had caught her attention or why there was a frown forming on her brow. It was dry, unstained and, sniffing it like a bloodhound that had just caught a scent, it smelled of fabric conditioner.

With her hackles raised, she searched through the rest of the bag. His shorts *did* look used but given that he often wore the same pair more than once, that wasn't enough to settle her growing unease. As expected, the towel was unused because he had said he hadn't showered at the gym and there at the very bottom of the bag was the small hand towel he took into the gym to mop up sweat while he was working out. That was most definitely used and she released a sigh of relief. What had she been thinking?

She was being silly, she told herself, and Paul deserved better. The man who had held her in his arms, looked deep into her eyes and told her he loved her, hadn't lied.

What had she been thinking? she asked herself again.

With a collection of shopping bags surrounding her like a force field, Helen was oblivious to the mutterings from fellow diners who tried to get past as she concentrated on sorting through the crisp till receipts acquired during her early morning shopping expedition.

'You've been busy,' Julia noted as she stepped over a Zara bag to reach a chair.

'And I've bagged a few bargains,' her friend announced proudly. 'In fact, I think I've got just enough left to be able to treat us to lunch, although it's a good job Phoebe couldn't join us because that might have pushed me over my allocated budget.'

Julia gave her a quizzical look. 'You? Budget?'

'Chris has been giving me some tips on how to manage my finances.'

'Has he now? And what else has he been giving you?'

'We've had a few meetings, that's all.'

It had taken a moment too long for Helen to assume her poker face and her smile gave her away.

'They're called dates, Helen, stop pretending they're not.'

Helen shrugged and said, 'We'll see.'

She liked Chris. In fact, she liked Chris a lot, but she couldn't be sure if he had entered her life at precisely the right, or precisely the wrong, time. She was going away just when she wanted to get to know him better, and they had certainly been getting to know each other intimately. But what if he lost interest while she was on holiday? On the positive side, she would have plenty of time to spare when she did get back – except, given how her stomach clenched whenever she thought of life without Milly the Millstone, it felt anything but positive. Helen was going to be a wreck when she came home to an empty house and no man could fill the void her daughter would be leaving behind.

After the waitress had taken their order, she steered the conversation back on track. 'The point I was making is that I gave myself a limit on what I could spend this morning and I've stuck to it.'

Julia took the hint and decided not to push the subject, for now at least, and chose instead to eye the shopping bags. 'But I thought the idea was we would take as little as possible and go shopping crazy while we were away?'

'Not all of it's for me. Most of it's for Milly to take when she moves in with her dad.'

'There's no chance she might still change her mind, is there?'

The desperation in Julia's voice was echoed in Helen's when she replied, 'Never say never, but John has spent a fortune doing up her bedroom. I was dragged in to see it

321

the other day.' She had been dropping her daughter off at John's and, oblivious to the knife twisting into her mother's heart, Milly had insisted she take a look. 'The house smelled of happy families, Julia, from fresh baking to muddy boots.'

'And baby powder?'

Helen nodded. 'Little wonder Milly's been tempted into their world, but I've bought some picture frames so she can put up photos of the two of us, all in the vain hope that she won't forget me.'

'She's not cutting you out of her life completely, Helen. You're simply reversing the arrangements you already have with John. You get the good bits and he gets the dirty laundry and the tantrums.'

'Nice try,' Helen said, 'but we both know it's going to be horrible.'

'I know.'

When the conversation risked becoming maudlin, Helen said, 'Do you want to see what else I've bought?' She delved into a bag and pulled out an exquisite red dress. 'I couldn't resist this and it was on sale. We are still sharing our wardrobe, aren't we?'

'If that dress is part of the deal then yes, most definitely. I'm taking that LBD you like,' she said, her voice trailing off as her face darkened.

'What?'

Julia was shaking her head. 'Nothing. Nothing at all.' She gave Helen a bright smile and then looked far too excited about the plate of pasta that had just arrived. 'This looks delicious.'

Helen didn't so much as glance at her food, she was

too busy dissecting the happy expression on her friend's face. 'What's wrong, Julia?'

Pushing the penne around her plate, Julia looked as if she was searching for the answer to the question Helen had posed. 'I think this holiday is way overdue,' she said at last. 'I need to clear my head and when I get back, I'm getting things back on track.'

'With Paul?'

Julia nodded.

'He must be finding it difficult,' Helen offered.

'This whole fertility business has left him feeling *emasculated*.' When Helen raised her eyebrows, Julia added, 'His words, not mine. And what does a man do when he feels his manhood is being questioned?'

Helen had taken a mouthful of food, which fortunately prevented her from saying the first thing that came to mind. With more time to think, she replied, 'Give his wife a good . . .'

The comment raised a fleeting smile but Julia wouldn't be appeased. 'I mean, as well as that,' she said and waited for Helen to try again. Still refusing to say what she was thinking, Helen shovelled another forkful of pasta in her mouth, and Julia was forced to say it for her. 'What he does is go out and prove himself with other women.'

Helen chewed on her pasta as if her life depended on it.

'I know what you're thinking,' Julia said. 'I've been more than a little insecure lately and I'm being irrational.'

'Paul loves you.'

'Yes, I know. He said that very thing to me last night.'

'But?'

'But he also said he was sorry. For what?'

'For not being able to give you babies, of course.'

'He said he didn't deserve me. Why? What if there's more to this than he's letting on?'

Helen felt some sense of relief. 'If the only damning evidence you have against Paul is that he said he was sorry without prompting then there must be a hell of a lot of guilty husbands out there. If there was such a thing as a Husband's Handbook, I'd say apologizing to your wife at least once a day, whether you've done something wrong or not, would be covered in the first chapter.'

Julia didn't look convinced. 'It wasn't the only thing, Helen. I was emptying his gym bag last night and his T-shirt was crumpled but it most definitely hadn't been worn. Other stuff in the bag had been used but that could so easily have been from the other night when we had gone to the gym together. If he was being clever about it then he would have kept the same shorts, not rinsed through his hand towel like he normally would and, knowing that I might pick up on him not changing his shirt – which he always does – he could have thrown in a clean one, crumpled it up and hoped it would look used.'

Helen opened her mouth to challenge Julia's theory but her friend hadn't finished. 'And he had a shower as soon as he got in. He usually has one at the gym.'

'Usually, but not always?'

'Not always when I'm with him because I'd rather get washed and changed at home. When he's on his own, he tends to shower there unless it's too busy.'

'And was it busy?'

'He says so.'

'And did he look like he'd had a workout when he

324

came home?' Helen asked before snapping her mouth shut. There was more than one way to get hot and sweaty.

'I didn't notice. I was in the kitchen and barely gave him a second look. All I could smell was the mint he'd been eating. What if that was part of his plan to cover his tracks? What if he was trying to disguise the smell of another woman?'

'But he loves you,' Helen said, only her argument wasn't holding together as strongly as it should.

'I keep telling myself I'm being paranoid and we're still coming to terms with what the consultant said. It's not like Paul could have gone out and found someone else so quickly, is it?' Julia had that desperate look in her eyes that pleaded with Helen to tell her that her suspicions were unfounded. 'Am I talking utter rubbish?' she asked.

'You? Always.'

'Do you think I should confront him?'

'If he's guilty then I'm sorry, short of sending his T-shirt off to forensics, you haven't got anything that he couldn't deny. And unless he gives you an outright confession, there's nothing Paul will be able to say or do that will put your mind at rest. You'll only make things worse and, not wanting to sound selfish, it's not exactly going to make a great start to our holiday.'

'Sorry, I shouldn't have opened my big mouth. You shouldn't have to put up with my neurosis on top of everything else.'

'It's OK. You had to tell someone and it was better me than Paul.'

'Yes, but still, I probably should have talked to Phoebe about it, rather than burdening you.'

'Maybe,' Helen said and wondered what her friend would have made of Julia's fears.

Phoebe hadn't been able to join them for lunch and they had barely spoken in the last few days. Someone with a suspicious mind might think she was being evasive, and unfortunately for Phoebe, that someone was Helen.

26

The Accident

'Julia, I don't know what to say . . .'

'Why don't you try saying *sorry*. That usually works, doesn't it, Paul?'

His mouth moved and when the words wouldn't come, Julia looked straight through the broken man standing in front of her and towards Anya. For a moment, it seemed she would retain her icy composure, but then Julia's face creased up with pain. The nurse stepped quickly towards the pump administering a steady stream of morphine to her patient. Her finger was already hovering over the booster button when she asked, 'Do you need more pain relief?'

Julia's eyes refocused, locking on the machinery. 'No, it's not that kind of pain! And I said I didn't want any drugs. Take this thing out of me,' she said, glaring at the cannula protruding from her arm.

'Until you're able to eat and drink properly, that has to stay. Your pain relief has been reduced, but you do need something.'

'Then why can't I think straight? I need to think straight,' Julia moaned but she was already giving up the fight.

'Let me explain, Julia, please,' Paul said.

When Julia shook her head, a tear slipped down the side of her bruised face. 'No, leave me alone, Paul. I can't bear to look at you.'

'He's right,' Phoebe said. 'We need to talk about this.'

'Shut up, Phoebe, just shut up!' Julia said. 'Haven't you caused enough damage? If I am ever ready to talk about this then it won't be with *you*. I'm not even sure it's going to be with *him*.' She glared at Paul briefly before turning her attention to Anya. 'How's Helen? Is there any news?'

'That's what I was coming to tell you,' Anya said. 'She's breathing on her own now and her sedation is being withdrawn gradually.' The relief on Julia's face was short-lived when Anya was forced to add, 'There's still some way to go yet. Her head injury is serious and we won't know what damage there is, if any, until she comes round.'

'Will you let me know as soon as she does?'

'She'll be fine,' Paul said.

'She'd better be.'

Despite the drugs, Julia managed to hold Paul's gaze and he was the one who looked away. 'I know, Julia. I know it's my fault.'

Julia's voice was a strangled whisper when she said, 'I loved you, Paul. We had—'

'Auntie Julia!' came a desperate cry.

Milly had pelted at full speed into the room and weaved between Anya and Paul to reach Julia. There was a gasp of pain as the little girl wrapped her arms around Julia's bruised body before anyone could stop her, but rather than push her away, Julia clung to her as the young girl began to sob.

'Oh, Milly, honey. Are you all right? What's happening with your mum?'

Milly's face was buried against Julia's shoulder and her words were unintelligible until Julia lifted up the girl's face and, with a few soothing words, managed to coax a coherent answer from her. 'She won't wake up, Julia. Everyone's so scared and they don't know if she ever will. I talked and talked and I told her I would do anything, *anything*, if she would just open her eyes but she's still asleep.'

Anya glimpsed an out-of-breath John Butler coming to a halt at the doorway after chasing his daughter through the hospital. He approached the group slowly and had to squeeze his nose between his thumb and forefinger to regain his composure before he could talk.

'They think she might have suffered brain damage,' he said, at which point his daughter's wails intensified.

Julia made soft, shushing noises and eventually Milly was able to speak. 'We have to wake her up, Auntie Julia,' she cried between rasping breaths. 'I need her to wake up.'

Turning to Anya, Julia said, 'I have to see her.'

'And me,' Phoebe added.

Before Anya could object, the two women began pulling themselves up, and paid no heed to the various tubes they were connected to.

'You can't,' Anya said, lunging towards Phoebe who was meant to remain immobilized until the surgeon was satisfied there was no further risk of her rupturing her spleen. The nurse hadn't been so concerned about Julia who had one leg completely encased in plaster and was therefore the least capable of getting very far, or so Anya thought.

'Paul, get me a wheelchair,' Julia ordered.

'No!' Anya said more firmly this time.

'Either you help me get to Helen or I'm discharging myself and I'll find my own way there,' Julia replied.

'I'm coming too,' Phoebe said.

27

Milly would be moving out on Saturday morning, giving her just enough time to work out if she had forgotten anything before Helen set off on the first leg of her holiday two days later. This meant they should have been spending Friday evening double-checking what Milly had packed, but it was their last night together before everything changed so, unsurprisingly, they found themselves snuggled up in front of the TV.

The American sitcom they were watching was one of a long stream of programmes that Milly would watch nonstop if she had her way, which wasn't very often, but tonight Helen raised no objection. Her mind was elsewhere, and as she kissed the top of her daughter's head she breathed in the scent of her and wondered if she would be able to recall that distinctive Milly smell when she wasn't there. She hoped so, but she wished she didn't have to.

'What was that for?' Milly asked. She had kept her eyes on the TV while upturning her face towards her mum.

'Because—' Helen had to stop, caught out by emotions

that had quickly risen to the surface and had to be swallowed back. 'Because I'm going to miss you.'

Still not looking at her mum, Milly dropped her head onto Helen's shoulder and pushed against her body. 'I'm going to miss you too.'

After the embarrassment had passed, Helen expected her daughter to relax back into a comfortable silence. It was only when she gave Milly a gentle squeeze that she realized her daughter was holding her body so taut it was making her tremble. 'Are you OK?' she asked.

Milly's body shook that little bit more in what was a poor attempt at a nod. Despite the roiling emotions, Helen was tempted to remind her daughter that this was all her doing. It had been her decision and her decision alone to go so there was no point moaning about it now. She had not only wanted to live with her dad, she had demanded it.

Their argument over the laundry felt like a lifetime ago and they had both come a long way since then. Helen had learned the hard way that her daughter had her own needs, her own opinions and her own way of doing things. As Milly's mother, Helen was meant to guide her towards independence, not control her every move and then complain when she rebelled, but she wasn't the only one who had learned a thing or two. Milly had been forced to realize that her mother wasn't perfect, that she had been making it up as she went along and sometimes she had got it wrong.

'It's going to take a while for us all to adapt,' Helen offered. 'Even though you've stayed with your dad and Eva often enough, it's going to be different – for all of us.'

'Eva's said she won't be trying to take your place.'

The thought hadn't even occurred to Helen and it pained her to imagine it now. When she gave Milly another hug, she squeezed shut her eyes. 'I'm glad to hear it. If I was going to be made completely redundant, I might as well stay in New York.'

This time when Milly lifted her head towards her mum, she did look at her. Tears were welling in her eyes. 'You will come home, won't you?'

'Of course I will. I couldn't live without you, Milly, and I'll be counting down the days until you get to stay with me.'

Milly's lips cut a sharp line across her face, albeit a sharp line that quivered. She continued to shake and when she did speak, her words came out in a trembling rush. 'And I can't live without you! I don't want to go, Mum, I want to stay here! I know Dad's spent loads of money doing up my room, but I don't want to live there.'

Her last words were choked, and as Milly began to sob Helen rocked her fiercely. Her first reaction was to imagine John and Eva standing in front of her so she could put two fingers up at them. There you go, she would tell them. You think you have your perfect little family but you're not stealing *my* daughter! Her second, more considered response was to accept that this might just be last-minute nerves. Whether she wanted to or not, Milly would be spending the next week and a half with her dad which gave her plenty of time to renege on any rash promises she might make tonight.

'The choice is still yours to make, Milly, and me and your dad will do our best to make it work, whichever one of us you choose to live with. But when you do choose, there are certain practical arrangements we have to make, so when you make your final decision, you're going to have to stick with it,' Helen said. She was surprised how sensible she sounded and wondered if Chris's influence was coming into play. This might not be a financial decision but Milly's choice would have financial implications and both she and John needed some certainty. 'Go to your dad's and see how it goes while I'm away. I'll let him know you're having second thoughts and we can all sit down and talk it through when I get back.'

'I won't change my mind again,' Milly promised. 'I keep thinking about what Phoebe said about her mum. You might drive me crazy but I'm so lucky to have you as my mum and I'd die if anything happened to you. I wanted to tell you ages ago that I'd changed my mind, but Dad was decorating my bedroom and I was scared it was too late. I want to live with *you*, Mum. I'm already sure and I'm sorry for making you sad.'

Pulling away, Helen waited until her daughter had wiped her eyes and was sitting up rather than cowering in a crumpled mess. 'Look at this face, Milly,' she said. 'Does this look like a sad face to you?'

Milly took her time scrutinizing her mum's features. Her nose wrinkled as she smiled. 'No, it looks like a happy face. A bit funny looking,' she added for fear of sounding too soppy, 'but not sad.'

Helen couldn't stop grinning and even after Milly had gone to bed and she had phoned John to warn him about their daughter's change of heart, she kept her smile. John must have heard it in her voice and while he was none too pleased, he couldn't and wouldn't go against his daughter's wishes. They both knew Milly too well to think they could force her into doing something she didn't want to without suffering the consequences.

It was only when she dialled Phoebe's number that the feeling warming her insides began to cool.

'How's the packing going?' she asked.

'Oh, you know,' Phoebe said with a sigh. 'I've packed and repacked everything three times and now I can't remember what I took out and what I kept in so I'll end up doing it all again tomorrow. How about you?'

'I think I'm almost there, and with Milly going off to her dad's tomorrow, I'll have more time to concentrate,' she said. She chose not to tell Phoebe about the latest development. She wasn't even sure she would say anything until after they were all back from holiday and she was certain that Milly was going to be true to her word this time. In reality, she knew there was no way she would be able to contain her excitement for that long, but it was an idea she would keep alive that bit longer. Besides, there were other things she needed to discuss with her friend. 'Speaking of being alone, how are things with you? You've been a bit hard to pin down lately. Have you been throwing wild parties and forgetting to invite your two best friends?'

'Not unless you count the teatime rush at Nan's new digs. Some of those residents would stab you with a fork if you tried to pinch the last piece of Battenberg.'

Helen gave a half-hearted laugh as she racked her brain to think of a way to broach the subject of Julia and Paul. 'At least you don't have those battles at home any more. But it must be weird living in a big, empty house,' she said.

'It won't be forever. I've convinced Nan that we should sell the house sooner rather than later, so I'll be looking for somewhere smaller and more practical in the New Year. It will be a completely fresh start for me, Helen.'

'But while you are there,' Helen persisted, 'you could always have a dinner party to fill the house.'

'A dinner party? Since when did you get all grown up? Does this have something to do with what's-his-name, Chris?'

'Maybe, but assuming you'd be inviting Julia and Paul too, that leaves us a bit unbalanced. We'd have to find a date for you to even up the numbers.'

'Hmm, I think I'd prefer being the wallflower, thank you very much.'

'Wouldn't it be awkward though?'

'No.'

Helen could forgive Phoebe for sounding a little defensive and a lot confused. Her attempt to shoehorn Paul into the conversation was at best crude and Helen grimaced when she said, 'I just meant about Paul being there. It can't be easy switching off your emotions, so don't pretend you have.'

'Helen, why are we even discussing an imaginary dinner party when there are more pressing needs like going on holiday?'

'Sorry,' Helen said. She bit her lip, disappointed that her first line of questioning had reached a dead end but she wasn't giving up. 'To be honest, I'm not sure it would be such a good idea inviting Julia and Paul out anywhere at the moment.'

'Why? What's happened?'

336

'She was telling me over lunch today how worried she is. I'm sure she'll tell you herself while we're away, but . . .'

'But?'

Helen was trying to sound as if she were letting Phoebe into a secret. It was, after all, what she desperately wanted to believe, but as she spoke, Helen's ears strained for any clue to Phoebe's reaction. 'She thinks he's having an affair.'

There was total silence at the other end of the line, not even the sound of breathing. Phoebe was holding her breath and when she released it, her words tumbled out. 'That's ridiculous!'

'That's what I said.' Pressing her phone hard against her ear, Helen wished she could see Phoebe's face. She could hear the odd click and tap and imagined her friend playing nervously with whatever was to hand.

'Is there something particular that's made her suspect him?'

Helen could feel her heart sinking, taking her good mood along with it. Phoebe wasn't asking about Julia's state of mind or the state of her marriage – she was far more eager to hear how Paul had slipped up. 'She thinks he's been going somewhere else rather than to the gym.'

'But that doesn't mean he's having an affair, it just means he's been skipping a session or two. How many people exaggerate their workouts?'

Helen thought long and hard about how to pursue the matter. Did she want to go on holiday with someone she suspected was not only lying to her but, worse still, betraying their friend in the worst possible way? No, she

337

might be wrong: surely Phoebe wasn't capable of such a thing even if she had admitted to still having feelings for Paul? But even as the debate raged inside her head, Helen was already talking. 'Where did he go, Phoebe?'

'What?' There was a loud clatter suggesting that whatever knick-knack Phoebe had been playing with had fallen over. 'Helen, I hope you're not suggesting—'

'Please, Phoebe, tell me I'm wrong. I'm sorry but I really need to hear you say that you wouldn't do that to Julia, that you wouldn't jeopardize a lifelong friendship. Make that *two* lifelong friendships.'

'Nothing's going on, Helen!' Phoebe said.

'Really?'

Phoebe's tone hardened when she said, 'Yes, *really*.'

Helen waited for the rush of relief but it didn't come.

'What else do you want me to say?' Phoebe demanded. 'I swear on my life that I'm no more capable of betraying our friendship than you are. There, is that good enough?'

It wasn't good enough, but Helen couldn't tell Phoebe that the oath was technically worthless because she herself was already guilty of the charge. She had betrayed Phoebe once and the past was catching up with them at a frightening rate. She felt herself bracing for impact.

There was a brief moment when Phoebe had felt rather smug with the answers she had given her friend, but her clever words couldn't ease her conscience. She had lied to Helen, but that wasn't the worst of her sins.

Paul had arrived unannounced on her doorstep the night before, demanding that she tell him everything. Judging by the way he kept his coat on, he had no intention of sitting down and chatting about old times. There was only one thing he needed to know.

'What you said the other day, Phoebe . . .'

She heard the doubt in his voice and reacted to it. 'Was it true? Do you really think I'd make something like that up?'

Paul had no follow-up question prepared and Phoebe was in no mood to offer any more information willingly. She turned her back on him and went into the kitchen to fill the kettle and make drinks that neither of them would want but it was better than looking at Paul's tormented expression.

Phoebe had never intended telling Paul about the baby, it was a secret she had thought she would take to the grave. It was only when Paul's infertility had been brought into question that it had begun to play on Phoebe's mind and she had racked her brain to find a way of telling him without telling him – to reassure him that the results would prove what she already knew, that he was capable of fathering a child. But the results had shown something else and the need to tell him had grown stronger and yet still she had resisted, right up to the moment she had stood at the side of the road and saw that look of horror on his face after they had kissed. She had forgotten all about wanting to help Paul, she had only wanted to hurt him deeply, and judging by the look on his face as he stood in the kitchen staring at the tiled floor, that was exactly what she had done.

'If I'd known . . .' he started, daring to look up briefly, before letting another sentence wither and die. 'Did you tell anyone?'

'I told Nan, and then the decision was taken out of my hands. There was no question about what had to be done. She had gone through the same thing with Mum, only Mum had got her way and kept the baby. Nan didn't need to remind me how badly that had turned out.'

'But was it what *you* wanted?'

'Why do you need to know that?' she asked while trying to make sense of not only her feelings but his too. 'What do you want from me, Paul? Do you want me to tell you I would have gone through with an abortion with or without you? That you're completely absolved? Is that what you want hear?'

He shook his head and, still looking at the damned floor, said, 'I don't know, Phoebe. I've spent the last few days torturing myself, wondering how different things could have been for all of us.'

'I was eighteen years old and I didn't know what I wanted,' she said, which wasn't exactly true. After years of neglect, Phoebe had wanted to be loved – it was as simple as that. She had wanted a little family just like Helen's, except she wasn't at all like Helen. Her friend might have complained about her imperfect life but she had had the kind of stability and security that Phoebe could only dream of. 'I was in no fit state to bring up a child, Paul. I was the one that needed looking after.'

'But it didn't have to be your nan looking after you, Phoebe. I don't know how I would have reacted if I'm honest, but I would have at least been able to give you another option.'

Releasing a sigh, Phoebe turned her back on the man who claimed he would have saved her but wasn't even brave enough to look her in the eye. She debated whether to take one cup or two from the cupboard. The discussion was going nowhere and she wanted him to leave. 'You'd already made your choice, Paul. Why pretend it would have been any different?'

'I don't remember it being my choice, Phoebe. You sent your henchwoman to tell me to keep away, remember? What else was I supposed to do?'

With a clatter of china, Phoebe turned to face him again. 'My nan went to see you?'

'No, I mean Helen,' Paul said, sharing her look of confusion.

'But I sent Helen to tell you— What exactly did she say, Paul?'

He laughed. 'You expect me to remember a conversation I had over ten years ago?'

'Try.'

He scratched his head. 'She said how you had been going through a tough time and that you weren't interested in anything long term and we should cut our losses. I got the impression that it was your nan you needed more than some bloke you barely knew – and it wasn't as if we were in a proper relationship. It was a few nights out, Phoebe, and it made sense to stop before things got too serious. At least it did at the time . . .'

'It's all right, Paul, you don't have to explain, but I think someone else might,' she said. 'That wasn't what I asked Helen to tell you at all. She was supposed to explain how I wanted to carry on seeing you; only it would have to be in secret. I was giving you the choice.'

'So why did Helen lie?'

Phoebe racked her brain to find an answer. 'I suppose she didn't want me to make the same mistake she had,' Phoebe said, her mind refusing to comprehend the full extent of Helen's betrayal. She gave a sad laugh, then added, 'She didn't know I already had.'

'But it wasn't a mistake, Phoebe. It was a new life! We could have – I could have . . .' As he spoke, Paul moved from left to right as if he couldn't decide which way to turn. 'So it was all down to Helen. She's the one who ended our relationship before it had even begun, ended our child's *life* before it had even begun.'

The kettle had begun to boil but it was Phoebe's emotions that were bubbling over. Her friends meant everything to her and she hadn't wanted to lose them, but how was she ever to face Helen again now that she knew the truth? Should she confront her? Would she tell Helen about the pregnancy? Would she tell Julia? Exposing the secrets of the present and the past would leave their friendship in tatters.

'But I was the one who had the abortion, Paul,' she said. 'I can't blame anyone else for that.'

When the boiling kettle switched itself off, it gave Phoebe a start and she had to lean back against the kitchen counter to keep herself from sinking to the floor. How different might her life have been if Helen hadn't interfered? With Paul's support instead of her nan's suppression, she could have been anything she wanted to be. She could have been a woman with substance, not someone who people simply looked though.

Except Paul wasn't looking through her now. He held her gaze as he approached, each tentative step a considered one.

342

'Do you hate me?' she asked.

Paul didn't answer until he was close enough to trail a thumb across her cheek, wiping her tears. 'Not even close, Phoebe.'

As he cupped her face in his hands, Phoebe tried to summon up images of her two best friends. She pictured Julia and Helen, not as grown women with all the hangups they had acquired, but young girls sitting on Helen's sofa watching Disney movies. It had been a long time since Phoebe had imagined herself a beautiful princess but that was how she felt under Paul's gaze.

'This is killing me,' he said. 'I haven't been able to stop thinking about what might have been if only we'd been given the chance.'

Phoebe squeezed her eyes shut and willed herself to disappear again, while fighting a much stronger desire to follow Paul's lead and summon up an alternate life where it wouldn't be wrong to let him do what he did next. When she felt his lips on hers she let out a soft moan and pulled away. 'It's too late,' she said.

'I know.'

With her eyes still closed, she sought out his mouth and kissed him briefly before adding, 'We can't go back, Paul. You love Julia, and I love her too. We can't do this.'

Resting his forehead on hers, Paul traced his hands down her body before resting them on her hips. 'I know,' he said without any attempt to step away. 'But we had something I may never get to share with anyone else, no matter how much I love them. I don't know how to deal with that, Phoebe. I don't know how to stop this ache inside me.'

'We can't . . .'

'Not even once?' he asked. 'I can't walk away, not this time. Not yet.'

When Paul pressed his body against hers, Phoebe offered no resistance and, as he kissed her, she let out a groan that was part pleasure and part frustration. She was done for.

Her body had been on fire and as they made love Phoebe had imagined herself a phoenix rising from the flames, but it was a fire that had burnt out all too quickly. By the time she had spoken to Helen, it was only the guilt that endured and she didn't know how she was going to face her friends.

It was Sunday, 14 February and the three friends had distinctly different starts to their Valentine's Day. Helen woke to find her bed a tangle of sheets and limbs. Chris was lying next to her fast asleep, having sneaked out of bed at some point during the early hours to place a card and a red rose on the bedside table next to her. She picked up the flower and trailed its baby-soft petals across his face, neck and chest. When he didn't wake up she considered hitting him with it but then a smile crept across his face and she giggled like a schoolgirl.

Julia woke with a start when she heard the front door closing and she opened her eyes to find a large pink envelope on the pillow in the place of her husband. Raising herself on her elbow she scanned the bedroom and noticed Paul's running shoes were missing. She checked the clock and hated herself for noting the time, knowing she wouldn't be able to rest until Paul returned, and maybe not even then despite telling herself that he didn't deserve her suspicion.

Phoebe wasn't at all surprised to open her eyes and find her bed as empty as her life. She had spent the last few days struggling to come to terms with what she had done and imagined Paul was doing the same. He had made no attempt to get in touch since leaving her sitting on the kitchen floor, both stunned by and ashamed of what had just happened, and she hadn't expected him to rush back for a repeat performance. They had agreed to forget it had ever happened, little knowing Paul had already aroused suspicion.

She needed to warn him and had tried to phone a number of times the day before, but because it was the weekend, she couldn't risk calling him on his mobile. She had phoned the house on the pretext of wanting to speak to Julia about holiday plans, and it had been Julia who answered each and every time.

Standing in the kitchen in a nightshirt, Phoebe made another attempt to speak to Paul, and yet again he evaded her.

'Hi, Phoebe,' Julia said brightly. 'That's good timing – I was about to phone you. I've just been checking with Helen and I *knew* we shouldn't have relied on her, especially now she's all loved up.'

Phoebe was tempted to make some comment about Helen having a history of being untrustworthy, but she was hardly in a position to criticize, and besides, Julia wasn't talking about the kind of fundamental character flaws that could destroy friendships and marriages. 'Don't tell me,' she said, 'she still hasn't managed to buy everything she was supposed to.'

They had decided to share the long shopping list of all their holiday essentials so they could spread the load and, as always, Helen had left hers until the last minute.

'How did you guess?' Julia said. 'Apparently she spent all of yesterday with Chris and he's still there now!'

'I'm going out to visit Nan this afternoon, so I suppose I could always do a detour to the shops.'

'No, I can do it. Paul's going to drop me off at the retail park for a couple of hours. I did try to persuade him to come with me but he says he'd rather stick pins in his eyes than listen to me twitter on about shampoos and conditioners. I don't think he should get off scot-free though, so I was thinking he could nip to yours and give you one last driving lesson.'

'Oh,' Phoebe said. She needed to speak to Paul but a repeat visit to the house was an entirely different proposition and one she wasn't sure she could deal with. 'I'm not sure I've got time.'

'Please, you'd be doing me a favour. Someone needs to keep tabs on him.'

'Have you actually asked him? He might have better things to do.'

'He'll have more free time than he'll know what to do with while I'm away,' Julia said. 'Honestly, Phoebe, he won't mind.'

Judging by the tone of Julia's voice, her mind was set. 'I suppose,' Phoebe said. She was running her fingers through her hair, which felt lank and dull. 'When were you thinking?'

'We'll be leaving in ten minutes so I'd say he'll be at yours within the hour. And if he isn't, I'll want to know why.'

Julia had yet to voice her concerns to Phoebe, but even if Helen hadn't told her, the playful comment couldn't disguise the fact that her friend's trust in her husband had been dented.

'So what did you want anyway?' Julia was asking.

'Sorry?'

Julia laughed. 'You phoned me, remember?'

'Oh, erm, nothing really,' Phoebe said, trying to remember the spurious excuse she had prepared. 'It was only to see if you wanted me to pick up any last bits and pieces but it looks like you've got that covered.'

Phoebe was on the move even as she ended the call and she was still blow-drying her hair when she saw Paul's car pulling up outside. Whatever the future held for them both, she had decided that she wouldn't spend the next decade being as invisible as she had in the previous. She still felt that need for Paul to look at her, *really* look at her, and to want her, if not as much as Julia, then just a little. The torture of what might have been was no longer hers alone.

'Do you want to go out?' Paul asked with a sheepish look on his face as he stood on the doorstep. He hadn't even ventured inside the porch. 'I have over an hour to kill.'

The idea of a driving lesson took Phoebe by surprise. She had completely forgotten that was why he was coming over and looked down at the high heels she had just slipped on. They were patent leather and went perfectly with the turquoise bodycon dress she was wearing, the one she had bought with the intention of strutting around Manhattan. 'I'd have to change into my boots first.'

Paul bit his lip as his gaze lingered over her curves before he could stop himself. 'It wasn't my idea to come over.'

She smiled at him. 'I know. Come in.'

Without asking, Phoebe led Paul through to the kitchen where, in a repeat of their last meeting, she switched on the kettle. There was an outside chance they might actually have a drink this time.

'Julia knows something's going on,' Paul said. 'I swear the guilt must be written all over my face because in the last couple of days she hasn't been able to look at me. I want to ask her what's wrong but at the same time I'm scared she might just tell me.'

'I can tell you,' Phoebe said as she carried on making the drinks as if this were a normal conversation. 'Julia's told Helen she doesn't think you were at the gym on Thursday. Apparently she's taken to sniffing your clothes.'

'Shit! I really would be rubbish at having an affair.'

'Then it's lucky that you're not having one.'

Continuing to avoid making eye contact, Phoebe looked inside the fridge, which was almost bare, and took her time finding the milk.

'I can't believe what we've done,' Paul said. 'I hate myself. You have no idea how much.'

She turned back and said, 'Oh, I think I do.'

'It can't happen again, Phoebe.'

'Would you want it to?' she asked, more out of curiosity than anything else.

Releasing a sigh, Paul looked around the kitchen as if

the evidence of his infidelity were on display. When his eyes settled back on Phoebe they managed to hold each other's gaze, but unlike Thursday evening there was no connection to be made with the past or the present, and certainly no more unfinished business.

'You're a beautiful woman, Phoebe, and I care about you, but I love Julia. You really do deserve better – and so does Julia. God knows what I'm going to do if she does find out. I suppose it's something that she doesn't suspect you're involved.'

'But someone does.'

Paul's eyes widened in fear. 'Helen? Have you told her?'

'While I would like nothing better than to confront Helen about what she did to us, at the moment I don't feel like I have the right to take the moral high ground.'

'Then how does she know?'

Phoebe turned her attention back to making the drinks, giving herself a moment to think. She didn't want to tell him that she had made a drunken confession about being in love with him. For one thing, she wasn't sure that was how she felt any more. Where once she had felt sick with love, now she felt sick with self-loathing. 'She just knew we were getting closer than we should, that's all,' she said.

'You can't tell her, Phoebe! We can't tell *anyone*,' Paul said. 'I don't know what I thought I was doing, and I'm not saying I don't have regrets about what happened all those years ago, but . . .'

Phoebe picked up two mugs and offered one to Paul while he continued to grapple with his words.

'Shall we go somewhere else?' she asked, and when she

saw the look of horror on his face she found herself smiling. 'I meant to the living room. I wasn't about to seduce you again.'

Paul took his drink and didn't speak until they were both sitting down. 'You didn't seduce me, Phoebe. If anything, I was the one who made the first move.'

Shaking her head, Phoebe said, 'We both have to take responsibility for our actions. It happened and there's nothing we can do about it. It was a moment of madness, a *really* bad one, but it's over now.'

Paul thought for a moment and then said, 'I know we're going to have to lie to other people, but can we at least be honest with ourselves? As moments of madness go, it was a pretty long and drawn out one. I'm not suggesting it goes right back through my entire marriage to Julia, but maybe since I started giving you driving lessons.'

'We'd forgotten how easily we could talk to each other,' Phoebe agreed. 'And you reminded me I once had a spark. You made me want to get it back.'

Paul made sure he was looking at his feet when he said, 'And you *are* getting it back. I just hope I haven't done something to set you back. If I could split myself in two—'

'Don't,' she interrupted, not because she didn't want to hear it but because, finally, she didn't have to. She had felt hollow and wretched for days, and her guilt had been the perfect antidote to her childish infatuation – or at least that was what she had to believe if she were going to move on from this. 'I will get that spark back, Paul, but it'll be through my own accomplishments, and not just a reflection in someone else's eyes.'

350

Paul finally lifted his head and looked at her.

'There is no *us*,' she continued, 'and if things had been allowed to run their course then we would have worked it out long before now. Let's leave it at that, shall we? Agreed?'

'Agreed.'

28

The Accident

Julia and Phoebe were briefly united in their stance. Despite their injuries, which should have slowed them down, they were both hell-bent on seeing Helen, and Anya didn't doubt for a minute that they would follow through with their threats to discharge themselves. She had managed to keep Phoebe in bed for the time being, but Paul Richardson had been less successful in restraining his wife who had made good her threat and already ripped the cannula from her arm.

'You don't seem to realize how serious your condition is,' Anya said to Julia. Turning to Phoebe, she added, 'Or yours. You've both had surgery, and neither of you are fit enough to get out of bed, let alone be discharged. You risk internal bleeding, or further damage that might stop you from making a full recovery, and not to put too fine a point on it, that damage could be fatal.'

During the commotion Milly had been all but forgotten, having flown into her father's arms while Anya and Paul fought to restrain the two unruly patients. It was the fragile child's suppressed sob that brought the group to their senses.

'I'm sorry!' Milly cried. 'I didn't mean to get you into trouble. You can't get out of bed. Please Julia, please Phoebe. I don't want *anyone* to die!'

Julia threw open her arms. 'Milly, it's all right, honey, no one's going to die, I promise.' When Milly failed to accept the hug being offered, Julia looked puzzled until she noticed everyone staring at her left arm where blood was streaming down her forearm.

'I'll get some gauze and call the registrar. He can talk to you about who's fit enough to get out of bed and who isn't,' Anya said.

'And in the meantime, you go back to your mum,' Julia said to Milly. 'Tell her we love her and that we'll come and see her just as soon as we can.'

'Tell her to hang on,' Phoebe added.

When Anya returned with the gauze, Milly and her dad had disappeared and she hoped the immediate crisis was over. 'This is just temporary,' she said to Julia. 'The registrar can decide if you need a new cannula inserted. He's with another patient at the moment but shouldn't be long.'

'Tell him not to bother,' Julia said. 'I'm not staying.'

'Julia,' Paul said, 'listen to what she's saying. You can't move.'

'Don't tell me what to do, Paul! Don't ever tell me what to do again.'

'Please, listen to your husband, Mrs Richardson,' Anya added.

'He's not my husband,' Julia said. 'Not as far as I'm concerned.'

'Please, Julia, I'm begging you,' Paul said, his voice shaking with emotion. 'I know you don't want to hear this now, but I love you. I messed up and I'll admit that for a while I lost sight of what we had because I was consumed by what we didn't have and, I'm sorry, but so did you. If we'd had the chance to talk yesterday before the accident then, if I'm honest – and I swear I'm being more honest than I have been in a long time, with myself as much as you – I probably wouldn't have been able to speak with as much certainty as I can now, but I still would have said the same thing. I know what I want, Julia, and it's you. I need you to give me a second chance. I'll do anything you ask.'

Paul was panting and his cheeks were flushed, but not as flushed as Phoebe's, Anya noted. The nurse was beginning to make sense of what was happening, but their private lives were of little consequence at the moment. She was only concerned with their medical needs and concentrated on cleaning Julia's wound.

'If you want to help, Paul, then find me a wheelchair, something that will cope with this,' Julia said, nodding towards her immobilized leg.

'Any ideas?' Paul asked Anya.

With a sigh, Anya said, 'You'd better ask Sister. She might be able to suggest something,' she said, knowing full well that he was more likely to receive a lecture rather than a wheelchair.

'I love you, Julia,' Paul said as he prepared to leave. 'And I won't rest until I've proved that to you. I won't rest until I make you love me again.'

'Don't hold your breath,' she muttered.

'What about a wheelchair for me?' Phoebe asked, but Paul had turned away and left it to his wife to answer.

'Hasn't he seen to your needs already?'

'Please, Julia, you don't know the whole story.'

Julia stared straight ahead, a snarl of contempt on her face as she watched Paul disappear out of the ward. 'Oh, but I can imagine.'

'No, you don't understand. Back when we first met—'

'I know, Phoebe,' Julia interrupted.

Anya couldn't help herself; she looked up and glanced from Julia's hardened expression to Phoebe's pained features.

'You knew it went further than Paul just giving me a lift home?'

Bristling, Julia said, 'You think Paul and I didn't talk about it? I accepted it was something you didn't want to tell me, but the thing is, Phoebe, you can't keep secrets from your friends as easily as you think. You should have known that before you started fooling around with my husband. Or is that what you wanted? Did you want to be found out?'

Phoebe's breathing had become rapid and Anya thought she might have another crisis on her hands.

'You knew about us?' Phoebe repeated.

'Yes, I know *everything*.'

'But that's where you're wrong,' Phoebe said, not sounding the least bit smug about correcting her.

29

The alarm had been set to give Julia an hour to get ready, have breakfast, then throw the last bits and pieces into her suitcase. They were due to catch the ten o'clock train to London and Paul had booked the morning off to take her to the station, picking up Helen and Phoebe along the way. She was already awake when the alarm went off, but she didn't move. With her back to her husband and her stomach in knots, she heard Paul begin to stir. He rolled towards her and when he kissed her shoulder, she tensed to such a degree that she wanted to be sick.

The warmth of Paul's breath against her skin as he released a sigh sent a shiver down her spine. He had risen up on an elbow and placed his hand on her bare shoulder. She bit her lip as she felt his fingers trail down the length of her arm before sliding over her stomach, which had clenched to hold back another wave of nausea.

'I love you,' he whispered.

The reply that would once have come so easily caught in Julia's throat. In the last few days she had developed quite a clear image of Paul in bed with another woman, one who wouldn't remind him of his failings as a man. She wished she could resurrect the unshakeable trust she had once held, but all she could think about was that unused T-shirt.

'This is where you're supposed to say you love me back,' Paul said.

They both held their breath as she rolled onto her back and looked up at him. 'Are you seeing someone else?' she asked.

Paul's jaw dropped. 'You're about to gallivant around the world and you choose now to accuse *me* of having an affair?'

She regretted the question immediately. 'I'm sorry, but something feels wrong, Paul, and it's scaring me.'

'Well, it doesn't help that you freeze up every time I touch you. Do you want me to find someone else, Julia? Is that it? You once said you were prepared to leave me so I could have children with someone else. Are you hoping I'll make the same kind of sacrifice?'

'No!' she cried. 'I don't care about those bloody fertility results. I care about *us*.'

Paul didn't look convinced and when he made a move to turn away she grabbed him. 'I love you,' she said.

He put his hand over his face and pushed a thumb and forefinger against his eyes, which were glistening. She pulled his hand away and said again, 'I love you.'

When he leaned down and kissed her, Julia kissed him back with more than a little desperation. She wanted so much to revive the passion she knew was buried deep inside but she remained fixated on the possibility that the hands that were gently caressing her body had been exploring another woman's curves. She froze again as another wave of nausea hit her. She felt Paul's body sag and when he pulled away he moved quickly and didn't stop until he had climbed out of bed.

'I'm sorry,' she said.

'I don't blame you. I have nothing to offer you, Julia.'

'Stop it!' she cried, pulling herself up so she was kneeling on the bed. 'Stop putting yourself down at every opportunity – that's what's wrong with us, *that's* why I feel like I'm this constant ball of apology. I'm sorry that we ever went through all those tests and I'm even more sorry that it wasn't me who had the fertility problems! Right now, I'm sorry for ever wanting a baby in the first place!'

'I wanted it too!' he yelled back, his eyes blazing with fear and pain. 'I still do, Julia. You have no idea how much!'

'Please, Paul,' she said, reaching out to him.

He shook his head, taking a step nearer the door. 'We both need some space,' he said. 'Maybe you going away is good timing.'

After he left Julia was tempted to hide back under the covers, but the mounting fear that her marriage might be over twisted her insides and sent her running to the bathroom. She stood with her hands on the white porcelain basin while her body quaked. She had never been so frightened in all her life. She had been racked with nerves on the morning they had been due to see the consultant, but at least then she hadn't felt so alone.

With time ticking by, Julia seriously considered calling off the holiday. Her marriage was more important and her friends would understand. If she went away there was a chance this other woman Paul was seeing – and he hadn't denied it, she noted – would sink her claws deeper into him. Should she stay and fight? Could she forgive him if he had been unfaithful? What if he was deliberately pushing her away? And if they did manage to get through this then how would their marriage stand up to the stress of fertility treatment? They had been offered counselling and perhaps that was something to pursue, but not yet, not until she knew exactly what damage her marriage had already sustained. Julia's body began to sway as her thoughts churned up her stomach. She wanted to trust her husband, even if at that moment it was only blind faith.

Retreating into the safety of routine, Julia began her morning ablutions. She was in a trance as she showered and it was only when she had wrapped herself in a towelling robe and opened the bathroom cabinet that she was pulled up short. The shelves were crammed with ovulation kits and pregnancy tests, along with the sanitary towels that had proven far more necessary. She had stopped tracking her menstrual cycle to the hour but she hadn't ignored it completely and she knew she would need supplies to take away. Picking up a pack, her movements slowed as she visualized a calendar. She was only a day, late and where once she might have paced the floor excitedly as she tried one pregnancy test after another, convinced the last one was faulty, now she knew the fault lay elsewhere. Paul reminded her of it constantly.

Taking a deep breath, Julia kept hold of the sanitary towels while pocketing another item from the cupboard. It was ridiculous to even think of using it, but the warm sensation of hope trickling into her heart gave her the momentum she needed to finish packing and to form a superficial truce with her husband that would paper over the cracks in their marriage, if only for the duration of the drive to the station.

'And relax!' Helen said, as if she and her friends had just completed a strenuous workout. By the look on Phoebe and Julia's faces, the task of dragging their suitcases onto the train had left them completely drained. They had reserved table seats and although that left one vacant space, their fellow passengers had chosen wisely to avoid it, leaving the three friends to enjoy the first leg of their transatlantic journey in relative peace.

Julia was struggling to squeeze her hand luggage into the compartment above the seats. 'Stupid bloody shelf! Why can't they make them bigger?'

'I think you'll find it's your so-called hand luggage that's oversized,' Helen said.

She had already grabbed the first window seat and was feeling decidedly giddy. There had been moments in the last couple of months, if not the last few days, when she thought the holiday wasn't going to happen and yet here they were. She was looking forward to the trip, which would give them a chance to regroup and have a damned good time in the process, especially now she wasn't dreading the return home.

When the whistle blew and the train pulled out of Lime Street Station with a gentle jolt, she added, 'You're going to regret bringing that by the end of the holiday, you mark my words.'

'I'm already regretting it,' Julia muttered.

'Here, let me help,' Phoebe offered.

Being the shorter of the bunch, Phoebe struggled to reach the shelf but the one thing she had that Julia was apparently lacking was a sense of determination. With an almighty shove, the case was forced into place. 'There,' she said, holding onto the back of a chair while the train rocked gently. She offered Julia a weak smile but the miserable look on her friend's face left it to wither on her lips. 'Would you like the other window seat? I don't mind where I sit.'

Julia shook her head. 'No, you take it. Looking out will only make me travel sick.'

Helen was watching them both intently. 'Well, this is a fine start to our holiday. Are you two going to stay this miserable for the entire trip?'

Phoebe and Julia took their seats. 'I'm not miserable,' Phoebe said, refusing to look at Julia. 'It's just been a bit hectic, that's all. But we're on our way now and we can put our troubles behind us.'

Julia's mouth twitched in a vain attempt at a smile, but she didn't speak. It had been impossible not to notice the strained atmosphere between her and Paul on the drive over. Of the two, Julia had been the more animated but it was becoming apparent that she had been putting on an act for her husband's benefit, and her 'happy mask' had fallen.

With Paul out of the way, Helen was about to ask what was going on but Phoebe spoke up first.

'What makes you so cheery anyway, Helen? Or shouldn't I ask?'

Helen had placed her mobile on the table in front of

her and she glanced at it briefly. 'I have some news,' she said.

'Oh, God, she's in love,' Phoebe said, trying to draw Julia into the conversation but only managing to raise another weak smile from her friend.

'Actually, that wasn't what I was going to say,' said Helen. 'My news is that Milly has changed her mind. She doesn't want to live with her dad any more. We had a talk the other night and apparently she's wanted to say something for ages but was afraid that the arrangements couldn't be undone. John's not happy, given how he's spent a small fortune getting her room ready, money he thought he would be saving by not paying child support. I've been trying not to get overexcited – a lot could happen in the next ten days – but she's sent me a text this morning saying she's missing me already and she can't believe she ever thought she could live without me. I'm under strict instructions to pick her straight up the moment we get home from New York.'

'That's wonderful news,' Julia said.

Helen took in the tears welling in her friend's eyes and the stricken look on her face. 'OK, what's going on, Julia?' she asked. 'I'm not going to spend the next two hours, let alone the entire holiday, looking at your long face. If you've fallen out with Paul then phone him now and sort it out.'

'Our problems can't be solved by a phone call, not when I don't know if the person on the other end of the line is telling me the truth or not. We've hit a few bumps in our time, but I'm starting to think we might not recover from this one. I think he's having an affair,' she said for

362

Phoebe's benefit in case Helen hadn't told her. 'I confronted him about it this morning and he pretty much ignored the question.'

Phoebe's eyes widened in shock, although Helen was more inclined to think it might be panic. Helen had thought long and hard about Phoebe's denials and she wanted to believe her lifelong friend, but it was a simple matter of mathematics. Phoebe's feelings for Paul had, by her own admission, been reignited, and Paul was acting suspiciously. Phoebe was feeling vulnerable and so was he. They had once dated and they had been spending time alone together. Two and two came to four every time.

Slow to draw her gaze from Phoebe, Helen asked Julia, 'Did you ask him where he was on Thursday evening?'

'We didn't really have time to go into the specifics,' Julia said.

'Then don't jump to conclusions. You're both under a lot of stress, which is completely understandable, but I have every faith in the two of you. You will get through this, Julia. Won't they, Phoebe?'

The anxious look on Phoebe's face became even more pronounced. 'Yes, of course.'

'Thank you both for putting up with me. I promise not to be a miserable cow for the entire holiday and I will phone Paul and clear the air – tonight. I know it's tough for him at the moment and I should be more understanding, and it's not like he hasn't supported me through my monthly devastations.' Julia's lip trembled as she tried to smile. 'And it doesn't help that I've got a raging dose of PMT at the moment.'

'There, that explains it,' Phoebe offered. 'It's just hormones.'

Julia's face contorted and she looked as if she were trying on various emotions, seeing which one fitted best. 'Sorry, I feel a bit queasy. I need to go to the bathroom,' she said. She picked up her handbag before heading down the aisle towards the toilet, her body swaying as the train jostled her from side to side.

30

The Accident

Lucy was used to feeling unwell but for once she was enjoying the sensation. She felt sick with nerves and had even gone as far as to throw up her breakfast, although she had done so quietly and discreetly. She wasn't ill, far from it. After years of being constantly aware of her mortality, today Lucy felt very much alive and, if anything, it was her mum who looked as though she wasn't going to make it through to the end of the day.

'Don't worry, it's not that heavy,' Lucy said when she noticed her mum testing the weight of her suitcase under the guise of moving it so she could sweep up around the front door.

'You won't push yourself too hard, will you? Let people help, Lucy.'

'Have we ever had a problem finding a helping hand?' Lucy replied, losing patience. The flight wasn't until late afternoon and there were far too many hours left for her mum to fill with anxious questions. 'People take one look at me and fall over themselves to help. I'm your typical charity case.'

'Well, make sure you accept,' her mum said with a sniff.

'I will, stop worrying.'

Her mum shook her head. 'You know I won't do that until you're home again.'

'And even then.'

'Are you *sure* you know what you're doing?'

It took a couple of breaths before Lucy had enough air in her lungs to answer her mum. 'I have to do this, Mum. Is it so wrong to want to live a little?'

'Don't go thinking you'll be able to keep up with your sister.'

'No, but I'd like to die trying,' Lucy snapped back.

Her mum's lower lip trembled. 'Please, Lucy . . .'

'It's for five days, Mum. *Five. Days*. Nothing's going to happen and I'll be back before you know it.'

Their eyes locked and Lucy felt her mum's fear slither towards her and creep up her spine. She wasn't so headstrong that she was ignoring the dangers. Something could go wrong so easily, as often happened in her life. A fever could appear out of nowhere or her heart could decide to go into arrhythmia just for the fun of it. Any one of a number of medical crises could strike at any given moment and if she were in the wrong place at the wrong time, then today might be the last day she and her mum spent together. And that was what she was seeing in her mum's eyes.

'I love you, Mum,' she said.

'And I love you, more than life itself. I just want you to be safe.'

'Can you at least settle for happy?' Lucy asked as she drew closer to give her mum the hug they both desperately needed.

31

The Pendolino train tilted into a bend and Phoebe glanced out of the window to see the countryside sweep past in a green blur. She knew there was a good chance Helen would start asking some more difficult questions the moment Julia was safely out of earshot, so she attempted distraction.

'I was thinking: we could check out the hotel's spa once we've dumped our bags in our rooms, maybe even book a quick session if we can. The show doesn't start till eight.'

'Hmm,' Helen said, not even pretending she had been listening to a word Phoebe had said. She was too busy scrutinizing her friend's face for the telltale signs of betrayal. 'How was the driving lesson?'

Phoebe managed to hold Helen's gaze for a second or two. 'Let's not have this conversation again, Helen.'

'Why? Is it not so easy to lie face to face as it was over the phone?'

'What do you want me to say?'

'I want you to tell me the truth,' Helen told her. 'I'm watching my friend's marriage unravel before my eyes and I'd really like to know if their relationship is under threat before I waste any more time telling Julia she's being paranoid.'

As the train rocked from side to side, Julia wasn't the only one feeling queasy. Phoebe had already received a desperate message from Paul that morning telling her how Julia had made a direct accusation. He was worried that Julia or Helen would wear Phoebe down during the holiday to the point that she might confess all and he had begged her not to.

'It's all such a mess,' she managed to say as she thought back to Thursday night, pressed up against the kitchen counter with her legs wrapped around Paul's waist. The memory churned up her insides all the more and, to her eternal shame, the sensation wasn't entirely without pleasure even if it was quickly overpowered by self-loathing. Her so-called love for Paul had been flawed from the start and she just wished she hadn't taken it as far as she had to find that out. There would be no risk of a repeat and they had parted on Sunday as friends, with a shared hope that the guilt etched on their faces wouldn't give them away. Judging by the frown on Helen's face, it already had.

'You *really* want me to tell you?' Phoebe asked. What she was actually asking for was Helen's permission to continue with the lie, because at that precise moment she was edging towards the truth and once it was out there would be no going back. Would that be such a bad thing? Could she ever hope to live with such a marriage-shattering, friendship-breaking secret?

'I want you to tell me that you put your friendship above any stupid idea you might have about being in love with

368

someone else's husband,' Helen said, but then saw the answer on Phoebe's stricken face. She put her hand to her mouth and her words were muffled when she added, 'But you're not going to tell me that, are you? Oh, Phoebe, what have you done?'

'It was only once,' Phoebe blurted out, 'and it wasn't planned. We both agree it shouldn't have happened, and—'

'Save it!' Helen hissed. 'I don't want to hear your pathetic explanations.'

Phoebe looked over her shoulder to make sure Julia wasn't making her way back from the ladies, before asking, 'What do we do now?'

Helen glared at her friend. 'Seriously? You've fucked your best friend's husband and you're expecting me to tell you what to do? It's a bit late worrying about the consequences now, Phoebe!'

Trying not to think about the carriage full of passengers, who must have overheard Helen's outburst and would be listening intently to their conversation, Phoebe asked, 'I mean, do we tell her?'

Helen was facing in the direction Julia had disappeared and would be watching out for her return. There was still time to salvage the situation although Phoebe had no idea how she was going to do that. She picked up her mobile phone as if it would hold the answers.

'Don't!' Helen warned.

'What?'

'Don't contact Paul. Keep out of it, Phoebe.'

'Why? It's not like *you're* going to keep out of it, is it?'

'That's where you're wrong. I'm not going to tell Julia what you've done. I couldn't do that to her, not with everything else they're going through. You say it's over? Well, make sure of it. You don't speak to Paul, you don't text him – and you certainly don't take any more driving lessons from him. What you're going to do is be the best bloody friend you can be to Julia. You make sure this disaster of a holiday is the best it can be and together we'll do everything we can to send Julia home to her cheating husband with at least some hope for the future. I can't believe you could have done this to her, Phoebe, or Paul for that matter, although I doubt he's the only idiot to have his masculinity questioned and thought he could prove it with the first slut who came his way.'

Phoebe ought to have been relieved that Helen was giving her the chance to carry on as if nothing had happened, but she was too busy being furious that her friend was not only absolving Paul, but conveniently ignoring her own culpability. 'Hold on! I'm not the only one at fault, Helen. What about you? My nan wasn't the only one who came between me and Paul, was she? If only we'd been given a chance back then, maybe we wouldn't have had all those unresolved feelings for each other.' When Helen's only response was to stare wide-eyed at her, Phoebe continued, 'And OK, yes, I had a choice to make this time and I made the wrong one, I know that, but I won't take the blame alone for the problems in Julia's marriage.'

It was only when she drew breath that Phoebe realized that Helen's glare had been a warning. Julia dropped her handbag onto the empty seat next to Helen before returning to her own seat. 'I'm such an idiot,' she said.

She was waiting for someone to ask why, but Helen and

Phoebe had been struck dumb. Phoebe had no idea how much Julia had overheard or how quickly she would jump to the right conclusion.

'I'm almost forty and it's time I realized there are no happy endings,' Julia continued.

Phoebe had no idea where the conversation was going but even if Julia hadn't picked up on what was going on, it wouldn't take long for her to realize something was wrong between her two friends. They couldn't carry on as if nothing had happened – it was impossible. Julia had been right to suspect her husband and the only thing she deserved now was the truth.

'I'm so sorry, Julia,' Phoebe began. 'I didn't mean to . . .'

'Do you want to know what I've just been doing?' Julia said when Phoebe had left too long a pause. 'I've been sitting on a tiny stainless steel toilet trying to pee on a white stick. It wasn't easy and I don't even know why I bothered. It's not as if aiming straight helps make that magical blue line appear.'

'Oh, Julia, I'm sorry,' Helen said, 'but at least there is a line we can draw, one between the past and the present. Isn't that what this whole trip is supposed to be about, preparing ourselves for the next decade of our lives? It's a fresh start for all of us.' She glanced at Phoebe before adding, 'Just as long as we can hold our nerve.'

'Maybe,' Julia said and then checked her watch as if she were already aware of time slipping away.

Phoebe was holding her nerve, but not in the way Helen hoped. Her body tensed as she practised the words, but as she opened her mouth to speak, Julia was already talking.

'I didn't even look at it,' she said to Helen. 'I know it's

a foregone conclusion so what's the point? I can already feel a bit of cramping.'

'Oh, right,' Helen said, eyeing Julia with suspicion. 'Did you throw it away?'

Julia shook her head. 'Do you think you could check it for me? I can't face looking at another negative result. I know what it's going to say but I'd rather hear the bad news from a friend.'

'I think you're so right,' Phoebe said, although no one was paying her any attention.

When Helen had found the pregnancy test wrapped in toilet roll in Julia's handbag, Julia said, 'There are two windows on the stick. One should have a blue line but please don't go getting all excited. That's just a control to make sure the test's worked. It's only if there's a blue line in *both* windows—'

'I know how these things work, Julia,' Helen said as she began to unwrap it from the folds of tissue.

Craning her neck to get a better look, Julia added, 'I just didn't want you screaming out "it's positive" the minute you saw a blue line, that's all.'

Helen's brow creased with a frown. 'Nope,' she said and immediately offered the stick to Julia. 'I can't work it out. I think you should look.'

Julia recoiled as Helen tried to pass it to her.

'Oh, for God's sake,' Phoebe said as she made a grab for the stick. She stared down at the two windows Julia had described and, to her credit, her heart soared even as it was breaking. 'You're going to have a baby, Julia,' she said.

*   *   *

As Julia glanced at the seemingly unremarkable white plastic stick in Phoebe's trembling hand, she felt irrational fear rather than the joy that had been denied her for so long. 'No,' she managed to whisper when Phoebe tried to pass it to her.

'At least look at it,' Phoebe offered, turning it so the two blue lines were clearly visible if only Julia would dare to look.

With her mouth agog, Julia didn't need to squint or strain her eyes in search of that elusive hint of blue. After all this time, there they were – *two* blue lines. 'But I can feel cramps. I'm coming on,' she insisted. 'It must be wrong.'

'That's your body preparing to blow up like a balloon over the next nine months,' Helen said in a soft bedside manner usually reserved for her patients. 'I'm pretty sure that if ever there's a false reading, it's far more likely to be a false negative rather than a false positive.'

In the last couple of years Julia had conjured up a thousand daydreams of this moment, and whether she was running into Paul's arms, jumping on the bed to wake him or letting him scoop her up in his arms, in each one of her fantasies her husband had been there. Not once had she imagined delivering the news, not only over the phone but while on a train travelling at high speed in the opposite direction from him. She should have taken the test earlier.

'I need to speak to Paul.'

'Do you want some privacy?' Helen asked. She was giving Phoebe a meaningful look but it was doubtful Phoebe could see a thing through the tears streaming down her face.

With difficult decisions still turning over in her mind, Julia said, 'No, it's all right. I can't break something like this over the phone. I need to tell him in person.'

She looked to her friends and hoped they would suggest what she was loath to.

'You want to get off the train, don't you?' Helen asked.

When Julia nodded, it was Phoebe who considered the practicalities. She sniffed back her tears and said, 'The next station is Crewe. You should be able to get a train back to Liverpool quite easily from there.'

'Don't worry about us,' Helen told her. 'Do what you think is best for you and Paul.'

'And you could always join us again in a couple of days before we set off for Paris,' Phoebe continued. 'It's a good thing we decided to do the trip this way around. If we'd started off in New York, I don't think it would have been quite so easy to drop you off mid-Atlantic.'

'Tell him you're on your way home,' Helen said. She had already fished out Julia's mobile from her handbag but hesitated before handing it over. 'Actually, why don't you tell him we're *all* coming back? I'm not going on this trip without you, Julia, not even one leg of it.'

Julia was stunned and turned to Phoebe for her reaction.

'Helen's right. I don't think any of us are up for this trip right now.'

Not trusting herself to speak to her husband without giving the news away, Julia's trembling fingers typed out a text message.

I'm about to get off the train at Crewe. Don't ask, just be there when I get home. J x

After sending the message, Julia's thoughts began to catch up with her. She wasn't sure if her friends heard what she said over the squeal of brakes, but then she could hardly believe them herself.

'I'm going to be a mum,' she said.

32

The Accident

'There, that should do for now,' Anya told Julia when she had finished cleaning and dressing the wound on the back of her hand. She had been forced to listen to Phoebe's confession about her teenage pregnancy and the nurse's presence had been as awkward as the silence that followed.

'I'll be back in five minutes with the registrar,' she warned, thinking this would be enough time for the two to continue their conversation in private.

Julia was lying back against her pillow, eyes closed.

Anya picked up her hand and checked her pulse. 'Are you feeling OK?'

Julia grimaced and said, 'I feel a bit woozy actually.'

'Is she all right?'

Anya turned to Phoebe, who had dragged herself out of bed while the nurse wasn't looking and was using her drip stand for support as she took in Julia's ashen features. 'She's probably realizing about now that her body isn't quite ready to cope with all her exertions, and the same applies to you. Please get back in bed,' she said.

'I will just as soon as I know she's all right.'

Anya was after the same reassurance and asked Julia, 'Are you in pain?'

Julia gave a tight nod of the head as if any movement were agony. 'I'll be fine in a minute.'

As Anya slipped on a pressure cuff to check her blood pressure, Phoebe asked, 'Will the baby be all right?'

'Our first priority is to look after Mum,' Anya told her, 'but we're being cautious.' When Julia peeled open her eyes, she told her, 'We've scheduled another ultrasound today but I promise you the drugs we've been giving you are because you need them. The registrar has said he would like to see you try to eat again. It's most likely you've been suffering from morning sickness, but if you can manage to hold food down then you won't have to go back on IV fluids. You'll still need to take the meds though and not just for pain relief. You need antibiotics and anti-inflammatories too. We don't want complications because anything that endangers your life also affects your pregnancy and that would include such things as discharging yourself and racing across the hospital. I'm sure your friend Helen wouldn't want you to take those kind of risks.'

'Maybe it wasn't meant to be,' Julia whispered. 'Life's unfair like that.'

As Anya checked Julia's vital signs, she went against her better judgement and let Phoebe remain where she was for the moment. She couldn't ignore the tension that had been building between the two bedfellows all morning and the strain in their friendship was tangible, so it came as quite a shock when Julia reached over to Phoebe with her free hand. After only a moment's hesitation, Phoebe grasped it fiercely.

'I'm so sorry, Julia. I hate myself for what I've done to you. If I hadn't been so stupid and selfish then things could have gone so differently yesterday and maybe we wouldn't have been involved in the accident. If you lose this baby then I'll never forgive myself.'

A tear trickled down the side of Julia's face. 'Maybe it's what I deserve.'

'You can't say that! *You* have nothing to feel guilty about.'

'Don't I? It was me, Phoebe,' she said. 'I was the one who made sure you broke up with Paul, not Helen.'

'What? I don't understand. You weren't around – how could you—'

'I was there for Helen and she was worried about you. Oh, God, Phoebe, I'm so sorry. We talked about the best way to help and, Helen being Helen, was more interested in pretending to be a judge on some talent show than worrying about the consequences. From what she'd said, you were set to go off the rails – I swear I was only trying to get you back on track.'

'Controlling me, just like Nan always did?'

'Yes, I'm afraid so, except I was far more devious. When Helen set off to meet Paul, I went with her,' Julia said. When she closed her eyes it wasn't clear if she was reliving the memory or trying to manage her pain. 'Paul didn't see me and never knew I was there. I was looking after Milly, standing guard to make sure Helen did what I'd told her to do. I had no idea how involved you were by then and I thought I was helping, Phoebe. You had such potential and I had to stop you throwing your life away,' Julia gasped. 'Oh, God, if only I'd known what I was doing.'

Phoebe swayed as though the revelation had been a

physical force ramming into her and her knuckles turned white as she gripped the drip stand to steady herself. Taking a deep breath she looked up to the ceiling in an effort to stem her tears and, only when she was ready, did she lower her chin and focus on Julia. Her voice was strong and resolute. 'You were being my friend, protecting me. You shouldn't feel guilty about that.'

'But if I'd known . . .' Julia persisted, her voice trailing off.

It was Phoebe's turn to wrestle with another kind of pain. 'You know, I've imagined what might have happened if Paul had stuck around, but the truth is, Julia, I don't think he could have changed a thing. No one would have been able to stand up to my nan. She wasn't going to let me make the same mistakes as Mum.'

'But *did* you want to keep it?'

Anya had finished what she was doing and went over to Phoebe, who was struggling to remain on her feet. The nurse tried to meld into the background as she helped her patient back into bed, which also gave Phoebe enough time to find her answer.

'No, Julia. No, I didn't,' Phoebe said firmly.

'And when did you tell Paul?'

'Last week.'

'How did he react?' Before Phoebe had the chance to answer, Julia added quickly, 'Actually, you'd better not answer that. We both know how he reacted.'

'Shouldn't you tell him about the baby – *your* baby – now?' Phoebe asked.

Tipping her head slightly, Julia looked towards the door. 'He's taking his time.'

'I expect Sister's giving him an earful,' Anya told her. 'Would you like me to go and tell them you've changed your mind about discharging yourself?'

'Yes, please.'

When Anya left the ward, she expected to find Paul Richardson arguing at the nurses' station with the ward sister, but the corridor was deserted.

33

The guard's whistle sliced through the cold February air and with a reluctant jolt, the train pulled away. In its backdraught, the three friends stood shivering on the platform watching their dream holiday disappear without them. Not one of them looked upset about it.

Phoebe had spent the last few days dreading going away with Helen and more especially Julia and she was relieved to be off the train. They were still talking about the possibility of resuming their journey in a couple of days, but no one spoke with any real enthusiasm and in the unlikely event that Helen and Julia did want to try again, Phoebe knew she wouldn't be going with them. She could feel the anger radiating from Helen, and it had only intensified once she realized that Paul hadn't only cheated on a loving wife, but a pregnant one at that.

However, it wasn't Helen's fury that pained Phoebe most but rather the expression of pure delight on Julia's face. Her friend was wearing a broad grin that would soon be making her cheeks ache as she pulled out her mobile and checked her messages.

'How about I go and buy our tickets home,' Phoebe offered.

'No need,' Julia said. 'Paul's already on his way. He should be here within the hour.'

'He's eager,' said Helen.

'I know, and he hasn't even asked why we're coming home, thank God.'

Helen gave Phoebe a meaningful look to add to the barrage she had already directed towards her, leaving Phoebe all the more determined to get away from her friends as soon as she could. She didn't know what would happen after that. Even if they could keep the secret from one of her best friends, she couldn't imagine being able to repair her relationship with the other. She didn't blame Helen for hating her, she hated herself. What the hell had she done?

'He's in for a shock,' Helen said, 'and I can't wait to see his face when you tell him.'

Phoebe was horrified at the idea. 'We can't be there!'

Helen began dragging her suitcase along the platform. 'We're hardly going to disappear with all this baggage. Besides, we've been part of this journey too. I think we *should* be there.'

Ignoring the next glare directed her way, Phoebe turned to Julia. 'You don't want us around when you tell him, do you?'

Julia was lagging behind as she juggled her hand luggage and suitcase. 'Helen has a point: you are both a part of this. But,' she added, 'I don't want the news going any further. Getting pregnant is only the first step. We've a long way to go yet.'

'Should you be pulling that?' Phoebe said with a note

382

of concern that surprised her. No one had been at hand to take care of her when she had been carrying Paul's child, but she refused to feel resentful. She cared too much about Julia, and Paul too for that matter, not to want this for them. It wasn't that long ago that she had convinced herself that the break-up of Julia's marriage was inevitable and, if she was brutally honest, it was something she might briefly have hoped for. But the baby was a game changer, and while it would break her heart for more reasons than she could yet fully appreciate, it would make two of the most important people in her life blissfully happy and she had to be happy about that.

'I'm no different than I was this morning when I dragged it into the station,' Julia said. 'Now come on, let's find a café and take the weight off our feet.'

'Yes, you are waddling a bit,' Helen confirmed.

They headed straight for a coffee shop and while Helen and Julia debated over what was the ideal refreshment for a mother-to-be, Phoebe made her excuses and headed for the toilets. She didn't bother going into a cubicle, she was only interested in checking her phone. She had felt it vibrating in her bag shortly after Julia had sent Paul the first text message, but she couldn't look at it with Helen watching her every move. There was no need to guess who it would be from.

Have you told her about us?

What was she supposed to say to that? She couldn't explain to Paul the real reason why the holiday had been called off. She considered telling him not to worry and suggesting he erase her number from his phone, but she didn't get the chance.

'Sending a message to Paul by any chance?' Helen said, catching a glimpse of the phone Phoebe had tried to palm when she heard the door open.

Phoebe had no strength left to evade the truth. 'He thinks I've told Julia about us.'

Helen's features were as cold and unfeeling as the tiled floor. None of her usual jokes or quips were ready on her lips to dispel the frosty atmosphere. 'What did you tell him?'

'I haven't replied yet.'

'Well, don't. It'll do him good to stew in his own juices for a while.'

'Helen, I'm sorry. Can't we at least try to recover from this?'

'No,' she said simply. 'I honestly can't see a way past this. Maybe if I had Julia to talk to she might offer some sage advice, but oh no, I can't do that, can I? What I'm really struggling to understand, Phoebe, is how you can go from being the kind of person who always put her friends and family before herself, to . . .' She shook her head, not prepared to describe the person standing in front of her. 'The only thing I am sure of right now is that, God forgive me, we keep it from Julia. This is her moment, the one that's been eating her up for the last two years and brought her marriage to the brink. She's having a baby and nothing else matters.'

'It's a shame you never gave me the same consideration.'

'Sorry?'

'You didn't just kill a relationship when you told Paul to keep away from me.'

Helen was shaking her head as if Phoebe had lost her senses. She couldn't begin to imagine the damage she had inadvertently caused, or perhaps she didn't want to.

'Do I need to spell it out, Helen?' Phoebe asked. 'I was pregnant.'

There was a moment when it felt like the world had stopped turning and time slowed until Helen let out a gasp. 'No!'

Phoebe remained silent and still. She didn't need to fill in the gaps; Helen could work it out for herself.

'Jesus, Phoebe, why didn't you tell me?'

'Truthfully?' Phoebe warned. 'I knew what you'd say. You were hardly the poster girl for teenage pregnancy, were you? You never stopped complaining about how it had wrecked your life. Nan wouldn't even enter into a debate about me keeping it, and thanks to you I didn't have Paul to turn to. Maybe if I'd let Julia back into my life a little earlier she might have been a better ally. Who knows?'

'You wanted to keep it?'

A sudden rush of emotion made Phoebe feel sick and tears stung her eyes when she said, 'How could I have looked after a baby?'

'But you wanted it?' Helen asked, determined to get a direct answer.

'Yes! Yes, I wanted the baby,' Phoebe cried, shocking them both by her answer. 'But I've spent the last eleven years trying to convince myself that I would have made a mess of it just like mum did, that my baby would have felt resented instead of loved.' Phoebe shook her head. 'But I would have loved my baby, Helen, and of all the things I regret, that's the thing I regret the most. Not what I might have had with Paul, but what I might have had with my baby if only I'd been given the chance.'

Helen's furrowed brow gave away the emotions she was wrestling with, but her words when they came remained harsh. 'I'm sorry, Phoebe, but none of that excuses what you've been doing with Paul.'

'Do you think I don't know that, Helen? It was a mistake and we both knew that as soon as it happened. You have no idea how sorry I am about it and if I could go back and change things I would. You and Julia are the closest thing I have to family left and I don't want to lose you. We will get past this, we have to,' she insisted. 'You said it yourself, we have to pretend everything is all right for Julia's sake.'

'And I think that's the point,' Helen said and to her credit there was more pain than anger in her voice now. 'It *will* be pretending.'

When they returned to the café, Helen took the seat closest to Julia. She was still reeling from the snatched conversation with Phoebe, and wished she had never followed her into the ladies. She had been carried along by a crimson tide of fury but Phoebe had turned it against her. For years Helen had felt justified in her actions, and even though Paul had turned out to be a decent and honourable man – excepting recent events of course – her conscience had remained clear. She and Julia had been acting with the best intentions at the time, convinced that they were protecting Phoebe from herself as much as the predator they perceived Paul to be. Little had she known that it was Phoebe's so-called friends that she had needed protecting from the most.

'She's lonely,' Helen had told Julia all those years ago when she had turned to her for advice. 'What's the harm in her having a bit of fun?'

'If that's the advice you're giving her then I'm more worried than I was before. It wouldn't be the first time she's followed your example and headed straight into trouble.'

Her friend had a point so Helen hadn't argued. 'She's actually admitted she envies me. God knows why!'

'Do you think she'd deliberately get pregnant?'

'Personally, I can't imagine *anyone* wanting to get pregnant, but I suppose she might be daft enough not to avoid it, if you know what I mean. She wants a family, one that doesn't just include her nan.'

Julia had shaken her head. 'But not everyone's like John,' she had said and before Helen could make some derisive remark about her husband, she added, 'If we stand back and let Phoebe get involved with this bloke, then what happens if, or should I say *when*, things go wrong? Would the life-model-cum-stalker hang around once there was a baby on the scene, or would he already be looking for his next conquest?'

'He probably thinks baby oil was only invented for rubbing on his chest.'

'Then we have to stop Phoebe from making a huge mistake.'

'Will you speak to her?' Helen had asked. It was the reason she had confided in Julia in the first place.

'She was nine years old the last time I saw her – she's hardly going to listen to me. No, what you need to do is speak to this Paul and put him off – tell him she doesn't want to see him.'

'I can't do that! What if Phoebe found out?'

'Then we tell her how we did it for her own good. Look, once he's out of the way we'll all go out together. I'll take Phoebe under my wing and convince her to go back to college and make something of her talents. By the time she finds out, if she ever does, she'll be a successful artist and will thank us for it!'

Helen didn't have to look at Phoebe now to know that there wasn't so much as a hint of gratitude showing in her face – not that she could bring herself to look at her.

'I know what you're thinking,' Julia said when she noticed Helen staring into space.

'Go on,' Helen replied cautiously.

'You're already wondering what it's going to be like when the baby comes.'

'Well, obviously *you* are,' Helen said and tried to give Julia her best smile, which she briefly directed at Phoebe. Even someone as cold-hearted as Helen could appreciate how painful it was going to be for Phoebe to sit there and listen to endless baby talk.

As they chatted, Phoebe did try to engage in the conversation but it was obvious, to Helen at least, that she was struggling. Julia was carrying Paul's baby and already looking forward to its birth. Had Phoebe briefly done the same before her nan had told her what needed to be done?

'I can't wait to tell Paul,' Julia was saying.

'I can't even begin to imagine how he'll react,' Phoebe said, a little too honestly.

'I can. In fact, I can't think of anything else,' Julia said. 'He's been in such a dark place lately and this is going to be like an explosion of light hitting him between the eyes.

I can picture the exact expression he'll have on his face.' She broke into a soft laugh. 'Everything else is behind us now. There's only the future.'

'I should think Milly's going to be ecstatic too,' Phoebe offered in an awkward attempt to move the focus away from Paul.

'Ooh, I never thought of that,' Julia said. There was a look of unrepressed joy on her face as the news kept getting better. 'If there was any remaining doubt in her mind about staying with you, Helen, then this has to be the clincher.'

Thinking of the good times ahead, Helen willed herself to believe that there was a chance they could all right themselves, and then Julia's phone beeped. It was a message from Paul to let her know he was waiting in a pick-up bay.

'Come on, let's put him out of his misery,' Julia said.

Phoebe moved quickly but only to grab Julia's hand luggage. 'I'll take that,' she said.

Julia didn't argue and Helen struggled to keep up with her as they hurried out of the station with Phoebe trailing behind.

'There he is!' Julia said.

Paul was standing next to the car, his head down and his hands in his pockets, looking for all the world like a condemned man. It was a poignant reminder of Paul's adultery and the warm fuzzy feeling that had been insulating Helen from darker thoughts began to cool until she couldn't feel it any more. It was impossible to escape the fact that Paul and Phoebe had betrayed someone who loved and trusted them and that Julia's life was at risk of being torn apart just when she was coming so close to getting her heart's desire.

Taking Julia's suitcase, Paul deliberately avoided making eye contact. 'Don't you want to ask what's going on?' she asked, momentarily taken aback by her husband's continued silence. It was his expression that gave away his guilt and Julia stopped looking confused and began looking fearful. Before he could answer her, she blurted, 'Let's get in the car first.'

As she disappeared to the front of the car, Helen handed Paul her suitcase. She wasn't sure if she was angrier at him for sleeping with Phoebe or for being such a terrible liar. 'You fucking idiot,' she said under her breath.

Phoebe had arrived just in time to hear the exchange and Paul glared at her. In a low growl, he asked, 'Why, Phoebe? We said it meant nothing. Why tell her now?'

'I didn't—' Phoebe started but then stopped, colour draining from her face as she looked over Paul's shoulder. Julia was standing behind him.

'I wanted the water bottle from my bag,' she managed to say, her voice hollow. She was staring at Paul.

'I'm sorry, Julia. I'm so sorry,' he said.

No one spoke another word as they forced the rest of the luggage into every available space before squeezing themselves into the overcrowded Beetle. It was probably a good thing that Julia and Paul were sitting up front so they couldn't see the tears slipping down Phoebe's face. If Helen had had more time to think she would have refused the lift and insisted that she and Phoebe take the train home to give Julia and Paul some space. It was too late now; they were all trapped in the car, wishing they were somewhere else.

Once they hit the motorway, the silence in the car became

as taut as a band stretched to breaking point. The traffic was heavy but moving, and although Paul had to weave across lanes once in a while, there was nothing else to occupy his mind other than the thickening atmosphere.

'Julia,' he said, 'please say something.'

'I'm not sure I have anything to say, Paul,' she answered faintly. 'Not any more.'

Paul kept looking at his wife with only one eye on the road while Julia stared straight ahead. Phoebe let out a brief sob until Helen silenced her with a glare and neither of them noticed the swarm of red brake lights appearing up ahead, or the tanker that had begun to jackknife. It was Julia who saw what was about to happen first and she let out a scream. Two cars closest to the tanker had no time to react and took the full impact of the collision as Paul turned the car violently to the left. Time slowed as they swerved to avoid the carnage and there was a split second when Helen thought they were safe. But then she saw a minibus spinning out of control and a moment later the world went dark.

34

Now

Phoebe had moved to the edge of her hospital bed so she could watch over Julia. Her friend had her eyes closed and her face was held in a constant grimace.

'Do you want me to get the nurse?' she asked.

'No, I'm sure she'll get to me when she can. They're busy enough as it is.'

'She said she'd be five minutes but that was over half an hour ago. You're in pain, aren't you?'

Julia gritted her teeth but left it to Phoebe's imagination to work out how much pain she was in, not all of which had to do with her injuries but rather the agony her husband and best friend had put her through.

'I'm going to find that bloody registrar.'

'Find Paul while you're at it,' Julia said.

'He was right, you know, about it not meaning anything. We were both trying to get back what we'd lost all those years ago and we realized too late that we were chasing something that never really existed. Paul and me were meant to be friends, that was all, and I'm so sorry I let things get as far as they did to find that out. It's no excuse but I think all this focus on having babies messed up my emotions too.'

Rather than agree or accept Phoebe's version of events, Julia simply said, 'Bring him back to me.'

Phoebe's hospital gown gaped open at the back and her feet were bare, but it was the site of the keyhole surgery on her left side that made her progress out of the ward tentative. Her legs trembled as she held onto her drip stand and the pain was so intense that it left her short of breath, but she pushed on. Anything was better than lying in the bed next to Julia, waiting for her friend to be strong enough to think about her future and decide if Phoebe deserved a place in it.

Helen had already made her feelings known on that score but right now Phoebe was more concerned about her surviving than she was about their friendship. She feared for Milly too. Phoebe knew what it was like to lose a mum at a young age and while Milly would be looked after, Helen's loss would create a fault line that would change the landscape of her daughter's life forever.

Reaching the corridor, Phoebe found the nurses' station deserted and briefly considered whether or not she could carry on all the way to the Critical Care Unit, even with a gaping hole in the back of her gown. But Julia still needed pain relief and at that moment a visitor's chair looked particularly inviting. She had just sat down when Anya appeared. Phoebe was surprised when the nurse didn't immediately order her back to bed but continued slowly and silently down the corridor towards her.

'Julia's in a lot of pain,' Phoebe said.

Anya's only response was to sit down next to her patient. She took hold of Phoebe's hand and gave it a tight squeeze. 'I'm afraid I have some bad news,' she said.

The taxi was waiting and the time for arguments was over. Lucy had been right not to let her parents see them off at the airport: standing at the door hugging her mum one last time was literally heart-wrenching but at least it was in the privacy of their own home.

Mrs Cunliffe showed no signs of releasing her and looked over her shoulder to her other daughter. 'You look after her.'

'I will,' Hayley said with the same catch of emotion that had made her mum's words tremble. 'Now can we please get going before the taxi leaves without us?'

The moment her mum let her go, Lucy was already missing her and couldn't bring herself to move away. They needed to take one last look at each other.

'Come back to me,' her mum said.

Lucy could only nod as she hurried to leave the house before the dam of tears burst through her resolve. She was aware that she was being watched as she and her sister loaded up the taxi, or to be more precise, when Lucy looked on while Hayley and the cab driver transferred the suitcases from the doorstep to the boot. She was shivering against the biting February wind and dared to turn back only briefly to wave at her mum one last time before getting into the back of the cab.

'I thought you might want to keep hold of this,' Hayley said before getting in beside her. She was holding the small shoulder bag Lucy had left with her luggage that held her passport and holiday money.

394

'Yes, I suppose I better had.'

Hayley put it to her ear before handing it over. 'Your phone's beeping.'

'It'll probably be a message from Dad wishing us luck,' Lucy said, although she suspected his message would be more along the lines of: *please don't do this to your mother*.

When she checked her phone, there was a missed call and a text message, neither of which were from her dad.

'Oh. My. God!' Hayley said as she peered over Lucy's shoulder to read the message she had opened.

'John Lennon Airport is it, love?' the cab driver asked.

Rather than answer, Lucy continued to stare in disbelief at the text message.

'What the—?' the driver said as he spotted Mrs Cunliffe racing out of the house with a phone pressed against her ear. With more drama than was entirely necessary, she threw herself in front of the stationary vehicle for fear of it speeding off. The driver took his hands off the wheel and held them up in surrender.

The car door opened and Mrs Cunliffe crouched down in front of Lucy who immediately grabbed hold of her hand. 'Mum? Is it really happening?' she asked and then burst into tears.

'The transplant nurse was afraid you'd already left. Look, it's not definite, it might come to nothing . . .' Lucy's mum stopped and tried to smile but she too let out a sob. 'Someone somewhere still needs to make a very difficult decision. God bless them, but I hope they know your life is in their hands.'

35

The only windows in the room faced inwards and gave no clue as to what might be happening beyond the clinical confines of the hospital. Julia had no idea of the time but she guessed that in another version of her life, she and her friends would be spending their second day in London indulging in some beauty treatment or other. Instead, she had been caught up in a warped version of reality that she was struggling to make sense of. She was sitting in a wheelchair with one leg sticking straight out in front of her, but at least she had dispensed with the need for a drip stand. She was on oral meds, having done everything the registrar had asked of her just so she could get here – even though it was the last place she wanted to be.

She wished she had stayed on the train yesterday, but then she wished for so many things. She wished she had taken the pregnancy test before leaving the house, or that she had simply left it until they had travelled too far for Paul to be able to pick them up. She wished she had phoned and told him the news instead of insisting it had to be in person. Perhaps if she had given him even the subtlest hint about what was happening, that it was good news she was about to impart rather than an accusation, then maybe . . .

As she released a sigh, Julia tried to let go of all those 'what if's' but they clung to her like leeches, draining her spirit and dragging her down into a dark world. There was only one person in her life who would be strong enough to pull her to safety, but he couldn't reach her, nor she him, even though he was lying in a hospital bed only feet away.

Paul had been taken to A & E along with the rest of them and it had appeared that he had walked away with only minor injuries. The minibus had hit the passenger side of the Beetle and Helen and Julia had taken the brunt of the impact. Once Paul's minor wounds had been dressed he had refused further treatment or tests and had become one of the many walking wounded who had remained in the hospital to be close to loved ones. By the time Julia had seen him the following day he had seemed fine. Or at least he had *looked* fine.

But now Julia could hear Paul's life force ebbing away, released with a hiss at regular intervals as the ventilator kept her husband's chest rising and falling. She stared long and hard as she tried to make sense of what she was being forced to witness.

'It looks just like he's sleeping,' she said.

A hand rested gently on her shoulder.

'I know,' Anya replied.

Julia's eyes were red and swollen but her tears had dried, leaving her skin feeling itchy and tight. She shook her head. 'What do I do now?'

The doctor had told Julia much of what she needed to

know, giving her the salient facts about Paul's condition and his prognosis. She could recall everything she had been told; she simply couldn't process that information. Her mind was pulling her towards the safety of an emotional vacuum and she had no reason to fight it, there was nothing she could do to save him.

'Would you like me to go through it again with you?' Anya asked.

Julia wouldn't take her eyes from Paul. 'We're going to have a baby,' she said.

'I know.'

Julia smiled. 'You must know more than you want to by now. Goodness knows what you think of us all.'

'I think you care very deeply for each other and, if I'm not mistaken, I'd say you're the one who looks after everyone. You've been the strong one, Julia,' Anya told her. 'And now you're going to have to be stronger than you ever thought possible, for you, your husband and your baby. But I promise you, I'm going to be here for you every step of the way.'

'Don't you ever go home?' Julia asked, keeping the conversation light as if it wasn't a life-and-death decision she were about to make.

'I'm going to stay as long as you want me to, but first there are some decisions you need to make. I know this is impossibly hard for you, Julia, but you do need to think about what's going to happen next.'

Julia nodded, but then in a contradiction of everything the doctors had told her, she said, 'He's going to come back to me, Anya. He's strong. He can do it.'

The nurse's reply was spoken gently but her words

were brutal. 'No, Julia. I'm sorry, but he's not. The brain haemorrhage was catastrophic and it's only the machines that are keeping your husband alive. His body is a shell.' She left a pause, as if that bitter blow had left her breathless too. 'The tests the doctors have now performed twice confirm brain stem death. I wish it could be different but he won't be coming back to you.'

'You don't know that!' Julia cried. 'The doctors don't know him like I do. They said we wouldn't be able to conceive naturally but Paul proved them wrong. And if he did it once, he can do it again. He *will* do it again!'

Julia knew she was being delusional, but she had to have one last chance to make things right between her and Paul because the alternative was unthinkable. If only she could go back in time! 'I should have told him. I shouldn't have been so pig-headed and made you all keep it a secret,' she said. 'This morning when he came onto the ward and tried to talk to me I knew he was in agony, that he was sorry for what he'd done, and I believed him when he said he loved me. He would have been so happy if he'd known I was pregnant, feeling twice as guilty but deliriously happy. Only I wanted him to suffer. If I'd known time was running out . . .'

When the nurse remained quiet and could offer no hope, Julia was forced to face the future head on. 'How long do we have?'

'The ventilator will keep Paul's body functioning for some time yet, but eventually his organs will fail and he'll pass away,' Anya told her in a low voice. 'We think it would be better, as much for you as for him, to switch off the machines before that happens.'

'No, no, no!' wailed Julia. She had continued to stare at Paul lying so still and imagined him listening to them.

'Julia,' Anya said with enough force to drag Julia's gaze towards her. 'Remember what I said about being strong? Now is that time.'

'But I don't have to decide now! You're jumping too far ahead.'

'I know,' Anya said, 'and you're right, you don't have to decide yet, but I wanted to give you time to think about something else.'

'What else?'

'Organ donation.'

Julia's face twisted with pain. 'No. Even if . . . even if Paul wasn't coming back, even if . . .' she said as she tried and failed to get her thoughts in order. How was this conversation even possible when their lives had been so normal yesterday? She took a deep breath and straightened up. 'We talked about it and he said he didn't want to donate his organs. He said it creeped him out.'

'But Paul is on the register.'

'I'm sorry, but your records are wrong. Helen tried to persuade him to register online a few months ago. We all did, but he said no.'

'He might have said no at the time—'

'He would have told me if he'd changed his mind. We told each other everything,' Julia said before snapping her mouth shut. That was blatantly untrue. Of course they kept secrets from each other, recent events proved that, and Paul wasn't the only guilty party. Hadn't she kept secrets right from the start of their relationship?

When Julia had first spied Paul at the gym she had

recognized him immediately as Phoebe's stalker and had been understandably suspicious of him. Only when she had succumbed to his charms did she tell him that she knew who he was and, responding to her honesty, Paul had been open about the extent of his liaison with Phoebe. At that point Julia should have told him how she had instigated the break-up of his relationship with Phoebe, but she hadn't. Things had been getting serious between them and once Phoebe had given her blessing, Julia concluded that there was no point raking up the past. She should have told him. They should have all talked about it instead of letting the lies fester.

'It's too late now,' she said. 'We can't talk about anything any more.'

'Are you saying you don't want to consider organ donation?'

'I threatened once that I'd donate his organs, with or without his consent,' she told Anya. 'But it's one thing to say you'll do it and another to sit here and agree to him being carved up. Listen – listen to him breathing.'

'It's a machine,' Anya said.

'It's my husband!'

Anya nodded. 'I know, and I'm sorry,' she said, 'I didn't mean to sound so harsh and no one will pressurize you. It's your decision and I genuinely don't know what I would do in your position. I really am sorry.'

Julia gave Anya an apologetic look. 'It's all right. And to be honest, if my friend Helen were here she'd be giving me such a hard time right now. I do want to do the right thing; it's just so hard when I'm not sure of Paul's wishes. I may have come across as the wife from hell, but Paul is

– *was* my life, my leading man. Although not perfect by any means.'

'I think I have one of those at home,' Anya said and rested a hand across her bare neck.

Julia stared at her for a moment and a random thought took her by surprise. 'I didn't imagine the necklace you were wearing before, did I? It was one I made, part of a collection for a client who had been happily married for fifty years. I envied him for being that secure. God, I still do.'

Smiling sadly, Anya said, 'That would be my dad. The necklace was a Christmas present. He seems to be under the impression that my marriage is from the same mould as his. But it isn't.'

'Are you still together?'

'Only just,' Anya said gently. 'But I still love him and I'm starting to think I should give it another try. We should make the most of what we have.'

'What do I have?' Julia said, turning her attention back to the lifeless body of her husband.

'You have the amazing gift your husband left you. A miracle baby, by all accounts,' Anya reminded her.

'He might have fallen from grace but he's still my hero,' Julia agreed, drawing her thoughts back to the difficult decision she was still wrestling with. 'And he could be for other families too.'

'I can arrange for someone from the transplant team to come and talk to you if you'd like. Will you think about it?'

'OK,' Julia said, her jaw set firm until her lower lip began to tremble. 'But just not yet.'

She turned from Anya and began pushing her wheelchair closer to her husband's bedside. Reaching out, she was surprised how warm and supple Paul's arm felt. There was no coolness of death, not even a suggestion. The doctors were wrong. Looking past the tubes and monitors, she searched for the slightest flicker behind Paul's closed lids that might give her hope. 'Do you think he can still hear me?' she asked.

'Maybe.'

After everything they had just discussed, they both knew this wasn't true, but Julia appreciated the lie. 'I need to tell him something,' she said.

'Would you like some privacy?'

When Julia nodded, Anya squeezed her shoulder and left without a word.

Forcing air past her constricted throat, Julia took a deep breath and held it. Only when her lungs burned did she force herself to speak.

'I know what happened, Paul. All of it,' she began. 'And I can't begin to imagine what was going through your mind when Phoebe told you about the baby. I can't get my head around it myself and while I don't understand how you could both do what you did, I forgive you, I have to.'

She took another shuddering breath, readying herself for Paul's reaction to the confession she was about to make as if he were actively participating in the conversation.

'You see, it was because of me that you weren't there for Phoebe when she found out she was pregnant. *I* was the one who persuaded Helen to feed you the lies. I thought

403

I was protecting Phoebe.' She gave a short laugh that was more of a sob. 'What a mess I made of that!'

Julia had to take another deep breath before she could continue. She wasn't as strong as everyone thought and would have to take this slowly. 'But at least I can say I didn't know what damage I was causing at the time. You, on the other hand, knew exactly what you were doing this time around, and I hate you – I hate you *both* for what you did. Honestly, Paul, while I can say I could forgive you, I don't know if that would have been enough to save our marriage, but I'd like to think it was,' she said, and then added quickly, 'Actually, that's a lie. I'd rather not think about it at all, not any more.'

Stroking his arm absent-mindedly, she said, 'Do you remember the day we got married? Do you remember how we stayed up talking until the morning? OK, maybe not *talking* all the time . . .' She took a few gasps of air to hold back the sob. 'We were like two excited children, planning out the rest of our lives together. We'd have a bit more time as a couple and then we'd start knocking out kids. We should have had at least two by now, and maybe we wouldn't have stopped there. It was meant to be . . . and then, when it didn't happen, I think we were both scared, scared that if we didn't have it all then we would have nothing. We were so wrong, Paul.' She squeezed his hand, wishing beyond everything to feel an answering pressure.

'We were so wrong because we already had everything we needed – we had each other. I need you to believe that before I tell you my news. I need you to know that *you*, Paul Richardson, are *everything* to me. You always were and you always will be.'

Ignoring the pain her movements caused, Julia leaned over to trail a finger across Paul's face. She expected to see a twitch at any moment before his cheeks pinched into a smile. He remained stubbornly unmoved but she was saving the best for last.

'You were so upset when you found out that the physical problem was with you, and maybe you did what you did because you wanted to push me away. Maybe it was your way of setting me free to find someone who could give me babies – I'll never know. But here's the thing, Paul, I didn't need anyone else.'

She left a pause, imagining that she had piqued his curiosity and he was about to peel back an eyelid. She thought she heard him say, 'Go on, then, tell me what's got you all excited?'

When Julia smiled, her eyes sparkled with unshed tears. 'We did it,' she whispered, her voice breaking at the last. She swallowed hard and forced herself to speak loudly and clearly. She needed him to hear this. 'We made a baby, Paul. I'm pregnant. You're going to be a dad.'

Pressing her palm against his cheek, her hand trembled. They had created a new life, proving that together anything was possible. 'Did you hear me, Paul? We're going to have a baby. So now you have to wake up. You have to.'

This was where Paul's eyes were supposed to open wide with shock. He was meant to jump out of bed and sweep her up into his arms, holding her so close she wouldn't be able to see the look of pure elation on his face but she would feel his body shaking.

He didn't move.

With a strangled cry, she shouted, 'Please, Paul! Please don't do this! I love you! Don't leave me!'

There was a click as the door behind her opened and Julia's head snapped towards the sound. She took a deep, mournful breath and just before she gave in to the sobs that would rack her body, she said, 'I can't do this, not on my own.'

'You're not on your own,' Phoebe said.

36

Helen had finally made it to see Take That. She was standing in a vast auditorium where the only light came from the stage but it was so far away that she couldn't see the band or even hear them properly. Desperate to get closer, she began climbing over people – and in the next moment she was crowd-surfing towards the stage where Robbie Williams was waiting for her. He reached out his hand and she was about to take it when the music stopped and the stage plunged into darkness. Helen spun around as she tried to get her bearings, only coming to a stop when a noise caught her attention and fear trickled down her spine. She could hear someone sobbing. The moment she recognized who it was, she began pushing back through the crowd, but there were too many people. She didn't know which way to go, but she would use up the last of her strength to get back to her daughter.

'Shush,' a voice said close to her ear. 'You don't need to panic, Helen. You're safe. We're here.'

The sobbing faltered then stopped.

'Mum? Mum, are you awake?'

Helen opened her eyes but couldn't make sense of the bright light and the moving shapes although she was fairly certain that none were Robbie Williams. 'Who switched off . . . the music?' she managed to ask. Her throat hurt, her lips were dry and she was struggling to make the connection between her brain and her mouth. 'Where . . . am I?'

'You're in hospital. There was an accident and you were badly hurt but you're going to be just fine,' the first soothing voice said, and Helen finally recognized Julia's calm tones.

As her eyes adjusted to the light, Milly's worried face came into view. 'You're going to get better now, Mum.'

'Yes,' Helen said and tried her best to put her arms around her daughter who was leaning in for a hug. 'Oh, Milly, sweetheart.'

Milly squeezed her fiercely and released another sob. 'I love you, Mum, and I'm never going to leave you again.'

'Except maybe now,' a man said.

It was John's voice, and although Helen couldn't see him he seemed some distance away, standing at the door perhaps, out of the way. 'Your mum might have been asleep for a while but she still needs her rest,' he added.

'If you do go back to sleep, you won't not wake up again, will you? Promise?' her daughter pleaded.

'Promise,' Helen said.

'Come on, Milly,' John said softly. 'We need to go and tell your nan and grandad. They'll still be in the cafeteria with Julia's mum.'

'But Mum doesn't know about . . . I should stay.'

'It's all right, Milly,' Julia said. 'I think your dad's right. Don't worry, I'll tell her.'

As Milly moved away reluctantly, Helen turned her head to face Julia.

'Tell me what? Oh my God, what happened to you?' Helen asked when she realized Julia was in a wheelchair.

'Nothing that won't mend.'

'The baby?' Helen said and willed her mouth to keep up with what she needed to ask. 'Are you all right?'

'So far so good. Do you remember what happened? Do you need me to explain?'

The events leading upto the accident flashed before her eyes and Helen swallowed a sick feeling back down. Only now did she notice Phoebe who was standing behind Julia's wheelchair, hiding in the shadows as if she wasn't sure she should be there at all.

'No, it's all right,' Helen said and then frowned as she took in the expression on her friends' faces. Julia's eyes were hollow and sunken and her nose looked red and sore. The shadows lurking around Phoebe accentuated the haunted look on her face too. 'Where's Paul?'

There was a pause that might have been deliberate or it could have been because Julia's lips were quivering too much to speak.

'He's gone,' Phoebe said.

'He can't! You have to stay together,' Helen said to Julia.

Julia was shaking when she said, 'No, Helen. Paul died.'

'What? But—' Helen made a move to sit up but Julia laid a hand her shoulder.

'Don't you move. You're not out of the woods yet and you need to take care of yourself.'

'But I want to take care of you.'

'Phoebe's helping me.'

Still squinting, Helen attempted a glare at Phoebe.

'Don't,' Julia said. 'I don't know yet how I'm going to come to terms with what happened, but I've taken a leap of faith. I'm still angry but I've forgiven her. I've forgiven them both, Helen, and I expect you to do the same. We need each other. *I* need you – both of you.'

Much of what Julia had said simply washed over Helen. She would try to make sense of it later. Only one thought remained. *Paul was dead.*

Helen wanted to cry but she was too weak. She wanted to scream but her throat wasn't up to the job. She wanted to punch someone but Phoebe wasn't within reach. There was nothing she could do but accept what she was being told and help her friend as best she could.

'He died a hero,' Julia told her. 'Did you know he'd registered as an organ donor?'

Despite herself, Helen smiled. 'Yes. We had a few private chats and I wore him down,' she whispered.

'He should have told me,' Julia said. 'I should have been more prepared to make that kind of decision.'

'But you did?'

Again her lip trembled when Julia said, 'Yes.'

Helen scrutinized her friend's face. 'Julia,' she said softly. 'Will you stop pretending to be so strong?'

When Julia leaned over and rested her head on the pillow, Helen began stroking her hair. Tentatively, Phoebe took a step nearer and, with her free arm, Helen didn't hesitate when she invited her into the group hug.

As the women clung to each other, they didn't notice Anya watching from the doorway with tears in her eyes and a trembling smile on her lips. The nurse imagined it was going to be near impossible to separate the three friends again.

37

As Lucy's senses were raised into consciousness, the first thing she became aware of was the noise around her. There was chatter and occasional bursts of laughter from people who were in the room but not close by. The voices weren't familiar and the acoustics suggested a room too large to be her bedroom. She couldn't remember where she was and as her eyes fluttered open, a face loomed over her.

'Hello, Lucy, can you hear me?'

Lucy couldn't answer because she was intubated, but she managed to blink a couple of times.

'You're in hospital and you've had an operation. Do you remember?'

Along with her returning senses came the power of recollection although everything was jumbled up. Yes, she remembered arriving at the hospital, she remembered sitting with the transplant team while she tried not to build up her hopes. She had been expecting there to be a last-minute hiccup and hadn't dared to imagine waking up and – and what? Unable to speak, the nurse second-guessed what she needed to know.

'The transplant went really well, Lucy, and you're doing fine.'

With a body still emerging from general anaesthetic and veins pumped full of painkillers, Lucy struggled to work out how she felt. Her ribcage had been cracked open and although she was aware of that pain, she couldn't *feel* it. What she was aware of was the strong, powerful beat of her heart, except it wasn't hers, not the one she was used to. Her thoughts turned to her donor. She knew he had been a man in his thirties but no more than that, and so, while the medical team continued to fuss around her, Lucy allowed herself to wonder about his life and the feelings he had carried in the organ beating steadily in her chest.

It was such an intimate part of another human being that she was sure she would be able to detect the residual emotions of its previous owner. Had this heart raced more often with passion or with fear? Had it ever been broken?

It might only have been her imagination, but there was a moment when she *felt* something. Of all her donor's emotions, it was love, the strongest one of all, she felt warming her heart.

Acknowledgements

Given the subject matter of this book, I think now would be a good time to thank everyone involved in the search for a bone marrow donor for my son, and most especially the donor himself – who I know nothing about except he was a man in his thirties. And even though Nathan lost his fight, the selfless deeds of our unknown hero are by no means diminished and I thank him with all my heart for giving us hope. I am also immensely grateful to the medical team at Alder Hey Children's Hospital and the Anthony Nolan Trust for their help in matching Nathan to his donor and giving him a fighting chance.

I could not continue to write without the amazing support from family and friends. My daughter Jessica is, as always, my foundation and I never tire of saying how proud I am of her, and I very much doubt I ever will. I would also like to thank my long-suffering family; my mum Mary Hayes; Lynn Jones; Chris Valentine; Jonathan Hayes; and the wider family who I keep promising to spend more time with but seem to fail at miserably. I might not show it enough but I don't take your love and support for granted and I'm blessed to have you all in my life.

Thank you to my friends and, in particular, one special group who have stuck together through some tough times. Thank you Nee Parker, Kathy Kelly, Tracy Wood-Burrows, Chris Broadfoot, Phil Quinn, Karen Lowe-McAlley and Sarah Evans as we raise a glass to absent friends.

Thank you as always to my agent Luigi Bonomi and all the team at HarperCollins, especially Martha Ashby, Kim Young and Jaime Frost for making the life of an author far more demanding, thrilling and rewarding than I could ever have imagined. Thank you so very much for giving me all those 'pinch myself' moments in what has become a dream job.

Finally, I would like to thank all my readers who invest their time and money reading my novels. I share a little of my heart in my books and I know I'm in safe hands.

READING GROUP QUESTIONS

What was the goodbye gift? Did you think
there was more than one, and if so,
what was the other one?

**What do you think are the moral
implications of organ donation?
Do you think it should be an opt-out
or an opt-in scheme?**

There are differences between the characters
and how they approach organ donation.
Where do you sit on that line?

**Julia, Helen and Phoebe make difficult
moral decisions throughout the book.
What were they? And who do you think
had the most difficult choice to make?**

Julia is scared that she won't be able
to conceive a child with her husband.
Do you think there is enough openness
in society about difficulties with conception?

**Julia is also terrified that her husband,
Paul, will leave her if she can't conceive.
Do you understand her fear? Do you think
that society places too much pressure
on women to be mothers?**

Helen discovers a secret in her friendship and must decide where her loyalties lie. What do you think was the strongest factor influencing her behaviour?

How do you think Phoebe's behaviour was influenced by her upbringing? What effect does her past have on her present and her future?

What did you think of the structure of the story? Why do you think the author told the story this way?

What do you think the author wishes you to take away from this novel?

An interview with
AMANDA BROOKE

1. Tell us about the inspiration for this novel.

Experience has taught me that life is anything but
predictable and I wanted to write a story that not only
dealt with the fragility of life but also touched upon the
miracles of modern medicine which give so many families
hope. My son's only chance of survival when he was
diagnosed with leukaemia was a bone marrow transplant
and, with no family match, we were lucky enough to find
an unrelated donor. I never had the chance to meet this
unknown hero, although I did write to him to explain that
while Nathan lost his fight, his efforts hadn't been in vain.
For a time we had hope, and that mattered so much to my
family. *The Goodbye Gift* is my way of thanking a complete
stranger for his amazing act of kindness.

2. Tell us about the experience of writing three different principle voices (five if you count Anya and Lucy). How did you go about creating these characters?

Even though I'm a writer, most of the time there's only
one voice in my head and that's my own. Understandably,
when I do sit down to write, it can be a bit of a challenge
immersing myself in the thoughts and feelings of
imaginary characters, especially when I'm making them

act and behave in ways that wouldn't necessarily come naturally to me. And because I was dealing with so many characters in *The Goodbye Gift*, it did get a bit crowded inside my head at times.

Julia was probably the easiest character to write because she was the nearest in age to me and my friends. She likes art which is another thing we have in common, and while I can't claim to have some of the good qualities I gave her, in some ways I would like to be more like her.

Phoebe and Helen were a little more tricky and for different reasons. Even though they're the same age, they have completely different attitudes to life and have been influenced by vastly different past experiences. Helen comes across as older and more mature, which is understandable because she is a single mother with a responsible job. I deliberately made Phoebe's character a little more difficult to unravel, only revealing aspects of her past much later in the novel. My intention was that once the readers knew more about Phoebe, they might be more understanding of her actions.

3. You always put your characters through the wringer emotionally. Do you find this affects your own emotional behaviour?

With a tight schedule, I write every day and so I'm never too far removed from my stories and my characters.

The issues I write about and the emotional journeys my characters go through are intense at times and the subjects often very serious, so you might assume that I'm a rather solemn person. To some extent, that's true, and not just because of what I might be writing at the time. Losing my son altered my perspective on life and changed my priorities, and I'm continually reminded of what tragedies other families face because I volunteer for a helpline that supports bereaved parents. That being said, there's only so much seriousness one person can handle. It may not come out so much in my writing but I don't take life, or myself, too seriously if I can help it, and once in a while my irreverent sense of humour does come out in a scene. And I do love writing cheeky characters like Beryl who Helen meets on the bus home from work.

4. Organ donation is a tricky moral question. Do you feel like there is a clearly right or wrong answer?

Organ donation is something I'm quite passionate about, and while I was writing *The Goodbye Gift*, I took a lot of interest in the debates and campaigns surrounding this subject. There has been much talk about changing the registration process for organ donors in the UK, so that people opt out rather than opting in and this change has already been implemented in Wales. There appears to be a good argument for an opt out system given that there are so many people who would be happy to donate their organs when the time comes, but never get around to adding their details to the Organ Donor Register. If a change in the system increases the number of donor organs then it has to be a good thing. However, what I think you might lose with an opt out system is the opportunity for people to make a positive declaration so that their loved ones are left with no doubt that they wanted to be donors. Whichever system we use, the most important thing is that our families know our wishes. So if you're reading this and you haven't had that conversation yet, what are you waiting for?

5. Was it important to you to keep the reader in suspense as they read the book? And how did you set about doing this?

It wasn't just the reader I was keeping in suspense when I began writing *The Goodbye Gift* – even I didn't know how it was going to end. I put off deciding which character would be the organ donor until I was about two-thirds of the way through the first draft. Because I was writing a story that reflected the unpredictability of life, I needed to write about Julia, Helen and Phoebe as if I expected their lives to continue as they were planning. I didn't want to fall into the trap of setting up one character to reach a neat conclusion in their life because that's the whole point of the novel – the future can't be taken for granted. The accident scenes interspersed throughout the book did come later and by that point I did know who would die and deliberately held back certain details to keep up the suspense.

6. Did you have to do any particular research for this novel? Can you tell us about it if so?

Even though I include very little reference to the organ donation procedure itself in the novel, I did research as much as I could about the process. It was very moving and inspiring to read the accounts of families who took the decision to donate their loved ones' organs, sometimes knowing the donor's wishes, and sometimes not.

With so many main characters in the book, there was a lot of other research required, particularly in relations to their jobs and interests. Fortunately it didn't all involve leafing through books and scouring the internet. I had some lovely meals in The Elephant in Woolton Village as well as a fabulous day visiting Martin Mere Wetland Trust. I also made time to go to the Andy Warhol Exhibition which I probably would have missed if I hadn't been so eager to share in Julia and Phoebe's love of art.

7. What are you reading at the moment?

I've just started reading *A Spool of Blue Thread* by Anne Tyler and it's a book I've wanted to read since hearing about it when it was nominated for the Man Booker Prize. It's written so beautifully and even though the family are introduced in the first chapter as not being a 'melodramatic family,' I'm so enjoying getting to know them.

8. Can you tell us a bit about your next book?

My next book has a working title of *The Affair* and is about a woman called Nina who has two teenage children. She has very recently remarried and the story opens with Nina's discovery that her fifteen-year-old daughter is pregnant. With growing horror, Nina realises that rather than one of her daughter's friends, the father is someone in a position of trust.

Look out for Amanda's next book,

THE AFFAIR

Coming
January 2017

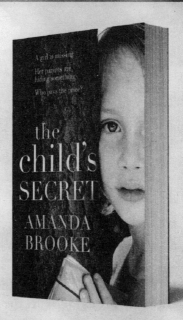

Everyone has secrets...

When eight-year-old Jasmine Peterson goes missing, the police want to know everything.

What is the local park ranger, Sam McIntyre, running away from and why did he go out of his way to befriend a young girl?

Why can't Jasmine's mother and father stand to be in the same room as each other?

With every passing minute, an unstoppable chain of events hurtles towards a tragic conclusion.

Everyone has secrets. The question is:
who will pay the price?

OUT NOW